I0747856

WHEN TREES FALL

THE WOOD AND WATER SAGA

BOOK ONE

DALE MAHFOOD

ROCKSTONE
PUBLISHING
HOUSE

ISBN: 978-1-7359083-5-9 (hardcover) | ISBN: 978-1-7359083-4-2 (paperback) | ISBN: 978-1-7359083-6-6 (e-book)
Subjects: | FICTION / Sagas. | FICTION / World Literature / Caribbean & West Indies. | FICTION / World Literature / Africa. | FICTION / Historical / World War II. | FICTION / Literary.

DEAR READER

The Jamaican Language

Even though I am a born-and-raised Jamaican, writing the native Jamaican Language, otherwise known as Patwa, for this novel has been a learning experience. I wrote the Patwa for the first draft phonetically, but most people who read the early manuscript—even many Jamaicans who speak Patwa regularly—said it made for hard reading, interrupting the flow of the story. So, I compromised, using mostly standard English spelling with Patwa grammar. I've done my best to keep the flavorful spices of the Jamaican language while still making it readable for a wider audience. As we say in Jamaican, *go easy wid me* where I have failed. In any case, while I've always loved to hear and speak Patwa myself, the experience of "playing" with the language for this novel has been formative in my new conviction that it actually is a language in its own right, with grammar rules, a vocabulary, and rich cadences of speech. It's also important to note that Patwa is a language that Jamaicans of all social standings can and do speak. I hope you enjoy reading it as much as I enjoyed writing it.

Endnotes

The endnotes in this novel will inform you of some aspects of Jamaican life, culture, and language. They also serve as a subtext for the novel. While they are not necessary to read, those who read them will enhance their experience and understanding of both Jamaica and the novel.

Character List

To assist you in keeping up with the characters in the novel, I have included a character list in the back of the book.

Setting

The small village of Oristano, Jamaica, was settled early in the sixteenth century by the Spaniards, who established the settlement on an abandoned Taino[1] site. The large bay and abundance of fresh water made it one of the prime sea towns for the Spaniards. Within one hundred and fifty years, the British conquered Jamaica, and, for a time, Oristano became one of their key ports. For the purposes of our story, *Oristano* is the name of a fishing village in the south-coast parish of Westmoreland.

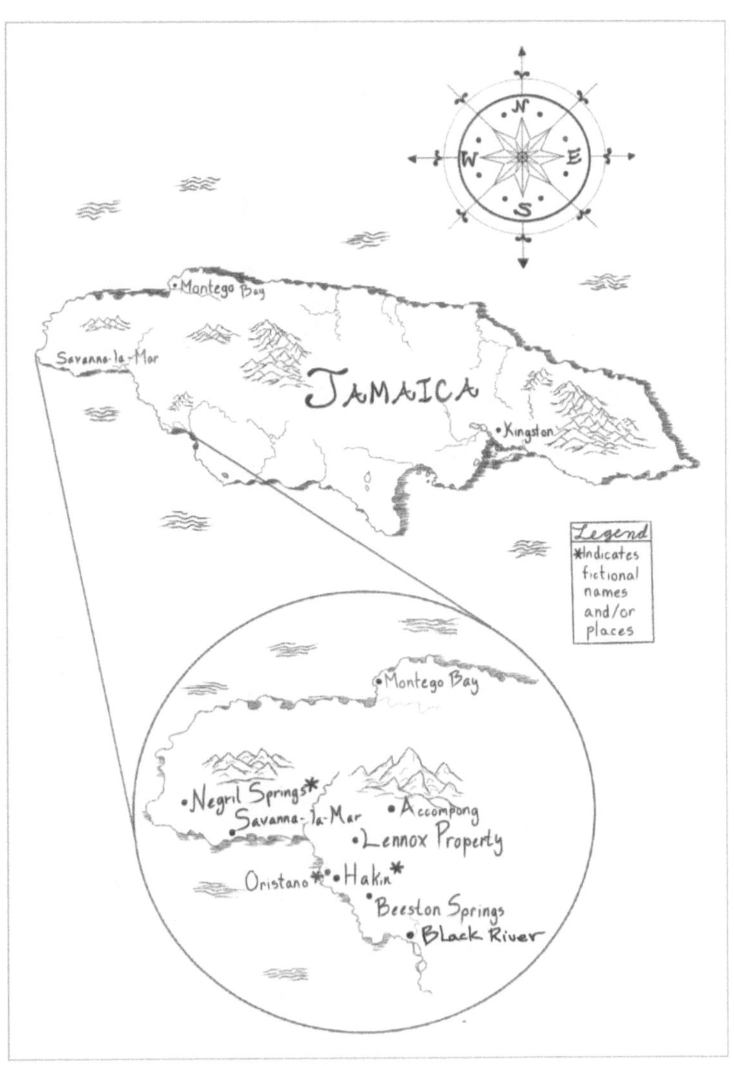

Map of Jamaica, 1944-1945

And he cometh to Bethsaida; and they bring a blind man unto him, and besought him to touch him. And he took the blind man by the hand, and led him out of the town; and when he had spit on his eyes, and put his hands upon him, he asked him if he saw ought. And he looked up, and said, I see men as trees, walking. After that he put his hands again upon his eyes, and made him look up: and he was restored, and saw every man clearly.

—Mark 8:22-25

1973

ailin Campbell wept. She wasn't sure of all the reasons. Maybe she cried because no one else did. Or maybe because of unrecognized tension bottled up inside her over the last forty-one years. One thing she knew for sure—she cried because she loved him. And today, standing by her father's grave, she was his little girl again. Thoughts swirled through her mind of times she vied for his attention with a silly joke or dance. She longed for that chance again, but it was too late. It had been too late for a long time.

The others drifted away from the graveside, walking back to the house. Only she and Archie Price remained, gazing down the slope past the lush lower foothills and on to the many layered hues of the blue Caribbean bay.

Quaco Sharpe, who used to be Cailin's father's property foreman, stood in the midday sun at a distance. With graying hair and neatly dressed in a starched, timeworn white shirt and black pants, he stood as if watching sentinel over the grave.

"How long has it been since you've been back?" asked Archie. When Cailin remained silent, he continued. "I've been gone so long, I forgot on a beautiful day like today the view seems to stretch from Black River to Negril Point. It really is breathtaking."

She gave no response.

He looked at her thoughtfully, then said, "The innocent, fair-haired girl I met years ago hasn't changed a bit—except, of course, for the benefits age brings a few fortunate individuals." He looked her up and down. "Your style reminds me of the women back in New York. I guess the big-city Kingston life-style suits you." He smiled.

Cailin returned a smirk. "Ever the sweet mouth." She turned to walk the short distance to the old silk cotton tree's roots, Archie trailing behind.

The silk cotton tree trunk lay fallen by the gravel road with the bulk of its leafless crown spread down the mountainside. It was said to have been the oldest and largest silk cotton tree in all the Caribbean. Now, it lay without interment, close to her father's unmarked grave. Only the stubborn roots of the massive, tentacled stump remained. The roots were as high as six feet above the ground at some points. When Cailin was younger, the maids would tell her ghosts—or what they called duppies[1]—lived in between the cotton tree roots. She chuckled, thinking how appropriate it was that her father now haunted these trunkless roots. That was the first lighthearted thought she'd had since her sister had called her two days earlier, informing her of her father's death.

Leaning against a root, with her eyes still moist, she sighed. "It's been sixteen years since I last came up here. I wanted him to meet his grandchildren." She looked over at Archie. "But you know Daddy. It was a brief meeting." She paused, and with a smile, continued, "But not as brief as when Harry asked him for permission to marry me. Daddy met us with a shotgun, yelling at Harry, saying he would never allow me to marry an Arab."

Archie laughed. "Sounds like Malcolm. I remember when

he wanted to usher me into manhood, to use his terminology. He had a certain lady of the evening—another one of his sayings—come over to Oristano Inn."

Cailin, rolling her eyes, responded, "Spare me the details, please." Remembering Archie in his youth—smooth words and a thick head of wavy brown hair—there was no need to imagine the evening ladies loving him. His hair was no longer thick, but his words were just as smooth.

Her thoughts returned to her father and involuntarily escaped through her lips. "You know I adored him?"

He laughed and replied, "Everyone knew that. I remember the first day I met you. When I asked you your name, you proudly said you were Cailin Campbell, Malcolm Campbell's daughter. It was like he was the governor of Jamaica."

That made her laugh. "Did I really say that?"

"You did. Just like that."

"I guess I did, then." She looked back out to the sea, then turned to him. "I was surprised to see you here. Last I heard, you took a job with a newspaper in New York."

"Talk about surprised." He reacted as if chafed by sandpaper. "I answered the phone at work to the operator saying, 'There's an Irma Campbell on the phone for you. Should I put her through?' She was the last person I expected to hear from. She told me she didn't want me to come, but Malcolm had insisted." He looked into Cailin's eyes. "He wanted me here. So, like I always do, I came running." He shook his head. "Anyway." Archie took her arm. "Come, I think we should head back to the house. We'll be missed."

She turned to look at Cawdor, the run-down great house, once the pride of the property. "I really don't want to go back in there...with Irma. His third wife! I don't care for her demeanor, and I can't stand the pleasantries, pretending everything's fine between us—especially at a time like this. For all we know, she could have killed him."

"I wouldn't put it past her, but I don't think so. When I got here last week, the doctor told me the old man's liver was giving out on him." Encouraging her on toward the house, he continued, "I'm sure it won't be long before she sells off all of Malcolm's property and heads back to Austria, leaving nothing for the family."

"Let's not talk about money," she urged, walking ahead of him. "It's the last thing on my mind today."

"I'm sure you're the only one who feels that way, especially since Malcolm wrote everyone out of the will, except Irma." He caught up to her. "As a matter of fact, did you notice Ian and Gus didn't come to the graveside?"

"Yes, I've been wondering where they've been."

"Malcolm's lawyer gave Ian a tip."

She looked at him with a furrowed brow. "What advice did he give Ian?"

"He told him Malcolm had money hidden in the ceiling above his bed. So, he and Gus stayed back to check while Irma was at the graveside."

She stopped in her tracks. "He told Ian that?"

"Yes."

She took a deep breath and continued walking. "Archie, I really don't want to talk about money or the will. He was just put in the grave. Let him rest. At least for a while."

"All right. I won't mention it again. Anyway, you're sure to hear about it."

Cailin didn't respond, feigning disinterest.

They found the others sitting at the old, long dining room table talking politely to Irma. Cailin looked at her sisters, brother, and cousin, and her mind took her back thirty years earlier when they would sit at that very table—old as it was then, yet polished and patinated—her father seated at the head, Auntie Abum at the other end. Presently, Irma sat at the head, old and stoic like the now dry, worn-out table, only responding with curt nods and occasional commands to the maid.

Cailin slid into a chair beside Ian and whispered, "Do Rowena and Heather know what you and Gus were up to?"

He leaned his head over. "We didn't find money. But we found something."

"What?" She looked at him.

"Just some old letters. They're addressed to Auntie Abum from the old man's parents. If I'd known what they were, I'd have left them up there."

"What are you going to do with them?"

"Why? Do you want them?"

"Yes. It may be a chance to learn more about Daddy."

"They're yours then. I put them in my car. I'll give them to you when we leave."

She squeezed his hand and gave him a smile. "Thanks."

Cailin looked over at Irma as she barked a command at the maid to put more lemon in the lemonade and thought it fitting her gray-haired bun was so securely wound that it appeared to pull at the skin on her face, giving her a taut, excruciating appearance. She wondered what her father had ever seen in her.

When she could bear the charade no longer, Cailin looked over at her sisters. They looked at Ian, and, as if reading each other's thoughts, they all rose. One by one, from the eldest to the youngest sibling and then their cousin, Gus, they approached Irma and shook her hand. Duty done, they headed toward the front door, leaving their past behind.

Cailin, realizing she may never see Cawdor again, stole out the doors to the back veranda to take one last look at the view she had taken for granted in her early years. The distant incoming ocean tide crashed against the barrier reef, foaming toward the shore. She closed her eyes. Memories from the past flooded in. She could hear as if it were yesterday—Malcolm's voice yelling at someone, anyone, during one of his tirades. A bubble formed in her throat. She held it back, deciding she'd done enough crying for one day.

She walked back down the hallway leading through the center of the house toward the front door. With each room she passed, her heart was awash with fluctuating emotions, flowing with bliss and ebbing with apprehension—her family around the supper table filling every seat with laughter and conversation; nights she and Rowena lay in their beds sharing secrets their father could never be allowed to hear; times she, Ian, or Gus were beaten for some infraction of her father's law. Again, a bubble formed in her throat. She swallowed hard.

She stepped onto the barbecue, a large, square cement slab almost the width of the main house and more than the depth of the kitchen house. In her youth, it had been used to sun-dry pimento seeds, one of her father's business ventures that helped make him the wealthy man he once was.

Cailin met Ian at her car, where he handed her a bundle of old, stained letters bound with yellowed yarn. She thanked him and gave him a goodbye kiss on the cheek. When they had all said their goodbyes, Cailin spotted Sharpe standing by her 1972 Camaro and headed toward him.

He opened the driver's door for her. "Thank you, Sharpe. This time, you ride in the front seat. We'll make Archie ride in the back. Bring his ego down a bit."

Sharpe chuckled. "If you say so, Miss C." He closed her door and made his way to the passenger side. Sitting back in the bucket seat, Cailin put the letters on the console and allowed her shoulders to sink. Sharpe sat in the passenger seat.

"I don't think I ever told you, but I always appreciated the way you ran the property—and especially how you managed my father." She smiled. "He was a lot to manage. How you put up with him, I'll never know."

"Hmm." Sharpe reflected. "The beginning was tough. And

sometime me thought say either him would fire me or me would fire meself. But eventually, when me got to understand Busha[2] and him understand me, we was alright."

She looked over at his aging face.

"In the end, a few year back, when him give up on the property, he wanted to mek sure say me and Essie was set, so he arranged with the owner of Oristano Inn to let us run the inn. The place was a sure mess. Nothing like when Mass Archie mother, Miss Gracie, did run it. But between Essie's good cooking and me fixing up the place, the guest start to come back again. Truth is, if it was not for Busha—"

Before Sharpe's eulogy on Busha was complete, Archie opened the passenger door and exclaimed, "You are the man now, Sharpe! You can come back and restore this place to its former glory!"

"Who, me, sah?[3] No, sah! My time at Cawdor done!" Sharpe got out and pulled the seat forward so Archie could get in the back.

"Yes," Archie responded, "you did your time."

"Well…" Sharpe paused. "Once I would have put it that way, Mass Archie, but now me think forward better than backward."

"You mean forward in the sense of leaving Busha behind!" Archie laughed.

"Archie," Cailin moaned. "Not today."

Sharpe and Archie were polar opposites—one tall and dark with low-cut hair, the other of average height and light with unkempt, wavy hair. In her youth, Cailin had admired them both for different reasons. Sharpe was pensive and respectful; Archie was sociable and cavalier. It was odd for her to be driving with both in the same car.

It took a full ten minutes to make it slowly down the rough, white-limestone gravel road leading from the Cawdor great house to Oristano. The sloping, cow-populated fields—currently absent of cattle and not even visible because of the overgrown bushes—had previously been maintained to greeting-card perfection. The low, almost-flawless stone walls that lined both sides of the meandering Cawdor road were now crumbling with gaps every so often, aiding in the erosion of parts of the road. The threesome bemoaned the loss of its beauty, wishing the property could have been seamlessly passed on to one of Malcolm's children before he was too old to manage it. But they knew they were speaking in could-never-have-beens.

At the bottom of the road, Cailin turned left onto a pothole-hampered road and traveled a quarter mile to a gate with a winding driveway that led to the Oristano Inn. Even though it was not as pristine as Archie and Cailin remembered, both agreed it still held its old charm, partially because of the impressive mountain backdrop.

Cailin pulled under the porte-cochère and stopped.

She picked up the bundle of letters and got out of the car while Archie remarked from the back seat, "You know I would have opened the door for you had I not been sitting in the back seat."

She laughed. "Yes."

"It's second nature," Archie responded as he climbed out from the back seat. "Living and working at the inn honed many a skill—valet, errand boy, chauffeur for drunks. Need I say more?"

"No," Cailin replied, not sure how else to respond.

They walked through the double doors and climbed the mahogany staircase.

"Hmm, something smells good!" remarked Archie.

"It's Essie's curry goat. She mek me buy one goat once she know say Miss C coming for lunch today."

"Well, I've been here for over a week, and nobody made me curry anything!" teased Archie.

"You will have to take that up with Essie. Besides, you know she was the chief cook up at Cawdor when Miss C was a girl."

Archie put his hand on Sharpe's shoulder. "You're just taking up for your wife. I remember those days when I came up to the house, you could be found hovering around the kitchen like a John Crow, hoping Essie would pay you some mind."

Sharpe nodded. "Well, the John Crow get him prize." He laughed and gestured toward the balcony. "Come, mek we go sit down on the balcony, and Essie can bring us something to drink."

He called out for Essie, then moved three mule-skin planter chairs from the gallery onto the spacious balcony that covered the width of the porte-cochère. Drained from the day's trouble, the three sat facing the bay in the inn's shade.

No one said a word until Essie came out to pay her respects.

"Miss Cailin," Essie took Cailin's hand, "I couldn't bear to see Mass Malcolm put in the grave."

Cailin looked up at her, noticing she had aged well. "I know, I know, Essie."

Essie went on expressing her sorrow until Sharpe tactfully interrupted, "Essie, why you don't bring some of that nice ginger-cane juice you made this morning?"

"Yes." She released Cailin's hand. "Let me go get it."

"None for me, Miss Essie. I'll have my usual rum and Coke. After all, what better way to honor the dead?" Archie raised his hand in a mock toast. "To Malcolm! In his next life, may it be done unto him what he did unto others." Then he drank down his imaginary beverage.

Cailin heaved a sigh. She had seen Archie like this before, but only after a few drinks. Having to be with Malcolm in his dying days must have been harder on him than she suspected. Now that it was all over, the temporary emotional blockade he had constructed dislodged.

Sharpe leaned forward, turning to Archie. "You sure you need liquor, Mass Archie?"

"Why?" He shot back in a commanding tone. "You think it'll drive me to kill someone—like Malcolm did?"

Visibly shaken, Sharpe replied, "Well…well, that's not what I'm saying."

Not liking the direction of the conversation, Cailin jumped in. "You know, Archie, we're all upset. But at least you spent time around him over the last few years. That's more than I got."

Archie turned to face her. "Believe me. It's been no winning day at the racetrack." He turned back toward the bay. "The only reason I ever tried with him is because of my mother. The elegant Gracie Price," he said with sarcasm. "She's still pining for him. All these years living in New York, and she can't forget him." Archie got up and walked over to the baluster, placing his hands on it. Leaning forward, he chastised himself. "And me! At my age, I'm still doing what the old woman tells me. That's the only reason I'm here."

Cailin dropped her head and played with the yarn on the letter bundle in her lap.

There was a dense silence until Essie reappeared with the drinks.

Looking at them, Essie interrogated, "What is going on here? Haul in you mouth them and mek me pass[4]. Me know say Busha dead, but these are the times to tell stories about him, not to fret yourselves."

Sharpe broke the threesome's silence. "Essie is right, you know. We all have stories about Busha, and it look to me like it might do us a whole lot a good to tell them—both the bad and the good."

Archie, still at the baluster, turned around to receive his drink. "My flight's not for a couple more days, and I have nothing special on my itinerary."

Cailin sat there fingering the letters.

"Miss C?" Sharpe inquired gently. "What about you?"

She hesitated, then replied, "I could call home to let Harry and the children know I won't be back today."

With that said, she pulled the bow, loosening the yarn from the letters.

1

CAPE TOWN, SOUTH AFRICA

22 FEBRUARY 1902

Dearest Abum,

We arrived in Cape Colony yesterday morning. The voyage from London was overall a pleasant trip. Cuddy complained incessantly about the cold in London, but he is pleased with the weather here in Cape Town. It is very much like Jamaica's weather at this time of year, even though February is Cape Colony's hottest month. I'm looking forward to experiencing their "winter" during June and July. Perhaps it will remind me of the cool air of Jamaica's Santa Cruz Mountains.

Upon disembarking the ship, we were met by a De Beers agent who transported us to Mount Nelson Hotel in a motorcar, which, I tell you, is quite a different experience from a horse and buggy. I suppose motorcars will come to Jamaica soon. You'll have your chance before too long. On our ride to the hotel, British military men could be seen everywhere, and the agent told us the hotel itself was being used as a military campaign headquarters.

Mount Nelson Hotel is marvelous. It only opened three years ago and is better appointed than the Myrtle Bank Hotel in Kingston. I was pleasantly surprised to find hot and cold running water in the lavatories. It is a pity we are only staying here for one night. Tomor-

row, we will take the train from Cape Town to Kimberly. Cuddy is itching to get started in his new position as physician for the diamond mines. As for me, I suppose I will be setting up house and home, relying heavily on the two maids and the gardener, who the De Beers agent says are waiting for us.

I cannot thank you enough for taking our six children. I am glad they are with you. I know it was a big request, but with the orange business failing—and you know your brother is not suited for business—Cuddy had to fall back on his medical training, and the offer from De Beers was too good to refuse. Now that we are here and have heard accounts of battles with the Boers, we feel we have done the right thing to support the British Empire. Cuddy's medical skills are in dire need here.

It was hard for me to leave my family and home in Jamaica, but I had to follow my husband. As you know, he is not one of those men who could make it on his own without female companionship. When he gets settled in his job, he plans to send money for the children's support. In the meantime, be sure to have them help around the house, and Kester, even though he is only nine, should be able to work around the property. Cuddy says they should learn to earn their keep.

Oh, how sad I was to have left before baby Malcolm's first birthday. I fear I will not recognize him when we return for the children and that Tam and Bonnie will not recognize me. At least I know Kester, Cameron, and I hope, Susan will not forget. This has been the hardest thing I have ever done. Remember me in your prayers.

Please read this letter to the children, or have Kester read it as he is such an accomplished reader for his age. I love and miss you all, my children. We will write again as soon as we are settled in our new home.

As ever,
Cuddy and Winnie

2

CAILIN

MONDAY, SEPTEMBER 4, 1944

Cailin sat on the sloped, sun-bleached shingle roof overlooking the ground level Cawdor House water tank, the upper quarter of the verdant mountaintops reflecting in its still waters. Staring from behind suntanned skin, her thoughts focused on whatever caught her attention at the time: the roof gutters leading to the downspouts which fed the water tank, the white-crowned heads of the two baldpate pigeons preening one another and flying off into the Poinciana tree behind the kitchen house, her younger cousin taunting her like a character in the silent movies she had only heard about, her favorite goat bleating down in the goat pen—anything but the history book she was supposed to be reading in the school-room she had her back to.

What did she care about the Etruscan domination of Italy in the mid-sixteen hundreds BC? She was only concerned with Ian and Gus and how she could join in their explorations of her father's endless property. Though now it would only be with Gus, as her father had taken Heather and Rowena to Hampton School and Ian to Munro College, both boarding schools located in the adjoining parish. The girls were returning to

Hampton, but it was Ian's first year away from home. He had tried talking his father out of boarding school so he could continue learning how to run the property. The impervious answer was always no.

Her train of thought jumped the track to her father. *Where is he?* He had left to take her siblings to school the previous morning, but hadn't returned. Her mother told her the schools were only an hour and a half's drive away. She wondered if he was okay, but told herself he must have spent the night at the Oristano Inn again. Her shoulders slumped at the thought. *What condition will he be in when he comes home today—if he comes home today?*

"Cailin! Get off the roof immediately! You know what your father would do if he caught you up there. Come down before he sees you."

Startled, she looked down to see her mother looking up at her with both hands resting on her full hips. She chuckled, thinking of her good-natured mother who was forever trying to protect her children from harm and trying to teach Cailin how to behave as a young lady.

"Okay, Mummy," she conceded.

Climbing back into the schoolroom through the shuttered window, she heard the rapid-fire blitz of her governess' shoes assaulting the narrow wooden stairway.

"Cailin Campbell! What am I supposed to do with you?" Miss Recas scolded. "You are ever dreaming and finding ways not to do your studies. Now, open the book to where I marked it and read your history lesson."

Cailin plopped into her desk chair sulking, then plucked up courage and said belligerently, "Why do I have to be up here when Gus is outside playing?"

"Angus finished his lessons a good two hours ago," snapped Miss Recas. Then it was as though the very mention of his name transformed her countenance. "He even read further in the science book than I required," she said with a gleam in her eyes, which were surrounded by imitation tortoiseshell horn-rimmed glasses. It was as if Gus was that once-in-a-lifetime student every governess prays for—the one who will hallow the halls of Oxford.

Cailin spent the next hour forcing herself to read the prehistoric history book and finish the mathematics problems she had skipped earlier. Miss Recas sat in her chair with one eye on a Dickens novel and the other on her pupil, prompting Cailin to promise herself she would never read Charles Dickens.

In the two years Miss Recas had been her governess, Cailin couldn't recall her laughing once and had only seen her crack a faint smile when it had to do with an essay Gus had written or a difficult mathematics problem he had solved. She was an odd woman who stayed cloistered in her room outside of school and mealtimes. On weekends, she went to her family's home in Black River.

The thought came to Cailin that Miss Recas probably didn't even have any friends in Black River. The thought gave her a disquieted feeling of satisfaction tinged with remorse. She shook it off and finished her last mathematics problem.

Free from the schoolroom, she hurried out of the house, asking Essie if she'd seen Gus. Essie pointed to the coffee bushes under the old silk cotton tree, saying, "Dinner is in an hour, and you know say Miss Helen is going to want the two of you washed up and ready." She paused. "And look out for your father. If him coming home today, it will be soon."

Sprinting as if to reclaim time, she cut across the barbecue, which was half covered with green pimento berries drying in the sun to be sold as allspice. Long-jumping off the edge, she ran barefoot on the grass until she reached her cousin amid the coffee bushes, who was focused on catching ground doves with a springe he learned to make from the yard man.

"You frightened her!" Gus said, annoyed, as he wiped the sweat from his forehead into his disheveled hair. "I almost had her."

"Serves you right for making fun of me while I was stuck in school," Cailin shot back with a jaunty smile.

"So sorry." He clasped his hands in pleading sarcasm. "I never realized the roof was your new schoolroom." He bent down to set the springe. "Besides, I wasn't the one who reported you to Auntie Helen. It was Essie. She saw you from the kitchen."

"Our problem is we have too many mothers here at Cawdor. Mummy, Essie, Auntie Abum, Auntie Bitsy, Ruby, and that darn governess. You can't do anything without one of them saying something about it." Looking further down the mountain toward the three small foothills, she added, "Maybe that's why I like to go exploring."

Gus pointed at the sun hovering over the western horizon and said, "I don't think we should go exploring. It's too late. We won't get back in time. I'd rather not take the chance of Uncle Malcolm coming back before we return."

Two years earlier, Gus's father, Tam Campbell, had left him in his bother Malcolm's care, taking off to England to enlist in Britain's Royal Air Force "to beat the Nazis!" as he had put it.

"You're right," said Cailin with a frown. "Then let me help catch a ground dove?"

"Okay, look at that one over there with the dark underbelly. It's a male."

Gus set the trap, and they hid between the cotton tree roots and waited. Time slugged slowly by, and Cailin got fidgety. Then, to her relief, the male lighted near the trap and worked his way toward it. Just as he was about to step under the basket, Gus pretended to sneeze, scaring the bird away.

"You did that on purpose!" Cailin reacted with a look of disbelief.

"Just returning the favor," he replied with a smirk that matched his mischievous brown eyes.

Before Gus had time to reset the springe, they heard someone down the hill exclaiming, "Hitler! Hitler! Him comin'!"

This set off a frenzied chain of events. Cailin and Gus took off sprinting toward the great house. One worker, who Malcolm nicknamed Samfie for his conman antics, emerged from under a tree and began chopping at an overgrown bush near the road. Cow Man, the one who had done the yelling, bound over the low stonewall further down the road and cut through the upward sloping meadow at racehorse speed in an effort to reach the cow pen in time. Essie shouted to Ruby, the housemaid, to set the supper table quickly. Helen busied herself brushing her hair and straightening her dress. By the time Cow Man made it to the pen and Cailin and Gus made it back home, a black, 1940, four-door Ford was pulling up the last stretch of the gravel road, turning left alongside the cotton tree and heading toward the barbecue.

Cailin and Gus stopped short as the car passed. With a last crunch of gravel from the rubber tires coming to a halt, the driver's door swung open and Malcolm Campbell—formally known to the property workers as Busha but informally as Hitler—stepped out. Of Scottish lineage, he was of average height and thin girth. His white, short-sleeved shirt revealed his tanned, toned arms. He always wore khaki pants, which complemented his sun-bleached brown hair and dark chestnut eyes. That he could and sometimes did work as hard as anyone he hired afforded him a fascist disposition.

"Where's Sharpe?" he barked to everyone in earshot.

Essie yelled through the kitchen window, "Sah, him down checking on the Kerry Mongoose them, since them never bring enough pimento to dry."

The yard man, who was grooming Malcolm's horse, looked up and added, "You know how them good to steal some of it."

It baffled Cailin how Essie seemed to know everything happening on the property at any given time. She knew some of it had to do with the fact that Essie, Ruby, and the yardman lived in rooms adjoining the pimento storeroom, just off the kitchen, but that didn't explain how she knew what was happening at the far reaches of the property. She settled on the hypothesis that Essie, being the head cook, was the wheel's hub —everyone had to come in contact with her at some point during any given day. And her commanding demeanor, next only to Malcolm's, had the effect of eliciting honesty. As Sharpe often said, "She little but she tallawah!" Meaning she was small in stature but knew how to manage anyone in her purview.

Looking around, Malcolm spotted Gus, who was still panting. "Gus, go get that lazy, good-for-nothing Samfie, and tell him to get up here, put the pimento in the boxes, and lock them in the storeroom. Anyone with an ounce of common sense would know rain is coming in the next half hour. That's money lying there on the barbecue!"

Gus took off running in Samfie's direction while Malcolm strode toward the front door where Cailin now stood with her mother under the front porch trying to decipher his mood. Had he been drinking? Was his stay at Oristano Inn agreeable?

"Glad you're back, Daddy," Cailin said in a sweet, young voice. Even though she was now fourteen, her father brought out the little girl in her. Being at a loss for something else to say —another effect he had on her—and wanting to influence his mood, she asked, "Would you like me to do a Highland jig for you?"

The corners of his mouth shifted slightly into a smile. "Not now, dear. Perhaps after supper." He turned to his wife and said, "Good evening, Helen," then walked into the house.

Helen exhaled relief.

Twenty minutes later, Ruby, about to place a large soup tureen on the supper table, jumped in fright when, out of nowhere, lightning flashed and a crack of thunder rolled across the sky. Seconds later, a sudden white sheet of rain, visible through the open doors and windows, came rolling over the mountain, surprising everyone—everyone except Busha.

After gaining her composure, Auntie Abum, in her usual pedantic manner, asserted, "A good storm shower brings the cool air," as if everyone didn't already know that. She then addressed Ruby, who had almost dropped the terrine, "Come, come. Finish the supper table. After all, it's nothing but a little rain."

Abum had inherited Cawdor House from her father, and even though she had long since transferred ownership to Malcolm, her youngest nephew, her voice still resonated with a commanding timbre.

Ruby filled the glasses with water, and on her way back to the kitchen, knocked on Malcolm's door, signaling everything was ready.

Looking refreshed from a brief nap, Malcolm took his seat and inquired about everyone's day. Thankful he was in a genial mood, each responded cheerfully, except for Miss Recas, who never spoke at the table unless specifically addressed.

Each night, supper commenced with Helen ladling a broth of some sort into bowls and passing them down the extra-large dining table. Tonight, serpentine ribbons of steam rose from the beef broth and vegetable-filled soup terrine, as the time-worn serving dishes passed around the table with the faded-blue, traditional British pastoral scenes camouflaged by the greens, yellows, and oranges of the island's cuisine. At least half of each supper was produced on the Cawdor property, with the rest purchased from market women and fishermen who came up to the house selling their goods.

The rain tapered off to a drizzle as the table conversation rambled aimlessly about the day's goings-on, with Gus interjecting witty limericks every so often.

Cailin, who had been unusually quiet, carefully broached the subject of Ian's arrival at Munro. "Daddy, how was Ian's first day of school?"

Malcolm's face stiffened. He drank some water. Forking a piece of fried breadfruit from his plate, he replied, "He's fine. He'll do just fine. And the girls got off well."

She thought to probe further, but decided against it.

Auntie Bitsy, nicknamed from her youth for her tiny stature, broke the tension with her genial nightly recitation, meant as a sort of rhetorical question. "There's one more piece of plantain. If no one wants it, I'll have it."

As usual, Cailin and Gus would play along by putting their fork above the plantain as if to steal it from the plate. Together they would say, "I'll have it," knowing very well Bitsy would end up with the plantain.

Bitsy was Abum's younger sister, who had returned to Cawdor after the untimely death of her husband to become the governess for the previous generation of Campbells, of which Malcolm was the youngest of six. When asked to teach the present generation, she softly declined, maintaining that her teaching days were long over.

At the conclusion of the charade, Helen, advancing cautiously into mine-laden territory, asked Malcolm, "How is your new venture progressing?"

With fork paused midair, he glanced over at her and asked, "What venture are you referring to?"

"Oristano Inn," she said, keeping her eyes fixed on the pastoral design on the rim of her plate.

He replied matter-of-factly, "Business has picked up. Gracie has put her touch on the place, and word has traveled from Montego Bay to Kingston that the inn is back in business." His tone lightened. "In fact, Bustamante will be in the area soon for one of his rallies, and he plans on staying at the inn. It's been a while since he visited Oristano. It should be quite an evening."

"Can me and Gus come down too, Daddy?" exclaimed Cailin, practically bouncing in her seat.

"Calm down, child," reprimanded Abum. "One would think you were a five-year-old. And, besides, it's 'Gus and I' not 'me and Gus.'"

"I'm sorry, Auntie Abum, but the last time we saw Mr. Bustamante, he sat both of us on his knees and told us jokes. He even reached into his coat pocket and gave us Paradise Plum sweeties."

Changing the subject, Abum inquired, "And, Malcolm, how are Ms. Price and her son finding Westmoreland?"

Malcolm glanced over at Abum, whose eyes locked with his for a moment before he looked down at his plate. "Gracie and Archie seem to be adjusting well."

"Where is the boy going to school?" she continued.

"Manning's School," he answered curtly.

"How will he get there every day?" she persisted.

"I've arranged for his room and board at the Witcombes during the weekdays."

She ceased her interrogation.

He exhaled his angst—leaving an uneasy specter presiding over the table.

Cailin, not understanding the silence that ensued, attempted to bring levity to the evening by offering Malcolm the Highland jig she had promised him earlier. He gratefully accepted.

She sprung out of her chair and kicked off her shoes, which thumped against the mahogany wall, eliciting a "Humph!" from Abum. Then, up on the balls of her feet with her left hand on her hip and her right arm curved so that her hand was above and just to the right of her head, she bent her right knee and swung her foot toward her left knee then out diagonally. Jumping rhythmically, her upper torso remained erect. She smiled brightly all the way to the finale, then gave a gentle curtsy, just the way Helen had taught her.

The entire table applauded, with Gus taking the opportunity to theatricalize by shouting, "Bravo! Bravo! Bravo!"

Malcolm smiled and said, "Well done, my little girl."

3

SHARPE

MONDAY, SEPTEMBER 4, 1944

With the tough soles of his bare feet to provide traction, Sharpe moved deftly down the tree-covered slope, avoiding ground cover that could signal his presence.

He heard a voice. "Lawd! Stop you foolishness and..." Then the voice softened till it was indecipherable. Moving with stealth in the direction of the voice, he soon spotted a handful of people standing in a clearing where he could hear them clearly.

"Mek me explain. Take the pimento and hide it in this here tree trunk. Then we take it little by little every day till it gone, and we sell it up at Newmarket." The stocky woman who said this asserted her authority with one hand on her hip and the other gesturing as though she were an orator. She never said a word when Busha was around, but in his absence, her opinion was law. The five men with her sucked their teeth in capitulation.

Sharpe moved into the clearing, purposely stepping on a twig to draw their attention.

"Quaco!" said one of the men. "Where you come from? You is like a duppy come out a nowhere."

Sharpe was born in Accompong, one of the two main locations on the island where the Taino Indians, and later, runaway slaves of various tribes, fled from the Spanish and English, respectively. His dark skin and six-foot plus height came from his mother's mostly African Mandinka side. The women in her family, proud of their heritage, made it a point to pass this information on to their offspring. His father, who worked hard and drank even harder, never spoke of his origins, but his mother—to whom these things were an obsession—inquired of his relatives, who informed her that he was mostly a mixture of Taino and Akan. His people were a mortar and pestle blend of various spices.

Quaco was Sharpe's first name, which he inherited from a tradition enslaved Akans brought with them from Africa. The day a child was born, he or she would be given a specific name that was related to that day of the week and the gender of the child. Boys who were born on Wednesdays were called Quaco. Regarding his last name, even though his family had lived in Accompong for generations, Sharpe's great-great-grandfather had been born on a sugar plantation in Saint James and was given the last name of his owner, who was also his father. On August 1, 1838, the enslaved people of Jamaica were emancipated, in large part due to the catalyst of the Christmas Rebellion of 1831 that was sparked by Samuel Sharpe's peaceful strikes. Sharpe's great-great-grandfather, who was not entirely satisfied with the conditions the British had spelled out for emancipation, took the opportunity afforded by the day of celebration and stole away to Accompong, the nearest Maroon town. From that time on, he never again said his legal surname but claimed the name Sharpe.

While working on the property, Quaco used the name Sharpe because he felt the name Quaco had a quashie[1] ring to it, which could give white people the false impression he was a bumbling Black idiot.

"What me hearing you going do with that pimento? It belong to Busha," Sharpe stated in his deep, clear voice.

"Look here, Quaco," said the orator, who went by the name Lucy. She paused, clasped her hands together in a stately manner, then mustering up her best King's English, and with a slight wag of the head said, "Or should I say, Sir Sharpe?"

The gathering broke out in raucous laughter.

Her Patwa[2] returned. "When since you switch side, eh? Don't forget, most of we know you from you was a boy come to Hakin. Now you working as the foreman for Busha, and you forget where you come from!"

Hakin, a small hillside village a half hour's walk from the entrance gate to the Cawdor property, was populated by the people nicknamed Kerry Mongoose. When Sharpe was about ten years old, his mother, pregnant with her fourth child, died of malaria. He was then sent to his father's sister, Phibbi, in Hakin.

"Me know where me come from," Sharpe responded, standing tall with his feet planted in the damp soil of the decomposing tree leaves. "Me also know who me work for and what is my responsibility." He pointed at Lucy and said, "You responsible…" then he panned his index finger from one worker to the next, "…to pick the pimento. Me responsible to see it get where it belong." He stuck out his hand, palm up, and demanded, "Now pass it 'ere!"

Sharpe strode forward, liberating the bulging pimento crocus bag from its captors. Lucy let out some ear-singeing expletives while the rest of the workers—now void of arrogance—parted like the Red Sea. "No mek me catch you do it again!" He turned and began his trek back to the gravel road and up to the great house.

As he walked with the sack on his right shoulder, Sharpe

entertained mental arguments. Justice required him to march up to the house with the bag of pimento, lay it down on the barbecue, call for Busha, and expose Lucy and the other workers. Mercy reminded him of the village that had taken him in when he was young, taught him to be a survivor at any cost, and brought him to Cawdor to work with them. Justice and Mercy were fierce rivals. His mind vacillated between the two as he struggled to mediate a settlement.

By the time he turned the corner at the cotton tree, he knew what he would do.

He found the storeroom on the far side of the barbecue from the house chained shut, so he leaned the bag of pimento against the door. Just then, a flash of lightning, closely followed by a clap of thunder and pelting rain, soaked the barbecue. Sensing it was one of those storms that wouldn't last very long —as though the sky needed to relieve itself of pent-up pressure —he sat down beside the pimento bag and waited it out.

When the rain let up, Sharpe headed to the kitchen to say good evening to Essie and Ruby before he left for Hakin.

Sweeping the floor with her head down, Essie responded, "Me see what you do."

At first he thought she was referring to the incident down the hill with the workers. Then he realized she couldn't have been there and gotten back before he did. Confused, he said, "What you see me do?"

Picking up her head and looking him squarely in the eyes, she replied, "You sneak and put the pimento against the door. And now you is leaving without notifying Busha."

At these words from Essie, Ruby quickly made herself busy washing pots.

"What business you have in that? How you know what me going do come morning? Miss Essie." Sharpe paused for emphasis before continuing. "Me tell you before, and me going tell you again, don't fass[3] up in me business."

"You always a take up for the Kerry Mongoose them. Them is a lying thief!" Essie began sweeping again and with a solemn tone continued, "The Bible say them is under condemnation for that."

"Not that again, Miss Essie! I would respectfully ask you to keep you Pocomania Wrap-head Church[4] preaching from passing me ears."

"That is just the problem! It passing you ears instead of going in them. Beside, I am not a Pocomania nor a Wrap-head. My Moravian Church people was here well before any of them other religion reach Jamaica."

"Yes, yes, Miss Essie," Sharpe responded with a grin. "You just go ahead and pray for me. In the meantime, I gone home to Hakin."

"This is what me will pray for you." She pointed in the direction of Hakin. "That you stop mix up with that devil Obeah[5] man in Hakin."

With a smile, he turned to leave, shaking his head and muttering, "She always have to get the last word."

"And you always pretend like say me can't hear you," she countered victoriously.

Heading down the long gravel Cawdor road with the now light rain dampening his clothes, Sharpe thought about Essie. He admired her feistiness and thought her an attractive woman, but he did think it odd that she rolled her socks down beneath her ankles, giving the effect of two large white rings resting just above her shoes. He laughed to himself, then breaking his thoughts, he heard cheering and laughter coming from inside the great house. He stopped and listened. He then continued his trek down the gravel road, allowing his thoughts to wander back to Accompong, back to the time when he was a little boy—when his mother was still alive and his father hadn't sent him away. He exhaled deeply, not realizing he had been holding his breath, then resumed walking.

That evening, Sharpe, whose hunger was not quite satiated from the savory ackee and callaloo dinner Marsha had cooked, sat with his Uncle Leroy, his friend Ram Foot, and three other men of Hakin, drinking cheap rum and smoking jackass rope—pipe tobacco rolled into long ropes and sold at the market by the yard. They were seated in a small, wooden, tin-roofed rum bar, which sat on the edge of a rocky, steep incline with its back protrusion elevated by stilts. After the patrons were gone and the door shut, the weather-worn wood boards would openly invite rodents of all types to a late-night social gathering. Most of the shops and residences of Hakin were in a similar condition.

Though it was now night, and most of the children had been routed out from secret play areas and corralled into homes, a little Jenkins boy wearing only a tattered shirt barely covering his protruding navel peered through the bar door with his gray mud-caked cheeks and imploring eyes. Before anyone could scold the boy, his mother seized his hand, jerking him from sight while chiding him for leaving her supervision.

Four of the five men Sharpe sat with had the surname Jenkins, as did the great majority of the people who lived in Hakin. This had puzzled Sharpe a few days after his arrival to the village. As he was introduced to his new neighbors, he discovered most of them had the same surname as his Auntie Phibbi and her husband, Uncle Leroy. When he questioned his aunt about this, all she said was that things in Hakin were different than in Accompong.

It wasn't until years later that he was able to piece together the patchwork of village gossip. Apparently, the lower plains of the larger piece of land the Cawdor property was eventually carved out of had once been used for growing sugar cane. Slaves, mostly of the Igbo tribe, were brought to the area to work the cane fields. After emancipation, Kerry Jenkins, an ex-slave, became the self-appointed leader of the people who remained on the property.

They eventually migrated from the meager dwellings provided them to meager dwellings they built for themselves on the steep, craggy hillside a short walking distance from Oristano. The only two advantages the location offered were isolation from intrusive outsiders and the palliative ocean panorama. Kerry was, for all practical purposes, the chief of the new village. Because of this, he had his way with most any woman he set his eye on. Thus, the popular, inbred surname Jenkins. Kerry was also the chief thief of Hakin and expected the same of all his people, bringing about the nickname Kerry Mongoose. Their infamy was known widely from Black River to Savanna-la-Mar.

When the rum had taken effect and the discussion in the bar was rambunctious, Ram Foot, confident only Sharpe could hear him, leaned over and said, "Quaco, why you did take the pimento bag from Miss Lucy? She can't stop run her mouth about it. You know how she always trying to cause trouble."

From the first day of Sharpe's arrival in Hakin, Ram Foot, a neighbor's son so named for his ability to swiftly ascend the steepest rocky hill, attached himself to Sharpe, becoming his how-to-maneuver-Hakin mentor. As children, they played together on the hillsides, and as they grew older and ventured down the hill to the small one-teacher, Methodist primary school, they were constantly one-upping each other in academics and sports. When they completed the primary grades and their opportunity for further schooling subsided—as there was no other free schooling available—their competitiveness transformed itself into a quest for girls. At the moment there was no interpersonal competition. Ram Foot had been forced to concede Marsha to Sharpe. Now, Ram Foot's only concern was that Sharpe was agitating the Hakin wasp nest.

"Yes, Ram Foot. Lucy good for that," Sharpe paused, "but it's high time we live down the Kerry Mongoose reputation."

Magus, who had antenna ears and was the resident village Obeah man, picked up on the confidential conversation and declared loud enough to be heard over the rum bar racket, "Kerry Mongoose reputation! What you know about Kerry Mongoose reputation?" As he said this, his face twisted into multiple deep crevices, reminding Sharpe of the claw marks vultures leave on carcasses.

All eyes in the bar fastened on Sharpe.

Realizing Magus's response was motivated by news of the pimento incident earlier that day, Sharpe knew he couldn't back down. "What me know is anytime me tell anybody me come from Hakin, them always have something bad to say about we. And mostly them walk—"

"How you use *we* so freely?" Magus interrupted, "Just because you live with we, don't mean you is one of we." Continuing his accusations, he turned to Sharpe's uncle and pointed at Sharpe, "And you, Leroy! You marry outside of we, and look what happen?"

Conducting his typical machinations, Magus dragged the rest of the rum bar into the controversy. The chorus bolstered his argument with great cacophony, drowning out Sharpe's solo arguments. Ram Foot wisely remained an onlooker.

It wasn't long before Sharpe got up from his seat and headed to his one-room shack. As he started the ascent up the path, he heard a voice shout from the rum bar, "Get you filthy Accompong Maroon rass[6] outa here! Him is nothing but a runaway slave, and him think him better than we."

Sharpe came to a slow halt, turning to see if he could tell who made the contemptuous slurs. Only silence came from the rum bar, with the cry of a hungry infant in the adjacent house. Several men stood outside the bar glaring at Sharpe. While he realized he had not been born in Hakin, and he was only in his early thirties, he also knew he had worked hard to gain the respect of the community; he was certain they had backed his decision to accept the foremanship at Cawdor. Now he felt like the rum bar—precariously perched between land and noth-ingness.

Not able to pinpoint the perpetrator, he thought it unwise to add kerosene to the glowing embers. Turning, he continued homeward.

Heading up the steep, water-furrowed, rocky path, he continued his Justice v. Mercy courtroom debate.

Mercy: The people of Hakin have labored, manipulated, and stolen to get what they barely have. But who can blame them? As a matter of fact, doesn't Busha owe them? After all, he made his money off the backs of these people. They deserve some kind of compensation—if not legally, then however they can get it.

Justice: That's exactly what Alexander Bustamante and Norman Manley are fighting for. Aren't all Jamaicans supposed to have the right to vote during the upcoming first general election in December? This will give the people of Hakin a chance to better their lot, instead of stealing what is not theirs.

His thoughts turned to himself. Feeling the ever-present ache increasing, he longed for relief from the miseries he felt in Hakin. While recalling with ambivalence the challenges of surviving the rugged and often hazardous Accompong Cockpit Country terrain, he also remembered the respectable sense of living as an independent people with the necessary resources surrounding them. He appreciated his aunt and the Hakin community taking him in, but he had tasted better fruit. The only way out of this present morass was to work hard and gain Busha's trust, living down the unasked-for reputation conferred on him upon his arrival to Hakin. Then he could move out of Hakin.

Marsha stood waiting at the threshold of their dwelling.

With hands on hips, she observed, "Me Black Giant, you is finally home." An attractive girl in her early twenties, her smooth golden skin illumined in the half moonlight, momentarily distracting Sharpe from his problems.

"Me hear the noise down at the rum bar. What happen?" she asked.

"Nothing. Let we just go sleep," Sharpe replied.

Determined, she continued her inquiry. "Does it have to do with what Miss Lucy was carrying on with before dinner?"

"Don't worry yourself about nothing. I will handle it." He gently put his hand around her waist to lead her inside.

She resisted. "Quaco, me have to worry. Me hear say Miss Lucy going set the Obeah man on you."

Taking the whole evening out on Marsha, Sharpe erupted like a pent-up volcano. "Chuh[7], man! Me say you not to worry youself. Me know one Obeah man that will turn Magus outside-in so a John Crow can pick out him insides. Anything Lucy want Magus put on me, me Obeah man can tek it off and send it back to her!" Sharpe, with his eyes now flaming, demanded. "Come now!" He picked her up and laid her on the bed.

Late into the night, as Marsha lay softly breathing by his side, Sharpe stared out the open window, his mind oscillating between Justice and Mercy.

4

ARCHIE

"*A* car's coming up the drive," Gracie said nonchalantly, addressing her son while sipping her nightly dram of whisky. "Go meet them."

"It's just Mick. He and Malcolm are the only ones with gasoline who come here," replied Archie with his left leg slung over the arm of a curved-back leather chair and his head of thick, wavy, brown hair resting on his light-brown arms. "He can let himself in."

"Just because he's an old friend, doesn't mean you shouldn't treat him with the same respect as the other guests. Now go downstairs and meet him, and don't call him Mick." She swigged the last of the whiskey, got up and went to the hallway mirror to examine herself.

With languid effort, Archie raised himself out of the chair and made his way downstairs to the porte-cochère where Mick McFagan was getting out of his car. A tall lanky man of Irish parentage, he always wore a well-fitted three-piece suit and a white fedora, which brought attention to his ginger hair. This he did even on the hottest day of August.

"Archie, my dear boy. Be a good lad and park the car, will you? Where's your mother?"

"Where you always find her. Dressed and ready for guests."

He laughed, handing Archie his hat, and replied, "Ah, but I'm not a guest."

"Try telling her that. Everyone's a guest to her, except—" Before he could finish what he was saying, Mick's stride had taken him through the doorway and halfway up the stairs. He finished softly to himself, "me."

He parked the car on the side of the house. While still outside, he heard his mother give one of her vaudeville laughs, putting him on edge.

Back inside, Archie resumed his position on the leather chair and watched the show. He'd been to the Strand Theatre often during the time his mother ran an inn on the outskirts of Montego Bay and had come to see his life at the inn as one string of performances after another. He had once seen an old silent film version of *The Great Gatsby*, in which, despite the antiquated acting and the lack of speech, he recognized characters like his mother and himself—characters pretending to be what they could never be.

A year later, he saw an American tourist at his mother's Montego Bay inn reading *The Great Gatsby* on the front veranda. Archie asked if he could read it when she had finished. On her last day there, she gave him the book. He read it that day and into the night, seeing himself between the jacketed cover. He was Jay Gatsby, ever masquerading as something other than himself—whatever his mother wanted him to be at the moment. Feeling a kind of bitter catharsis, he read the novel multiple times, underlining and memorizing sentences. It then became a game he played with himself to see how often he could use quotes from the story in conversations with others.

Even more, he saw in his mother the pitiable Myrtle

Wilson. Reaching beyond her limits. Disguising her loosely coiled black hair with a red wig. Accentuating her tall, thin, light-skinned body, notwithstanding her full lips. Toiling to climb social classes—using any means possible, including her son.

"What can I get you to drink?" Gracie offered Mick.

"The usual," he absentmindedly answered her as he sat down on the sofa and picked up the paper he had been eyeing on the coffee table.

"If you brought me more of the usual, I could give you some of the usual."

"My dear, you know how hard it is to get hold of Scotch these days. Those damn Nazi U-boats keep sinking British merchant ships." Pointing at the open paper he continued, "Here's another one in today's *Daily Gleaner*[1]." Then, remembering his role as a liquor salesman who traveled the island from hotel to inn, he attempted to overcome her objection. "Appleton Estates has addressed the problem by producing their new blend of rum. Most of my clients use words like 'heavenly' or 'extraordinary' or, as my father often says, 'toothsome.' Before you know it, you may never touch Scotch again."

"Yes, yes. You've told me that. And some do find it as a replacement, but it's not quite toothsome to me yet. So, you have the rum, and I'll stick to the Scotch."

Gracie handed Mick his drink, and he turned his attention to Archie, "So how've you adjusted to Oristano, my dear boy?"

Not liking the way Mick always referred to him as "my dear boy," Archie bristled. "If it was up to me, I'd still be in Mobay."

"Yes. I understand why." Mick swirled the ice in the glass and took his first taste of the rum. "Um, smooth," he said with eyes closed in concentration while Gracie shook her head and smiled. He continued his focus on Archie. "Your mother tells me you'll be attending Manning's. Very good school. Very good school. One of the best on the island, my dear boy." He raised his glass as if to toast the school.

"So I've been told," Archie responded with a smirk.

"How do you plan on getting to Sav-la-mar[2] with so few cars on the road these days?"

"Mr. Campbell is going to take me there on Mondays and pick me up on Fridays."

"Ah, the Thane of Cawdor." He glanced over to Gracie, then continued addressing Archie. "So, you won't be here to help your mother during the weekdays, then?"

Archie, wondering about Mick's Thane of Cawdor comment, didn't reply.

"And where will you be staying?"

"With a man and his wife that Mr. Campbell knows," replied Archie, curious why Mick was so interested in his affairs when he usually only gave hellos and goodbyes. A general unease came over him. He sat forward, taking the opportunity the silence offered, and excused himself, saying he was still hungry from dinner and wanted something from the kitchen.

Abbie had just about finished cleaning the kitchen when Archie walked in. Taking one look at him, she said, "What is the matter with you, Mass Archie?" She had been the cook at the Montego Bay inn and had come along with Gracie and Archie to Oristano at Malcolm's insistence. Feeding Archie for the sixteen years of his life, she knew him even better than she knew her own children, who lived in the parish of Hanover, a half hour's drive from Montego Bay. She certainly knew him better than Gracie did.

"Nothing that a piece of your potato pone won't fix," he smiled.

"Ah, it's the Alleluia In Between you looking." She laughed.

Archie looked puzzled.

"You don't know what me talking 'bout?"

"No."

Motioning with her hands, she said, "Them say, 'Hell a top, hell a bottom, alleluia in between.' When we cook the potato pone in Hanover Parish, we put hot charcoal on top of it and under it, and what come out is so good, you must praise God!" She laughed again and handed him a good portion of her sweet potato pone. "Now, tell Abbie what is bothering you so."

Archie's brow was weighed down in thought. "I don't exactly know…except that…Mick gets me upset."

"What him say to upset you?" She pulled up a chair and sat with him at the small kitchen table.

"Nothing really, except he was asking me about me, and he's never shown any interest in me before." He looked down at the table.

"Me can tell you thinking something. What is it?"

"Maybe Mick's intentions toward Mummy are more than just to sell her liquor."

"As smart as you is, is a wonder you never see that before," Abbie responded.

He continued, engrossed in his own thoughts, "Yes, why didn't I see it before? Over the years, Mummy has had quite a few gentleman friends—some at the same time—but I thought she had finally settled on Mr. Campbell. He's practically set her up as proprietor of this inn. I know he has a wife up the hill, but I also know how things work. Now I finally understand what people mean by what's sauce for the goose is sauce for the gander." He sat up straight. "Well, what's sauce for the goose is also sauce for the gosling!"

With a puzzled look on her face, Abbie asked, "What is a gosling?"

"A baby goose," he replied, as if everyone should know.

"Sound to me like you know too much for you own good. Be careful, Mass Archie. I been round this inn business a long time. De best thing for you is to go to school tomorrow and study to do something other than the inn business. Is a good thing you staying in Sav for most of the week. If you can stay for the weekends, me advise you to do so."

He got up from his chair, bent down, and gave her a big hug and a kiss on the cheek. Her soft plump body partially enveloped him, and her sweat from the kitchen stove and the summer heat smudged his face. He didn't care. Her listening ear and astute words had lifted his spirit.

The next morning, Archie was up early, dressed in his new school uniform, eating a hearty breakfast Abbie had prepared for him.

"I'm sure the food won't be like this at the Witcombes. I'll be thin as a stick when I come home at the end of the week, and you'll have to fatten me up again," Archie said to Abbie while wiping egg yolk off the plate with his last piece of johnnycake.

"Me will do just that." She stopped what she was doing, turned around, looked at him with a smile, then continued. "But you mek sure to eat whatever the Witcombe them put before you, for dog that eat nothing can't bark at no one."

"Just when I think I've heard all your proverbs, you come out with another one," he chuckled. "Don't worry, Abbie, I have plenty of bark—and bite—in me." He got up from the table and gave her a long hug. "I'll miss you, your food, *and* your sayings."

She was silent for the duration of the hug, then said with a lump in her throat, "Go on now. You know say Mass Malcolm want you waiting when him get here."

"You're right." He headed out of the kitchen.

"Me will see you Friday. You favorite dinner will be waiting," Abbie called after him.

He looked back and replied with a smile, "If personality is an unbroken series of successful gestures, then there is something gorgeous about you, Abbie."

Her face reddened, then she sucked her teeth and said, "Go along with you Gatsby foolishness."

Archie grabbed his small suitcase and was heading toward the stairs when he saw his mother standing on the veranda looking out toward the ocean that glinted through the bright orange lit Poinciana canopies. He was surprised but pleased she had gotten up to say goodbye to him. Admiring her beauty, long and lean with a constant sun-brushed glow, he could see why so many men were attracted to her. He put the suitcase down and walked toward the veranda. He was about to say goodbye when he realized she wasn't looking at the ocean but at the driveway. Wasn't that just like her? A puppy waiting for any morsel of attention from its master.

"Goodbye, Mother," he forced the words out of his mouth.

She looked around. "Oh! Archie." She laughed softly, as if embarrassed for being discovered daydreaming. She looked him over. "You look like a fine young man in your Manning's uniform. I'm proud you're going off to school, even though I'll miss your help around the inn. I'm not sure what I will do without you. Yet, I know a young man needs his education." She paused, looking back at the driveway. "Don't forget what we spoke about. Take full advantage of the time you have to curry favor. He's your ticket."

"Yes. I know, Mother. We've had this conversation many times." He looked toward the road. "I have to go now. Malcolm wants me to be waiting when he gets here."

"Yes." She lightly kissed his cheek. "Don't keep him waiting."

With that, Archie collected his bag and headed down to the porte-cochère.

~

The ride to Savanna-la-Mar, which usually took just under an hour, seemed especially long. Archie had driven with Malcolm before, but never alone. They sat in silence for most of the drive with the scenery transitioning from the spray of south-coast waves crashing against the sea wall, to steep hillsides pressing against the gravel road, to impenetrable vegetation enshrouding them, and then repetitions of the same.

When they passed Ferris Cross and the vista widened, revealing the cultivated lands signaling their approach to Savanna-la-Mar, Archie dared to breach the silence. "Mr. Campbell?" He paused until Malcolm acknowledged him, then continued, "How will my things get to the Witcombes' place?"

"I'll drop them off."

Archie waited a while longer before asking another question. "What time will you be picking me up on Friday?"

"I wouldn't know."

They drove further, then without prompting, Malcolm instructed, "Go straight home after school on Friday, and be ready for me when I get there."

"Yes, sir," he replied immediately. Something about his instinctive reply to Malcolm irked him. This isn't how Gatsby would have responded. Yet something about Malcolm's demeanor required it. Archie's conflicting feelings of repulsion and attraction unsettled him. Then he remembered his mother's incessant reminders to "curry favor." He shook off the ambivalence and went into performance mode. "I'll be waiting, Mr. Campbell, and I want you to know how grateful I am for all you are doing for me."

Malcolm responded with a barely perceptible grunt.

5

KIMBERLY, SOUTH AFRICA

10 MARCH 1902

Dearest Abum,

I trust you and the children are well. Cuddy and I are settling into our new life here in Kimberly. I've never seen such a place. It's a big enough town to get needed supplies and has many people coming and going via the Cape Town Railway, including British military men stationed to keep the Boers at bay. The landscape is primarily rocky and flat, with large mounds of debris from the mines here and there. Cuddy says they look like boils rising from the land longing to be wrapped in a poultice. I'm sorry for that distasteful image. I thought about starting the letter over without it, but after thinking on it, that is exactly how it looks to me as well.

Our new home is situated close to the mines for proximity to Cuddy's infirmary. It's not a bad house. It had been occupied by the previous physician, who was incapacitated during the Boer attacks on Kimberly three years earlier. After that, he saw patients with minor illnesses at the house and had an assistant take care of the colored laborers at the infirmary. He and his wife left Kimberly the week before we arrived, so we were greeted by a well-kept house that only needed my touch to make it a home for Cuddy and me. Don't misunderstand me, it is not Jamaica, and I often find myself wishing the orange business had not failed. However, I am trying to make the best of the situation. Cuddy plans on eventually sending for the children, but I'm not sure it is the best place for them to grow up. This flat, endless plain is unfit for much but mining diamonds.

Every evening, since it is only Cuddy and me at the dinner table, he occupies my mind by telling me about his day at the infirmary. Most of what he does is tending to broken limbs and wounds from falling rocks in the mines. He was told from time to time there are outbreaks of tuberculosis and other diseases caused by the poor housing conditions of the fenced compounds in which the colored laborers live. There is only so much he can do in these cases, so he'll have to send them to the Kimberly Hospital where they have their own wards, separate from the white wards.

The part of his job he finds distasteful is the holding cell. When a colored worker has completed his six-month contract and wants to leave the mine to return home, he has to go into a cell, strip naked, and stay that way for three days and nights to ensure he has not swallowed any diamonds. These stories do indeed take my mind off my present situation. The poor devils.

Well, how are the children? I miss them so. It gets so silent sitting in a home with no one but a cook and a maid. I used to get over-whelmed with the noise and needs of the children, but now I miss them in the silence. The only noise is from the maid clanking pots in the kitchen and the gardener snipping at the bushes. There are also the explosions that come from the mines. They always catch me off guard.

Please give my love to the children and do write letting us know of how they are.

As ever,
Cuddy and Winnie

6

―――――

CAILIN | SHARPE

TUESDAY, SEPTEMBER 5, 1944

"Cailin. Cailin," Gus whispered, gently shaking her out of a deep sleep. He'd taken a chance coming into her room without knocking. She was his cousin—and practically his sister—but as of late, she had taken to being modest about her body.

With groggy eyes and molasses speech, she sat up looking at him befuddled, and croaked, "What...what...?" She looked around then continued, "It's...still dark. Go back to bed."

"The bird trap—we left it there—a bird could be trapped—I couldn't sleep," he spewed his phrases in desperation. "I've been thinking about it all night. Suppose a mongoose gets to it?"

Cailin looked at him blankly, flopped back on the mattress, and replied. "A mongoose can't lift the trap." She turned over on her side, pulling the covers over her head and repeated with more volume, "Go back to bed!"

"Shh," Gus quieted her and continued his plea. "You don't know mongoose like I know mongoose. If they can't lift it, they'll burrow under it." He waited for a response, but when he got none, he shook her again, whispering urgently, "Get up! You have to go with me!"

She sighed. "Go by yourself."

"I can't. It's dark." He paused, then admitted, "I'm afraid."

"Well, I'm sleeping!" she said, raising her voice again.

"You have to," he said, shaking her, then added, "If you don't, I'll tell your father you were swimming in the pond yesterday."

She threw off the sheet and sat up. "You wouldn't dare do such a mean thing!"

Gus responded, "And why shouldn't I?"

"You snake! You can't tell. If Daddy found out, he would kill me! I told you what he did to Ian for swimming there."

"I don't want to tell, but you give me no choice." He folded his arms. "Or you can get out of bed, get dressed, and meet me outside."

About mid-afternoon, a car came to a stop on the Cawdor road. Sharpe had been helping Samfie cut back the overgrowth along the roadside when he turned to see who it was. Seeing it was Busha, he swallowed hard. While he knew a talk with Busha was inevitable, he wasn't mentally prepared. His mind had been preoccupied with ways to deal with Lucy and Magus.

Malcolm leaned his head out the car window. "Sharpe, get in the car," he ordered.

"Yes, Busha," he responded promptly.

Samfie looked at Sharpe with questioning eyes.

Without another word, Sharpe got in the car. They drove in silence up to the house, parking in front of the barbecue.

Malcolm threw his arm over the car seat and turned to Sharpe. "Where's the pimento bag?"

Sharpe, looking straight ahead, answered, "In the storeroom, sah."

"Who put it there?"

Sharpe's eyes fixed on the red ginger lily plants the yard man was clipping. "Me put it there, Busha."

Malcolm opened the car door. "Come with me."

Malcolm marched across the barbecue toward his office. Sharpe followed. His mind raced. Would he be demoted? If so, how could he go back to Hakin and face them? Or, worse yet, would he be told to leave Cawdor altogether? If so, Lucy and Magus would be sure to stir up the people and run him out of Hakin. What would he do then? Where would he go?

Inside the office, Malcolm glared at Sharpe with a corrugated brow and tightened thin lips. Sharpe had seen him wear that face before when castigating other workers publicly. Back in Hakin, they would often mock Busha, impersonating his facial expression and the things he had said as a way of appeasing their brooding shame. The only puzzling thing for Sharpe was why Busha was chastising him in private.

Malcolm's words were deliberate and direct. "I chose you, Sharpe. I chose you out of that den of thieves. I didn't choose you because you're a big black bastard! I chose you because I saw in you a seed of myself. A man who would do anything to get something." His mouth opened again to speak, but he paused as if taking another route and asked intently, "Am I right?"

Looking at the ground in front of him in order to maintain a submissive attitude, Sharpe felt the sting of Malcolm's demeaning words. *Big Black bastard*, he thought, *what give one man the right to speak to another man this way?* The only answer Sharpe could muster to his own question—unsatisfactory as it was—was that Busha had always been this way.

Though he also wasn't sure about the *do anything to get something* part, Sharpe replied. "Yes, Busha."

"Look at me and speak up, damn it! Don't take me for a fool, like one of those baccra[1] white people. I wasn't born yesterday. I know how you people put on a quashie act to make us think you're daft and dutiful. Now I'll ask you again. Are you the right man for the job?"

"Yes," Sharpe replied with his head still bowed. Catching himself, he straightened his posture, looked Malcolm squarely in the eyes and said, "Yes. Yes. I am the man for this property." Then, for good measure, he added, "I will do whatever it takes to run it right."

His eyes locked with Sharpe's, Malcolm responded, "That is what I need to know." Satisfied, he sat down at his desk. Then looking up at Sharpe, he warned, "Never try to samfie me again. Now get out of here, and do whatever you have to do to show them you're their boss!"

"Yes, sah."

Outside, Sharpe exhaled, relaxing his shoulders. He hadn't been demoted or lost his job. They wouldn't be able to mock him or drive him out of Hakin. With a sigh of relief, he decided to go back down the hill to make sure Samfie finished the job. The walk down would give him the time to sort through what had just happened.

When he turned the corner just past the cotton tree, with no eyes on him, he felt free to think—to talk out loud—to gesticulate if need be. His first uninhibited thought surprised him: *I chose you because I saw in you a seed of myself.* He remembered the statement word for word. Why would those words from Busha, of all things, be his first thought? He mulled it over for a time. His father came to mind.

As a young boy in Accompong, Sharpe was intent on being like his father. He tried imitating his facial expressions, his mannerisms at the dinner table, even his gait. When his father was at work, Sharpe would boss everyone around, which only worked on his two younger sisters. His mother would always laugh as she came to the girls' rescue. But he didn't do it to be funny—he wanted to be like his father. When he was sent to Hakin, he tried imitating his uncle. It was taken as mockery, for which he was punished. After that, the only other man he had looked up to was Mr. Aldridge, his schoolteacher. But when he tried imitating Mr. Aldridge, the other boys ridiculed him. From then on, he'd had to patch together, from afar, what he thought a man should be like.

It dawned on him now, for all practical purposes, Busha had offered him an invitation to imitate him.

This revelation unsettled him. Busha was a white man—a property owner who treated his workers as little more than slaves. He didn't treat his family much better, either. To boot, in his youth, Busha was rumored to have shot and killed a property worker for defying him.

Sharpe stopped, threw his hands up in the air, letting them fall and clap against his thighs, and questioned aloud, "Do I really want to be like him?"

He stood fixed in place and time. His thoughts roiled around his head like rice and peas in boiling water: *Yes. No. Here's why...Here's why not...But what about this...Yes, but don't forget about that....* As grains and legumes soak up liquid and begin settling into a temporary whole, so his thoughts began to calm. While he was not yet able to accept or reject Busha's implied offer, he told himself there was no rush. He didn't have to decide then and there. He figured he would test it out, see if there was really a seed of Busha inside him.

He started walking again.

When he reached the spot he had left Samfie, he didn't see him, nor did he hear the expected chopping of a machete. Instead, he heard laughter. He followed the sound and found Samfie with Fisha, a fisherman who usually brought fish up to Cawdor to sell. They were sitting on the trunk of a fallen tree, with Samfie exhaling a plume of smoke toward the tree canopy.

Seeing Sharpe, Fisha said, "Come, man. Come join we for a smoke."

Samfie held a ganga spliff[2] out to Sharpe.

Sharpe's only thought was, *The first test is sooner than expected*. Then he barked at Samfie, "Get up! Smoke ganja on you own time!"

Samfie jerked his head back and countered, "Look, Quaco. No take you talk with Busha out on me."

Sharpe took two quick steps, grabbed Samfie by his scrawny arms, and hoisted him up. "Don't ever talk back to me again! And while on the job, my name is Sharpe to you! Now put the spliff out and get back to work! If you don't finish the job by sundown, it's me you gwane deal with." He turned to Fisha. "And you! Get up to the house with the fish!"

Sharpe handed Samfie the machete while Fisha took off up the road as fast as his fish-laden donkey would allow.

Sharpe stood watching Samfie chopping bush like he'd never seen him do before and marveled at what just happened. Maybe he had it in him after all—that seed of Busha. Even though it was only Samfie and Fisha he had dealt with, the incident served to bolster his confidence for the other tests that would surely come—Lucy and Magus.

But Lucy first.

He let Samfie finish the job on his own and headed to the east side of the property to check on the pimento pickers, where he knew he'd find Lucy.

It had been a humid day. Sharpe's sweat-stained clothes were beginning to dry as a welcome breeze blew up the mountainside from Oristano Bay, and the westward sun hid itself behind a tall thicket of mahogany trees, indicating the pimento workers had a good hour more to finish picking and bagging the pimento.

On his way there, he practiced his gait, marching as he'd seen Busha do, less than an hour earlier. For extra measure, he threw his shoulders back. It wasn't natural to him, but he thought he might need it when he approached Lucy and the other pimento pickers.

When he spotted them, he didn't see Lucy. He sighed with relief, but then decided not to let his guard down.

"Where is Lucy?" Sharpe asked. "Sitting down on some log making you do all the work?"

"She in her bed suffering with woman problem," replied one of the women.

Sharpe thought it odd as Lucy seemed well past that time of life. He checked their pimento pickings, then said firmly, "Mek sure all the pimento get into the storeroom before dark." He made firm eye contact with all five of them. "I will be up at the house waiting for you."

In Lucy's absence, there was no backtalk.

Walking away, Sharpe felt satisfied with this second test, though it didn't quite give the release putting Lucy in her place would have. Nonetheless, he had to admit he was partially thankful for her absence. He'd have to deal with her soon enough.

On his way back up to the house, walking through a small wooded area, he heard the splashing of nearby water.

Sharpe recognized Gus's voice saying, "Why'd you do that?"

Cailin laughed and replied, "For waking me up at four this morning."

There was another splash of water followed by Gus's defense. "We saved the ground dove, though."

"That dove was never in danger. It could have waited until morning."

Sharpe was relieved it was only the children. So as not to surprise them, he cleared his throat with a cough and walked toward the pond.

A "Shhh!" came from the water.

When Sharpe reached the pond, he saw ripples and bubbles of air rising to the water's surface. He waited patiently. In less than a minute, Gus popped out of the water gasping for air with Cailin immediately following. After she caught her breath she said, "Good job, Gus. You can't even hold your breath long enough to keep us a secret."

Sharpe bridled his urge to laugh. He knew how Busha felt about the children swimming in this pond. Because one of his cousins had drowned in the pond at a young age, Busha had forbidden his children to even go there. Sharpe had heard about the thrashing Ian received when Busha caught him swimming in the pond. The same would come of these two, no matter that Cailin was a girl.

Here was the next, but unexpected, test—Busha's children. Could he do it? Would he turn them over to Busha? He thought of his own sisters. He could only see them as they'd been when he'd left Accompong—young and innocent. Would he have wanted someone to report them to his father? He wavered for a moment. This was going to be a harder test than even dealing with Lucy. But he knew he had to pass it. He had to show Malcolm he could be trusted.

~

"Into my bedroom!" Malcolm growled, standing on the barbecue.

The two children ushered themselves reluctantly into the house.

Cailin, with her hands covering her bottom, leaned over to Gus and whispered, "Do what I told you, and it won't be as bad."

The only time Cailin saw the inside of her father's room was for beatings. It had been a while since she'd been there. She'd forgotten how plain the furnishings were—a dark chest of drawers with a washbasin, shaving gear, and a small mirror; a simple bed, not much larger than her own single bed; and a brown iron safe sitting on the floor with an oval brass name-plate inscribed with *J. Cartwright & Sons*. The safe doubled as his bedside table. The only pleasant thing about the room were the two windows, one looking toward the cotton tree and the other overlooking the ocean. Her mother had her own room and had not been called to Malcolm's room in years—she had done her duty in giving him his respectable white family.

"Pull down your pants and bend over the bed," he ordered Cailin. While he opened the top drawer of his chest of drawers, Cailin turned to Gus and mouthed, *Remember*. Ian, who had received more beatings than there were stones on the Cawdor gravel road, had once offered his sister sage advice—*Make your bottom as tight as you can, and yell louder than it hurts.*

Malcolm had made a cat-o'-nine-tails some years earlier, specifically intended for Ian. The cowhide, which was from the property, was cut into twenty-seven thin strips, braided three at a time, and bound with a long strip of leather to a hand-carved handle. The nine tails extended two and a half feet from the handle, each with a knot at the end.

Cailin tightened her bottom as Malcolm brandished his whip. When the first stroke hit, she gave a small whimper. With each stroke, her whimpers increasingly evolved until they were at last bellows. By the ninth blow, she screamed, "Daddy! Please stop!" and she began to cry.

He dropped his arm to his side and said with steel in his voice, "Don't you *ever* go swimming in that pond again! Do you hear me?"

She let out a brief sob and replied, "Yes, Daddy."

Without turning around, he barked, "Angus! Get in position."

With his face fixed in a scowl, Gus walked to the bed, pulled his pants down, and bent over. Cailin could tell by his leg muscles he had tightened his bottom. She was relieved to know he was following her suggestion.

Malcolm brought the whip down for the first blow. No sound came from Gus. The second…the third…the fourth…the fifth, and still not even a moan. Cailin looked at Gus's face, saw the unbending alloy of pain and defiance, and wondered why he was doing this. Was it because her father was not his father? Was it because he didn't understand why her father hadn't gone to war with his father? Was it because his father was suffering at war, and he felt he needed to suffer too? Or maybe it was just something boys did. But Ian was tough, and he was the one who'd come up with the idea to yell. She was confounded.

By the tenth blow, Malcolm was getting angrier. "Pull your underpants down!"

Cailin turned around, embarrassed for him. She heard the lash of the whip—eleven…twelve…thirteen. Still no sound from Gus.

"Right then! The legs."

Fourteen. Malcolm grunted as he brought the whip down with all his might on Gus's legs. A slight groan escaped from Gus.

Cailin could take it no longer and left the room, crouching just outside the door. Still hearing the lashes, she groaned softly with tears welling in her eyes, "Daddy…Daddy…Daddy."

On the twenty-fourth lash, Gus finally surrendered with a flood of tears and sobs.

~

Sharpe stood on the hilly slope just beneath Malcolm's window, legs unsteady. He heard it all. His heart vacillated between malleable clay and metamorphic rock.

7

ARCHIE

FRIDAY, SEPTEMBER 8, 1944

"Coming back for more next week?" a tall, white-skinned boy yelled as Archie walked out the Manning's School gate and turned right on to Beckford Street. Archie pretended not to notice him, but inside he was burning. It had been a brutal week, which he had expected but had forgotten how it felt. Four years earlier, when he entered first form at Cornwall College in Montego Bay, he had experienced the customary initiation rites: "The Dance," where one had to remain in the same spot while jumping about in order to avoid his feet being pulverized by propelled rocks; "The Arm Wrench," where one arm was painfully twisted behind the back while the other surrendered whatever was in the money pocket; "The Grovel," where one had to assume the role of a personal servant—the final test for anyone desiring to enter a particular circle of boys.

This was different, however. He was a new boy going into the fifth form of a new school where he didn't know a soul. Entering Manning's as a fifth former, he was too old to start back at initiate, yet, being a newcomer, he was an unknown entity and, therefore, might as well have offered himself up for archery practice. To make it worse, Manning's had girls! He wasn't sure how that affected relations between boys in school, but he knew it had to.

On Monday of that week, Malcolm had dropped him off at the school gate and pulled away as soon as Archie closed the car door. His eyes followed the car down Beckford until he heard a voice ask, "Who's that boy?"

"He must be new," answered another.

Archie stiffened his back, took a deep breath, and thought to himself, *Here we go*. Turning around, he saw two boys dressed as he was in khaki short-sleeved shirts tucked into their khaki short pants. One boy was tall and white-skinned; the other was about Archie's height but dark-skinned.

Archie had rehearsed this for the past few days, knowing of the impending first contact—the contact that would determine the direction of at least the first few weeks of the school year. He wasn't sure which of his well-honed approaches he needed to use: the cocky, I'm-going-to-rule-this-place or the chummy, we're-going-to-be-best-friends. He stood there for a moment. Going with his gut, he walked past them with chest puffed out and chin high.

"Well, look at that! Not even a nod of respect for fifth form-ers," declared the taller boy. His accent carried an air of what Archie would come to know as the Savanna-la-Mar estab-lishment.

Archie continued walking up the gradual hill with mostly colored boys and girls scattered around in groups, heading toward the schoolhouse. The building diverted his attention. There was something symmetrically pleasing about it—two wings on opposite ends which extended forward out of the main edifice and a stately cupola rising from the middle of the steep shingle roof. While thinking he may like it there, he felt an impact on his upper back and tripped over something. His schoolbag went flying while his face careened toward the lime-stone gravel path.

After a moment of smarting pain, he opened his eyes to see a wave of legs surging toward him dressed in short-khakis and navy-blue dresses. He heaved himself from the ground, stood up, and brushed his clothes off while looking around to see who the perpetrators were. The swelling crowd seemed like one massive tentacled entity.

"Did you lose this?" someone asked to his right. Archie looked over and saw his schoolbag in the hands of the shorter of the two boys he had seen at the gate. The crowd broke out in turbulent amusement. So much for his I'm-going-to-rule-this-place strategy, and it was too late now for the other. News of this event was sure to spread quickly throughout the school.

The tone was set for the rest of the week. The two boys led a pack of wolves who saw Archie as their prey. Clive Taylor, the taller of the two, was the head of the pack. Being captain of the football team the previous year, all the girls loved him. It didn't hurt that he was the only fully Caucasian boy in the school. There were a handful of boys, like Archie, who were question-ably white, but to be obviously white was an anomaly at Manning's. Clive, whose father owned a large cattle property just west of Savanna-la-Mar, was only attending Manning's because he'd been expelled from Munro College. Nobody knew why. Nor would they dare ask. Devon Blake, the pack's second in command, was the son of a prominent businessman in Savanna-la-Mar. Devon's father, the son of a property owner in the Darliston area who had an affair with a colored woman in Savanna-la-Mar, had himself attended Manning's. The rest of the pack ran in whatever direction these two were going.

The rest of the week was filled with adolescent pranks aimed at embarrassing Archie in front of girls, teachers, and the student body in general. He figured he was going to have to

ride it out until he had the opportunity to gain the students'
respect through sports or, more probably, a good fight. This
was not the way he had anticipated starting the school year.
His one reprieve was his return to Oristano for the weekend.
This reminded him of Malcolm's words to be ready and waiting. Being that it was Friday, he shifted from saunter to sprint.

Beckford Street merged into Rose Street, which quickly
merged into Great George Street. The Witcombes lived in a
roomy two-story house behind their store, Great George
Street Haberdashery, about half a mile from the wharf.
Malcolm had taken Archie to meet the Witcombes two weeks
earlier, where Archie found the accommodations agreeable,
albeit not quite like his mother's inn. His room had everything
he needed: a comfortable bed, a desk to study at, a cushioned
chair to relax in, and a window overlooking Mrs. Witcombe's
flower garden in the back of the house.

His initial assessment of Mr. and Mrs. Witcombe was
favorable. He was sure he could navigate these waters. Mr.
Witcombe was a tall, slim man with thick, grey sideburns. He
wore a waistcoat with a chain draped from one pocket to the
other. One end of the chain sported a gold-plated watch his
wife had given him as a wedding present, while attached to the
other end was a fob his father had used for embossing his
initials in wax letter seals. His ribbon lips smiled affably, and he
gave Archie a firm handshake. Mrs. Witcombe, slightly on the
rotund side with graying, bunned hair and wearing a soft
cotton floral frock, held Archie by his shoulders and expressed
her great pleasure at having him there. She made much of him,
as though he was her son coming home from an epic journey.
On his first day living there, Archie asked the cook about the
Witcombes' children and was told, "The good Lawd never seem
to want them to have pickney[1]. It's been a great burden on the
both of them—specially for the misses."

Upon Archie's arrival from school, he hurried behind the

haberdashery to the house, where he half expected to see Malcolm's car parked. Glad the car wasn't there yet, he dashed into the house and up the stairs.

"What's all the rush about, dear?" Mrs. Witcombe called upstairs.

"Mr. Campbell should be here any minute to pick me up," Archie yelled down as he changed his clothes and shoved a couple of last-minute things into the bag he had packed from the night before.

"Be sure to put your uniforms and anything else you need washed in the clothes hamper. And don't forget to bring your schoolwork with you," she called up.

Archie looked at his schoolbag thrown by his desk, thought for a moment, then turned, picked up his small suitcase, and headed downstairs. He found Mrs. Witcombe in her wingback parlor chair, crocheting a doily, which was her perpetual pastime. This made sense to Archie as the haberdashery was filled with doilies. Earlier in the week, on his way home from school, he had stopped in the store to see what they sold. He found an abundance of sewing paraphernalia: bolts of cloth, thread, buttons, and yarn—nothing of interest to him. On his way out of the shop, he spotted a shelf in the window laden with doilies made in multiple patterns, colors, and sizes.

"Goodbye, Mrs. Witcombe. Thank you for your kindness this week. Mr. Campbell should be here any minute to pick me up." He bent down and gave her a customary kiss on the cheek.

"My," she exclaimed with a chuckle, her head down and not skipping a stitch. "It's as if you're leaving, never to return."

Archie's cheeks reddened. "No, no. I apologize. I'm thankful to be here. It's just that I'm eager to get back to Oristano and see everyone again." *Well, at least Abbie,* he thought to himself.

She looked up at him with a tender smile. "I understand." After a pause, she suggested, "Why don't you sit on the couch while you're waiting? I'll have Pressy get you a slice of ginger-bread and some lemonade."

"Thank you, but I'm going to wait on the front steps. He told me he wanted me ready when he got here."

She laughed again. "Go ahead then. I'll have her bring it out to you."

On the steps, he thought about the Witcombes. He liked them. They seemed to be what he imagined actual parents to be like—kind, concerned, protective. Maybe too protective. He had to be home right after school, have all his homework done before dinner, and keep a curfew of seven thirty, which didn't give him much time to explore as dinner started promptly at six thirty and wasn't over until seven. And his lights had to be out by nine! Yes, that was another reason he couldn't wait to get back to the inn.

After a while, Pressy brought him the gingerbread and lemonade. He had hoped Malcolm would have been there before she came out, figuring he'd get some of Abbie's cooking that much sooner. But after his first bite of the dark, sticky cake, fragrant with ginger, he was glad for the delay. Pressy lingered long enough to enjoy the look of pleasure on his face, then returned to the kitchen. Archie was not the type to scramble down his food. As his mother's inn always had an abundance of food, he never felt the need to devour his. He savored the gingerbread, washing down every couple bites with a swig of lemonade. With every swig, he imagined he was at one of Gatsby's over-the-top parties. After the last of the lemonade, he got up, feigning intoxication, and yelled, "It's a great advantage to drink among hard drinking people."

Mrs. Witcombe, stirred from her crocheting, got out of her chair, looked out the window, and asked, "What are you going on about, son? Is everything alright?"

He stopped in the middle of a spinning stupor and replied

with a chuckle, "Yes, Mrs. Witcombe. It's something to do with a book I've read."

"Books are good, son. But one has to be ever so careful about reading the right books, as some lead to moral decay," she sermonized.

Thinking it better not to contradict her and take the chance of her possibly telling Malcolm, he sobered his demeanor and sat back down on the stairs. His mind was now back on Malcolm, wondering where he was.

He began pelting stones from the gravel driveway at the occasional bird that would perch on the electrical wire that came from the street to the house. It wasn't very long before Mrs. Witcombe's head popped out of the window again admonishing him for throwing the driveway gravel, saying, "At this rate, there won't be anything to prevent the rain from turning the dirt into mud." He stopped throwing stones and sat down again.

Archie sat fidgeting, looking toward where the driveway passed the haberdashery and led to Great George Street. Getting impatient, he asked himself, "Where is Malcolm?" Then, to pacify himself, he thought, *He must have been held up on the property. Something urgent has come up. He'll be here soon.*

Realizing he needed something to occupy his mind, he got up, left his suitcase on the porch, and went inside the house and up to his room. He sat down at his desk and started his homework.

Archie had always done well in school. The reason could be traced back to Abbie. She required him to complete his homework daily, and she checked his report cards religiously. The real incentive, though, was her system of rewards and withholdings. He was rewarded dessert on the days he did his homework before dinner, and she baked him his favorite dessert on the days he received a report card with all A's and B's, which gave him the opportunity to earn his own personal lemon meringue pie during Christmas and Easter holidays and when school let out in May for the summer. Her system of withholdings denied him dessert accordingly. His mother left his education in Abbie's capable hands, mostly because she was more concerned about his service to the inn than anything else.

He spent the next couple hours completing his homework, then he sat in his cushioned chair, staring blankly out his window, watching the slow sunset. He heard the dinner bell ring promptly at six thirty. When he didn't appear for dinner, Mrs. Witcombe sent Pressy up to his room. He told her he wasn't hungry, that the gingerbread had filled him up, and he was saving his appetite for his favorite meal that Abbie had promised to cook for him. Pressy gave him a look of compassion, then retreated downstairs to report to Mrs. Witcombe.

At eight thirty, Mr. Witcombe took a plate of food and Archie's suitcase up to his room. Mrs. Witcombe had encouraged him to bring the food up and offer Archie any consolation he could, but Mr. Witcombe found him sprawled out on his bed fast asleep—shoes and all. He set down the plate and the suitcase, pulled off Archie's shoes and left the room, closing the door behind him.

Archie was up early the next morning. The smell of ackee and saltfish and johnnycakes drew him down to the kitchen, where he voraciously made up for the previous evening's missed meal with the healthy portion Pressy served him. On his way out of the kitchen, he told her he was going to explore Savanna-la-Mar. Before she could tell him what time lunch was served, he was out the door.

Savanna-la-Mar was established during the eighteenth century. Being one of Jamaica's larger towns, it was sizable enough to spend the day exploring. When Archie got to Great

George Street, he already knew which way he would turn. He was curious as to what lay to the right where he had been told the wharf was, but he headed left, toward Manning's, as he had daily passed by a store with an item that caught his eye. But during the week, he dared not stop on the way back to the Witcombes, not being sure if they would tell Malcolm he had not returned directly after school. Today, he didn't care what they told Malcolm.

The street was lined with a mixture of houses, businesses, and churches in a great variety of shapes, sizes, and building materials—wood, cut stone, rough stone, and cement—each adding to the flavored history of the town. Abbie had once told him that Savanna-la-Mar used to be a slave-trading port. Though he looked, he saw no sign of it.

He got to the store he was looking for, Chester and Holt Hardware, which was on the corner of Beckford and Lewes Streets. There it hung on the back wall, easily visible from the street—a hunting rifle. He thought, *That's the kind of gun Gatsby would have*. He went into the store, which was filled with hammers and nails, nuts and bolts, and tools of seemingly unending varieties. Archie had done light repair work with the gardeners of the two inns his mother had run, but none of the tools appealed to him. He was only interested in the gun. He had always wanted to go bird shooting and heard Malcolm went every year. Maybe he'd take him next season. The thought of Malcolm upset him. He left the store.

As he stepped on to Beckford Street, he saw a boy from Manning's walking in his direction. He wanted to pretend he hadn't seen the boy and cross the street, but their eyes had met.

The boy, looking uncertain, said, "Hello," and paused. "I believe you're the new fifth former at Manning's. Archibald Price, isn't it?"

Archie, taken aback that the boy spoke to him but wanting to take advantage of it, answered, "Actually, I prefer Archie."

"It's Archie then." The boy glanced around as if to be certain no one was watching then said, "I'm Robert Thompson. Everybody calls me Robby."

Making the most of the opportunity, Archie threw out some bait. "As you said, I'm new here, so I'm taking the grand tour of Sav."

Robby chuckled. "Not much to see, but have you been down by the wharf area?"

"Not yet. Is there anything interesting down there?"

"Well, there's the market and the wharf, but not far from there is the square with the Doric Cinema."

"A cinema! I haven't seen a picture show since I left Mobay. What's playing there?"

"Last Saturday I saw *Sherlock Holmes Faces Death*," Robby said with a glimmer in his eyes. "It's a war movie with Sherlock Holmes. He solves some mysterious deaths at a big home that was used for wounded soldiers. I would see it again. You want to go see it today?"

Satisfied that Robby had taken the bait, Archie said, "I would love to, but I don't have any money on me. Can we do something else, like go down to the wharf?"

"Rhaatid![2] Don't worry about money! I never pay. I know how to get into the Doric. After we've watched the movie, we can go to the wharf."

On the way to the Doric Cinema, Robby filled Archie in on the stores and homes they were passing, including his own home on Ricketts Street, not far from the Witcombes. The boys spent the rest of the day watching the movie, walking around the open-air market assuming the roles of Charles Dicken's characters the Artful Dodger and Charley Bates—nicking a coconut drop here, a piece of peeled sugar cane there—and sitting on the wharf throwing stones into the sea while Robby told Archie about British and American naval ships he'd seen frequent the area.

Evening approached, and Robby suggested going into Saint George's Parish Church. The suggestion came with a dare to see how long they could stay in the church building once it got dark. When Archie learned they would trespass, he told Robby he couldn't because he had to get back to the Witcombes. Even though he was upset about Malcolm not picking him up, trespassing was definitely not the way to curry his favor.

On reaching the Witcombes' closed store, Archie addressed Robby using one of his cavalier Gatsby phrases. "Well, old sport." He patted Robby on the back. "Thanks for showing me the highlights of Sav. It wouldn't have been the same without you."

"Not a problem for me. It was good to have an accomplice," Robby replied.

"So can we do it again tomorrow?" asked Archie.

"Maybe. It depends on what my parents decide to do after church."

"If not, I'll see you on Monday morning, then," Archie said with a light punch to Robby's shoulder.

Robby hesitated, making Archie feel as though he had overstepped his bounds with the friendly punch, but what Robby went on to say caught him off guard. "Well, you know…um…I think it's better if we just see each other on the weekends, outside of Manning's. You understand, don't you?"

Archie's countenance stiffened. "Yeah. I understand. See you around then," and turned down the Witcombes' driveway.

Robby stared at him for a moment, then headed toward Ricketts Street.

Kicking the gravel as he walked toward the house, Archie thought of Malcolm. He picked up a stone and hurled it at the electric pole, hitting it dead on. The stone rebounded back onto the gravel with a crack. He climbed the stairs and entered the house just in time to be late for dinner.

8

KIMBERLY, SOUTH AFRICA

23 JUNE 1902

Dearest Abum,

I received your letter in the post yesterday and am glad to know the children are doing well. I remember how hot it can be there in June. At least you are high on the hill and get the benefit of both the elevation and ocean breeze. It is chilly here in Kimberly, which is such an odd feeling, knowing it is June. It makes me think of the British Empire. Not only does the sun never set on it, but it always maintains varying degrees Fahrenheit at the same moment in time. Long live King Edward!

That brings me to some good news. If you have not yet heard, the war with the Boers is over. Under the new treaty, the people of the Orange Free State and the Transvaal are at last under the Crown. Although I had not mentioned it before, I now feel at liberty to say I was concerned for our safety, but, thank God, we are under no threat. I will say it again. Long live King Edward!

Cuddy and I have discussed the matter you broached in your letter. He says he will send money for the children's support when he is able, but he wants to remind you that your father left you the prop-erty as he had sent Cuddy to medical school in Edinburgh and Bitsy was married, even though she is now widowed. He said until he is able to send money, the property should produce more than enough to support you and the children.

What wonderful news to hear Kester is excelling in school. I always knew he had it in him. Being her pupil, Bitsy must be every bit as proud of him. Please thank her for her dedication as governess to the children. Regarding her recommendation that Kester be sent to a school to further his studies, Cuddy suggests Potsdam School in the Saint Elizabeth parish. Potsdam was established for poor children. Under the circumstances, they should take him in.

The only other child you have written about is Malcolm. I am happy you have taken an interest in him. It is easy to love the baby of the family. However, Cuddy wants me to warn you against favoritism. He says it never comes to any good.

As always, please give our love to all the children and write back soon.

As ever,
Cuddy and Winnie

9

CAILIN

SUNDAY, SEPTEMBER 10, 1944

"Let's go, Gus! You haven't saddled your horse," Cailin called from the front of the house.

Dressed in long khaki pants, a plain white short-sleeved blouse, and her only pair of dress shoes, Cailin was ready for church. It bothered her that the other girls would be in dresses, but she would never admit it to anyone. And besides, she had no intention of riding sidesaddle.

When it became apparent Gus was not coming, she went to investigate and found him on the back veranda staring at the ocean far below. "What in the dickens are you looking at?"

He turned to her with a pair of binoculars in hand, exclaiming, "I think I saw one!"

"Saw one what?" she asked, frustrated.

"A U-boat. A German U-boat!" he replied with rising fervor.

"That doesn't make sense. You told me yourself that the Allies destroyed the German U-boats. Nobody's seen one around here for some time. You're just imagining things. Now come on, or we'll be extra late to church."

"Well…" his face reddened, "you may have a point. I did say that. I wasn't sure if it was the fin of a U-boat or a small fishing boat. He took one more look through his binoculars. "It doesn't hurt to be vigilant. Those Germans are stealthy. Anyway, I'll bet Daddy dropped a few bombs on those U-boats himself."

"He probably did. But enough of your big words. Let's go."

Cailin headed down the Cawdor road on her horse with Gus trailing behind riding one of the property horses. She patted Prime Minister's shiny coat and ran her fingers through his well-groomed white mane. He had a dark-brown upper coat with white on the bottom half, making him look as though he had waded into a vat of white paint that went almost up to his torso.

Prime Minister was her prized possession. Two years earlier she had begged her father for a horse. He said if she planted carrot seeds in her mother's garden and could bring in a consistent crop for an entire year, he would give her a horse. He forecasted a brilliant takeoff, a turbulent flight, and a crash landing. But Malcolm didn't know his own daughter. With dogged devotion, she daily tended the carrot patch that year, until Helen shamed Malcolm into giving Cailin his oldest stud. His only stipulation was it would still be used for breeding. Cailin eagerly agreed and cared for Prime Minister diligently, just as she continued to tend and reap a harvest from her carrot patch.

Sunday mornings were her weekly diversion—the serene, filtered early morning light lending credence to minimal movement on the property; Prime Minister's leisurely amble down toward Oristano with his hoofs beating out the gentle cadence to "Beautiful Dreamer," while Cailin softly hummed the tune, browsing the tropical foliage and landscape looking for every color on the spectrum. Occasionally, especially after receiving a letter from Rowena, she thought about what it would be like to leave Cawdor and go off to boarding school. She tried her best to ward off such thoughts as she did with any other notion of consequential weight. Her only thoughts were reserved for her cherished Cawdor, her paradise.

The only reason she didn't mind Gus coming along on Sundays was their shared appreciation for the way tranquility amplifies and sharpens the senses. His senses, though, were tuned to less evident things: spotting various birds, who seemed to be the only creatures presently employed in the business of life—hoping to see a potoo, a nocturnal bird that positions itself on trees in such a way that it looks like a dead branch; identifying plants with their botanical names; and anything he could tie back to what he read in his venerated schoolbooks.

He didn't always accompany her to church, though. The main reason he consented to go today was that she agreed to stop by Mr. Lyn's store, which doubled as the Oristano post office. Even though the shop was closed on Sundays, Mr. Lyn didn't mind giving the Campbells their mail. Malcolm was his best customer. Besides providing groceries to Cawdor, Mr. Lyn's rum bar, attached to the grocery store, was one of Malcolm's main watering holes.

Besides the peaceful morning ride, Cailin anticipated the time spent at the church. The first time she had ever been to church was when Rowena returned from her first term at Hampton. The school's chapel priest had read from the Gospel of Saint Matthew and spoken about Christ. Rowena was so intrigued she went back to her dorm room and spent the rest of the day reading Saint Matthew. On her visit home, she took Cailin to church. It was the first time Cailin had ever been.

Cailin loved the old stone walls of the Anglican Church and the way the windows and doors rose into uniformly pointed arches with darker colored stonework accenting them. Inside the building, she often found her gaze rising to the vaulted wooden beamed ceilings. She imagined the notes of the organ music and congregational singing, bounding and rebounding off the walls and angled ceiling, eventually finding their way through the open stained-glass windows to be broadcast to those who had not come to church. Sometimes she wondered if they could hear it up at Cawdor. Then she would remember she had heard nothing on the Sundays she had not attended. How she wished they could hear the music. The content of the homily was of some interest to her, but it was the priest's holy intonations fluctuating from bass to tenor and soft to loud just at the times he was driving home a serious point that made her face give way to an irrepressible smile.

There were only two things that bothered her. The first was more of an inner twinge. It irritated her to see how everyone dressed so nicely. Even if she wanted to wear a dress, she had nothing to compare to the dresses of the other girls and their mothers. She had only to ask, and her mother would have gladly taught her to sew a nicer dress than the one presently hanging in her closet. But sewing was irksome to her, and she had no intention of wearing a dress of her own volition.

The second thing bordered on a gut wrench. She disliked the way the mothers would glance at her and whisper to their girls. If she greeted any of them, they would barely acknowledge her, then act as if they'd been called away. At times, out of the corner of her eye, she would see a cluster of girls staring at her and giggling as if they had snuck and drunk the remaining communion wine before the priest did. She didn't understand their cold reception but figured it must have something to do with the way she dressed. After two Sundays of this, she decided it was better to arrive at church late, slip into the back row, and leave before the benediction. Yet, when all was said and done, the contentment she felt while attending the little church outweighed the bother she had to endure.

When she and Gus reached Oristano, they took a left before the inn and continued up the road a quarter mile, where they dismounted and tied the horses to the iron fencing.

"Why do we always have to tie the horses so far from the gate?" Gus queried.

"Why do you have to ask so many questions? Suppose I like to walk a little before I go in the church," she quipped. "Now remember to stand and sit whenever everyone else does, and don't ask me any questions once we're inside."

They slipped quietly through the large opened wooden doors and slid into the back pew occupied by an elderly couple. The gentleman turned and smiled, but his wife elbowed him, whispering to pay attention to the prayer. Right at the last syllable of the priest's "Amen," the organ rang out the first melodic notes of "Rock of Ages." Cailin, who knew the first verse by heart, began singing while turning to the page number shown on the hymn board. Notwithstanding Gus's U-boat episode, they had made it in time for the first song, and it was her favorite.

After the singing of hymns, wording of prayers, readings from the Gospels, and the priest's excitable oration, it was time for Holy Communion. This was something Cailin was drawn to but never dared go up to the altar to receive. She was intrigued by the idea that someone would die for her. Figuring her mother and maybe her father would risk their lives for her, she didn't understand why Christ would. She didn't even know him. Plus, why would he even need to die for her, or anyone? Even though she had these unanswered questions, she still desired to take part in the ritual. What deterred her, though, was having to walk to the front of the church and be seen by everyone. She imagined the stares, the snickers, the mothers telling their daughters to avert their eyes. Maybe there was something she needed forgiveness for. Maybe there was something about herself that she was blind to. She wanted to go forward—but she just couldn't. Her stiff shoulders loosened and fell.

During the last verse of the final song listed on the hymn board, Cailin signaled to Gus. They slid out of the pew.

Once outside, Gus, who had been holding himself back, blurted out, "Why don't we ever get to hear what he says at the end? You always make us leave."

"It's not anything important. Now come on. Let's get to our horses before they come out."

"Before who comes out?"

Cailin ignored his question, walking briskly. Gus let out a harrumph and ran after her.

They mounted their horses and headed down the road for the post office. There was silence for a short time then Cailin said, "You've got that look on your face."

"What look?"

"I can tell you're thinking about something."

He hesitated. "Yes. I am. It's about what the priest said. He said the Americans reached Germany's western border four days ago, and the war's going to end soon, and that God's always on the side of the righteous. I was just wondering what the German priests say to their people."

"Do the Germans even have priests?" Cailin asked half rhetorically.

"I imagine they would have. At least before Hitler took over."

"How would you know that?"

"I read my history lessons. Unlike someone we both know." Gus leaned to the right, expecting Cailin to pelt him. After a few more hoof clops, he continued, "I only wished it had been the Brits that made it to the border first. Then Daddy might have been there." A few more clops. "At least he must have been there on D-Day. Flying ahead of the troops. Dropping bombs to distract the Germans, so the Allies could land on the French beaches."

Cailin laughed. "You have it all figured out. Like you were there."

"As I said," Gus countered, "I read my books and the *Daily Gleaner*. Plus, I actually think."

This time Cailin did strike, causing Gus to spur his horse into a trot.

Mr. Lyn's grocery store sat on the opposite side of the road from the ocean. Cailin stood stroking Prime Minister's neck and watching a fisherman, halfway in the water, hauling his paint-chipped boat ashore. Gus dismounted and ran in. Mr. Lyn's little shop carried the necessary groceries, plus a few luxuries. Both Cailin and Gus favored his Chinese sweeties: dried, flavored plums that were either moist and sweet or thoroughly dried and sour. She preferred the bite of the sour ones, which caused her face to pucker. Whenever they came to the store, Mr. Lyn, enterprising as he was, offered each of them one.

Before Cailin could enter the store to claim her treat, Gus ran out waving an open letter in his right hand with a newspaper tucked under his left arm. "He's written! I knew he wouldn't forget me!"

Tam Campbell, Gus's father, second youngest of the Campbell children, had enlisted in His Majesty's Royal Air Force through a series of distressing events. A relative, who Tam had lived with in his mid-teens, had sent him to study agriculture in London. While there, he met an English girl who was preparing to be a pediatric nurse. He immediately fell in love with her fervor for life and her passion for dancing—they were inseparable! After graduating, they got married. Tam was offered a job in Westmoreland with the Frome Sugar Estate, and he persuaded her to move back to his homeland, telling her that as a British colony, Jamaica had everything an English lady could desire.

She hated Jamaica the moment she stepped foot on the

island, not seeing the remotest resemblance to England or British society. As time passed, she missed many of the comforts she was used to. She often cried. Within the year, Gus was born, and Tam was certain their bundle of joy would brighten her disposition. Her depression only worsened. She lived in a state of on-again-off-again depression for years. She dutifully cared for Gus, and almost never slept with Tam.

Late one afternoon, shortly after Gus's ninth birthday, Tam arrived home from work to hear the maid screaming, "Mass Tam! Mass Tam! She gone!" The maid handed him a letter from his wife that said she was sorry, she could do it no longer, she was no good for him or Gus, she had taken a boat out of Savanna-la-Mar that afternoon, he was not to follow her back to England, and she would arrange for the divorce.

After two months of sitting at home drinking, Tam lost his job. He took Gus to Cawdor and begged his brother to take care of him until he could find another job. Malcolm thought the boy should go to Kester or one of his other brothers. Tam wanted him to be with Cailin, his favorite cousin, and there was a governess at Cawdor. Only because of Helen's pleading for the boy's sake did Malcolm eventually capitulate.

Tam took a job in Saint Catherine at the Caymanas Sugar Estate and sent word to Malcolm that he would send for Gus once he had found a suitable home. He started going out at night to the Glass Bucket, a popular Kingston dance club that U.S. military men frequented and became friends with a U.S. Air Force pilot who showed him some basics about flying a plane at Vernamfield, an air base Britain had leased to the U.S. as a result of the 1940 Destroyers for Bases Agreement. Tam's love for flying grew, and because he was still hurting over his pending divorce, he moved to England and signed up as an aircraft crewman. He had been told there was a growing need for pilots in the RAF. He wanted to "fill the gap," is what he told Malcolm, although he didn't share his other motivation—to make a go at reuniting with his wife before the divorce was final. Malcolm would have disapproved.

Cailin and Gus led their horses by the reins and walked along the side of the road as he read the letter aloud to her.

26 August 1944

Dear Boy,

I cannot begin to tell you how much I miss you! Every night I lie on my cot thinking about my lad and how you must have grown and all the things you must know. I am sorry to be missing that. I am also sorry I have not written in a while. The war is going well for us, and there is little time for anything else other than work and sleep.

I know you have read about it in the Daily Gleaner, but I have to write it. We are clobbering the Nazis! I go on regular bombing missions, and I went on a series of them earlier this month. For three days straight we bombed the Germans in France between Mortain and Falaise. We decimated them! I know you will look up those places on a map. I know my boy.

I still have not flown a plane into combat. My pilot training is almost complete, at which time I will be commissioned as an officer, and then I will have a go at the Nazis myself! In the meantime, I am still able to go on bombing campaigns as a navigator. I have enclosed a photo of the crew and me. The fellow on my left is my best mate, Sal. He has a boy just older than you. We talk about the both of you every day.

I long to see how you have grown. Until then, say your prayers like your mother taught you to do, and pray for me as well.

Love,
Daddy

"I knew he hadn't forgotten about me," Gus said, looking up from the letter.

"I'm just glad he's alive. We've heard reports of too many dying. I can't imagine what it must be like—"

Gus broke in sharply. "Why would you think that? Before Daddy left, he specifically told me, 'I'm going to kill the Führer and bring your mother back.' He's coming back, you know!"

"I'm sorry for what I just said. I was just thinking out loud. Yes. He's coming back. As soon as the war's over." There was silence for a while, except for the clopping of horse hooves. Then Cailin continued, "Be careful not to mention your mother in front of my father. Remember what he said the last time you brought her up."

He carefully put his letter back into the envelope, folded the envelope once, and slipped it into his back pocket. Then he took the newspaper from where it had been under his arm and looked at the front-page headlines. To his annoyance, there was nothing about the war. He refolded the paper, then asked, "When is the wireless coming back? I wish the man in Black River would hurry up and fix it. I miss the daily BBC reports."

They mounted their horses to head back home.

When they reached the entrance to the Oristano Inn, Gus said, "Let's sneak behind the inn and go for a swim in the river. Maybe we'll meet the new boy, and he'll want to play with us."

Cailin had overheard Essie telling Ruby about the new boy at the inn. His name was Archie, and he was sixteen years old, two years older than her and four years older than Gus. While she was curious to meet him, she replied, "I have no desire to meet the new boy. Besides, what would Daddy say if he finds out we've been playing with an older boy? Come, lunch will be served soon. It's best if we head back to the house."

10

ARCHIE

FRIDAY-SATURDAY, SEPTEMBER 15-16, 1944

Archie sat on the front steps waiting for Malcolm. Mrs. Witcombe had cautioned him about getting his hopes up, and he knew she was right. But he had to get away from Savanna-la-Mar. School had been no better this week; in fact, it had been worse. Clive and Devon had been relentless in giving him no reprieve. They did nothing but laugh at Archie's "misfortunes." They were the puppeteers who stealthily manipulated the entire school. Reacting on cue to the surrounding ill will, even the teachers seemed to be under their control. Robby alone remained unnoticeably detached.

As the quarter hour went by, with bitterness vining up the walls of his heart, Archie resigned himself to another weekend away from home. He went back up to his room to get his homework done. Maybe Robby would grace him with his presence, and they'd watch another film show. Perhaps he'd even take Robby up on the dare to sneak into Saint George's Parish Church and see who could stay the longest in the dark. He opened his mathematics book, flipping to the assigned page. While he was calculating the second problem, he heard a car pull up in front of the house. He flipped the book shut and grabbed his suitcase, remembering Malcolm's words: *Be ready for me when I get there.*

Malcolm was standing by his car talking with Mr. Witcombe, and there was an exchange of money with Malcolm announcing, "This is for last weekend, which I told you would happen from time to time."

"That was no problem, Mr. Campbell. The boy is a pleasure to have around the house." Mr. Witcombe neglected to inform Malcolm about Archie being out all day Saturday, even though they had expressed their disapproval when he had arrived back after dark, saying they may need to let Malcolm know. This admonition prompted him to stay on the premises the whole of Sunday, despite the fact he wanted to do more exploring with Robby.

Archie put his suitcase in the trunk and got in the car, not knowing how to respond to Malcolm, who had not yet acknowledged him. They drove in silence.

On the outskirts of Savanna-la-Mar, Malcolm finally spoke. "I suppose everything is going well at Manning's."

Archie wasn't sure what Malcolm meant. Was it a question? A statement? Whatever it was, how could he begin to reply? *Oh, yes. I am the Three Stooges of Manning's. It's been one hell of a ride! When can I go back for more?* He doubted Malcolm had ever been to a film show, much less known who the Three Stooges were. He settled on a vague reply. "Yes."

He wasn't looking for conversation with Malcolm. What he wanted—what was really eating at him—was the lack of admission that he had been left stranded the previous weekend. Archie stared out the window at the gently sloping sugar cane fields that melded into the Westmoreland hills. On the other side of those hills was Montego Bay, his old life. The life he had begged to keep—but for his *dear* mother and her forever scheming.

Turning his head, he looked in the direction the car was

going. There was no use longing for what wouldn't be. He fixed his thoughts on the inn and Abbie and her food. The closer he got to home, the more the bitter vine receded down the walls of his heart.

"My dear boy is home!" cheered Gracie, mincing toward him with her arms stretched out Betty Davis style. With an embrace, she kissed him and tousled his wavy hair. She pulled back to inspect him, then gave her appraisal. "You know, I forgot how handsome you are! The spitting image of your father."

Archie gave her a dubious look. "Hello, Mother."

"One day. If the stars are all aligned…"

"Yes, yes. I know. If the stars are all aligned perfectly, I will meet my father," he mocked. "Where's Abbie?"

"In the kitchen, as always." She looked past him. "Where's Malcolm? Why didn't he come up?" She sounded irritated.

"I don't know. We hardly said two words to each other."

"Oh. Was it about him not picking you up last weekend? He was very busy, you know."

"I wouldn't know. Like I said, we barely spoke."

"By the way, I'll need your help. We have a full house tonight, including Mick."

Just then Malcolm shouted up the stairs from the porte-cochère, "Gracie!"

"Exit, stage right," said Archie, turning toward the kitchen.

Gracie caught him by the arm. "Malcolm's staying, too."

Abbie was waiting at the kitchen door. "Mass Archie! Me was praying say you would come today!" She smothered him with her hug, giving him a sweaty kiss on the cheek. He didn't mind. He missed those kitchen-sweat kisses. "How you been, Mass Archie?" she asked cheerfully. She held him at arm's distance and looked into his eyes. He didn't reply. "Okay...okay..." she nodded and pointed to the kitchen chair. "First me will feed you. Then we going talk. Donkey never do no work till him belly full."

Archie chuckled, shaking his head. "It's good to laugh again."

There was a full table that evening, comprised of Archie, Gracie, Malcolm, Mick, and four other inn guests. Dinner was exceptional. Even Gracie commented on it. Abbie had cooked rice and peas, plantain, callaloo and okra, just the way Archie liked it, and for a special treat, roast beef, which she later told Archie had come from Mr. Campbell's property. He ate two healthy portions of everything.

"My, don't they feed you at the Witcombes?" Gracie asked with a smile.

"They feed me well. There's just nothing like Abbie's cooking." He shoveled in another forkful of roast beef with rice and peas piled on top.

"That's not how I taught you to eat. Is that the way they eat in Sav-la-mar these days?"

"Leave the boy alone. For God's sake!" Malcolm snapped. "Let him enjoy being home." He got up to fix himself another drink.

Everyone glanced around, confused; Gracie alone understood the outburst. Amicably, she touched Archie's arm, saying, "Sorry, my dear."

Mick broke the ensuing silence. "Never mind, my dear boy.

When I would come home from boarding school in Britain, I would eat at least as much as you, if not more."

Continuing to steer the conversation elsewhere, Archie asked, "You went to boarding school in England, Mr. McFagan?"

"Not in England. Ireland. Campbell College, Belfast. A member of Price's House," he declared with a pretentious air.

Malcolm looked up from pouring his drink. "From Campbell College, Ireland, to selling liquor. I'll drink to that!" He raised his glass and downed the rum.

Gracie called out for Abbie to clear the table and bring the lemon meringue pie. Taking the opportunity for a breather, Archie volunteered to take the dishes to the kitchen while one of the other guests began talking about the war.

Later that evening, after all the guests had retired except for Mick, Archie was sitting at the dining table with one eye reading the *Daily Gleaner* and one eye and two ears on the affairs in the drawing room.

Malcolm groaned as he pushed himself out of the drawing room chair and motioned for Gracie to follow him.

"I'll come tuck you in shortly, my dear," she said in response to Malcolm. "It would be rude to go to bed while our guest is still up."

"Guest indeed," Malcolm muttered as he waved his hand down at Mick and stumbled off to his room.

Mick sat stirring the ice in his glass until he heard Malcolm's door shut. "You know you could do better?" He looked up at her.

"Are you referring to the whiskey?" She didn't let him answer. "That's exactly what I've been telling you. Where's the Scotch I've been asking for?"

"You know what I'm referring to." He glanced down the hall, as if expecting Malcolm to suddenly appear.

"Yes, I do. We've had this conversation before, darling, and I told you I could never be stuck up in that secluded house in the back-a-wall hills of Saint Ann's. No matter how much money your father has."

He made a motion as if to talk, but she cut him off. "Look, Mick. You're fun to be with and you have stability to offer, but I have everything I need right here."

"Do you? Do you really? Let's see—you're running an inn you don't own. Your philandering lover comes and goes between here and his white wife, who sits enthroned, surrounded by the four children she bore him. And who knows how many others he has on the side. Is there something I've overlooked or you're not saying?"

"Perhaps."

"Well, fill me in then." He sat back, waiting for the new revelation.

"I can't. And in any case, walls have ears," she said, motioning her head in the direction of the dining room.

"Oh." He looked toward the dining room. "I see." He took a deep breath. "So, Malcolm, or should I say, 'Macbeth the Thane of Cawdor,' it is then?" He got up out of his chair. "I guess that makes you Lady Macbeth." He smiled with a slight smirk. "Good night, milady. I'll be sure to lock my door."

The next morning, Archie woke to the smell of Abbie's "for Archie only" banana fritters sprinkled with sugar and drizzled with fresh lime juice. He ate quickly, so he could tend to the departing guests' luggage and valet their cars under the porte-cochère. After the last guests had left, he walked down to Mr. Lyn's store just to see if anything interesting was happening.

He chuckled to himself, remembering his outing the previous week in Savanna-la-Mar. While he didn't wish himself back there, he missed the goings-on of a larger town. He was reminded of the time he and his mother visited her sister in Kingston. Now *that* was a city. When he graduated from Manning's, he fully intended on moving to Kingston. Maybe his aunt would put him up until he could find a good job and afford a place of his own.

Seeing nothing interesting happening around the store, he walked over to the beach. No action there either; it was too early in the day. He took off his shoes and walked along the shoreline, kicking the lapping waves, skimming stones on the water's surface, and attempting to catch minnows schooling around the shallow end. Eventually, shoes in hands, he raced down the shore, competing in his mind against fellow athletes, who were trailing a yard or more behind. After breaking the ribbon with chest protruding and a shoe in each victory-raised hand, he headed back to the inn.

He sat at the kitchen table talking with Abbie, filling her in on the previous two weeks and laughing about some things he and Robby did. She must have sensed he was holding back something because she asked him, "Is there anything you not tellin Abbie?"

"No," he replied. He didn't want to worry her. He wanted to deal with this one on his own. Then he would tell her about it.

Following lunch, Archie went down to the small river running through the property behind the inn. The riverbanks were rounded shoulders outfitted with verdant foliage and umbrellaed with numerous trees. He went to a spot he had located when he first arrived in Oristano a few weeks ago. There was a mahoe tree that stretched over the river, reaching down almost to touch it. Just in that spot was a foot-high ledge where water cascaded into a basin, creating a mild whirlpool. Being barefooted since the beach that morning, all he had to do was take off his shirt. He threw it on a shower-of-gold shrub, with its yellow flower sprays brilliant in the sun, and took a running leap into the river pool. He loved the brisk mountain water, which always sent shock waves through his body. To acclimate to it, he dove underwater and swam around the pool with broad strokes.

Soon enough, he was floating on the water, looking up at the leaf-mottled sky. He felt safe here. The thought bothered him. Why would he need to feel safe? He was a man. He could manage. Yet he couldn't deny he was glad to be cushioned by the cool water and blanketed by the shading trees. Just then, he heard some laughter.

Not seeing anyone in his immediate view, he hid behind the mahoe branches, submerging his body up to his mouth. He heard talking. Not adults. Two of them. Then a boy and an older girl emerged from behind a thicket of high unkempt bushes. They were white. Archie wondered where they'd come from. The boy pulled off his shirt as if planning to swim. Archie's first reaction was to shoo them away, but then he decided he could have some fun with this.

Archie moved into their view and said, "Welcome to the Oristano Inn River! Delighted to make your acquaintance."

Wide-eyed, Cailin and Gus were speechless.

Seeing they were taken aback, he toyed with them further. "Let me introduce myself. My name is Archie, the firstborn and the only son and heir of the proprietor of this fine establishment, the Oristano Inn. And who might you be? Who is trespassing on my property?"

Cailin and Gus looked at each other. Then Gus looked back at Archie with squinted, focused eyes and asked, "If your father is the proprietor of the inn, then why does my uncle—" he pointed at Cailin, "—her father, own it?" The question was simultaneously one of curiosity and challenge.

Cailin interjected, "Actually, he doesn't really own it. He rents it and has someone run it for him."

It was Archie's turn to be speechless, but only momentarily. "Well, old sport, it's actually my mother who runs it for him."

There was a brief silence, which Cailin broke. "That means your mother is Ms. Price?"

"Yes. And what would your name happen to be?"

"Cailin Campbell. Malcolm Campbell's daughter," she responded with pride.

"I'm Gus Campbell, Cailin's first cousin."

"Well, Cailin and Gus Campbell, come and join me in *your* river, then!" Archie said, splashing the water toward them.

At the invitation to frolic, Gus jumped right in, intending to make a sizable wave. Archie laughed heartily and began a splash fight while Cailin sat on a large rock protruding from the bank's shoulder and watched.

When Gus noticed she wasn't coming in, he called out, "Cailin, come in!"

"I don't feel like swimming anymore."

"But you were the one with the idea to come down and swim. You have your swimsuit on under your clothes."

"Well, I've changed my mind. I'll get my amusement watching the two of you."

Archie hadn't much experience with girls, but sensing something about Cailin's reaction, he put his hands on Gus's head and said, "That's girls for you, old sport," and pushed him under water.

After a good splash fight, a few rounds of chicken with Gus on Archie's shoulders fighting and winning against many teams of imaginary opponents, and a breath-holding competition which Archie let Gus win two out of the three times, the boys sat on the bank near Cailin. There was conversation—mostly between the boys. They spoke about the inn, their parents, school, Savanna-la-Mar, and the Cawdor property. Gus told Archie about all the fun they have on the property—climbing trees, riding horses and donkeys, catching soldier crabs, trapping birds, climbing the hill behind the house. He went on and on. Eventually he said, "Why don't you come join us one day? We'll take you to all the good spots. It'd be great fun!"

"Well," Archie said, looking at Cailin with raised eyebrows, "it's up to Cailin Campbell, Malcolm Campbell's daughter." He elbowed Gus good-naturedly.

Cailin looked at the waterfall for a long moment, during which time its splash seeming to increase in volume, until Gus said, "Why not, Cailin?"

Looking over at Archie, Cailin explained, "It's just that we've never had anyone come over to Cawdor before. Except family, that is."

"That's okay," Archie said. "I have lots to do here at the inn. My mother keeps me busy."

"No," Cailin said softly. "It actually would be good to have someone else join our adventures. When Ian's away at school, we do miss our third leg."

"That's right!" Gus jumped in. "You can be our third leg! It'll be great fun!"

Archie reached down and splashed them with river water, as if a sign of accepting his membership.

Cailin felt something she had never felt before, and not knowing what to do with it, she turned to Archie and said, "On another topic, is Archie your real name?"

"Actually, it's Archibald."

Gus looked at him in surprise, exclaiming, "Your name is almost as bad as mine! Angus. I got named after a cow."

"Gus! That was rude," scolded Cailin. She turned to Archie. "Never mind him. Archibald is also my father's middle name."

Gus interjected, "I've never heard that before!"

"Well, he doesn't like anyone to say it. So don't you repeat it to anyone. I shouldn't even have said it, except you made Archie feel bad."

"No, no. I'm used to it," Archie said.

"At any rate, Angus," she said his proper name with emphasis, "we should be getting back."

"But we haven't been here very long."

"Don't leave on my account," appealed Archie.

"No," she replied, averting her eyes, "we must be going."

"Well, the both of you are welcome to swim in my river any time," Archie said, winking at Gus. "You're also invited to the inn." Before Cailin and Gus reached the opening in the bushes, Archie called out, "Until next time, old sports."

11

SHARPE

SUNDAY, SEPTEMBER 24, 1944

While property workers rarely worked on Sundays, occasionally the foreman would tend to an urgent need. Sharpe left Hakin for Cawdor early that Sunday morning. Marsha had encouraged him to stay home, saying he needed the rest, but he made up an excuse. He had to get out of Hakin. Sharpe had increasingly expected more from those who worked on the Cawdor property—which Busha acknowledged and affirmed, even offering Sharpe a shot of rum in his office on one occasion. The workers, unhappy with the increasing expectations and recognizing the influence Busha was having on him, spread resentment toward him throughout the Hakin community. Even Marsha's mother, who had previously doted on Sharpe, treating him as a son-in-law, had recently expressed uncertainty about him.

When he got up to the great house, Essie questioned him about being there on a Sunday morning. He gave her an evasive answer about work needing to be done. When he was still there in the afternoon, she gave him a squinted-eye, head-cocked look, which he ignored, continuing to work.

Late that afternoon, on his way back to Hakin, Sharpe made

a detour to visit Mr. Aldridge. Linton Aldridge was the minister and schoolteacher for the Methodist church and primary school in Oristano. His father had been a Methodist minister in one of the poorest neighborhoods in Kingston. Seeing the way his father had faithfully labored to educate and lift the surrounding community out of poverty, Mr. Aldridge took a post with the then four-member Oristano church at the age of twenty-two. In his thirty-three years of service to the community, the church had fluctuated in attendance, growing only to eighteen parishioners at its largest. But, as the only free school for miles around, he had educated innumerable children.

Sharpe recalled that on the last day he attended the school, after dismissal, Mr. Aldridge had asked him to stay behind. He told Sharpe he was sorry the school did not go beyond the primary level as Sharpe had a good mind but that there were other ways to succeed in life, and he knew Sharpe would find his way. He also told him his door was always open should he want to talk.

While Sharpe had seen Mr. Aldridge from time to time since his primary school days, he had not taken him up on his offer to talk.

Sharpe knocked on the little wooden two-bedroom manse behind the church building. Though it had been a while, he vividly remembered two things about his visits there when he was young: the well-maintained small house, both inside and out, and the warm hospitality he felt from both Mr. and Mrs. Aldridge.

After a brief wait, the door opened. "Quaco! How good to see you!" exclaimed Mrs. Aldridge. She shook his hand eagerly. He noticed her dark-brown face had worn well for a middle-aged woman with minor wrinkles at the corner of her eyes, most probably due to her jovial countenance. Mr. Aldridge met her soon after he arrived in Oristano, and they married within two months. In his younger years, Sharpe had wondered what an educated Kingstonian saw in a common Westmoreland girl. The longer Sharpe had known Mrs. Aldridge, though, the more he recognized that behind her smiling demeanor was a determined woman who was right at her husband's side through all the challenges and nuances of ministering to a small country community.

"Good to see you again, ma'am," he said, smiling.

"Please come in. Linton is inside reading another one of his books." She grinned. "Go ahead. You know where you're going." His mind flashed back to his many visits where Mr. Aldridge would help him with his schoolwork or lend him a book to read or feed him both body and soul.

When he walked into the room, Mr. Aldridge was already standing waiting for him, looking a little older but just as physically fit as the day they'd met. With a firm handshake, he declared, "What a pleasant surprise! How are you, Quaco? It's been a good while since I've seen you."

"It's good to see you, Missa[1] Aldridge," Sharpe said, shaking his hand.

"Do me a favor, nuh? It's time you call me by my first name. A big horse-staring[2] man like yourself still calling me Mr. Aldridge?" he laughed.

"Me guess you right, Missa...I mean, Linton." He hesitated. "It just don't seem right to call you by you first name. I have to put the handle to the cup[3]."

Mr. Aldridge laughed. "You'll get used to it. Now sit down and tell me to what I owe this visit." He made a hand gesture toward a small bench with homemade cushioned seating, and called out to his wife, asking her to bring them tea.

After some small talk between the two, Sharpe then switched the subject to how things had changed for him in Hakin since he took over the foremanship at Cawdor. He spoke about the pimento, Lucy and Magus, the rum bar incident, the threats, and his need to be firmer with the workers to get them to do their job properly. He thought about it but neglected to talk about the discussion between him and Malcolm or Cailin and Gus's thrashing.

When Sharpe finished, Mr. Aldridge shifted his gaze to the wall of books he was facing. The only sound he made was, "Hmm." Sharpe sat sipping his tea, knowing Mr. Aldridge's thoughts would not be immediate.

On the third "Hmm," Mr. Aldridge turned toward Sharpe, who recognized the look on his face. It was the look he had come for. He was confident it would bring the direction he sorely needed.

"You are well aware of the history of Hakin. You know they are a people who see the world through narrow eyes and walk with a chip on their shoulders."

"Exactly. Them always think say everyone out to get them."

"Yes. So, in turn, they strike back when they think they're being samfied. And, unfortunately, it only makes things worse for them, like the pimento incident." He blew on his tea, then took a sip. "And you are not really one of them. It doesn't matter that you've lived with them since you were a boy. Now that you are their foreman, and especially now that you've challenged their ways, what is happening should not be a surprise." Mr. Aldridge stopped, seeming to wait for a response from Sharpe. But none came, so he continued, "In many ways, you are fortunate to have come from Accompong, and maybe just as fortunate to have left Accompong and come to Hakin."

Sharpe donned a quizzical look.

"Hear me out, now. From all you've told me in the past about the people of Accompong and from what history tells me, you come from a fiercely independent people. A self-governing people—like no other in Jamaica. That is something to be proud of and carry with you."

"Me understand that, but in what kinda way should I be

proud to come from Hakin? When me go to Sav or Black River, me would never mention the word Hakin. Them would take me for mock[4] and watch to mek sure me no thief nothing."

"I know what people outside of Hakin think about the villagers, and sometimes with good reason. And I don't envy you having to bear that reputation wherever you go. But there is something more important I'm pointing out here. You know what it's like to feel pride—the pride of knowing you come from an independent people. Now, in the same way, let the shame you feel about Hakin conceive in you compassion." He said the word "compassion" with emphasis and paused as if to let it penetrate. He continued. "Compassion for the very same people of Hakin."

Sharpe sat in silence, not sure how he should respond.

Mr. Aldridge pressed on. "If you let the two feelings of pride and compassion become intertwined, like two trees planted so close to one another that from afar they look like one great tree—Humility—you will become a man worth following."

"Me? Who gwane follow me? The only reason them do anything I tell them to do is cause dem know say Missa Campbell behind me. Them afraid of Busha."

"I hope you don't misunderstand me, Sharpe, but what I'm encouraging you to do is to have compassion for where the people of Hakin have come from while appreciating that coming from Accompong, you have a heritage of inborn self-governance."

Leaning forward, Sharpe thought, *Me heritage of inborn self-governance.*

Mr. Aldridge added, "Both of these qualities will enable you to lead successfully as a foreman and, perhaps, in the village itself."

Sharpe heard Mr. Aldridge's words, but his own thoughts

replaced them: *Me inborn self-governance. Inborn self-governance. This is what me come for!*

"Let me explain further," said Mr. Aldridge. "When I came to Oristano from Kingston, I had a lot to learn about country people. If it wasn't for Norma, I'm not sure…" He kept on speaking, but Sharpe was only hearing his own thoughts repeating—*inborn self-governance.*

Sharpe's thoughts were interrupted when he heard Mr. Aldridge ask, "And where does Mr. Campbell fit into all of this? I know he can be a hard man to work for. Talk about reputation, his has spread far and wide. How are you managing under him?"

Sharpe sat back in the chair and looked up at Mr. Aldridge. The muscle under his left eye twitched. He took hold of himself and replied, "Him is a hard man, for true. But as 'long as me do what him tell me to do, everything good."

"Are you certain there's nothing you need to get off your chest?"

"Yes, Missa Aldridge, sah. Me sure."

Mr. Aldridge pushed no further.

"Well, thanks for the tea. It's time to go." Sharpe stood up, extending his hand for a goodbye shake.

"Before you leave, I have a book I'd like to lend you." He got up and walked over to his library, passing his palm over the spines until he found a collection of poems by Claude McKay.[5] He pulled out a small brown book and ran his fingers along the worn edges as if recalling its every word. He paused before putting the book in Sharpe's hand. "I want you to go home and read this, thinking about the circumstances you find yourself in. Consider the totality of your circumstance and those from Hakin."

"Homework." Sharpe half chuckled to himself.

"No. I'm serious. Read the whole book, but especially consider the poem that has the same title as the book, 'Harlem

Shadows.' It's Hakin." He handed the book over slowly, as if passing on a legacy. "Come see me again when you've finished reading it."

Sharpe, sensing the gravity in Mr. Aldridge's tone, took the book graciously. "Thank you, Missa Aldridge." Then, shaking his hand, he said, "Forgive me for not calling you Linton."

At the front door, Mr. Aldridge said, "Oh yes, one last thing. This Thursday, Norman Manley will be in Sav holding a rally."

"For the election against Missa Bustamante?"

"Yes. The whole election is historic. A general election where adults of all ages and colors, both men and women, can vote. It's not only for the male landowner anymore." He said this with an air of satisfaction. "And Mr. Manley will explain why we should vote for him."

"Me no hear much talk about Missa Manley up at the big house. Them mostly talk about Busta."

"That is to be expected," replied Mr. Aldridge, putting his hand on Sharpe's shoulder. "Some of us are heading down to Sav in the afternoon. Would you like to join us?"

"Massa![6] Me no think me can get off. And if Busha ever know say me gone to hear Missa Manley, me nah go hear the end of it." As Mr. Aldridge reached out to shake his hand, Sharpe said, "One more thing, Missa Aldridge."

"Yes, what is it?"

"If you could stop call me Quaco and just use me last name, Sharpe."

"I think I can do that, Sharpe." He firmly shook his hand and with a warm smile said, "But try getting used to calling me Linton."

~

On his way back to Hakin, Sharpe's mind fixated on his epiphany—inborn self-governance. He thought about the community he was born into with a history of those who resisted both Spanish and English slavery. He remembered the stories of Colonel Cudjoe, the most famous of the rebel leaders, who united the Maroons in Accompong under the Kindah, an ancient mango tree. He remembered his mother telling him the word "kindah" was an African word meaning "one family." These were Sharpe's memories. These were his people—a people with inborn self-governance. At this moment, he felt more than ever connected to Accompong. He too was of the Kindah—of the people of inborn self-governance.

Of what were those in Hakin? They were of anything but inborn self-governance. They were of inbred selfishness! A nest of scorpions clawing at one another and stinging anyone from the outside. Yet, conflicting thoughts came to him: His aunt and uncle had been nothing but good to him; Ram Foot had been his friend from childhood; Marsha had embraced him. He rebutted these easily: His aunt had connections to Accompong, so she was different; Ram Foot had pulled back since the rum bar incident; Marsha was in love.

Besides Mr. Aldridge, the only truly self-governed person he knew was Busha. Even the often-told infamous story about Busha in his youth killing a property worker and being sent to Cuba for five years spoke volumes to Sharpe about inborn self-governance. He knew this incident had fermented a mixture of hatred and fear toward Busha in the Hakin community. Sharpe had to admit it stirred the same reaction in him. But if he had to choose between emulating Mr. Aldridge's self-governance and that of Busha, he knew there was only one real option. He had no opportunity to better himself through education as Mr. Aldridge had, but he could follow Busha's path in his present role as property foreman, even if it meant provoking hatred and fear in the people of Hakin. He had no other choice. He would have to play this role for a time and then move on as better options opened to him.

Sharpe stopped on the craggy path. He held the book Mr. Aldridge had lent him in both hands and, reading the title out loud, wondered what revelation he would receive from this book. If it was anything akin to what he had just received from his old teacher, he was impatient to take hold of it.

It was almost dark by the time Sharpe got home. Without questioning his whereabouts, Marsha set a plate of yellow yam, okra, and fried fish on the table, making small talk about her day. He tried to pay attention to her, but his mind was on other things. After dinner, he set the Tilley lamp beside the bed, lay down, and opened the book to where the pages naturally parted. There on the left page was the poem with the same name as the book: "Harlem Shadows." He remembered Mr. Aldridge saying, "It's Hakin." Sharpe did not want to read about Hakin. He was more interested in reading what to *do about* Hakin. But, out of respect for his teacher, he read:

I hear the halting footsteps of a lass
In Negro Harlem when the night lets fall
Its veil. I see the shapes of girls who pass
To bend and barter at desire's call.
Ah, little dark girls who in slippered feet
Go prowling through the night from street to street!

Through the long night until the silver break
Of day the little gray feet know no rest;
Through the lone night until the last snow-flake
Has dropped from heaven upon the earth's white
    breast,
The dusky, half-clad girls of tired feet
Are trudging, thinly shod, from street to street.

Ah, stern harsh world, that in the wretched way
Of poverty, dishonor and disgrace,

Has pushed the timid little feet of clay,
The sacred brown feet of my fallen race!
Ah, heart of me, the weary, weary feet
In Harlem wandering from street to street.

Vaguely comprehending the poem's meaning, he read it again. While there were a few words he was unfamiliar with, the second reading brought more clarity. He closed the book. This is not what he was looking for. He had no intention of feeling sorry for the people of Hakin. That was Mr. Aldridge's business. His former teacher didn't have to live among them every day, feeling their palpable glares as he walked by, hearing their loudly whispered verdicts. Sometimes he wished they would yell at him instead! No. This poem was not what he was looking for.

For Mr. Aldridge's sake, he again opened to the table of contents, scanning for titles that caught his attention. He read "The Wild Goat" and wondered what the point of the poem was and whether Hakin or he was the wild goat on a barren hill. "The Tired Worker" caught his attention. By the end of the poem, he realized he was a doubly tired worker, for he had no rest when he returned to Hakin and did not dread the dawn; rather, it meant a reprieve from the scorpion nest. Scanning the table of contents further, his eye caught the title "If We Must Die" but then decided he didn't want to read about death. The only other title that intrigued him was "Tormented." He certainly felt that! After reading it, however, he decided that the person in the poem was merely a dreamer who would continue to be squeezed like a piece of sugar cane until the last drop of juice was extracted. He would not allow Hakin to do that to him!

Before closing the book for good, he thought about the poem he hadn't read, though it had caught his eye. He figured he'd give it a try. He flipped back to the table of contents, found the page number—53—turned there, and began reading "If We Must Die":

> *If we must die—let it not be like hogs*
> *Hunted and penned in an inglorious spot,*
> *While round us bark the mad and hungry dogs,*
> *Making their mock at our accursed lot.*
> *If we must die—oh, let us nobly die,*
> *So that our precious blood may not be shed*
> *In vain; then even the monsters we defy*
> *Shall be constrained to honor us though dead!*
> *Oh, Kinsmen! We must meet the common foe;*
> *Though far outnumbered, let us show us brave,*
> *And for their thousand blows deal one death blow!*
> *What though before us lies the open grave?*
> *Like men we'll face the murderous, cowardly pack,*
> *Pressed to the wall, dying, but fighting back!*[7]

Seized by what he had just read, he reread the poem to make sure it said what he thought it did. *Yes! This is it!* He read it again, analyzing each line. *This is Hakin! More than that, this is me!* The poem's aggressive tone kindled within him until he reveled in it. While he was the only one of his Kindah kinsmen, he would not let himself be hunted by these mad dogs. *And for their thousand blows deal one death blow!* Sharpe interpreted this to mean he only needed to deal with the main scorpion—Magus—and the others would back down. Malcolm's words came to mind: *I chose you because I saw in you a seed of myself. A man who would do anything to get something.* Sharpe was ready to do what he knew he had to do.

He sat up, outed the lamp, and got out of bed.

Marsha stirred from her half sleep and asked, "Where you going, putus[8]?"

"For a walk. Me need to consider me mind."

"Someting in that book Missa Aldridge give you bothering you?" she said in a mothering tone.

"It's alright, mama, a little walk will do me good."

In his newly found euphoria, Sharpe trooped further up the hill to Magus's house, where he found him sitting on his favorite rock in his rock-infested yard, smoking a ganja spliff. Every night after dinner, Magus would take a generous amount of ganja from his well-guarded old Cuban cigar box and care-fully roll it into a dried banana leaf skin, then set it on his bedroom windowsill. It would patiently wait there for his return from the rum bar, when he would take it from the windowsill and sit on his favorite rock to smoke it. Everybody in Hakin knew it was there. No one dared disturb it.

Magus's attention was on his woman, standing in the doorway of his dwelling, soothing her crying baby, so he didn't notice Sharpe until he was standing right in front of him. Looking up, he said in disgust, "What you want, Busha boy?" He took a drag of his spliff.

Sharpe looked Magus in the eye. In his rashness, he hadn't thought through what he was going to say.

"Why the hell you come up in me yard this time of night and just look on me so?" Ganja smoke was exhaled with every word. "What you come up here to say, ee?"

"Me come to say this—Stop stir up the people them against me!"

Magus let out a maniacal laugh and yelled to the surrounding houses, "Help me! Help me! Busha boy out to get me!" He leaned back and continued cackling.

Seeing the opportunity, Sharpe gave Magus the extra thrust needed to accelerate his backward motion, slamming him to the rocky ground. Magus let out a moan while rubbing the back of his head.

"Me warn you, Magus! Next time it going be worse!"

Child in hand, Magus's woman ran to help him, shouting, "Lawd, have mercy!"

Magus's neighbors stared at the commotion from their dwellings, then watched Sharpe disappear into the dark night while Magus yelled, "You forget who I am! You forget what I can do!" Then he let out a string of obscenities, the last of which was "Quaco!"[9]

12

CAILIN | ARCHIE

SATURDAY, SEPTEMBER 30, 1944

Cailin woke up earlier than usual that morning, anticipating the day's adventure with Gus and Archie. Lying in bed, going over the plans for the day, she found herself getting uneasy about having a visitor on the property who wasn't family. She calmed herself, thinking about the fun the three of them had had at the river.

After a quick breakfast Essie had insisted on, Cailin and Gus went out to the barbecue, looking toward the cotton tree, waiting for Archie.

"Do you think he'll come?" she asked Gus.

"He said he would when we asked him at Mr. Lyn's shop yesterday. Seems like an honest fellow to me. Besides, he's not due to be here for another five minutes."

Not long after, Archie appeared, coming from the side of the house. "I had to take a shortcut through the cow pasture. That was a long walk!"

Gus laughed. "I told you we would ride down to get you."

"Come on. Let's get going," directed Cailin.

The threesome walked across the barbecue toward the upward slope of the hill.

Essie called out from the window. "And who is you friend?"

"Archie, from the inn," replied Gus.

"Good fi meet you, Archie from the inn."

"Nice to meet you, Miss…"

"Essie," filled in Cailin.

"Yes, Miss Essie," finished Archie.

Essie's eyes followed them until they disappeared behind the pimento room.

It had been mid-summer since they had ventured up into the hills beyond the house, to a tiny village called Relax located a short distance from the northeastern Cawdor property line. Some people who lived in Relax often travelled a dirt path through the property to their desired destinations. Occasionally, just after dusk, while people from Relax and other surrounding areas were heading home from Oristano, Ian, Cailin, and Gus would stage a duppy scene in the small family cemetery that was at the intersection of the Cawdor road and the path that led to Relax.

Gus always volunteered to be the duppy. Sitting on a gravestone, he would hold a dimly lit lamp and cover himself with a white sheet. Before Gus came to live with them, Ian always volunteered Cailin to be the duppy. She hated it because it was hot and stuffy under the sheet. Since Gus's arrival, she'd been promoted to the tree branches where Ian made low moaning sounds while she rattled a bulky chain. Men and women passing by on the path would shriek, and more than one dropped their belongings—fish, vegetables, and, once, a small bag of money—and ran yelling, "Rolling calf! Rolling calf!"[1] The trio would laugh all the way back to the house, where they had to pretend nothing had happened.

Now, Cailin, Gus, and Archie hiked halfway up the slope to the sugar mill shack where they took a machete that was inside the doorway. From there they hiked the rest of the way to Relax, clearing underbrush that had grown since their last hike.

Since Archie had never done anything like this and Cailin seemed to be in charge of the adventure, he mostly walked behind them. Gus even joked about him really being the third leg.

On the way to Relax, they passed by Tawny, an Indian man tending his crops. Malcolm had loaned him a piece of hilly land for two years. During that time, it was his responsibility to clear the land of trees and plant crops. Yams, sugar cane, callaloo, whatever he thought would turn a profit. After the two years, he was to plant grass on the land and hand it back to Malcolm, who would use it to graze cattle. Malcolm would then loan him another piece of land for another two years to do the same. This was a deal Malcolm had with several other people, including Ol' Man Russy, who operated the sugar mill. In this way, Malcolm steadily increased the productivity and value of the Cawdor property.

After hiking for three-quarters of an hour, they spotted Relax from a distance, with its few and small shacks and the one shop it claimed. To Gus they looked like matchboxes perched on the hill and propped up with crooked matchsticks.

The trio lay low, not wanting to be seen. In the past, Ian, who was braver than they, paraded them through the village, stopping to talk with each person they saw. He wasn't afraid that the people might know they were the duppies from the cemetery. Cailin and Gus didn't want to imagine what the residents of Relax might do to them had they known. The truth is, even if the people knew it was the children who had scared them on those evenings, they would never have bothered them for fear of retaliation from Busha.

They saw two boys leaving a shack with large tin pails. Cailin knew that meant they were headed to get water and would pass by them to go to the brook a quarter mile away, a tributary that fed into the Oristano River. The threesome retreated from the rock they were spying from and began their trek back down to the sugar mill.

Upon arriving at the sugar mill, they found Ol' Man Russy in his little dwelling attached to the side of the mill shack, sitting on the only piece of furniture in it—a wooden bed not much wider than a bench. He lived there during the week working the land and went home on the weekends. Cailin wondered why he was there on Saturday and, for the first time, where his actual home was. She asked him if he would squeeze some sugarcane juice for them. He smiled and took a few pieces of sugar cane into the mill, tied his mule to the timber attached to the post, and urged it slowly around the mill while pushing the cane between the two rotating mill stones. The juice splashed into the empty vat where normally it would be boiled down into syrup. He scooped the juice up with a cup and offered it to them. Each took their gulp of the smooth liquid sweetness. Cailin allowed hers to linger in her mouth, growing sweeter, just long enough to satisfy her. Archie marveled at the taste.

After thanking Russy, Cailin asked if they could borrow the mule for a ride back to the house.

"Not that foolishness again, Miss Cailin?" said Russy.

"What are we doing?" asked Archie.

"You'll see," replied Gus. "I get the tail!"

Cailin led the mule to the front of the mill shack and stationed the donkey with its head pointing downhill. After Gus mounted it backward, facing its rump, she told Archie to mount behind Gus, facing the same direction as him.

"Have you lost your mind?" Archie asked as she lowered her interlocked fingers to offer him a hoist.

When the boys were both seated on the mule, Cailin slapped its rump, and off they went downhill, backward. Gus took hold of the mule's tail, pretending he was Billy the Kid in the last movie his father had taken him to. He whooped and hollered and shot at the trees with his two-fingered pistol, claiming he had rescued Archie from the Indians. Archie held on tight. Cailin laughed, running behind them.

Out of breath from running down the hill, Cailin found the boys sitting on the edge of the barbecue waiting for her. She flopped down beside them, and the three of them looked at each other and burst into laughter. She couldn't remember the last time she had so much fun.

Cailin noticed her grandfather's car parked by the barbecue, a black Ford with a running board. She had forgotten her grandparents were coming. Had she remembered, she would have waited at the bottom of the road and rode the running board up to the house.

She turned to Archie and said, "Mass Whim—I mean, my grandfather is here. He's my favorite person in the world—everything a grandfather should be. Would you like to meet him?"

"He is wonderful." Gus added. "Even though I'm not his grandson, he treats me like I am. You have to meet him!"

"I don't know." Archie pushed himself off the barbecue wall. "Maybe another time. I'd better be getting back to the inn. My mother has chores waiting for me." He walked off, then turned around and said, "Thanks for the adventure." He cut down by the side of the house, heading toward the cow pasture.

Cailin and Gus found their visitors on the back veranda. There, Mass Whim sat beside Cailin's grandmother, whom he called Cissy. Cailin was not surprised to find him laughing, presumably at some joke he had made. She tumbled into the armchair he sat in, which his frame filled, leaving her more lying on his side than seated beside him. Auntie Abum was sitting with Helen and Auntie Bitsy and was quick to point out that Cailin was far too old for such childish conduct and should get up promptly. Ignoring Abum, Mass Whim locked his arms around Cailin, giving her his old mischievous grin. How she loved him!

Essie appeared through the doorway and addressed Mass Whim, "You call for me, sah?"

"Yes, Miss Essie. Good to see you!" he said with delight.

"Good to see you too, sah," she responded with a timid smile. It always caught Cailin off guard to see Essie's response to her grandfather. He was the only one who could break through her in-charge demeanor. Then again, he had a genuine way of making anyone he spoke with feel special.

"Did you get the snapper I sent to the kitchen?"

"Yes, sah."

"I bought it from the neaga[2] man who was at the bottom of the road heading up with his donkey to the house to sell fish. I saved him the bother of coming up." He laughed. Then, with a pleading smile, he said, "I know you can cook a sweet brown-stew fish. Will you cook it for lunch with some green banana and dumplings?"

Essie glanced at Abum, who had given orders earlier that morning as to the lunch menu. Abum gave a capitulating harrumph. Then Essie affirmed Mass Whim's request and headed back into the house. Shortly after, she was heard yelling, "Samfie! Go to the banana tree and pick six green banana and bring them come. And mek haste!" Everyone except Abum laughed. Even Cissy gave a chuckle.

As jovial as was Mass Whim's countenance, Cissy's was more often than not stern. Cailin would never have referred to her grandmother by her first name as she did her grandfather, calling him "Mass Whim." Her grandmother didn't approve of such informalities. She wanted to be called Grandmother. When Cailin was younger, she thought her grandmother, who always seemed to carry an expression of pain on her face, was mean. Cailin later learned from her mother that this was not without reason. She suffered from a debilitating form of rheumatoid arthritis. To add to the "mean" impression, once when the family went to visit their grandparents at Lennox, Cailin was wearing shorts and had to spend the whole visit sitting in the car because her grandmother believed girls should always wear dresses and that shorts were a modern indecency. By that time Cailin knew of the arthritis, so she wondered if it also affected her grandmother's soul. Knowing her grandmother loved her, the thought pricked Cailin's conscience.

Ruby rang the dining room bell announcing lunch was ready.

After all were seated and Mass Whim had said grace at Cissy's insistence, Cailin and Gus recounted their adventure up to Relax and back. There was laughter and hand clapping at the children's vivacious narration, especially regarding the backward donkey ride. Abum and Cissy didn't crack a smile, though. Cailin knew her grandmother disapproved of her tomboy antics, but figured she held her tongue as her husband was heartily enjoying the stories. However, Abum, who never held her tongue, remarked, "It's a good thing your father is not present to hear this, Cailin. He would not approve of you inviting a boy up to the property."

Mass Whim responded with a downward wave of his hand. "Oh, Abum, there's no harm done. These are children playing children's games."

Abum gave one of her inveterate harrumphs.

War inevitably came up during the table discussion. Disappointment hovered as Mass Whim recounted the recent loss of Allied forces to the Germans in the Netherlands because of the failed attempt of British and U.S. airborne divisions to secure bridges over three important rivers. What was hoped to be a move toward the end of the war had proved a failure. Mass Whim, in his ever-optimistic way, assured them it was just a setback. The war would be over soon enough.

Like a German Messerschmitt, Abum dove in. "Tam is in the RAF, is he not? I wonder if he has been taken captive, or worse."

Everyone's heads pivoted toward her in distaste. Gus's father, Tam, was raised by Abum, along with Malcolm and their four other siblings, three who were spread over the island and one who had moved abroad. The only relatives Abum felt any warmth for were Malcolm and his eldest daughter, Heather. Cailin often heard her walking back and forth on the veranda praying repetitively, "God bless, Malcolm. God bless Heather."

Helen spoke up. "Now, let's not go putting things in our heads that ought not be there. The thing for everyone to do is to hope for the best and busy ourselves with our own affairs here at home."

Everyone understood Helen to be silencing Abum's abrasive tongue for Gus's sake. To intercept any further smarting comments from Abum, Gus addressed Mass Whim, "Grandpa, our wireless is broken and has been sent to Black River to get fixed. Uncle Malcolm said the man at the shop told him he was waiting for a part to come in." Gus always called Mass Whim Grandpa. He had known none of his grandparents, and Mass Whim had once offered to fill those shoes.

"I'm sure it will be fixed in good time, son," responded Mass Whim, smiling affectionately at the boy. "Until then, the *Daily Gleaner* will tell you everything you need to know."

Turning to Helen, Mass Whim asked, "I meant to ask this earlier, but young Gus here has reminded me of him. Will we have the pleasure of Malcolm's company before we leave today?"

"I don't think so," Helen responded, then turning toward the children she said, "Go find something quiet to do while the adults retire to the veranda."

Cailin got a board game from her room and set it up close

to the veranda door. She wanted to be within earshot of their conversation.

While she and Gus played, the adults spoke softly. Gus would celebrate his wins so loudly, she felt she was missing important parts of the conversation and was thankful when her mother reminded him they were to play quietly.

Gus chided Cailin when he noticed she was not paying full attention to the game, but she kept on eavesdropping. The more she listened, the more she pieced together a dim picture. Mass Whim seemed to be concerned for her mother. What about, she couldn't decode. He said something to the effect of her father renting the inn from someone, which Cailin already knew, and bringing a mixed woman over to run the place. There was something Mass Whim seemed to insinuate—she couldn't figure it out. She thought about her father and mother…Miss Gracie, the "mixed woman"…Archie, her son. She couldn't put it all together. *Why is Mass Whim concerned?*

Archie rested on his haunches at the back corner of the Cawdor great house, listening to everything on the veranda above him. The warm greetings. Abum scolding Cailin. The old man's jovial voice. The family chatter. Everything he wanted. He sighed deeply.

When Essie's urgent call for Samfie to pick the six green bananas rang through the air, Archie snapped back to reality. He took a deep breath, got up, and resumed his trek back to the inn.

13

SHARPE

FRIDAY-MONDAY, OCTOBER 6-9, 1944

"Come. Sit down and eat," Marsha pressed Sharpe. "It's been a hard week. You need some food and rest." She pulled him by his hand to the table. "See me mek salt fish, ackee, and green banana—you favorite."

Sitting down to a food-laden plate, he questioned her, "How you get the salt fish?"

"Jus like you have your ways them, me have my ways," she bantered.

"Well, since you know how to pull cat out of pregnant dog[1], me will eat the food respectfully." He pulled her into his lap and began kissing her.

"That is for later." She swatted him with the dishrag and got up to serve herself dinner.

As they ate, Sharpe inquired, "You read the poem I taught you to read?"

She sucked her teeth. "No, sah! You know say me can't read. No matter how you try to teach me. What is more, me no see how that poem is about Hakin. If anyting, it's about Magus, for is him cause most of the trouble around here. And mek me add to that," she continued, looking him full in the face, eyebrows raised, "What you did to Magus the other week is stirring the pot. Me afraid for what him is boiling up."

He casually looked back at his food and, after putting a piece of yam in his mouth, replied, "Nothing can't happen. Magus not going want to deal with me again."

She hesitated and said, "Me have to tell you something."

He looked up. "What? Somebody bother you?"

"Not really. It's Muma." She hesitated.

"Something happen to her?" He sat back. Her mother had been good to him since he and Marsha had been together. He had even begun to think of her as a mother. "Is what happen to her?"

"Nothing. It's just that she have a little talk with me a couple days back. Me did never want tell you, but me sort of see what she talking about."

"Go ahead and say it, woman! You carry on like you going say you pregnant."

Head hanging, she said nothing.

"It's that?" he exclaimed, shocked at the possibility.

"No. It's not that, thank the Lawd." She looked up then said, "She say me must leave you and come home. She scared of Magus. She say people talking what Magus going do, and she no want me mix up in it."

Sharpe's countenance fell, like that of a wounded puppy but then transformed into that of a rabid wolf.

Marsha took a step back.

He immediately masked the wolf, stepping towards her with a gentle embrace.

She calmed down. "You know how me love you, but sometime it hard." She paused. "But even though you is me Black Giant, me know say you still need me." She chuckled, flirting with him.

"Go along and clean the dish dem. It's almost time for what you did say was for later," he responded with a grin.

She playfully swatted him once more with the rag. "You too rude again. Maybe me not going give you nothing at all."

Sharpe woke from his sleep. His stomach ripping with pain and his body drenched with sweat. Outside, he heard a retching sound. Someone was gasping for air and then heaving. He felt the bed beside him. Marsha wasn't there. He forced himself from the bed into the dark night where he found her on her knees, hunched over a large rock, struggling. His stomach ripped again, along with the rising sensation of his innards pushing their way up through his esophagus. He tried to hold it back; he needed to help Marsha. But out it surged, and with it came more stomach-tearing agony, bringing him to his knees.

When there was nothing left for either of them to expel, Sharpe took hold of Marsha and helped her back into the house and onto the coconut husk-filled mattress. While doing so, he caught sight of their neighbor, Nana, peering through her window. Sharpe called to her for help. She disappeared.

That whole night they lay in bed unable to speak—groaning, shaking, sweating, and occasionally just about making it outside to heave what they did not have to heave. In the morning, no one came to help, although Sharpe found a pail of water just outside the door. Marsha recognized the pail as being Nana's. It was the only gesture given until about midday when Marsha's mother came. As soon as the rumor had made it round to her house, she hurried over to help. Ram Foot, too, heard but didn't rush over. A couple hours later, he approached the house, stopping fifty yards away and looking on. When Marsha's mother saw him through the window, she told him to run to Cawdor and let Busha know Sharpe was sick and wouldn't be able to come to work for some days. Without stopping to see how Sharpe and Marsha were, he quickly ran the errand.

In the late afternoon, when Sharpe and Marsha were stable, her mother went to get a chicken to make broth with. Sharpe, lying on his back, face to the ceiling, addressed Marsha, "Was the ackee[2] pod them fully open when you did pick dem?"

With a dry mouth and still weak, Marsha replied, "What you take me for? Yes, every last one of them was open."

"Then where you did get the salt fish?"

"Is Nana give it to me. She say she did buy too much and want to give me the balance of it." She thought for a moment then continued, "What you saying? You think the salt fish poison us? But I see Nana cook her piece, and she even taste little bit of it."

"That is just the point! Who is Nana related to? Nuh Lucy is har cousin?"

"But why? And how would Lucy get the poison?"

"Magus! That's what Obeah man do—him mix up in every kind a herb and plant and things that spin head and can even kill we."

"If it's Magus, then thank God we no dead." She exhaled and lay back on the mattress, staring at a faraway cloud floating past the open window.

Sharpe began slowly reciting, "If we must die—let it not be like hogs hunted and penned in an inglorious spot..." He continued reciting the poem slowly and methodically increased his volume and speed as he had heard Mr. Aldridge do in school during chapel, until his crescendo, "...And for their thousand blows, deal one death blow!" Before he could conclude, Marsha reached over and capped his mouth with her hand.

He pushed her hand away. "What you do that for?"

"Me can't take it no more." She inhaled deeply, then

expelled the air she'd taken in as though she were a tire worn thin that finally punctured and flattened to move no further.

Early Sunday morning, Sharpe, still weak from Magus's poison, readied himself to go to Cawdor. Marsha begged him to stay and rest, but he insisted, saying he couldn't lie around while there were things to be taken care of at Cawdor.

Like walking out of a smoke-filled rum bar, being away from Hakin brought him clarity. On his way down the craggy path, his mind crystalized. There were no more jurors deliberating in his head. There was only a judge who knew his mind and was ready to execute justice. The verdict? Guilty. Lucy and Magus's sentence? Forthcoming.

On arriving at Cawdor, Essie, whose ears had already picked up on the rumors about Sharpe's sickness, realized he was still not well and told Malcolm, who reluctantly sent him home to rest. Instead of heading back to Hakin at the bottom of the Cawdor road, he aimlessly wandered down to Mr. Lyn's store. He saw a few people hanging about, mostly at the rum bar, and sensed their stares. He turned back and found himself heading toward Mr. Aldridge's house. On his approach to the church property, he heard the singing and remembered Mr. Aldridge would be leading the service. He momentarily toyed with the idea of going into the church, sitting on the back pew, and waiting to speak with Mr. Aldridge after the service concluded. He laughed it off, thinking he didn't belong in a church. What had God ever done for him? Besides, what more could Mr. Aldridge tell him?

He took the long way back to Hakin.

Walking through Hakin, some men jeered at him, making comments: "Me 'ear you trow up all night!" "Hey, Busha boy!" "Watch how the food mek him face favor like when John Crow draw breaks!"[3] Bandwagon laughter followed. This was more reason to exact revenge, yet the time was not now. He ignored them, trying to appear healthier than he felt.

He walked into the house and found Marsha and her belongings gone. Her words came back to him, *She say people talking what Magus going do, and she no want me mix up in it.* A scowl came over his face. He stepped out the door to go get her back. By the time he was a quarter way to her mother's house, he stopped and turned back. He had been rehearsing things he was going to say to her but realized none of them would have worked, short of taking her by the arm and dragging her back. That would never do. Besides, he didn't want something like this, or worse, to happen to her again. He needed to face the demon alone. Then, maybe, he could win her back.

He returned to his house, lay down on the mattress, and slept until early the next morning.

~

The sun was not yet up when Sharpe reached the Cawdor house, and he was drawn to the only glow of light—Essie was in the kitchen, busy with preparations for the day.

She didn't see him standing in the doorway.

Sharpe cleared his throat and said, "Good morning, Miss Essie, how come you up so early?"

She looked up, unsurprised, and said, "I could say the same thing to you. But for me, I looking to catch the worm. Now, what about you?"

He hesitated.

Before he could think up an answer, she said, "No worry mek up anything, for Essie already know. Me tol' you 'bout the Kerry Mongoose dem." She motioned him toward a stool. "Now, come sit down. Me guessing you no eat nothing. Them say a hungry man is a angry man."

Essie fixed him eggs, toast, and coffee. He ate in silence, wondering how she knew.

When he finished the meal, Essie took the plate and said, "Busha want to see you. He will be in the office once the sunrise."

～

Malcolm spotted Sharpe approaching his opened office door and said, "You look somewhat better today."

Sharpe stepped into the office and stood at attention, as if awaiting orders. "Yes, sah. It was something me did eat."

"Yes. Salt fish, I hear."

"Yes, sah," Sharpe responded, realizing Essie must have told him.

Malcolm continued casually, "And do you have any more details you need to let me know?"

"Not really, sah," he replied, a little shaken.

Malcolm glared at Sharpe. When it was obvious he was not going to be forthcoming, Malcolm slammed his fist on his desk. "Damn it, Sharpe! I know what happened! A little food goes a long way with these Hakin people. I know what Lucy and Magus did to you and your woman."

Sharpe stood, head hanging.

"Pick up your head! What are you, a boy?" Malcolm came from behind the desk and faced Sharpe. "Now, as foreman of this property, tell me what you need to do about this situation?"

"Me no rightly know, sah."

"He doesn't know." Malcolm shook his head then repeated, "He doesn't know." Locking eyes with Sharpe, he demanded, "The first thing you will do is fire Lucy! The next thing is to deal with Magus. That will be more difficult as he doesn't work at Cawdor. But whatever you do, watch your Black hide. Stay far away from his reach."

Sharpe tensed at Malcolm's demeaning words, "He doesn't know," "your Black hide," thinking, *It never get any easier to hear him bad mouth me.* Yet, his conversation with Mr. Aldridge came to mind. The conversation that led him to the conclusion that even though Malcolm's way was harsh, Sharpe had no other option than to follow that path, for the time being at least. *Beside*, he thought, *Lucy and Magus bring it on themself.*

Sharpe looked at Malcolm. "Me will get rid a Lucy this very day. And as for Magus, me working on a plan to deal with him."

"Be careful, Sharpe. Obeah men are dangerous, as you now know. Walk that walk carefully."

"Yes, sah."

"Alright. Go do what you have to do."

Sharpe turned to leave, and Malcolm added, "And don't worry about your girl. One woman is as good as the next."

Sharpe chafed but replied, "Yes, sah," and headed back out onto the property.

After firing Lucy, living in Hakin became increasingly difficult for Sharpe. The only people who talked with him were his auntie and uncle—and that was with one eye on the lookout. Even Ram Foot avoided him. On the Cawdor property, the Hakin workers only responded minimally to his questions and never looked directly at him. He craved authentic human interaction, so most days he found himself at Cawdor before dawn, sitting in Essie's kitchen.

With little to no communication, Sharpe had too much time to think. His thoughts of retaliation intensified. Lucy and Magus had ruined what little life he enjoyed at Hakin. At first he was going to include Lucy in his exaction of revenge, but the more he thought, the more he realized she had already received hers. Since losing her pimento picking job, she was subdued—not running her mouth all over Hakin. And, from the little he could observe, there seemed to be a distance between Lucy and Magus. She had played with the devil and been burned.

Conversely, Magus was to be dealt with, and Sharpe knew how. He decided he would go to Accompong and procure from the Obeah man there a more dangerous potion than what Magus had dispensed on him. He would deal with Magus decisively, but he realized he would have to wait for Ian to return from school for the holidays, as Ian was the only one Malcolm would trust the property to in Sharpe's absence. Now was not the time to make those arrangements, though. Closer to Christmas. He would wait patiently. Time would bring revenge.

14

ARCHIE

"Archie! Come down for dinner," called Mr. Witcombe from the bottom of the stairs. "It looks as though you'll be missing dinner at the inn. If Mr. Campbell is even coming."

In two minds and with a furrowed brow, Archie came down and sat at the table.

Mrs. Witcombe put her hand on Archie's. "There, there. Why don't you see if your friend will do something with you tomorrow?"

Robby was his contingency plan; what he really wanted was Oristano. But remembering Malcolm had picked him up six weekends in a row, he figured he could live without the inn for one weekend if he had to, especially if Robby was around.

"Do you mind if after dinner I go over to Robby's house to see if he'll be around tomorrow?"

Mrs. Witcombe looked at Mr. Witcombe. He breathed heavily and said, "Only if we don't have a repeat of the last time the two of you spent Saturday together. You must be home before dark. That goes for now and tomorrow. I didn't tell Mr. Campbell last time, and I don't want to have to."

"Yes, Mr. Witcombe," Archie replied, then added, "I'm not feeling very hungry. May I be excused from the table to go over to Robby's now?"

Before Mr. Witcombe could say anything, Mrs. Witcombe chuckled and answered, "Certainly, dear."

Archie got back to the Witcombes just as Savanna-la-Mar had half slipped on her evening robe. The Witcombes were sitting in the parlor while Mr. Witcombe theatrically read what Archie recognized to be *David Copperfield*. He thought it appropriate they were reading one of Dickens's orphan novels. Mrs. Witcombe interrupted the reading to tell him Pressy had left him a slice of jelly roll on the kitchen table. He ate it, went to his room to do his science homework, and made it an early night in preparation for an early morning.

Savanna-la-Mar was their domain. Robby eagerly introduced Archie to haunts he'd not shown him on their last expedition. His favorite was a small restaurant on the outskirts of town, where the Indian proprietor let them sample the best curry goat Archie had ever tasted. He told them to come back when lunch was ready, but it was too out of the way. They headed down to the open-air market and stole coconut drops while a street vendor was tending to a customer. They threw rocks into the ocean until they hit a small fishing boat and were chastised by two fishermen. Then they went to the Doric and watched a cowboy film twice.

When they left the movie theater, Savanna-la-Mar was again slipping on her robe. Robby gave Archie a mischievous look. "Do you remember last time?"

"Last time, what?"

"When you chickened out on my dare to go into Saint George's to see who could stand the dark the longest."

"I didn't chicken out. I had to go home, like I should now."

"Rhaatid! You're afraid of the dark, aren't you?" Robby taunted.

Archie thought. It was one thing to trespass in the cinema, but to do it in a church? The parish church at that. What if they got caught? In addition, he'd be breaking his word to Mr. Witcombe. He would surely tell Malcolm. Or would he? Was he just bluffing like he did the last time? Yet, he didn't want to appear a sissy to Robby. The decision was made in the moment.

"Okay. I'll do it. Sounds easy."

"Took you long enough to decide."

"How do we get in?"

"There's a side door that isn't locked until about seven o'clock, sometimes later. The parson is probably preparing for church tomorrow."

"How do you know?"

"It's the church my family goes to. I know him, and I know the building inside out."

"Okay. Let's go."

The church interior was dark except for a faint light peeping under a door—presumably the parson's study. Robby led the way to a small room off the vestibule. "This is where they keep the dead bodies before funerals. If we can stay here, there's nowhere we can't stay."

The thought of dead bodies didn't scare Archie. He was now more concerned about his body being dead if Malcolm found out he'd disobeyed Mr. Witcombe.

For the next hour, Robby did his best to scare Archie, whispering the most gruesome, duppy stories he could devise. Amused, Archie sat against the stone wall, glad he had stayed in town. Robby and he were becoming fast friends. If only he would talk about the goings-on at school. At one point, Archie brought up the subject, but Robby told him not to spoil the spooky atmosphere and continued telling his stories.

During a lull in Robby's storytelling, they heard the creak of a door opening and closing, then some echoing footsteps. Archie froze. Robby whispered, "It's just the parson. He must be leaving."

Another open-and-closed door, then a key turning in a latch.

"He's gone," said Robby, returning to his normal volume.

"And so is the key to the door!" remarked Archie. "How the hell are we going to get out of here? Did you think of that?"

"Well…ah…no, but neither did you. We'll figure something out."

They stepped into the vestibule, where just enough light shone through the stained-glass windows for the boys to make their way to the side door. They checked, and it was locked. Archie cursed.

"Watch your mouth, Archie. We're in a church."

"I don't care if we're in Buckingham Palace!"

They split up with the mission of finding an open window. Robby said he would check the right-side windows, leaving Archie to check the left ones.

At first, Archie could hear Robby shuffling around trying windows. But after a short while, he couldn't hear any movement coming from the right side. He called Robby's name. There was no reply. He told him to stop playing games. No reply. He searched under every pew, in every room, in every space, but couldn't find him. Eventually, he realized Robby must have found an open window and left him there.

Trying the windows on Robby's side, he found his escape route. He hoisted himself up, slipped through, and let himself down gently, being careful not to attract the attention of anyone who may be in earshot. He looked around for Robby and called his name softly. There was no response. Once on the street, he looked around, but, seeing no sign of Robby, he ran back to the Witcombes'. Outside the haberdashery, he caught his breath, straightened his clothes, and headed for the house.

The Witcombes' were waiting, seated side by side on the parlor couch. He glanced at the grandfather clock in the corner; it was eight forty. Mr. Witcombe's thin lips were locked tight, giving him the appearance of having a surgical incision for a mouth. Mrs. Witcombe's tortured face oscillated twice between Archie and Mr. Witcombe, finally fastening on her husband.

"What is the meaning of this? You disobeyed my rule. I gave you specific instructions to be home before dark. The sun set before six o'clock."

While running back home, Archie planned a response to the sunset argument. Now was the time to use it. "Yes. Mr. Witcombe, but my curfew is at seven thirty. Six o'clock was an hour and a half before that."

Mr. Witcombe looked down for a moment then, raising his head, continued, "Whether six is too early is not the point. You deliberately disobeyed me. It's as though you want me to talk to Mr. Campbell about your impudence. This is the second time you have put me in this situation." He shook his head. "This time I will have to speak with him."

Almost on cue, Mrs. Witcombe put her hand on her husband's arm and pleaded with him, "Please, Edward. Can't we give him one more chance?"

He looked at her and explained, "One more chance will lead to many more chances."

There was something odd about the way he looked at her and made the last statement. It seemed as if Mr. Witcombe was softening up a little too quickly. Archie decided to let things play out further before he said anything more.

"Yes, Edward. But you know what the minister said last

Sunday, 'If thy brother trespass against thee, rebuke him,' which you have done."

Then again, on cue, Mr. Witcombe completed the quote, "And if he repents, forgive him."

By this point, Archie had deduced the Witcombes had preplanned this conversation just as he had his earlier comment. Were they giving him another way out? Did they know something about Malcolm that was preventing them from telling on him? Whatever the case, he was going to play along.

"I do repent." Archie hung his head. "I'm sorry that I disobeyed you, Mr. Witcombe."

Out of the corner of his eye he saw Mrs. Witcombe look up at her husband with a big smile. His suspicion was confirmed.

"Good," said Mr. Witcombe, "That being dealt with, I will tell you of a new rule we have made."

Archie looked up.

"Every weekend you stay with us, not only must you be home at the time I say, but you will also come with us to church."

Mrs. Witcombe swiveled her head toward Archie as if to see his response.

This new rule blindsided him. Church! Tonight was the first night he had ever set foot in a church. Other than that, the closest thing had been the mandatory school chapel meetings. Those were unbearable. Abbie had told him amusing stories of the church she attended. But he was sure the Witcombes' church was more like a school chapel than Abbie's church. He had to put his foot down here.

"Mr. and Mrs. Witcombe," he made eye contact with them both. "Thank you for allowing me to repent. And I do so wholeheartedly." Then he held both his hands to his chest, slowly casting his eyes down and bowing his head. "However, I am not the religious sort and would fear God's wrath on you both and on me if I should step foot in a church."

"Look at me, my dear," Mrs. Witcombe entreated him with gentle eyes. "Nothing is further from the truth. God wants sinners to come into his fold."

"Right. There you go," said Mr. Witcombe. "We'll be ready to leave for church at quarter to eight in the morning. Be ready. Come, Emily. Time for bed."

Archie, realizing his act had not worked, broke character and objected, "I will not go! I cannot go to church with you every Sunday Malcolm leaves me here!"

Genuinely angered, Mr. Witcombe stood up, raising his voice, "You will go! Or I will tell Mr. Campbell. And, besides, when did you start calling him Malcolm?" He pointed his index finger at Archie. "One word of advice, young man. Of all people," then in staccato, "don't—cross—Malcolm—Campbell!"

The next morning, Archie was up and dressed for church in the best clothes he had brought to the Witcombes.

"I hope I'm dressed okay," Archie said to Mrs. Witcombe.

She replied pleasantly, "You're fine, dear. The Bible says to render your heart, not your garment."

Mr. Witcombe raised his eyebrows. "Actually, my dear, the passage says 'rend' not render. It would be preferable if the boy did not tear his clothes. Now, come along. We don't want to be late. It takes at least ten minutes to walk there."

After the church service, the trio stood under the covered front entrance, and Mr. Witcombe said, "Let's wait right here." Then, addressing Archie, he said, "There's somebody I'd like you to meet."

Archie wasn't eager to wait as he had seen some of his class-mates sitting in the service, so he turned his back on the people exiting the church, hoping to avoid any contact. While they waited, he wondered who the person they were waiting for could be, so he asked, "Is it the priest? I don't think I'd like to talk with him. He seems like a stern fellow." Archie was disturbed by what the man had said about God being a father and all the things he had done for mankind and how, in turn, he wanted their unreserved obedience. He thought to himself, *No one gets my unreserved obedience. Not even my mother!*

"Actually," replied Mr. Witcombe, "he's not a priest. He's a pastor. And, yes, he can be stern at times, but I assure you, he has the heart of Jesus. If you only knew the good he's done for the poor of this town. But he's not the person I want you to meet."

That subdued Archie's irritation.

Shortly after, he heard a voice coming through the doorway. "Sorry to keep you waiting. I was just wrapping up some details with the collection."

Archie turned around to see a well-dressed gentleman carrying a Bible in one hand and a hat in the other. Beside him was an attractive woman around the same age.

The man put the hat on his graying head and reached out to shake Archie's hand. "So you must be young Archibald. The Witcombes have told me about you. It's a pleasure to finally meet you."

Looking up at him, Archie saw an oddly familiar face. He wondered where he might have met him before.

"Archie, this is Mr. Kester Campbell and his wife Jane," said Mr. Witcombe. "He's a deacon in the church, and he's also Westmoreland's finest doctor." Mrs. Witcombe nudged him. "Oh…and he's Mr. Campbell's—that is, Malcolm Campbell's oldest brother."

"Well, there's more to the story than that," Mrs. Witcombe chimed in with an elated smile. "While attending medical school in London, Mr. Campbell met his wife." She touched

Jane Campbell's arm as though she were a porcelain doll. "She was an English girl who was studying to be a nurse. Through her influence he became a devout Baptist, and through his influence she married him and moved to Jamaica."

Mr. Campbell chuckled and said, "Thank you for the commendation, Mr. Witcombe. And Mrs. Witcombe, may I recommend you become one of those romance novelists? You do make an ordinary courtship sound beguiling." He pulled his wife to him, wrapping an arm around her shoulder.

The two couples gave a pleasant chuckle, but Archie stared at Mr. Campbell, the puzzle snapping together. Apprehension gripped him. He was being turned over to the oldest brother to be dealt with. He froze, not knowing what to say.

"Well?" said Mr. Witcombe to Archie. "Have you lost your tongue?" He looked at Mr. Campbell and said, "This is a first."

Archie turned to the Campbells. "I'm sorry. Pleasure to meet you, Mr. and Mrs. Campbell." Then looking closely at Kester, he said, "I was only surprised by the resemblance between you and Mr. Campbell...your brother."

"Not to worry. You aren't the first." Mr. Campbell smiled warmly. His countenance seemed to melt a layer of Archie's armor. Archie had never thought of himself as wearing armor, but with some of his defenses down, he felt vulnerable. This was not a sensation he cared for.

15

KIMBERLY, SOUTH AFRICA

12 APRIL 1903

Dearest Abum,

I must start my letter with a sincere apology for not writing for these many months. You see, I gave birth to a beautiful baby girl last month. I was as surprised as anyone to realize I was pregnant. I thought I had caught a stomach bug, but after the second day I realized what it was. Then I cried for days, thinking about raising a child in this wilderness. My only consolation was that I would have one of my own children with me again. Now that I can touch her, wrap her tight in a blanket, and smell her sweetness when I hug her, I am content. I believe you will be pleased that we have named her Alexandra, after the Queen. Since Cuddy has seen me with her, he thinks we should have one more to keep her company. I reminded him that was God's business.

I did not write to you sooner as I was unsure how to tell you I was expecting another child when you are raising my other six. I will admit, we have placed you in an awkward position. Yet, I have no doubt the children are better off with you at Cawdor House than they would be here in Kimberly. I am indeed grateful to you.

As it is, you have successfully petitioned my brother, Alfred, to pay for Kester's education at Potsdam School. It brings joy to my heart that he is getting an excellent education, which will open many doors for him. Cuddy is particularly pleased to hear Kester wants to be a doctor. He says, Kester is a chip off the old block.

I am sorry for the brevity of this letter, but I am still recovering from childbearing, and Alexandra is having problems with colic. I don't know what I would do without the colored nanny Cuddy hired. She has a natural way with Alexandra.

As ever,
Winnie

P.S. Because we had to hire a nanny, Cuddy says we are unable to send the money he promised, but we have not forgotten.

16

CAILIN

FRIDAY, NOVEMBER 17, 1944

"No, dear," he said with a laugh. "Miss Longbridge is not my wife. But she's the only person who can keep up with me. She's pure gold."

In response to Cailin's reddening face, Miss Longbridge said, "What he means, Cailin, is that I'm his personal secretary. And truth be told, I am the only one brave enough to keep up with him, or should I say, put up with him."

Everyone laughed except Archie.

Cailin felt as though it was her they were laughing at even though she knew it was Miss Longbridge's response to Alexander Bustamante's comment. This feeling was exaggerated because Archie was sitting in the corner across the room from her, looking indifferent. The antithesis of the escapades at the river and Relax.

On the horse ride from Cawdor, Gus had said he hoped Archie would be there since Uncle Malcolm had said he was going to Savanna-la-Mar and would be back before Bustamante arrived at the inn. Gus informed her that Archie sometimes came home for the weekend on a Friday—as if she didn't already know that. Her ambivalence confused her. She found herself thinking about him every day. She didn't want it to be so—it just kind of happened. But if Archie was there, she wouldn't know how to act around Busta. Last time Busta had visited the inn, she'd sat on his knee and he'd spoken with her like a grandfather, giving her Paradise Plum candies. It would be embarrassing if Archie saw that.

Ambivalence had given way to insecurity—Archie was now a front row spectator.

"What can I get you two to drink?" asked Gracie.

Miss Longbridge answered, "Mr. Bustamante will have Scotch on the rocks, and I'll have a Coke."

"Coming right up!" said Gracie, heading to the kitchen to serve Bustamante from her personal hidden stash of Scotch. Her alacrity was appropriate for an innkeeper tending to her guest, Alexander Bustamante, who she hoped would be the first chief minister of Jamaica as the British Empire began the long and apprehensive process of letting go of her favored jewel.

"Oh, and Ms. Price," said Miss Longbridge, "Just to confirm. I won't be staying at the inn as a family friend is picking me up in a while to spend the night in Ashton, up Darliston way." She turned to Bustamante and said, "She promised to get me to the rally in Sav an hour early. So, I'll be waiting for you. Don't be late!" She grinned.

"See what I mean?" Bustamante said, spreading his arms out to everyone in the Oristano Inn drawing room, garnering attention to himself. As if he needed it, being that he was well over six feet tall with mostly salt-colored, combed-back, wavy hair that was unruly and bushed out uncontrollably at the sides. That was Busta, as Cailin had fondly grown to know him.

"So, Busta," Malcolm said with comfortable deliberation as he leaned back on the leather couch and smiled, "I hear Bustamante is finally your legal last name."

"Yes, yes. I've been using it for years, but I finally got around to changing it. Now it can appear on the election ballot."

"You mean your real name isn't Busta—I mean, Bustamante?" Cailin said with surprise.

"Well, it is now, but it used to be Clarke," answered Bustamante.

Malcolm jumped in. "My father knew old man Clarke back in the day when he oversaw the property in Hanover. It's over by Lucea, eh?"

"Yes, yes. Blenheim." Bustamante reflected. "He wanted to train me to be the overseer when he retired, but I didn't care to be stuck running a property." He turned to Malcolm. "My apologies, it wasn't what I was made for."

Feeling the grandfatherly kindness in Bustamante, Gus took a chance and asked, "Mr. Bustamante, what were you made for?"

By then, Gracie, who had served the drinks and was sitting with Malcolm, answered for Bustamante, "The leadership of Jamaica is what he was made for!"

"Well, thank you, Ms. Price."

She smiled. "Please. Gracie is just fine."

"Well, Gracie, I have to say I'm glad you've got this old inn back in business. It's in better condition than before and it's providing some much-needed employment here in Westmoreland." He paused, then said, "I trust you're paying your people a fair wage?"

Gracie smiled and replied, "Well, that is Malcolm's affair. I just run the place and keep the patrons happy." She looked up at the wall clock. "Speaking of keeping the patrons happy, supper will be served at seven o'clock. Will that do, Mr. Bustamante?"

"That sounds wonderful! And would you return the favor and call me Busta? That's what they call me from the King's House to the Sav-la-mar wharfs."

Gracie gave her Betty Davis laugh.

Malcolm elbowed her, and she calmed down.

Not one to let silence steal the moment, Bustamante picked up the conversation where Gus had left off, "Actually, young Gus," then pointing his thick, dark eyebrows toward Archie and then over to Cailin, he said, "This is for you too, young people." He paused. "And before I go on, might I add that since the last time I was here, you have grown into quite the young lady, Cailin."

"Thank you, Busta." She blushed for the second time.

"See, Gracie," he announced. "If the young can call me Busta, then so should the middle-aged." He looked at Malcolm and said, "And the old ones." He gave a jovial laugh.

"But I digress. Back to Gus's question." He took a drink of his Scotch and leaned forward. "You see, I left Jamaica at the age of twenty-one—along with many others—to find work in Cuba. I worked in the sugar business and later in the army, serving in the security police for both President Zayas and President Machado." He paused rhetorically. "Then I spent some ten years in Panama, where I met my wife, Mildred— God rest her soul. We moved to New York City where I worked as a dietician in a hospital and was able to use my business mind to make gains from the unfortunate Wall Street crash. Eventually, with some money in my pocket, I returned to Jamaica and opened a loan business." He inhaled deeply, signaling a transition to a subject worthy of sermonizing. "Because of the poor people's misery that I encountered on my various visits to colonial countries and then on my return to Jamaica, I began writing letters to newspaper editors on a daily basis. Those letters, all the union worker strikes I've orchestrated, and the two times I spent in jail because of the strikes are what got me into this mess of running for political office!" He laughed boisterously. "And, oh! Did I forget to tell you why the name Bustamante?" He looked at the children with wide eyes, expecting an answer.

Archie, playing along with thinly veiled sarcasm, replied, "Yes, you forgot, Sir."

"I thought so." He waited as if he was about to reveal something august. "While I was in Spain, a fisherman adopted me." He looked around as if to choose someone and settled on Gus. "Gus, guess what his name was?"

"Busta!" replied Gus, to the adults' amusement.

"Yes, yes. Almost. It was Bustamante." He sat back, obviously pleased with himself.

Miss Longbridge pursed her lips, rolled her eyes, and said, "See what I have to put up with?"

To which Bustamante replied, "But you wouldn't miss the action for the world, would you?"

Just then, horse hooves were heard coming up the driveway.

Getting up and looking through the balcony doors, Archie said, "It's a horse-drawn carriage."

"Oh, that would be for me. My cousin has come to collect me," said Miss Longbridge, relieved of the Busta-banter.

After Miss Longbridge left, the conversation turned to politics. Cailin and Gus were "silent and not heard," not because Auntie Abum had drummed that into them but because it was hard to fit together the political puzzle pieces. Gus understood a bit more than Cailin because he read the *Daily Gleaner* regularly, examining it for word on the war. Archie was likewise silent. Not because he had nothing to say on the subject—he read the newspaper and would have political discussions with his friends when he lived in Montego Bay—but since he had gotten home, his mother had put on his metaphorical servant liveries and had him rushing around to ready the inn for Bustamante. He realized this was why Malcolm had picked him up—and early at that. He was agitated.

Malcolm asked Bustamante his thoughts on Norman Manley promising to destroy "Bustamanteism." That lit Bustamante on fire. He reemphasized his passion for the poor man, who needed representation to increase the minimum wage rate and to receive workman's compensation and retirement pensions. As the leader of the Jamaica Labour Party, these were his imperatives. He said that while these were demands that would be made on big businesses, he was not against big businesses. The poor man needed the jobs the business sector supplied, even as the business sector needed the poor man for labor. Furthermore, he saw Manley's push for Jamaica's immediate independence from Britain as premature. He felt that time was needed for education and preparation regarding the operation of local governance. For all these reasons, Bustamante was sure the lower and upper classes of Jamaica would not let Manley win the election.

Gracie asked him why he and Manley—who he had worked so well with and was even related to—had parted ways and started their own political parties. To this, he answered that Manley had been greatly influenced by socialist associates. As such, Manley and the People's National Party were more concerned with the brown middle class than the poor Black man. Their socialist ideology was nothing more than a ploy to enslave the poor by taking away their lands under the guise of public ownership. In addition, Bustamante said he was against the PNP's support for birth control, seeing it as another form of poverty population control.

Bustamante, still in oratory mode, turned to Cailin and Gus, who had been so attentive, and asked, "What about you children? Do you have questions for me?"

Gus promptly piped up as though he had been waiting for the opportunity. "Yes, Busta. What do you think about the war?"

Malcolm chimed in, "I find the BBC's reports on mysterious

explosions that left lots of people dead in South Britain suspicious. I wouldn't put it past the British government to pull the wool over the people's eyes."

"Well, I'm not sure I would make that accusation myself," replied Bustamante, choosing his words carefully, "but I will say it wouldn't be the first time the Brits have covered up—especially the British officials within the colonies and how they report back to the motherland. That's why the '38 labor strikes were so necessary and why Britain sent a delegation to find out what was really going on with its British appointed officials here in Jamaica. If not, we wouldn't have had this opportunity for the universal suffrage vote this December." Turning to the children, he said, "I'm only sorry the suffrage vote isn't for children. Otherwise, I know you would vote for me."

They all laughed.

"In any case, son. Sorry for yet another digression. Do you have someone dear to you in the war, Mass Gus?"

"Yes, sir. My father, Officer Tam Campbell. He's a pilot in the RAF. He's been involved in bombing the Germans all throughout Europe."

"Well, with a son as proud as you, I wager your father's plane is going to be the one to bomb the old rascal himself! Then he'll be back in no time!"

Gus looked up into Bustamante's eyes. "That's my prayer, sir."

"Come here, the both of you." Bustamante called Cailin and Gus. "Here, up on my knees. I have something for you."

"Isn't Cailin a bit old for that now?" questioned Gracie.

"Yes, I believe Ms. Price is right," Cailin said softly. She blushed for the third time, but with considerably redder than before.

Gus sat on Bustamante's knee as he requested.

"First, I must tell you something I saw in Kingston last week. You know how gas is scarce—except for your uncle, of course. Well, this last Monday, I saw a man driving a car without an engine."

"How is that possible?" Gus quipped.

"The car was being pulled by a jackass!" He laughed. "Boy!" He shook his head. "That's Jamaica for you!" Then he reached his hand into his coat pocket, pulled out small packets wrapped in wax paper, and gave Gus a few. He threw some to Cailin and Archie.

"What are these?" asked Cailin.

"It's a new sweetie they're making in Kingston. It's called Bustamante Backbone." Then he laughed hilariously.

Gus had already unwrapped one of his and stuck it in his mouth. "Mm. It tastes good. But it's hard as rock," he said, slurring from the candy in his mouth.

"That's because they say Busta backbone hard as rock stone!"

Just then the dinner bell rang, and Archie got up to help Abbie serve the dinner.

Cailin watched his nonchalant stroll into the kitchen, wondering if he'd even noticed her.

17

SHARPE

SATURDAY-SUNDAY, DECEMBER 2-3, 1944

As was his habit at the end of every day, Sharpe made sure all tools were put away and everything was as it should be. He then made his way to Busha's office to present a request he'd had tucked away in his mind since early October when Magus had poisoned Marsha and him. The door was open, so he knocked on the frame to get Malcolm's attention.

Malcolm looked up from the ledger where he was recording figures and gave Sharpe a blank stare.

"Sorry to bother you, Busha, but me did want to talk with you about something."

Malcolm put his pencil down. "What is it?"

Sharpe began to fidget but realized Malcolm would not respond well to that posture, so he stood up straight and said, "Well, sah, it's been about twenty year now that me no see me father. And me would like go see him."

"And where is he?"

"In Accompong." Sharpe stood a little taller. "That's where me really come from."

"Yes. I know." Malcolm steepled his fingers, brooding at Sharpe for what seemed a long minute. Finally, he sat back with his arms resting on the chair arms and said, "But what I don't understand, Sharpe, is why in the world a man like you would want to go look for his father," then with emphasis, "who sent him away. And—what you are telling me confirms what I already know—he never cared to visit you or send for you to come visit him."

Sharpe, wondering how Busha knew all these details about him but figuring it best not to ask, continued his petition. "Me know what you a say, Busha. And you correct. But when me mother did die, she left me and two sister with me father, but him couldn't manage all of we. So him did the next best thing him could do and send me to me auntie."

Without a word, Malcolm sat forward and went back to adding numbers.

Knowing he had to get Malcolm to agree to let him go so he could exact vengeance on Magus, Sharpe braced himself, then spoke his next words with an air of authority. "Mass Campbell." He paused and waited for Malcolm to lift his head and look him in the eyes. "Me need to go Accompong to see how me father and sistas them doing. I know Mass Ian coming back for the Christmas holiday, and you trust him with the property. Me will take off without pay." He breathed in deeply, causing his already full chest to expand. "Me have something important me have to take care of, sah."

With that, Malcolm pushed his chair back, scraping it against the wooden floor, made his way around his desk, and stood in front of Sharpe. A half smile slowly formed on his face while he reached out for Sharpe's hand.

Defensive yet confused, Sharpe took Malcolm's hand and Malcolm gave him one firm downstroke handshake.

"Well done!"

Still confused, Sharpe replied, "What me did, sah?"

"You stood your ground! With intelligence and firmness,

you stood your ground! I can only imagine this is how you treat the property workers."

"Yes, sah. Me learn the lesson from you, sah." Still confused about Malcolm's response, Sharpe pushed further, "So, me can go to Accompong then?"

As if Malcolm had forgotten why Sharpe came to see him, with a deep sigh he answered, "Yes." He turned around and headed back to his chair while saying, "But only because Ian will be here to take your place. You can leave the day before Christmas, but be back by the new year."

"Thank you, sah."

"Remember this, though. Don't forgive your father for what he did. Not for one minute do you forgive him!"

Not knowing how to respond, Sharpe nodded and turned to leave.

"Before you go," Malcolm said, seated again, "I know you fired Lucy, but what have you done about Magus?"

Caught off guard, Sharpe replied without forethought, "That's what me going Accompong for."

The following silence felt thick to Sharpe, until Malcolm responded, "Now I understand your urgency."

Malcolm opened a drawer and pulled out a bottle of rum and two small glasses. He poured rum into the glasses and offered one to Sharpe. Then standing up, he said, with his glass held high, "How do you fight an Obeah man? With another Obeah man!" Then he drank the contents in one swig.

Sharpe did likewise, feeling the burn of the alcohol as it went down.

Malcolm sat back down, picked up his pencil, and returned to the ledger, saying, "Go do what you have to do."

A chill ran down Sharpe's spine as he realized his plan was now in motion.

Confident, Sharpe stopped by the kitchen hoping to see Essie. He looked in the door and, feeling good from the rum that had begun to lighten his load, inquired, "Good evening, Miss Essie and Miss Ruby. Howdeedo?"

They both acknowledged him.

"So, Miss Essie, what you cooking for suppa tonight?"

Stirring a pot of pepper pot soup, she asked without looking up, "Why you asking? The boss invite you to dinner?"

That knocked Sharpe down a notch. "Not really," he replied with an embarrassed grin. "Me did just come by to tell you good evening."

"Well, you already said it." She continued stirring the pot with what Sharpe perceived to be a delighted grin. "Besides, you only coming round cause you woman left you and gone back to her mother."

Ruby, who was peeling potatoes, shot a surprised look at Essie.

"Who tell you that?" Sharpe reacted with a lion's instinct.

Not fazed, Essie answered, "It's my job to know everything about everyone on this here property."

"You mean, it's your self-appointed job." He smiled, pleased with his comeback.

"Actually," she said, "It's me God-appointed job."

Sensing playful banter, he laughed.

"Me no really jokin, you know." She turned to him with the wooden stirring spoon in her right hand, using it as if directing traffic while she continued with emphasis. "I am not looking a dog who bitch send him away with him tail between him leg." She turned back to the pot. "And beside, any man I interested in must be a Christian man!"

Finding a possible breach in her argument, Sharpe interjected, "That's not a problem for me. Me go to church."

Taken by surprise, she asked, "What church is that?"

"The Methodist church down the hill. Missa Aldridge is the preacher man. I know him this long time," he announced, satisfied he had quelled her concern.

She crossed her arms and cocked her head to the right. "Now listen here. It's not all the time I like to repeat myself. But me will say it again: I know everything going on round these parts." She paused for effect then said slowly, "The only time you ever set foot in that there church is when you was a boy… and only because you teacher, Missa Aldridge, mek all a the pickney them sit for chapel time."

He was annoyed. How did she know so much about him— even his childhood? Now he was certain where Busha got all his information.

Sharpe countered her, "As a matta a fact, me was talking with Missa Aldridge just the other day."

The truth was, the last time he had spoken with Mr. Aldridge was over two months ago. He decided, if Essie knew this, he was giving up. Who wanted a woman who tracked your every move?

She narrowed her eyes at him, then said, "Well, the only thing me will say to that is when you Missa Aldridge preach, him add house and land[1] to him sermon. That man is more interested in the politics of man than in the religion of God." She pursed her lips. "Hmph!"

The rum loosened his tongue, so Sharpe read her "hmph" as a reluctant surrender and declared, "Me like how you so facety![2] Give me some time and me will win you for meself!" Then he looked up while stroking his chin, as if in deep thought, and said, "Sharpe and Essie. Hmm. Me like the sound of that." He laughed and walked away.

"That will be the day!" Essie yelled after him.

She went back to stirring the pepper pot soup and watched him walk across the barbecue, to the cotton tree, and around the bend until he disappeared down the Cawdor road. The entire time she mouthed what sounded like prayers.

The next morning, Sharpe cleaned the only pair of shoes he had, which he saved for going into Savanna-la-Mar, put on a white shirt with collar stains and a faded-blue pair of pants, then left Hakin. He had decided to go to church so he could tell Essie all about it when he saw her on Monday.

He arrived at the entrance to the church property early but didn't want to be the only one waiting around as others got there, so he took a walk down to Mr. Lyn's store where he bought coconut water. He briefly chatted with Mr. Lyn, who asked him about the goings-on at Hakin. Sharpe gave him general pleasantries, which he knew Mr. Lyn wasn't looking for, then downed his coconut water and left.

There was the faint sound of clapping and singing coming from the direction of the Methodist church. He had heard the Anglicans sing before, and the difference between the Methodists and the Anglicans was the difference between a waterfall and a slow river. He himself had not cared for singing since his school days when he was required to sing along during chapel, so he took his time walking to the church.

There was an unavoidable disturbance among the small congregation when Sharpe walked through the chapel doors. It rippled as one person elbowed the next until everyone was looking at him. He had seen most of the people around Oristano and recognized a married couple from Hakin, who usually kept to themselves. The congregation continued singing as Mrs. Aldridge got up from beside her husband, took Sharpe by the arm, and led him to where they were sitting.

Shaking his hand, Mr. Aldridge greeted him. "Good to see you here, Sharpe."

Sharpe reticently replied, "Thank you, Missa Aldridge."

A man in a faded brown jacket and a matching tie walked up to the pulpit, opened his Bible, and began reading from it. The reading became increasingly choral as the congregation recited the passage from memory. After the man had returned to his seat, Mr. Aldridge, wearing a black robe and clerical collar, mounted the platform, laid his Bible and sermon notes on the pulpit, surveyed the congregation, then began his sermon.

Sharpe admired Mr. Aldridge's ability to speak as though he were speaking the very words of God with confidence, cadence, and clarity. He spoke from the Bible passage the jacketed-and-tied man had read. It was about Jesus having the Spirit of God and being appointed to bring "good news for the poor and deliverance for the captives." This became Mr. Aldridge's constant refrain throughout the sermon, which his baritone voice trumpeted louder with each iteration.

The crescendo came after his application of the sermon, in which he spoke about his attendance at the People's National Party rally in Westmoreland, where Norman Manley had spoken so passionately about Britain granting Jamaica universal adult suffrage so that every Jamaican man and woman over the age of twenty-one—no matter their race, no matter their education, no matter their social status or whether they owned land or not—could vote on the twelfth of December. He emphasized that Jamaica was the third country, after Britain itself and New Zealand, to be granted this right and that this historic event was enough to inspire everyone to vote.

Mr. Aldridge concluded his sermon by saying, "In just nine days, we will be able to vote. And in my humble but well-read opinion, I can only encourage you to vote for Norman Manley. He has spent the last six years educating Jamaicans, so we can understand the issues. It is Mr. Manley's ultimate mission to win independence for Jamaica, which is," he paused, cueing the congregation to join him saying, "good news for the poor and deliverance for the captives."

He grasped the sides of the pulpit while panning the congregation and slowly said, "However, Alexander Bustamante's mission is to remain under British rule."

He gave a moment for his audience's reaction, which comprised ambivalent mumbles.

"Bustamante says he is for the poor man," he said, his volume increasing, "but Bustamante is really for Britain and for Jamaica's upper class."

This time there was more of a rumble from the congregation.

"Now, some people say they don't understand Norman Manley's big words."

The jacketed-and-tied man called out, "That's true!"

"But listen to me! Don't let Busta's charm and loudmouth fool you! Busta is for the rich, and Manley is for the poor! As Mr. Manley said, vote for causes, not for men. So go out and vote PNP on the twelfth of December! Because a vote for the PNP is a vote for the poor!"

Then, in a grand baritone crescendo, with the congregation joining unprompted, he trumpeted, "Good news for the poor and deliverance for the captives!"

Immediately, a girl, who had an obvious gift for musical composition, jumped to her feet, clapping rhythmically and singing impromptu, "Good news for the poor and deliverance for the captives; Good news for the poor and deliverance for the captives; Good news for the poor and deliverance for the captives!"

The congregation caught on quickly and were up on their feet, singing and clapping and dancing around the small chapel. Only Mr. Aldridge refrained from dancing, which Sharpe figured was for his sake. Sharpe stood, clapping halfheartedly while observing the merriment.

After the service was over, Sharpe was bypassing the line that was forming at the door to give Mr. Aldridge the customary handshake and "Thank you, Reverend," when Mr. Aldridge put his hand on his shoulder and asked him to wait a few minutes.

As the couple from Hakin passed through the doors, they acknowledged Sharpe with a smile and nod and kept on walking. The thought came to him that he didn't remember ever speaking to them before. They seemed like pleasantly respectable folk. They made him think of other people in Hakin who didn't fit the Kerry Mongoose mold. *Why them live there? Couldn't them move and find a life away from the Magus cauldron?* The thought boomeranged back to him. He was stuck there, too. And he had more of a chance of getting out than anyone in Hakin. His blood boiled. *Me know what me need to do. Me must deal with Magus, the wicked Obeah man! Him is the one who gave Lucy the herbs to poison me and Marsha. He is the one who poison everyone mind against me. Magus is the root of every kind of evil in Hakin!* He calmed himself with the thought that Christmas was just around the corner.

After the last handshake, Mr. Aldridge came over to where Sharpe was standing and said, "What a nice surprise. What brings you to church today?"

Knowing he couldn't lie to him, with a sheepish look, Sharpe answered, "Well, to tell you the truth, Mr. Aldridge, me really did come cause somebody up at the big house want me to go to church."

Amazed, Mr. Aldridge asked, "That wouldn't be Mr. Campbell, would it?"

"No, sah!" Sharpe chuckled. "People say the big cotton tree up there going fall before him set foot in church." He looked down and shuffled his feet. "Actually, is Miss Essie, the cook."

"Well, I don't know Miss Essie, but if she gets you to go to church, she must be something special," grinned Mr. Aldridge.

He led Sharpe out of earshot and, with a concerned look, said, "Some people from Hakin recently spoke to me about you and your predicament up there. They're worried about you. Is there anything you want to talk about?"

Sharpe was thankful to know people were on his side. Not

that there was anything any of them could do, including Mr. Aldridge. He knew what he had to do must be done on his own. Recalling a well-memorized line of the poem from the book Mr. Aldridge lent him, *And for their thousand blows deal one death blow!* he answered Mr. Aldridge, "Nothing we never talk about already."

"You're sure there's nothing?" he asked, looking into Sharpe's eyes.

"Me know what me need to do. But if you want, you and Mrs. Aldridge can pray for me."

18

KIMBERLY, SOUTH AFRICA

3 JANUARY 1904

Dearest Abum,

It is just over two years since we turned past the cotton tree and caught the last glimpse of you and the children. Jamaica is now a faint memory. I forget what it is like to see mountains, to see the ocean. I'm even forgetting what my own children look like. As it is, they'll all have changed, as children do so fast in their youth. As a favor for Cuddy and me, would you have a photograph taken of the family? I don't want to forget their faces.

Alexandra is growing beautifully. She is ten months old now and has recently discovered Cuddy as her playmate. Her birth has changed him. He never paid much attention to children before, but now he is concerned for her every move. Perhaps he is getting softer as he ages. He wants to know if I am ready for another child yet. I keep putting him off, though.

The real reason for this letter is to let you know Cuddy sent money for the children's care. It has been sent to the Colonial Bank of London on Harbour Street in Kingston and is addressed to your name. By the time you receive this letter, you should be able to collect it.

One last thing. I thank you for keeping us abreast of how the chil-

dren are faring. However, Cuddy and I are concerned that you are still favoring Malcolm. Down the road, it could spoil him for anything good. Please consider these words.

Do give my love to the children.

As ever,
Winnie

19

SHARPE

SUNDAY, DECEMBER 24, 1944

The journey from Oristano to Accompong was long and arduous. While there were roadways that led there, none of them were paved. The day before, a woman at Mr. Lyn's shop had told Sharpe he could either take the coastal road to Black River and cut up from there into the hills or start in Oristano and take the roads through the hills, where he would have a better chance of making it before sundown. The Black River way appealed to him as almost half the way was at sea level, and he thought he might get a ride from a passerby. He quickly dismissed the idea when he remembered there were few cars on the road because of the war rationing of gasoline and, even so, why take the chance of not getting picked up? So, he chose the route through the hills, which the woman dictated to him while he wrote on a piece of paper.

He left his house with a small bag an hour and a half before sunrise, accompanied by the cool night air and the half-moon casting enough light for him to see the familiar way toward Newmarket.

As he approached Newmarket, the sun had been up for some time. Sharpe noticed there were no hefty market women with produce-laden baskets swaying on their heads or slim donkey-pulling men with trailing carts full of the same. While passing the empty market area, it made sense; he had never been to New Market on a Sunday.

The rest of the way would be unfamiliar. He barely remembered the trip from Accompong to Hakin some twenty years earlier. His father had sent him with a man and a donkey who were headed to Savanna-la-Mar. He was fortunate enough to ride a good portion of the journey on the back of the donkey.

The woman who had given him directions for the shorter route told him he could ask someone in Newmarket about an off-the-beaten-path shortcut. He found an old man sitting outside the closed Chinese grocery store. The man told him of a path that cut through some privately owned lands that would shave off a good three hours from his trip. He stood up, pointing to his right, and directed, "Go roun that deh bend to the rum shop. A couple chain[1] afta the rum shop you we reach the mash down wall on you lef. That path wi take you through Missa Beckford land." He put his hand on Sharpe's shoulder. "If anyone ask you what you doin there, tell dem say Old Man Ronnie send you that way. Everybody know me round these part." He resumed his directing. "Once you come to a road, Missa Beckford land done. Just swing so," the old man curved his hand to the right, "and about one chain down the road, the path continue on the other side a the road. If you get to the guinep tree, you gone too far." The man continued giving directions about a precipice, an old iron pump, another stone wall, and a river, which he called Y.S. When he reached the junction of the path and the river, Sharpe was to take the road heading east, and he would be back on the route the woman had originally given him. Sharpe added the shortcut directions to the back of his paper as best he could and thanked the man.

Sharpe appreciated the path, which ambled through the less-than cultivated land, traveling slowly up and down and around tree-canopied hills. It reminded him of boyhood adventures into the Accompong's Cockpit Country. There were countless cone-shaped hills with deep pits in between, filled with exotic plants, stunning birds, and insects he had never seen the likes of in Westmoreland. Some hills had caves he and his friends had explored regularly. As a boy transplanted from Accompong to Hakin, he immediately noticed the difference between the two place.

On reaching the Y.S. River, Sharpe found the road he was to take. By this time, the sun was around the eleven o'clock position. Based on what he had been told, he had another couple hours on this road, then he would take a left where the road met the Black River. Another hour to the road that led to Accompong, and then less than an hour until he was home with his Kindah people. Cudjoe's people. The people of inborn self-governance.

When Sharpe had walked for almost six hours, he cursed the sun for its heat and the road for its lack of tree cover. Physically drained, his mind played contrary tricks on him, and he began brooding over what had driven him to the journey—Lucy…Magus…Busha…Mr. Aldridge…the people of Hakin. In some way, they had all played their part in the Justice vs. Mercy proceedings. In an eleventh-hour makeshift retrial, Sharpe relived each account multiple times, until he realized he was rehashing the same facts over and over with no new insights.

On reaching the Black River junction, he washed his face in the river and took a long drink. Then, sitting on the riverbank, he gazed blankly at the languid water drifting by. It lulled him to passivity. A thought had been slowly growing in his mind and now took the opportunity to work its way out: Could he go through with the Magus mission? Could he really kill a man? Magus was an evil man, yes, but his blood would be on Sharpe's conscience for life. Maybe he could approach the situation from a different angle. He could go back to Hakin and win the people over from Magus by trying to help them in any way he could—like Mr. Aldridge had encouraged him to do the day he had visited him. Then they would listen to what he had to say, and he could help them out of their miserable circumstance. Magus would be forced to go along with it, or he'd have to leave the village.

He picked up three smooth pebbles lying beside him and skimmed them one by one on the river's surface. After the third rock took its fourth skip and dove into the water, he made the decision not to visit the Obeah man when he got to Accompong. When he returned to Hakin, he would help the people. Resigned to this new plan, he stood up with his bag and resumed the journey.

After a mile, the sun resumed its assault on Sharpe. His mind again gave way to the Justice vs. Mercy proceedings. He couldn't stop them. Slowly and with rhetorical care, Justice presented arguments: What would Busha do if Sharpe didn't follow through on his promise to deal with Magus? It could cost Sharpe his job. And why should Magus go unpunished for what he had done? Or, for that matter, what he continued to do to the Hakin community—keep them under oppression. Sharpe realized that he had been fooling himself with the idea of going back to Hakin and winning the people over, as though he were Alexander Bustamante. He laughed derisively at himself when he recalled all the sneers and jeers he'd received from them over the past few months.

He recalled three words from the "Harlem Shadows" poem that described Hakin—*poverty, dishonor, and disgrace*. For Sharpe, Magus represented a long line of evil that had subjugated these people for generations past. Magus had kept them in that state. He was the guilty party. Sharpe didn't need to recall lines from "If We Must Die," but for good measure, his mind tracked the most relevant line for the last words of his closing statement: *And for their thousand blows deal one death blow!*

The gavel struck like a clap of thunder. The retrial was decided. The verdict: For Mercy to take its natural course, Justice must remove the obstacle.

With this, Sharpe put the case behind him for good and turned up the final road leading to Accompong, where he would find his family and his Obeah man.

When Sharpe passed the first dwelling on the outskirts of the small Maroon settlement of Accompong, he heard a deep voice call out, "Aye! Who is there?"

A man with a full head of gray hair appeared in the doorway. "Me say, who is there? Me no recognize you from these here parts."

"Me name Sharpe. Me come from here."

"Sharpe who?" the man called back.

"Quaco Sharpe."

The man stretched his head forward, squinting dark-brown eyes set above high cheekbones, and said, "But wait. You is Manu first boy?"

"No, I am his only son," Sharpe corrected him.

The man laughed and retorted, "Son, what kind of man you is? You must be gone bout two decade now. Then you think you pupa don't got plenty more boy pickney?" He laughed again and called into the house, "Mama Ginni! Come! Manu Sharpe boy pickney come back!"

An older woman popped her head out the doorway and exclaimed, "Lawd God! It could be him for true! Her head popped back in the house, and Sharpe could hear her command someone, "Run down to Missa Sharpe house and tell them say Quaco return." A boy came out of the house, glanced at Sharpe, then took off up the road at top speed, shouting, "Missa Sharpe boy come home! Missa Sharpe boy come home!"

The news instantaneously covered the region like an October rainstorm, and as Sharpe walked the short distance to where he remembered his home being, young and old spilled onto the road to see if what they had heard was true.

A beautiful woman approached him, saying, "Is that you for true, Quaco?" She studied his face. "Me can't believe me eyes! Me own brother!" She kissed him and began weeping.

Sharpe, knowing which of his sisters it was from her dark complexion, lifted her chin and said, "Bena." He observed her for a moment. "What a way you favor Muma."

She smiled, wiping the tears from her cheeks, and said, "Come. Me will bring you to Pupa and Ama. She is taking care of him, or else, me know she would have come to greet you."

"What happen to Pupa?"

"Him not so good. You will see when we get home." She held on to his arm as they walked. "If you ever know how we miss you this long time."

"Me know." A tear ran down his cheek.

He spent that evening in his old home with his two sisters and his father. Older community members, who remembered him well, stopped by unannounced to see him. Women he did not remember put their palms on his face, exclaiming, "Lawd! But you is the spitting image of you father," and "You remember me, Quaco? Me did help nurse you." The men shook his hand and beamed as if he was their own son. Along with them came gifts of potato pone, ripe plantains, and whatever they were able to muster up from their yards.

Bena's husband and children, and several people younger than himself claiming to be his siblings, also came by. These claims were confirmed by his sisters. The youngest of Bena's children pulled on Sharpe's hand. When he looked down, the child asked, "You bring something for me, Uncle?" Everyone laughed, causing the child to hide behind his mother.

When the last visitor left, Sharpe settled his attention on his father. He saw only remnants of the man who had been a strong worker and a good provider for his family. But what was mostly left was evidence of his nonstop drinking. Were it not for Sharpe's mother's control of the money, Manu might have drunk it all away. But now, around fifty years old, alcohol had worn him down, and he was no better than a set of old field clothes ready to be discarded. While he wasn't over-weight, his lower body was bloated and his eyes were eerily yellow. He lay there in a stupor. Sharpe couldn't decide whether his father looked like a half-living cadaver heading to the grave or a duppy coming out of it. When he had arrived in Accompong earlier that day, before seeing his father, resent-ment toward him had begun building as he thought about all he had missed—his sisters and the community, which seemed agreeably different from Hakin. Now that he had seen his father, he was unable to feel bitterness. *What a sad old man*, was the only thought reverberating in his mind.

Although his father had welcomed Sharpe and his facial expressions had shown he was genuinely glad to see him, his disease had prevented him from saying much to his son. At one point that evening, the old man pointed at an old mahogany chair with a broken leg. Ama told Sharpe it had been their mother's chair that she would sit on and shell gungo peas. She said their father had always loved how industrious his wife was, and how she held the family together. After Ama said these things, their father began to sob. Wiping his face, he reached out for Sharpe's hand and, squeezing it, said, "Forgive me for sending you away."

CAILIN

CHRISTMAS HOLIDAY, 1944

Gus agreed with Cailin. This Christmas holiday was different from any other. It wasn't the food or the presents. There were the same people who had always been there, which included Heather, Rowena, and Ian, who were back for the holidays. The same war continued just as it had last year. Even the artificial Christmas tree with the tiny clip-on wax candles they lit on Christmas Day was the same. As they discussed it, they decided the family was going through changes. Gus called it a metamorphosis. As usual, he made a meal of the educational opportunity, explaining in detail the life cycle of a butterfly: egg, larva, pupa, adult. He added that moths go through the same cycle. She sat there patiently indulging him.

The first opportunity to have Ian to themselves, Cailin and Gus asked what night the three of them would go down to the graveyard to duppy-scare the residents of Relax as they passed through the Cawdor property. Ian told them he couldn't do that anymore. He was going to be working as foreman of the property in Sharpe's absence, and if the property workers found out he was in on it, they wouldn't respect him. Cailin noticed an air of authority about him she had not seen prior to this. He had bossed the two of them around many times before, but now she could see he was ready to do the same with her father's workers.

The following day, Rowena and Cailin were dancing round and round about the house singing the words to "Harbor Lights." They called Heather to join in as she usually did, but she answered from the back veranda, where she sat reading, saying it was child's play. Yet, later that evening Rowena walked into the bedroom and found Heather singing the same song and dancing as if she had a partner.

Then, the next day, as if Rowena had time travelled a few decades forward, she turned down Cailin's suggestion for them to ride down to the river to swim. Instead, she chose to spend time with their mother and Heather sewing dresses. Cailin only realized why on Christmas morning during the church service when a boy kept looking back at Rowena. Rowena told Cailin that the boy had danced with her at the Munro-Hampton dance earlier in December.

The clincher, though, was when she noticed changes in herself. Two days before Christmas, Malcolm had dropped her, her mother, and her sisters at the steps of the Doric Cinema in Savanna-la-Mar, where her mother announced she was treating her girls to a matinee show. Cailin was ecstatic. She had only ever been told about films, mostly by Gus, whose father had taken him to the Doric at least once a month since he was five. *Meet Me in Saint Louis* was playing that week.

She loved and hated the film simultaneously. Esther was relatable—an independent girl who had a crush on the new boy next door. The similarities didn't escape her. The parts she disliked were the kissing scenes. But it wasn't really the kissing; it was that she was sitting beside her mother in the theater. Both times Esther and John kissed, she thought of Archie, then she thought of her mother, then she went flush in the face.

After the film, still embarrassed about the kissing, Cailin tagged along behind her mother and sisters as they walked to the Witcombe haberdashery to purchase sewing paraphernalia. While the three seamstresses sorted through zippers, buttons, and threads, Cailin found herself looking at the small selection of cotton fabrics. The patterns all seemed to be floral. She loved flowers. She even had a corner of her mother's flower garden where she grew Gerbera daisies, four o'clocks, and marigolds. But she couldn't bear the thought of looking like a flower arrangement. Behind the floral patterns, she found a bolt of plain sky-blue cloth, similar to what Esther was wearing in the film when she and John first kissed. Lifting the loose flap of cloth, she put her hand against it like she'd seen her sisters do. She liked the match! Rowena, who had been watching her with interest, caught the beam on her face and came over to her. Before Cailin knew it, all three of them were surrounding her oohing and aahing, and shortly after, the fabric found itself in a bag with matching blue buttons.

Mrs. Witcombe invited them for tea in her home behind the store. Knowing this was where Archie boarded during the school year prompted Cailin to wonder what he was doing back at the inn. Her attention drifted from Archie to her sky-blue dress. She could take it to her grandmother in Lennox and have her embroider the neckline like Esther's dress in the film. Then she would wear it to church and boldly walk forward to take communion. Those girls would be sorry they had ever snubbed her. Drifting from church to the inn, she thought of Archie again and his possible reaction to her in her new dress. She envisioned the kiss. This unsettled her, bringing her back to the tea gathering.

Of course, Cailin withheld the kiss and blue dress from Gus, but she realized a metamorphosis was indeed taking place. She couldn't decide whether she was changing into a butterfly or a moth. The thought made her chuckle.

On Christmas morning, a cool hillside breeze swaddled Cawdor House. Cailin, who had long since stopped believing in Santa Claus, remained in bed comparing what she had seen on snow-blanketed Christmas cards to the present cool air, which was the best Jamaica had to offer. She wondered what it would be like to see a snowy vista but decided it could never match up to the beauty of the Cawdor landscape.

After breakfast, the Christmas tree lights were lit and the presents opened. Malcolm refrained from going to his office so he could watch the children open their presents. It always pleased him to see their delight, especially when Cailin would do a droll dance about the room, plop in his lap, and adorn him with a kiss.

Cailin and Rowena dressed and rode down to the church for the Christmas morning service, then returned home in anticipation of their grandparents' arrival. Like clockwork, around noontime, Cailin and Gus heard a car coming up the road and ran down past the cotton-tree bend, where they hitched a ride on the running boards of Mass Whim's car.

After big hugs and kisses for her grandparents, Cailin nodded at the bulging, tied-down car boot and asked, "What's in the boot?"

"A-ha!" exclaimed Mass Whim. "That's for Cissy and I to know and for you to find out!" He looked around for Ian. "Where's that big, strapping young man?"

"I'll carry it, Mass Whim!" Gus jumped up and down like he was the runt of the rugby team begging to be played.

"Well, I suppose Cailin can help you," agreed Mass Whim.

"Whim, dear," Cissy appealed, "Cailin is a young lady now. She should not be doing a man's work."

He winked at Cailin but deferred to his wife's female protocol. "Alright, dear." Then he directed Gus to fetch Ian to help him.

Cailin sulked.

Her grandfather wrapped his arm around her shoulder and led her into the house, saying, "Don't worry, kitten, you'll have the honor of opening it." The two of them continued whispering and giggling together.

While Heather assisted Cissy into the house, Cissy called after them, "You do spoil her so, Whim."

Shortly after, Kester and his wife, Jane, walked through the doorway to the back veranda. Cailin and Gus had been so engrossed with Mass Whim's jesting, they had not heard the car coming up the road. Everyone was now out on the veranda. The five children got up to greet their uncle and aunt with handshakes and kisses. Heather and Rowena, who admired their Auntie Jane's elegant sense of fashion, led her to where they had been sitting. Kester joined Malcolm and Ian as they discussed the Jamaica Labour Party's twenty-two seat win over the People's National Party's five seats. Malcolm expressed thankfulness due to his concern for the People's National Party's strong socialist leaning; Ian saw things differently. He liked what he had read about Norman Manley's ability to reason thoughtfully and that he wanted an independent Jamaica sooner rather than later. Malcolm scoffed at him. Kester remained neutral. Helen, her mother, and the two aunties rambled from topic to topic, catching up on one another's news, while Cailin and Gus remained fixed to Mass Whim.

When the veranda conversations had drifted into praise for the weather and the Cawdor sea vista, Auntie Jane brought out presents for the children. The boys each received a pair of trousers and a long-sleeved shirt with a tie. The girls received beautiful dresses. Everyone knew the clothes were intended to be used for church. The intent of everything Auntie Jane did was to nudge the family toward God. Excited for the thoughtful gift, Cailin decided to wear it to church the following Sunday.

Mass Whim said it was time to unveil the present they had brought. Cailin jumped up to get it, but her grandfather told her Ian and Gus would get it and she would open it.

Before half the brown wrapping paper was removed, Gus, with more excitement then he could contain, yelled, "A wireless!" He looked around at everybody while pointing at the box and repeated, "It's a wireless!" Then he buried his head in Mass Whim's large pillow stomach and wept out the muffled words, "Thank you. Thank you."

Mass Whim rubbed his back, saying, "There, there, lad. Your father will be home soon."

The extra-large supper table was at maximum capacity laden with food. Everyone agreed Essie had outdone herself with the roast beef and the turkey. Cissy said the coconut flavor in the rice and peas was just right and she wished Essie could teach her maid how to cook.

Auntie Abum was in one of her rare good moods. She loved Christmas because the table was full, and family was all around. Last year at Christmas dinner, Cailin had commented that it should be Christmas Day every day if it were only so that Auntie Abum would be in a good mood. Auntie Bitsy had chuckled under her breath. Cailin got sent to her room. She thought about it but resisted the temptation to bring it up this year.

With lunch over but dessert yet to be served, Mass Whim suggested the boys move the radio to an electrical outlet and tune it into the BBC.

While they were doing so, Malcolm asked, "Mass Whim, where in hell did you get the radio?"

"Through a well-connected friend living in Kingston."

"What are his connections?" pried Malcolm.

"I don't know. And I didn't ask." He turned to Ian and Gus. "What's the delay, boys?"

Gus replied, "We're almost up and running."

"Nonetheless," Mass Whim continued, "The market seems to be loosening up as rumors of the war's imminent end trickle in."

The radio spat out static while Ian tuned the dial to the frequency the BBC news was normally found. There was nothing but continual static.

"It doesn't look as though the broadcast is on yet," Ian reported.

"I thought that might be the case," responded Mass Whim. "We'll have to try again later on."

Disappointed, Gus asked, "What's the last report you heard on your wireless, Mass Whim?"

"A couple days ago, Lord Mountbatten's speech from the front. I'm supposing he was somewhere near what they're calling the Battle of the Bulge. He said we were a long way from the end but that victory is sure."

"What else is he to say?" countered Malcolm. "He has to put on a good face for the Empire."

Helen, who rarely contradicted Malcolm, much less reprimand him, cried, "Malcolm!" and shot her eyes toward Gus.

With a blank face, Malcolm replied, "He must face things as they are, Helen."

Sitting on the floor beside the wireless, Gus dropped his stare to the mahogany floor.

Shortly after, Ruby brought in the Christmas fruitcake, flaming from the white rum that had been poured at its base and lit on fire. Cailin and Gus were the only ones who cared to ceremoniously blow out the fire. Then it was laid in front of Helen, who cut, plated, and plopped a healthy dollop of brandy butter on top of each slice.

The rest of the holiday gathering was spent back on the veranda relaxing and talking. At about three thirty, the gathering came to an end when Mass Whim said they needed to leave if they were to get back to Lennox by sundown. Kester and Jane agreed it was time for them to leave as well. Everyone went out on the barbecue for the grand send-off of their Christmas family guests.

Malcolm went to his office with thoughts of going to the inn later that evening. Gus began reading *Journey to the Center of the Earth*, a Jules Verne novel Miss Recas had left for him as a Christmas present. Cailin found herself wondering what Archie was doing.

21

ARCHIE

CHRISTMAS NIGHT, 1944

*L*eaning against the column of the porte-cochère holding one of his mother's cigarettes between his thumb and index finger, Archie took a drag while raising it against the pitch-black sky to see the tip glow then fade. He exhaled, making an almost-perfect smoke O. He envisioned Jay Gatsby doing that with a girl hanging on one arm, admiring his skill. The image of the girl came into focus. It was Cailin. He shook his head. His mother wanted him to get close to Malcolm, but he was sure this would be overstepping his bounds.

Headlights entered the gate. He thought, *Mick is already here, so it must be Malcolm.* He dropped the cigarette and stepped on it. His mother didn't like when he smoked, and he wasn't sure if Malcolm would tell.

Malcolm pulled under the porte-cochère with Ian in the passenger seat. Leaving the key in the car, Malcolm greeted Archie with an "Evening" and headed through the door.

Just before ascending the stairs, Malcolm turned to Archie and asked, "Can you shoot bird?"

Puzzled, Archie paused, then responded, "I'm sure I could."

Malcolm turned and headed up the stairs, leaving Archie suspended in confusion.

Ian nodded at Archie and followed his father.

Two days earlier, Archie had met Ian while Ian was at the beach with Cailin and Gus riding their horses. Gus had introduced them, telling Ian that Archie was the innkeeper's son and that he, Cailin, and Archie had had great fun at the Oristano River and Relax. Ian had quickly changed the subject and, after a brief conversation, said they needed to leave.

Archie parked the car, went upstairs, and prepared himself for what he knew would be an unusual evening.

Before he could finish climbing the stairs, Gracie mildly scolded, "Archie, you didn't announce Mr. Campbell and Ian's arrival."

Knowing there were no real guests staying at the inn, Archie's sarcasm reigned. "I didn't realize this was a palace. I'll do better next time, Your Highness." He bowed.

Gracie glared at him.

"Don't worry on my account. I'm only here in case Daddy needs a ride home." Ian said with slight sarcasm in his voice.

For a moment, there was a strange-bedfellow connection between Archie and Ian.

Gracie walked over to the bar. "Drinks?" She glanced at Malcolm. "Your rum is coming right up."

Mick glanced at Malcolm then spoke to Gracie, "I'll have some of that Scotch I brought you."

Gracie pouted. "But I thought that was for me."

"It is, but I think I'll need a stiff one tonight," Mick replied.

Malcolm eyed Mick with suspicion, then asked him, "Why are you here, on Christmas night? Shouldn't you be at home celebrating with your family?"

Looking at Malcolm, he grunted and looked off through the open window. "I could ask you the same question."

"Now, boys," said Gracie. "Let's be civil."

Both men settled back in their chairs, and Gracie gave them their drinks.

"Now, Ian. Would you like a drink?"

"I'll have a ginger ale," he replied.

"Archie, be a dear and get Ian his drink," said Gracie as she sat beside Malcolm.

"As you wish." He got up and bowed again.

"That's enough, Archie," Gracie responded. "It's getting tiresome." She looked at Ian and said, "So, how do you like Munro?"

"It's good. But most of the time I'm there, I'm thinking of working the Cawdor property."

"Well, I hear you have the opportunity to do just that over the holidays," said Gracie.

"Yes. And I'm enjoying it while it lasts," he said, looking at Malcolm.

"Gracie," Malcolm said, holding her left ear. "Where did you get these earrings? I've never seen them before."

"Why? Do you like them?" she asked, teasing him. "They are rubies." She turned her head to show him the one on her right ear.

"Yes, I can see that," replied Malcolm, who was becoming agitated. "Where did you get them?"

"Well," she answered nervously, "Mick was so sweet and drove all the way from Saint Ann's to be here for Christmas—"

Malcolm interrupted, "To bring you special Scotch and ruby earrings!" Looking at Gracie, then over to Mick, he burst out in a boorish laugh.

Flustered, Gracie said, "He just brought me a gift for buying so much liquor for the inn. You know. You've seen the bills."

Malcolm calmed his laughing and said, "Gracie, Gracie." He shook his head. "You're not fooling anyone, except maybe him." He looked at Mick, who was fuming on the edge of his seat, causing Malcolm to laugh again.

Red in the face, Mick barked, "It's more than you ever gave her!"

Gracie sat petrified.

Archie and Ian were taking in the drama.

Malcolm didn't bite Mick's bait.

Mick stood up, appealing to Gracie, "Is that all they are to you? A gift in exchange for purchasing my liquor? You know they're more than that. Why did you accept them then?"

Gracie looked at Malcolm, as if for direction. He just sat back, waiting to see what she would say. With a deep breath, she turned slowly back to Mick and calmly said, "Because I never look a gift horse in the mouth." Then she said, "Mick, we've had this conversation too many times."

"Mr. McFagan," Malcolm said, "a gentleman always knows when he's been beaten." He laughed.

Mick stepped toward Malcolm, but not knowing what to do, said, "That's fine coming from a man with a bastard!"

Archie was confused by Mick's remark and figured he must have said something like "...a man who's a bastard." But that didn't sound like what he'd heard.

Malcolm got up to defend his honor, but Gracie stepped between them, facing Malcolm, and said, "It's not worth it. Let's not start a ruckus and turn the inn into a rum bar!"

Mick yelled, "More like a brothel! Archie! Get my briefcase. I'm leaving." He turned to Gracie and said, "Keep the earrings. They'll remind you of what you could have had when this one leaves you!"

Malcolm went after him again, but Gracie held on to him from behind and whispered something in his ear.

When Archie got back from his valet duty, he found his mother pouring Malcolm and herself another drink, and Ian fixing one for himself.

When Malcolm noticed Ian picking up the rum bottle, he said, "No, Ian. You're going to have to take me home tonight."

He slugged down the drink Gracie had just given him and told her to make him another.

Shortly after, Malcolm took Gracie by the hand and pulled her into her bedroom.

Archie and Ian sat there alone.

Ian broke the silence. "I guess I'll be here a while."

KIMBERLY, SOUTH AFRICA

16 FEBRUARY 1904

*D**ear Abum,*

I received your letter yesterday and spoke with Cuddy as soon as he returned from the infirmary. He understands things are difficult for you and they are not your children, but he says this is no place to raise a large family, and Jamaica is a more settled environment than Cape Colony. Even though I have expressed a similar sentiment in my past letters, when I heard him say it so absolutely, I had a good cry.

You don't mind keeping them, do you? From what you write, they seem to be doing well and, even though you have never married, you have proven yourself to be well-suited for motherhood. I expect there is nothing either of us can say about it at this point. Cuddy has made up his mind, and you already have the children.

I am sorry the sum of money Cuddy sent was small, but he says it is all we can afford right now. He plans on sending more as soon as he is able.

Do give our love to the children. I hope they remember us.

As ever,
Winnie

2 3

SHARPE

MONDAY-THURSDAY, DECEMBER 25-28, 1944

Sharpe woke to the crisp, high-elevation air. He ate a quick breakfast then asked Ama where to find the Obeah man. She told him where Papa Rufus lived but corrected him, saying he was not an Obeah man but Accompong's Myal[1] man. She explained Papa Rufus had been an Obeah man in his earlier days, but when he learned the Myal way from his great-grandmother, he ended up converting most of the Accompong community. Sharpe was unconcerned with Papa Rufus's religious associations. He only wanted to know that the Myal man could help him. Ama assured him Papa Rufus could take care of whatever he needed.

He thanked Ama and headed for Papa Rufus's home. On arriving, he knew he was at the right place. Based on Ama's description, the gate and the windowsills would be blue to ward off evil spirits, and there would be a tall bamboo flagpole, which would have a different colored flag depending on the spiritual needs of the day. Sharpe noticed the flag was also blue. He also noticed the flat, open yard she'd told him about, where spiritual meetings were held, and a big, thick wooden table near the house that would be laden with food and drink offerings and other spiritual articles during the yard meetings. That morning the table was bare, except for a machete lying beside a green coconut and a big pot filled with uncooked callaloo leaves draped over one side.

Sharpe spotted a man of light-brown complexion with loosely curled salt-and-pepper hair falling to his shoulders. He was sitting in a high-back wooden armchair, head back and eyes closed.

Sharpe called out to him, "Papa Rufus?"

The man opened his eyes. "Come in, Quaco. Me was expecting you."

Sharpe wasn't surprised Papa Rufus knew his name. By now, everyone in the area knew he was in Accompong. He was also not surprised Papa Rufus had said he was expecting him. From years of knowing Magus, Sharpe understood these types of men enjoyed their little games.

Papa Rufus pointed to a large enamel jug filled with water and resting on a tree stump just inside the gate. "Wash you hands before entering," he said in a serious tone, not to be disobeyed.

While Sharpe poured water over each hand successively, he glanced over at Papa Rufus, who was watching him, and noted he seemed to be older than Magus; Sharpe hoped that would translate to more wisdom and more tricks up the man's sleeve.

Sharpe approached him slowly, being sure to show due respect for his office. "Good morning, Papa Rufus."

Papa Rufus, who had kept his eyes fastened on Sharpe since his arrival, said, "Me know why you come. But before we talk, we must take care of some business. The evil spirit them prowling round you like lion ready to pounce. Them want you, Quaco. Them want you bad."

Sharpe felt a coldness run down his back.

"Me will mek a bush bath for you out of coconut water and callaloo. The mixture, especially the coconut, will send the spirit them out of you. Evil spirit no like coconut at all. Come." He put his hands on the armrests to push himself out of the chair. "Everything ready. It just need to cook down."

"A bath for what?" Sharpe balked.

Papa Rufus relaxed his weight back into the chair and squinted his eyes as though in disbelief. "Man, where you born? You no know it will drive out the evil spirit them?"

"No, sah! It's not me need evil spirit drive out."

"You sure of that?"

"Me sure!"

Papa Rufus shrugged and raised his hands, palms up. "That is your business. But don't come crying eye water to me when the spirit them catch you."

Sharpe raised his brow. "No spirit nah go catch me!"

Papa Rufus cut his eye and sucked his teeth, then said, "Wherefore let him that think him stand, take heed, lest him fall."

Sharpe resisted rolling his eyes at Papa Rufus's mystic saying.

Papa Rufus folded his arms across his chest and said slowly, "Well, that is your business. Now, even though me already know, me want to hear from your mouth why you come back to Accompong."

Doubting Papa Rufus knew why he was there, Sharpe realized he had to play the game to get what he wanted, so he answered, "Well, Papa Rufus, me come back to find you cause me know say you can give me something to fix a man."

"What kinda fix? And what kinda man?"

"Well," Sharpe fidgeted with his hands for a moment. "It's really like this. The man is a Obeah man who try to kill me and me gal."

"How him try to kill you?"

"Well, him poison we till we throw up everything we had in we belly, and we lay in bed for three days!"

Papa Rufus burst out laughing, slapping his hands on the chair arms. When he calmed down, he said, "Listen here, massa. If that Obeah man did want to kill you, you and you gal woulda dead long time. Him was just ruffling you feathers!" He laughed again.

"Me can't call that ruffling when me lose me gal and the whole village against me cause of this one Obeah man."

"So, what you want me do about it?"

"Give me something going fix him." Sharpe's face tightened as he spat out the next words. "Fix him for good!"

Rufus closed his eyes and recited, "If Satan cast out Satan, how him kingdom going to stand?"

With a look of confused desperation, Sharpe pleaded, "You must can do something for me! Even if it fix him for a little while."

With his eyes still closed, Papa Rufus began to hum a tune. He did so for quite some time while Sharpe stood there trying to be patient.

When Papa Rufus finally stopped humming, he opened his eyes, stood up, and moved close to Sharpe, saying in a coarse whisper, "One thing me can do for you." He pointed and looked toward the cockpit landscape. "There is a bush…one leaf will mek the Obeah man vomit and lay in bed for the same three days."

"And what will two leaf do?" inquired Sharpe.

"Two leaf will mek him think him foot slip into the grave," Rufus said, still looking toward the cockpit landscape.

"What will four leaf do, then?"

"Four will find him bawling out in hellfire." He looked back at Sharpe. "But Myal man no mix up in that. Me will only get you two leaf."

Sharpe nodded slowly and said, "Okay. Me will take what you give me."

Papa Rufus sighed, then said, "Come to the Kindah tree this

evening. Me will have it for you. You can either make a tea with it or chop it up and put it into a ganja spliff. Me know how Obeah man love him ganja." He looked at Sharpe with steel eyes. "But this one thing. Cover you mouth! Never let no one know where you get the leaves from."

When Sharpe returned from his meeting with Papa Rufus, Ama told him there would be a gathering at the Kindah tree in his honor that night. Sharpe objected, saying he had not come to Accompong to be honored. Ama said he had to attend as the preparations were already well under way. She told him most meetings were held at Papa Rufus's yard, but as the entire Accompong community would be sure to attend the celebration of the return of a son of Accompong, the meeting would be held at the Kindah tree where there was room for everyone.

Near sundown, Bena and Ama accompanied Sharpe to the festivities, each holding on to one of his arms. They were both dressed in colorful robes and head wraps—reds and yellows and shades of blue. Bena said she was wearing their mother's meeting clothes. With a deep sigh, he gave her a hug, imagining he was hugging his mother for just a moment.

As they drew near to the Kindah tree, Sharpe chuckled.

"Why you laughing?" Bena asked.

"Nothing really. It's just that I forgot the Kindah tree is a mango tree. I thought of it as a big silk cotton tree." He laughed again.

"No laugh!" Ama scolded. "A cotton tree is where duppy live. This mango tree is over two hundred years old. Captain Cudjoe united us together against the British under this here old Kindah tree!"

Bena smiled and gave Sharpe's arm a squeeze. "Ama is fierce about our Kindah people."

He bent over and kissed Ama's forehead. "Thanks for the lesson, sister."

Much of the town had already gathered and was milling

around waiting for the meeting to start. Sharpe was glad to see he was not the only one who was not clothed in meeting garb. There were quite a few plain-clothed attendees. Yet, there were many other village folk, young and old, wearing robes with wraps on their heads. When he expressed his amazement at the variety of the clothing colors, Ama told him each person wore colors that the spirits had revealed for them to wear. As an example, she said Papa Rufus wore mostly white, as he was the shepherd of the community, and blue, to ward off evil spirits since he used to practice Obeah.

The gentle breeze that had been blowing to the north switched direction for a moment and Sharpe smelled curry in the air, which prompted him to look and see that, on the other side of the tree and down a slope, there were women and men tending to fires and pots. One woman lifted a lid, stirred the contents, tasted from the wooden spoon, and shouted, "Glory!"

With that, an older gentleman, who Sharpe recognized as someone who had come to the family's home to meet him the previous night and had introduced himself as the colonel of the Accompong council, welcomed the crowd and asked where the guest of honor was. A woman and a man, who were close by, took hold of Sharpe's hands and pulled him away from his sisters and into the crowd, which parted as if for Moses. When the parting opened at the center, Sharpe saw a very large table arrayed with lit candles, food, and drink. From the size of the table, he recognized it as the one he'd seen in Papa Rufus's yard. He wondered how many men it had taken to transport the table to the Kindah tree.

As Sharpe was led along the table, in the center he saw three large loaves of bread made in Trinitarian shapes—a dove, a cross, and a crown. The shapes were animated by flickering candles, which also cast swaying shadows from the many jars of flowers set on the table, making the crowd appear as spirits. There were also rum bottles, water bottles, soft drinks, and fruits, all set out in patterns across the table. Sharpe felt a sense of wonder at what had been prepared on his account—a table weighed down to the extent of which he had never seen.

He was taken to one end of the table where, to his surprise, he saw a large open book that looked like a Bible and a smaller open book that reminded him of the hymn books back at Mr. Aldridge's Methodist church. He thought to himself that this was like no Methodist church service he had ever attended.

The colonel, who was standing to Sharpe's right, shook his hand as a symbolic gesture and gave a short welcome speech, proclaiming Sharpe to be Accompong's prodigal son come home. Sharpe had heard the Bible story of the prodigal son and didn't agree with the colonel's depiction of him. After all, he had not left willingly; he had been sent away. But the sentiment was appreciated, and Sharpe nodded in response. In fact, Sharpe was more than appreciative, he was again moved by the extent to which his Kindah people had gone to welcome him, and under the Kindah tree's watch at that.

Papa Rufus, in his white and blue garments, raised an intricately carved staff and gave his own welcome to Sharpe. He stepped up to the Bible and read from one of the open pages, "Remember ye not the former things, neither consider the things of old. Behold, I will do a new thing; now it shall spring forth; shall ye not know it? I will even make a way in the wilderness, and rivers in the desert." He bowed his white-and-blue turbaned head and offered up a prayer of thanksgiving and deliverance for Sharpe.

This irked Sharpe, as he distinctly recalled telling Papa Rufus that morning that he had no need for deliverance from evil spirits.

Following the prayer, Papa Rufus raised his head, his staff, and his loud voice in an a cappella song, "There were ninety and nine that safely lay..."

The crowd immediately finished singing the line, "...in the

shelter of the fold." They continued to sing with Papa Rufus, "But one was out on the hills away, far off from the gates of gold—" Sharpe felt someone gently press against his right shoulder then noticed the assembly moving collectively, to the left, around the table.

"…away on the mountains wild and bare,
away from the tender Shepherd's care,
away from the tender Shepherd's care."

When the hymn was over and Sharpe had made it almost around the whole table, Papa Rufus, still on Sharpe's left, raised his staff and brought it down hard on the ground along with his left foot, creating a thumping sound. The thump was repeated in what felt like the rhythm of Sharpe's own heart-beat, while the crowd continued to move in the same circular fashion, now stomping their left feet in sync with Papa Rufus, creating a stomp, move-to-the-left, swaying effect, which Sharpe quite enjoyed. He felt safe, enveloped, part of the whole.

Out of nowhere, Papa Rufus began chanting in a mournful wail, catching Sharpe off guard, causing the person to his right to bump into him. The wail had rhythm and, at times, a staccato intensity. Sharpe had never heard anything like it before. It quickly became apparent that he couldn't understand a word Papa Rufus was saying.

The assembly joined in with Papa Rufus's curious chant, increasing the intensity of their stomping and loosening their upper bodies so that their arms began swinging by their sides. This was Sharpe's cue to ease his way out of the inner circle.

The farther he got from the table, the more he noticed that fewer people were dressed in robes and wraps. He stayed in the outer ring with the participants who danced but weren't moving to the left and stomping.

After a time, Sharpe observed that in between the stomps a few people in the inner circle were making a guttural exhalation sound. A young man standing beside Sharpe informed him that the inner circle was groaning. Soon the volume of the groans increased and the rest of those who were not in robes and wraps backed away, as did Sharpe. He could see the inner circle clearly now, with everyone stomping then bending forward as they made the groaning sound. The young man told him what they were doing was called laboring. The longer they labored, the more Sharpe realized they were working themselves into a frenzied state, making him uneasy. He backed out of the outer ring and found a place by the trunk of the Kindah tree where he sat down.

As the night progressed, the repetitious rhythmic chanting lulled Sharpe into a half trance filled with the shifting emotions of longing and dread. He fell into a deep sleep. In a dream, he saw himself saying goodbye to his father with tears flowing down his face, splashing to the ground and transforming into a stream of blood. The stream made its way toward his father, up into his bed, across his body, and into his mouth. Suddenly, the image of his father changed into that of Magus choking on the blood, eyes widening with horror and flowing with bloody tears, filling the crevices of his deeply wrinkled face.

Sharpe woke with a start and jumped up. Looking around terrified, he heard the familiar chanting and saw the figures dancing by candlelight. He spotted Bena's face lit up for a moment and then Ama's. He exhaled.

In the late hours of that night, Sharpe lay on the cold blanket-covered ground, listening to his father snore. The images from his gruesome dream filled his head. He wondered what the dream meant and if it was caused by the evil spirits Papa Rufus warned him about. He thought he would ask him in the morning, but then he remembered

Rufus telling him not to come back to him if he had dealings with the evil spirits.

Propping himself up on his elbow, Sharpe unwrapped the banana-leaf package Papa Rufus had slipped him at the end of the Kindah tree meeting. When he saw the shape of the leaves, he recalled, as a boy, shortly before his mother died, meeting a man he recognized from the village at the bottom of one of the cockpits. The man was collecting leaves and vines. Young Quaco joined him in the collection, and soon the man expressed his amazement at the boy's knowledge of plants. He had told the man his mother used various plant leaves to cook and heal and would often take him to collect them. Sharpe now realized the man had been the younger Papa Rufus, who had told him to stay far away from the plant that grew the leaves now laying in the open banana leaf package in the palm of his hand. Sharpe sat up. He knew what to do. He knew where to go and what to look for!

Up early the next morning, remembering the way to the nearest cockpit, Sharpe hiked with his banana-leaf package safely stowed in his pocket. After searching the bottom of three cockpits for nearly two hours, he found what he was looking for while making his way up the steep slope to explore the adjacent cockpit. A young vine with the same-shaped leaves that were in the package was making its way up the narrow stalk of a black lancewood tree. Being careful not to touch the leaves, he used a broad leaf from a nearby tree to pick four of them. With the two leaves he already had, that would make six. Papa Rufus's words resounded in his head, and he spoke them aloud with added emphasis. "Four will find him bawling out in hellfire!"

~

Sharpe spent the next two days repairing things around his father's house and talking with neighbors who were constantly stopping by to see him. Through them, he learned what it was like to live in the Accompong community. They all asked him if he was there to stay. He said no. Ama pleaded with him, saying she needed help with their father. Her pleas broke his heart, but he had a mission to accomplish. He thought about returning after the mission, but he knew there was no work for him in Accompong. He also realized, as a result of his conversations with the Accompong community members, that his idea of independent self-governance was more of a romanticized notion he had fabricated in his own mind. As far as he could see, while they were better off than the people of Hakin, they were not much different than most people he knew in Oristano. He loved his family and the heritage from which he came, but as he had once heard Essie say, "Come see me, come live with me, is two different thing."

Satisfied he had reconnected with his family and his people but feeling the urgency to return to Oristano, Sharpe informed his family he would be leaving early the next morning. That night, they reminisced about their mother with pride, laughter, and tears. Before going to sleep, Sharpe presented his father with his mother's mahogany chair, which he had mended and polished. When his father saw it, he reached out to hug Sharpe and smiled for the second time since Sharpe had been home.

24

——

SHARPE

FRIDAY-SUNDAY, DECEMBER 29-31, 1944

*A*rriving at the outskirts of Oristano before dark, Sharpe didn't want anyone to know he was back, so he hid in a long-abandoned, vine-infested shack. It was Friday, so people would be spending their week's pay at Mr. Lyn's shop before heading to their respective homes and communities for merrymaking.

While he waited, he took the leaves out of the banana leaf wrapping and minced them with his ratchet knife, then scraped the substance back onto the banana leaf and refolded it.

When the sun went down, Sharpe stepped out of the shack into the light dusting of the tree-filtered rays of the full moon. The moon would make it more difficult to conceal himself as he made his way to Hakin. On the other hand, it would be helpful while he added Papa Rufus's leaves to the ganja spliff. He retreated back into the shack and waited another hour, giving the locals time to be off the roads and engaged for the evening.

He judged the hour by timing in his head what people in

Hakin would be doing. Women would be adding last-minute flour dumplings to their soups while yelling at the top of their voices for their children to come home and help with dinner and for their men to find more kindling for the fire, which they might do if they hadn't already gotten an early start at the rum bar.

He envisioned every move Magus would make. Magus's prominent position in the village meant that most people could recite his daily schedule. During the evening, he ate shortly after sundown; painstakingly rolled his ganja spliff, which he put in the same spot on the same windowsill every night; headed for the rum bar, which he drank at until the doors closed; then returned home for his nightcap of ganja, which he got from his windowsill, then sat on a rock and smoked. After that, he was usually dragged to bed by his woman, where he slept into the late hours of the morning.

There were no more preparations to be made. The plan had been laid and incubated for three months, and it was ready for hatching. Sharpe thought further back to the insemination. He still remembered Busha's words clearly: *I chose you because I saw in you a seed of myself. A man who would do anything to get something.* Now was the time for the *anything*!

Sharpe left the shack and made his way toward Hakin with stealth. On two different paths, he almost came into contact with people. Both times he turned into wooded areas and hid among the underbrush. As he got closer to Hakin, he departed from the road and made his way up and around the village's periphery until he got to the top, where Magus lived.

He crouched and scoped out the situation. He could see the back of Magus's two-room dwelling. There was a lamp flickering at the kitchen side, but the bedroom, where the spliff would be resting on the windowsill, looked dark. He knew he had to get to the front of the house, but that was the side the moon was illuminating. He had to take the chance.

Panning from the dwelling on the left to the one on the right, he could see no one except a woman's back to a window. He deftly made his way down the rocky hill to the back of Magus's house. He checked once more to see if anyone was looking from the house on Magus's bedroom side: someone passed inside that house's doorway. Sharpe stayed in the shadow of Magus's house. A moment later, the path was clear.

Stooped and staying close to the wooden wall, he moved quickly toward the front. He peered around the corner and saw the spliff jutting out from the windowsill in arm's reach. He snatched it and reversed his steps to the back of the house, where he easily made his way back to his lookout.

After studying the roll of the spliff in the moonlight, he untied a string that cinched the bottom end and carefully unraveled the dried banana leaf just enough to see the ganja. He sprinkled all the minced leaves from his package alongside the ganja, then rolled and tied the spliff as it was before.

He knew Magus wasn't expected back for a while, but the rum bar was in full swing with punches of raucous laughter forcing its way up the rocky pathway, putting him on edge; he wanted the job over with. Repeating the procedure of panning the surrounding dwellings, he made his way down the hill behind the house, crawled along the side and carefully rested the spliff back on the windowsill, just where it had been. On the way back to the lookout, he saw a momentary silhouette of someone's face through the window of the adjacent house. He froze, then pushed himself forward, telling himself the person had not seen him.

Sharpe had no desire to wait around to see the outcome of his operation. He quickly worked his way back to the abandoned shack, being extra careful not to be seen now that the deed was done. There, he ate a piece of fried bammy[1]—the last of the food his sister had packed for him. He would have to do without food until he came out of hiding the following afternoon, making it known he had just arrived in Oristano from Accompong.

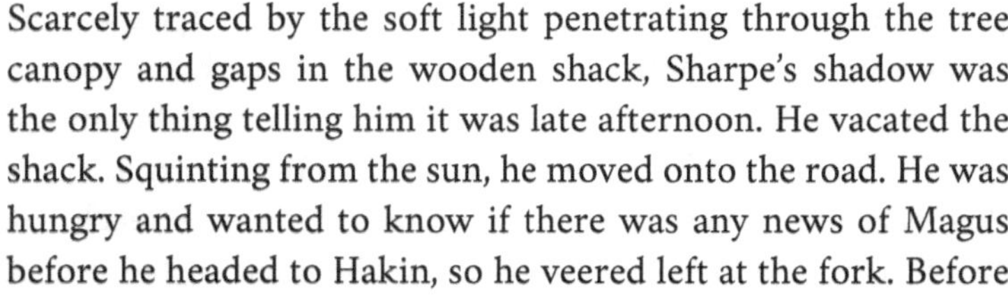

Scarcely traced by the soft light penetrating through the tree canopy and gaps in the wooden shack, Sharpe's shadow was the only thing telling him it was late afternoon. He vacated the shack. Squinting from the sun, he moved onto the road. He was hungry and wanted to know if there was any news of Magus before he headed to Hakin, so he veered left at the fork. Before reaching Mr. Lyn's shop, he saw two fishermen cleaning lobster traps. They looked up and greeted him with the usual "What a gowan?" He greeted them and kept walking. *Maybe Magus never dead*, he thought.

At the grocery store, Mr. Lyn welcomed him back from Accompong. Sharpe thanked him and bought a tin of bully beef and a gizzada[2].

At the counter, Mr. Lyn asked him, "Did you hear what happen up in Hakin last night?"

Sharpe jerked his head slightly, then slowly looked up at Mr. Lyn and replied, "No. Me just reach back from Accompong. What happen?" He leaned forward, trying to look concerned.

"The one them call Magus dead."

Sharpe widened his eyes and said, "How?"

"Nobody no know."

Sharpe handed Mr. Lyn money for the food.

"Me never did much care for him. But a life is still a life," said Mr. Lyn, shaking his head. "Them say, one a him neighbor did see somebody sneaking round the house."

Sharpe's stomach tightened. To seem casual, he bit the gizzada and spoke with his mouth full. "Them recognize the man?"

Mr. Lyn looked at him. "'How you know say it's a man? Woman can murder too." He laughed.

Sharpe relaxed and said, "True. Nuh true?" and he laughed, then said goodbye.

When he left the store, his laugh echoed in his head. It troubled him. Not that he had laughed—that served well as part of the coverup. It troubled him because he had laughed genuinely. He thought to himself, *A man dead...No, me kill a man and laugh about it!* It was just a laugh, but it was also the genesis of an infected needle pricking his soul.

As he walked through Hakin, he felt more than the usual stares. A man at the rum bar amplified his voice when talking to those around him, who included his Uncle Leroy and Ram Foot. "Look who rolling into town like a overripe turpentine mango. Him no good at all. Him spoil."

Sharpe was expecting raucous laughter, but all he heard was an assortment of disgusted groans, grunts, and sucking of teeth. These sounds knocked the air right out of his lungs. He wasn't sure why, but today he would have preferred the mockery.

He made his way to his desolate dwelling. Pushing the door open, he sat at the table and opened the tin of bully beef he had purchased from Mr. Lyn's shop. Preoccupied with his new circumstances, he ate slowly, right out of the can, picking at the bully beef with his fork, staring blankly at the wood grain of the table. *Me kill a man...murder a man. That mek me a murderer!* He dropped his head into his hands. He didn't know what he felt. There was neither elation at the kill nor remorse. He was flat. He had done this out of vengeance for Marsha and himself...and for the people of Hakin. But all he felt was flat.

He knew he was going to have to leave Hakin, but he

couldn't just get up and leave. That would be suspicious. He would have to feel things out some more.

Just then, there was a knock at the open door. He looked up and saw his Uncle Leroy and Ram Foot wearing somber faces.

"Come in." Sharpe got up from one of the two seats in his shack. "Please take a seat."

"No, no." Leroy said, raising his right hand. "We come to tell you something."

Ram Foot was looking at the ground and shifting nervously from side to side.

Leroy continued, "Not because we want to, but some of the men them give us the responsibility to tell you that you have to leave out of here…for good." He joined Ram Foot in staring at the floor.

Even though Sharpe took this as an answer to an unspoken prayer, he asked, "Them want me to leave my house?"

Ram Foot looked up. "Yes, Quaco. We sorry about it."

Playing innocent, Sharpe said, "Uncle Leroy, please look on me and tell me why them want me to leave?"

Leroy stood silent for a while, then replied, "Dem believe say you murder Magus."

With a questioning expression, Sharpe dramatized his response. "Me? Them say me murder Magus?"

"Yes," replied Ram Foot.

"Just one hour ago, when me come in from Accompong, Mr. Lyn did tell me say Magus dead. Then how them can say me do it?"

"Somebody live round Magus house say someone favor you was sneaking round Magus house last night," replied Ram Foot.

"It's a lie! How them going prove that?" Sharpe began shouting, hoping his neighbors would hear. "You know the truth! Them want to get rid of me this long time now! Plenty people nuh like Magus—you think it's me one have problem with him?" He sucked his teeth. "Every snake have somebody want to kill him." He calmed himself, "But me? Is nuh me do it."

"I don't say I doubt you, Quaco, but the fact is, them still want you to leave." Leroy looked up at Sharpe, "You kill dem Obeah man…or at least that is a what them think. And Lucy gone mad! If you never know it before, her boy pickney come from Magus. If you nuh leave, them going mek you life a living hell." He paused. "Neither me nor Auntie Phibbi want that for you."

"Me agree, Quaco," Ram Foot chimed in. "Me know we no really talk no more, but me nuh want nothing bad happen to you."

Sharpe, purposely relenting, said, "If me leave, them must know them have to still work with me as them boss."

"Yes," said Leroy. "Me already tell them they have to work hard or else them going lose them job."

Sharpe picked at his bully beef with his fork, knowing what he was going to do but stalling for effect. Finally, he said, "Me will leave with me few little things before daylight, but tell them, me nah go easy on them. If them think Busha bad—Huh! Them have no idea what going to lick them!"

The sunrise illuminated the cotton tree just as Sharpe turned the corner, carrying a large, bulging crocus bag. Standing at the kitchen window grinding coffee, Essie spotted him and furrowed her brow.

Sharpe placed the crocus bag outside the storeroom and walked over to the kitchen doorway. "Morning, Miss Essie."

She looked up and acknowledged him. "Me see you is back." She went back to her coffee grinding.

"Yes. Me did get back yesterday afternoon."

"So, you must hear that Magus dead, then." She glanced up to see his reaction.

Paralyzed momentarily, Sharpe couldn't breathe. He wasn't expecting this so soon. Finally, "Yes," is all he could say. He collected himself and decided to confront this head on. "Me nuh suppose you heard who them say do it?"

She looked up at him. "Who did it?"

There was an edge to her response. Sharpe realized she already knew. One of the Hakin property workers must have told her.

"Who did it?" she prodded.

"Dem say me do it." He hesitated. "Them say somebody favor me was sneaking round Magus house that night."

She put a pot on for the coffee. "Well?" She looked at him. "Did you do it?"

With a mixture of hurt and beguilement, Sharpe responded, "Miss Essie! You really figure me for a murderer?"

With fire in her eyes, she defended herself. "Me never figure you for nothing! But the Good Book say, 'The wicked flee when no man pursueth.' If you never do it, then just say so!" She ended with a "Humph!"

Sharpe didn't fully understand Essie's Good Book quote but caught the word "wicked." He stood there for a few moments, then turned to go.

As an addendum, she added, "In any case, as soon as Busha wake, you better talk with him."

Sharpe busied himself around the vicinity of the house, keeping an ear out for Malcolm. Around seven o'clock, Malcolm called out to Ruby for his morning coffee. Sharpe's body went erect. He knew what he had to do. He caught Ruby going into the house with the coffee and asked her to tell Malcolm he needed to speak with him.

Within moments, he heard Malcolm say, "What the hell is he doing here so early on a Sunday morning?"

He heard Essie in the kitchen say, "Uhuh! Same so."

Malcolm appeared on the front porch with his steaming coffee cup in hand.

"What are you doing here?" Malcolm asked, bothered. "It's a Sunday and the day before a holiday. Go back home and enjoy the time off." Malcolm looked past Sharpe and asked rhetorically, "Who left that crocus bag over there?" And without giving Sharpe a chance to answer, said, "That damn boy! I told him to make sure everything was put up before he finished!" He shook his head and turned around to go back into the house.

"It's that me come to talk with you about, sah. That is my bag me just put down there."

Malcolm turned back around. "Sharpe, what you trying to tell me? Does this have anything to do with Magus's death?"

"Well…yes, sah. The people in Hakin think me do it, and them send me uncle and me friend to tell me to leave the village."

"Leave? They threw you out of Hakin?"

"Well…yes, sah. Them say them was going mek me life a living hell. And to be honest, sah, them was already doing that. The only difference is Magus not in the picture anymore."

"That's for the best." Malcolm slapped him on the shoulder. "When I told you to take care of him, I didn't exactly mean this, but he's not the first to be dealt with this way." He blew on his coffee then took a sip of it. "For now, you can live with the gardener in his quarters, and you should immediately begin clearing a small piece of land farther up the hill to build a cabin. You can use lumber from the property, but the cost will be taken out of your pay. After my breakfast we'll go pick a spot for the cabin."

Before heading back into the house, Malcolm said, "If the people of Hakin give you hell, double it right back!"

2 5

CAILIN

JANUARY 14-28, 1945

On the second Sunday of the new year, Cailin attended church without Gus. No matter how she begged him to go, he said he'd been to church too many Sundays in a row. Rowena had gone back to school with Heather and Ian over a week earlier. Without Gus or Rowena, she felt more like a spectator than a congregant, and most times she felt like a spectacle when snickered at by her peers.

As was her custom, she left the church service at the beginning of the last hymn, even though she had worn her new dress from her uncle and aunt the previous two weeks and even gone forward with Rowena to receive communion. But without Rowena, she felt she couldn't face her female foes, so this Sunday she snuck in and out of church in her long khaki pants and plain white short-sleeved blouse. She decided she would save her dress for special occasions. Her sky-blue fabric was still in the brown paper bag it left the Witcombes' haberdashery in during the Christmas holidays. Her mother's rule for sewing was *Mother helps those who help themselves*. She had been too busy with her adventures on the property to bother to sew. She promised herself she'd get to it before Easter.

While riding Prime Minister down the road from the church, she noticed Archie standing at the bottom of the hill. Her first thought was to turn Prime Minister around. She remembered Ian telling her not to talk to Archie after Gus had introduced Ian to him at the beach. Still not understanding why Ian didn't want them to talk, she shook it off and put on her best smile.

When she was close enough to hear him, Archie bowed his neck while pretending to tip his invisible hat. "Top of the morning to you, Cailin Campbell!"

"Good morning to you, sir," she played along.

"Lady on horseback, may I walk you to your gate?"

At that moment, he looked so boyish and adorable she giggled, even as her heart beat faster.

"Would the lady prefer to remain on the horse, or would she like to walk?"

She dismounted, and he attempted to take Prime Minister's reins from her, but she insisted, "I've got it, thank you."

Prime Minister's hooves clip-clopped rhythmically ten times before either of them spoke again. Archie started, "Where are you coming from on a Sunday morning?"

"Church," she replied, keeping her eyes on the Cawdor gate not far away, wishing she had a dress on. This was the impetus she needed to submit to her mother's dressmaking rule.

"Church…" Archie thought back to Savanna-la-Mar and Kester Campbell. "That's good. I've been to church in Sav a few times recently. I met your Uncle Kester there."

"Uncle Kester?" Cailin looked at Archie in surprise.

"Yes. He seems to be somebody at the church."

"Uncle Kester and Auntie Jane are two of the most kind-hearted people. I could see them being important in their church."

"Yes, I can see that. He goes out of his way to greet me

whenever I go." He looked at Cailin and asked, "What about your family? Why aren't any of them with you?"

"Oh," Cailin began, sighing, "that's a long story. Gus comes to keep me company most Sundays, and one of my sisters comes with me when she's here on holidays. But that's it."

"Perhaps I'll come with you some Sunday." Archie raised his eyebrows and smiled.

She blushed. "I—I suppose that would be okay," she responded, wondering what Ian would say if he ever found out they went to church together or that they had been walking together.

When they reached the bottom of the Cawdor road, Archie tipped his make-believe hat again. "Well, I guess this is adieu."

Before she could catch herself, she blurted out, "I'll be going to Negril Springs tomorrow." Her immediate thought was, *Why did I say that?* Then, trying to sound cavalier, she followed it up with, "So I won't be at church for the next two Sundays."

"Where's Negril Springs?"

"It's a property my father owns west of Sav. We go bird shooting every year." She chastised herself with another why-did-I-say-that? He was sure to ridicule her for being a girl who goes bird shooting.

He didn't. Instead, he said, "Oh…your father said something about bird shooting." He hesitated, then added, "Happy shooting!" And then something that took Cailin off guard. "Wish I was going."

On her way up the Cawdor road, she let Prime Minister take his time as she repeated Archie's last words out loud, "Wish I was going." From that point until Prime Minister's hooves clopped on the cement barbecue, the words replayed like a scratched sound disk on a gramophone. She played multiple scenarios in her mind of her and Archie as a couple. Realizing she was getting carried away, she settled the matter by half convincing herself it was an innocent remark on his part. Even so, she had to admit she would miss him, too.

On Monday, Cailin sat silently in the front passenger seat of her father's car while Gus read silently in the backseat. She wondered how fun it was going to be without Ian there this year. Her only solace was that she'd get to fill his shoes, assisting her father on shoots. She thought of her mother, how she'd left her along with the aunties. It was the first year she had even thought about leaving her mother. She wondered why her father never took her to Negril Springs. It hit her that he never took her anywhere. *Why?* She was about to ask him when she realized she dared not risk raising his ire at the start of the trip. Otherwise, it could be a long two weeks.

A few miles out of Oristano, she saw her father's herd of cattle ahead of the car. The herd was mostly made up of cows and a few expensive bulls Malcolm had bought from Britain for breeding. The herdsmen and Sharpe had left Cawdor with the cattle at sunup, and they were expected to arrive at Negril Springs about sundown. When the breeding season was over, they would be herded back to the Cawdor property. Malcolm stopped the car and called Sharpe over. They discussed some logistics, and Malcolm drove off.

Savanna-la-Mar was the halfway stop between Cawdor House and Negril Springs. Malcolm parked the car outside Chester and Holt Hardware and went in to purchase supplies for the shoot. Cailin and Gus followed him into the store. Gus spotted a book on trapping animals, so Cailin left him and browsed the merchandise. She picked up a tool she had seen Sharpe using to smooth some of the planks of wood he was building his house with.

"That's a plane," she heard someone beside her say.

She looked up and saw a boy who looked to be a few years older than herself. She was struck by his full jet-black hair and eyebrows. *He's handsome,* was her first thought. She'd never seen anyone like him before.

Her only response was, "Oh," and she looked back at the plane, pretending to inspect it.

He chuckled and said, "My name is Harry, but my friends call me Rollo."

Still inspecting the plane, she said, "Those are interesting names."

"Yes. Harry comes from Harrison, which is odd because my parents are from Lebanon, and Rollo is because I was chubby when I was younger."

"I would never have guessed you were chubby," she spouted, then looked away blushing.

He smiled warmly, then asked, "Are you from around here?"

"I'm from Oristano. It's not far from here." She looked at him again. "Where are you from?"

A tall, thin, buxom woman with the same thick jet-black hair called from the store doorway, "Harry! Buy the shotgun shells and come. Your father's waiting in the car."

"Kingston," he replied. "I'm in Westmoreland visiting my grandparents."

Before she could ask him where in Westmoreland, he said, "Sorry, but I have to go."

As Malcolm pulled away from the store, he asked, "Who was that boy you were talking to?"

She sucked in air and sat up. "Oh. He said his name was Harry. His family's from Lebanon."

"I figured as much. With those looks, he must be an Arab." He turned to look at her and said, "Cailin, stay away from boys. And definitely stay away from Arab boys!"

"But, Daddy," she protested, "he was the one who spoke to me first!"

"Did you hear what I said?" Malcolm erupted.

She looked down at the floorboard and replied, "Yes, Daddy."

Negril Springs was on the flat planes that spread out from the hill country like the emerald train of an elegant evening gown. The flat, grassy lands fed by delta-like tributaries were perfect for grazing and breeding cattle. There was a section of the property that was too marshy for grazing cattle, so Malcolm rented it to Indians who grew rice.

The modest great house was perched on a mound easily visible from the road. Cailin loved it there because there wasn't a swarm of women dictating her every move. The housemaid, who doubled as the cook, spoiled her and her siblings whenever they came. She felt truly free!

They were up before daybreak the next morning and out on the plain with rifles in hand. Sharpe had asked Malcolm if he could join him for the shoot before heading back to Cawdor. Cailin was disappointed, as Malcolm chose Sharpe to be his assistant and was given her gun for the shoot. One of the Negril Springs property workers was told to oversee Cailin and Gus's handling of their shared gun. This further aggravated Cailin.

Overall, the shoot that day was a success. It brought in a plethora of birds that had escaped the North American cold, only to end up hanging on a rope bunched together. Gus tried to carry the carcasses himself but soon passed them off to their overseer, who gave a hearty laugh, embarrassing Gus. Dinner was a feast that night. Although there was not always a lot of meat on the birds, Cailin loved the wild taste. She thought it preferable to chicken or turkey.

For most of the two weeks, the schedule was the same: up

early, shoot birds, help the maid defeather them, go exploring on the property, eat dinner, and go to bed early for the next day's shoot. There were a few days of no shooting. On those days, Malcolm had usually been out drinking the night before and couldn't wake up for the shoot.

One evening during the last week in Negril Springs, Malcolm took the children crab hunting. On the way, he stopped in a small village to pick up a young Black woman and her brother to assist them in the hunt. From there, Malcolm drove down a small path that led toward the sea. The path was barely wide enough for the car to pass through, with wild bushes brushing against it. At a clearing, he told the four of them to get out and walk in front of the car as he drove slowly. From time to time the headlights illuminated a crab walking across the path, and the woman and her brother held it down with one foot while picking it up by its back, and then dropped it into a crocus bag. Cailin and Gus quickly caught on.

On the way home, Malcolm dropped the boy back to the village, but the woman, who Malcolm had sit in the front seat, went back with them to Negril Springs. Knowing the awkwardness of the situation, Malcolm announced the woman would help the maid cook the crabs the next day. He never said where she would sleep, but that night, Cailin heard some laughter coming from her father's room. She thought this odd as she'd never seen her father in his bedroom with anyone, not even her mother. She tiptoed to his door and heard the young woman's coy voice, "Mass Malcolm!" and then her giggle.

Confused, Cailin walked back to her room and laid awake until the wee hours of the morning.

～

On the morning before they were to return to Cawdor, Malcolm was sitting on the front steps pulling off his bird shooting boots when the maid handed him an envelope and informed him, "The man tell me it's from one Missa Witcombe."

Malcolm looked at the writing on the envelope, then opened it and pulled out the note. The next thing out of his mouth was, "That damn boy!" He got up, kicked his boots, and repeated, "That damn boy!"

When Malcolm came back from Savanna-la-Mar that afternoon, he was in a dour mood and said nothing to anyone for the rest of the day.

ARCHIE

SATURDAY-MONDAY, JANUARY 27-29, 1945

"All you've been talking about for the last hour is bird shooting!" complained Robby. "Have you ever even been bird shooting?"

"No!" said Archie defiantly, exposing the angst he'd been blanketing since the previous afternoon when Malcolm hadn't shown up for the second Friday in a row. What really angered him was his unrealistic expectation that Malcolm would even consider taking him to Negril Springs to go bird shooting. He'd foolishly held on to the only words Malcolm had spoken to him on Christmas Day, *Can you shoot bird?*

Robby slapped him on the back, exclaiming, "Rhaatid! A new recruit! Welcome to training, Private Price. You can call me Sergeant Thompson. Or just Sergeant will do. If you step right this way, we'll acquire the necessary training weaponry." He laid his hands on Archie's shoulders, turned him around, and gave him a shove up Great George Street.

Complying, Archie asked, "Where are we going?"

"I'm going to teach you to shoot birds, but first we have to get some shotgun shells."

When they passed Ricketts Street, Archie asked, "Why aren't we going to your house?"

"Are you joking? We can't use any of my father's shells. He'll hit the roof!"

Archie stopped walking and faced Robby. "So where are we getting them from?"

"The hardware store," replied Robby, prodding him on up the road.

"Chester and Holt Hardware?"

"Same one. Nowhere else sells them."

"How are we going to pay for them? I don't have much money on me."

"We're not going to pay for them." Robby donned an impish smile.

Furrowing his brow, Archie attempted to stop again, but found himself being pushed forward by Robby. "Are you saying we're going to steal them?"

"I prefer to use the word 'pinch.' It sounds less..." he searched for the right word, "...less criminal."

"Pinching, as you put it, at the market was one thing, but we could get in big trouble for this."

"Don't worry yourself. I've done this before. We'll use the same plan we used at the market. You distract the clerk until you see me walk out the door. It's like shooting birds in a cage." He elbowed Archie. "Nothing can go wrong."

"If you get caught, I don't know you."

Robby slapped him on the back again. "Don't worry. I won't."

Once in Chester and Holt, Archie and Robby branched out in different directions. Archie pretended to browse, then made his way to the counter.

"Do you need anything, young man?" asked the store clerk.

"Ye...yes," Archie said. He hadn't premeditated how he would distract the clerk. The first thing that came to mind was the gun he'd been eyeing for months. He asked, "How much is the gun that's hanging up back there?"

The clerk looked to the back wall as Robby nonchalantly stuffed a small box of shotgun shells under his shirt.

"Thief!" yelled the clerk. "Thief!"

Archie saw Robby freeze with his hand under his shirt.

Seconds later, a man rushed through a doorway in the back of the store and blocked Robby from getting out the front door.

A crowd was gathering outside the store, and the clerk shouted, "Someone get the constable!"

Archie and Robby sat on the parlor couch with their heads hanging while Mr. Thompson and Mr. Witcombe took turns castigating the boys. The men's wives sat in the armchairs, woeful, with handkerchiefs in hand.

"I'm a bank manager in this city!" Mr. Thompson declared, pacing back and forth. "Your mother and I are respectable citizens of Savanna-la-Mar! That's the only reason the manager of Chester and Holt is not pressing charges."

Robby's mother let out a wail. "Oh! I can't believe my boy is a thief!"

Mr. Thompson put his hand on his wife's shoulder, sighed and said, "Settle down, dear."

"And as for you, Archie," joined Mr. Witcombe, "God knows what Mr. Campbell will do when he realizes you've been mixed up in this nefarious business."

Like the chorus of a Greek tragedy, Mrs. Witcombe quavered mournfully, "He was like a son to me!" And she sniffled, blowing her nose.

"Please, dear," chided Mr. Witcombe. "It's not as if he's dead."

Outside, car tires could be heard crushing rock.

Mr. Witcombe pulled the sheer curtain to the side to get a better look. It was Malcolm.

Before Mr. Witcombe could make it to his front door, Malcolm threw the door open and marched in. "Where is he? Where's that damn boy?" Mr. Witcombe motioned to the parlor. Seeing Archie on the couch, Malcolm grabbed him by his upper arm and said, "Up to the bedroom!" Malcolm propelled Archie forward by the arm.

The two ladies gave a choral whimper.

When they reached the stairs, Mr. Thompson called out, "Mr. Campbell! The boy is far too old for that. Come back down, and we'll find another solution."

Ignoring him, Malcolm thrust Archie up the stairs and into his room.

The door slammed.

All the audience in the parlor heard coming from the second floor were wall thuds and furniture scraping the floor, consummating in what sounded to be a belt striking flesh in tandem with Malcolm's voice booming, "Never! Embarrass! Me! Again!" over and over. The women blocked their ears; the men paced the floor; Robby hung his head.

Kester, who had been sent for earlier but was out on his rounds, knocked on the front door. Mr. Witcombe promptly opened it and frantically explained what was happening.

Kester double-stepped it up the stairs and tried to open the door, but it was locked. He knocked forcefully and called, "Malcolm! Open the door! You've made your point clear! Open the door!"

The door swung open; the two men faced each other. Malcolm thrust his way past his brother and proceeded down the stairs.

Kester pushed the door further open and saw Archie keeled

over on his bed. Shirt ripped. Pants hanging on one ankle. Welts all over.

"Whoever is there, please leave me alone," said Archie with restraint in his voice.

Kester pulled the door closed. Before he made it down the stairs, the key in Archie's door turned.

All Archie heard from that point on were voices rising and falling like waves rumbling against the cliff shore.

That day, no matter how Kester and the Witcombes appealed, Archie stayed in his room with the door locked. He left lunch and supper trays untouched outside his door. Late at night, Mrs. Witcombe heard his door open. She presumed he went into the kitchen and perhaps used the lavatory. Shortly after, she heard the door lock again.

It wasn't until suppertime the next day that Archie appeared downstairs. When Mrs. Witcombe saw him, she let out a gasp, covering her mouth and looking away. Archie ignored her reaction and sat in his seat at the dinner table.

After Mr. Witcombe gave thanks for the meal, Archie spoke up. "I have one thing to say, and then I would rather not speak about it again."

"Go ahead," prompted Mr. Witcombe.

"Mr. and Mrs. Witcombe," he looked at them for a moment each and then fixed his eyes on his plate. "I'm sorry for the trouble and embarrassment I've caused you."

Mrs. Witcombe responded, "It's alright, dear."

"No," contradicted Mr. Witcombe. "It's not alright." He paused. "But we can see that you have more than paid the price of your offense, so we do accept your apology." He hesitated, then said, "Mr. Campbell and Mr. Thompson agreed on one rule for both you and Robby. You are not to speak to one another in school, nor are you to see one another outside of school."

Archie had already figured that would be the case, but it still smarted to hear it. The school part didn't bother him, as Robby wouldn't give him the time of day there, but on the weekends when Malcolm didn't pick him up, Robby was his only consolation. After what had happened, who knew if Malcolm would even pick him up again?

Mrs. Witcombe tried to stimulate light conversation, but neither Archie nor her husband took the bait. The rest of the dinner was spent in silence except for Mrs. Witcombe calling out to Pressy to bring the dessert and then to clear the table.

Archie didn't want to go to school and face what he was sure would be the worst day of his school career. But he knew he had to face it head on. If he put it off a day or more, he would only effuse the scent of blood into the school's atmosphere. The wolf pack would be that much wilder and more ravenous. He had to go. He planned on getting there just before his first class.

Lingering outside the school gate, he heard the bell ring for the first class to begin and waited until the last of the students entered the buildings. He made his way up the gravel path to the main building, through the hallway, and into his physics class without incident. Normally he bemoaned physics being his first class, but on this day, he was thankful. No one in the wolf pack took physics. *They're too stupid,* he thought to himself and chuckled, then gasped and held his right ribcage.

The girl beside him asked, "Are you alright?"

He straightened up and replied, "Yes," with a strained smile.

After roll was taken, the teacher announced there was to be a special all-school assembly, and the students were to form a line and follow her to the assembly hall.

That caught Archie off guard. He was sure the assembly had

something to do with the Saturday incident. Were he and Robby going to be paraded in front of the entire school?

Clive and Devon, the alpha and beta of the pack, were seated with their respective classes on opposite sides of the hall. Devon noticed Archie walk in first and yelled, "There he is!"

Spotting Archie, Clive echoed in response, "The thief!"

Half the assembly, who were privy to the gossip, burst out in laughter then turned to the bewildered ones explaining the situation, which caused another wave of laughter. The teachers' attempt to quell the mirth failed until Mr. Pritchard, the headmaster, stepped up to the lectern and called for silence. The laughter died to a low rumble and then to only one young voice at the back of the room who could be heard asking, "What was that all about?"

Mr. Pritchard boomed, "I'll tell you what that was all about!"

There was pin-drop silence in the room.

Archie sat stoic. This was more belligerent than he had anticipated, but he had to hold himself together, as much as he felt like getting up and yelling at them all.

"Two of Manning's very own students were caught stealing this Saturday. I don't need to mention names, as I can see most of you already know who they are. Besides, the names are not as important as the fact that they are Manning's students." He paused, looking around at the student body. "This is not acceptable behavior for any student attending this school!"

"Here! Here!" yelled Clive, triggering a round of snickers through the assembly hall.

"That's quite enough, Mr. Taylor! One more disruption and you'll see me in my office." Mr. Prichard gripped the lectern. "As I was saying, Manning's standards are high, and anyone who tries to follow the example of these two boys will be dealt with severely! As it is, we have sent for their parents to meet and discuss their behavior."

"And who is Archie's father?" called out Devon.

There was a brief silence, then the room filled with a mixture of oohs and guffaws.

"Mr. Blake! You can go straight to my office...now!" demanded Mr. Pritchard. He gave a throat-clearing cough, then concluded, "Well, I have said what needed to be said. I expect the best out of each and every one of you because you represent Manning's School." Then he said, "Teachers, please escort your students back to your classrooms."

Exiting the assembly hall, Archie and Robby saw each other. Robby's eyes shifted to the back of the boy's head in front of him. Archie laughed to himself in ironic frustration.

Archie didn't hear a word his teachers said throughout the day. All he heard were whispers and snickers in the classrooms' subterranean stratum. It got to the point that he wasn't certain if what he was hearing was from the classroom he was in or from the aftershock of previous classrooms. To shore up his crumbling dignity, he pretended to listen to the teacher and take notes. What he really wrote was, "If I make it through this, damn everyone!" and variations on that same theme.

Lunch was a repeat of class time with greater tremors and agitation. No one spoke directly to him, but he knew their conversations were all about him. He sat at the end of a table with his head bowed to his plate.

The greatest seismic shock came at the end of the school day. Archie, whose focus was on making it out of the school gate, had made it halfway down the gravel drive and was passing a circle of boys. The circle opened and quickly closed in on him. Realizing this was the wolf pack, he dropped his schoolbag, ready for a fight.

"Cool down. Cool down," said Devon.

Three girls gathered on the outskirts of the circle.

Clive said, "We have a few questions for you. That's all."

Archie stood rigid.

Devon asked, "Why did Mr. Campbell beat you?"

Archie felt momentarily winded. He had hoped Robby wouldn't have told anyone. He figured they must have ganged up on him when they realized he and Archie were weekend friends. Archie didn't respond to the question.

Another boy continued the interrogation. "Is he your father?"

"No! He's not!" Archie protested involuntarily. He tried to push out of the circle, but the boys locked arms, preventing him.

"Why so defensive?" mocked the same boy. "Who is your father, then?"

There was silence. Archie looked above their heads, avoiding their penetrating stares.

Devon pushed further. "You know what I think?" He looked around the circle, landing on Archie. Then he said in a low, casual voice, "I think you're a bastard of a murdering womanizer."

A girl gasped.

"I have no idea what you're talking about!" Archie objected, shaking his head.

"Maybe you don't," said Clive, "but that proves all the more you're a bastard!"

The circle broke out in laughter, joined by the growing crowd.

Clive, emboldened by the laughter, loudly broadcast, "You're a bastard of a neaga woman!"

Archie didn't comprehend what they had been saying about his supposed father, but this he understood. They were talking about his mother. He was about to strike Clive with his hardest blow when two of the boys grabbed him from behind. He struggled to get free but was overpowered.

Just then, a teacher dispersed the crowd, finding the two boys holding Archie.

"Why are you holding him?" inquired the teacher.

"He was about to punch Clive," answered a boy.

"Why?" asked the teacher.

"He hasn't liked Clive since the first day he came to Manning's," replied Devon. "He sees him as competition."

"Mr. Price, please come with me," ordered the teacher. "The headmaster will deal with this. As it is, your parents have not responded to his request to have a meeting."

Mr. Pritchard was not concerned about the averted fight. Instead, he questioned Archie as to Malcolm's whereabouts. Archie told him he could send a message to the inn where his mother lived, which Malcolm often frequented. Other than that, Archie had nothing else to say.

On his slow walk to the Witcombes, Archie brooded over the wolf pack's inquisition—*Is Mr. Campbell your father? Who's your father then? You're a bastard of a murdering womanizer.*

What was he to think? *Is Malcolm really my father? How could such a heinous man be my father?* He wrestled with the allegation. Then he constructed his defense. *I refuse to believe it! I would rather accept Hitler as my father!*

KIMBERLY, SOUTH AFRICA

5 JUNE 1904

bum,

We have received your many letters requesting more money, even though Winnie has written you that I will send money whenever I am able. If what I have sent is not enough, then it is not enough. You have the family property, which, as the oldest male, should have been mine. Instead, when I came back from medical schooling in Scotland, I was given the orange orchard in Saint Elizabeth to run alongside my medical duties.

Because of your incessant requests, I have forbidden Winnie to correspond with you until such time that you show gratitude for what I am able to send.

And one last thing, I know you say Malcolm needs a father, so I must either return or send for him. From what I can see in your letters, you are the problem! He is only three years old, yet you have already spoiled him. It is time for you to lay down the law. Spare the rod and spoil the child.

Cuthbert

2 8

CAILIN

SATURDAY, FEBRUARY 10, 1945

"*L*et me see them," insisted Gus.

Cailin lifted the letters Mr. Lyn had handed her over her head so Gus couldn't reach them. She read the name of each recipient. "Malcolm Campbell…" She skipped the next one and shuffled it to the back.

"Cailin!" Gus demanded. "If that's for me, give me!"

"Give me, give me, never get," she taunted, and a moment later announced, "Here's one for me!" She handed the other letters to Gus and remarked, "It's from Row."

"It's him!" exclaimed Gus, waving a letter. "Daddy's written at last!" He shoved the remaining letters into Cailin's hand and asked Mr. Lyn for a knife to cut open the airmail letter.

They sat on the bench outside the grocery store and silently read their respective letters. Cailin's letter read:

6 February 1945

Dear Cailin,

I'm sure you are surprised to hear from me. I have not been the best at writing with all my schoolwork and the activities here at Hampton and even at Munro.

Speaking of Munro, that is why I am writing. There is something I simply must tell someone, or I'll burst! But first, before you read another word, you must swear yourself to secrecy! Stop now and do it.

Cailin stopped reading for a moment and put her hand on her heart, silently mouthing an oath of secrecy.

Gus looked up at her and asked, "Is everything alright with Row?"

"Yes. Everything is just fine."

She continued reading.

Now that you have sworn secrecy, I can tell you. Remember the boy who was looking at me in church on Christmas Day? Remember, I told you he danced with me at the Munro-Hampton dance? Well, this past Saturday, some of us girls from Hampton went over to Munro for the Munro versus Jamaica College football game. He spotted me and came right over. He spent the whole game talking to me! Heather saw us, but I could not tell if she disapproved. During the interval, he bought me an aerated water, and we sat under a tree. We stayed there talking during the second half of the game. It felt scandalous. Before the game ended, he was sitting close and asked if he could kiss me. That certainly was scandalous! I wanted to kiss him, but I know what Hampton gossip is like! I declined. Fortunately, he was a gentleman about it, and he told me he was already looking forward to seeing me at the next school event.

Well, there you have it. Remember, you are sworn to secrecy! I thought of talking with Heather about it, but I am not sure if she would tell Mummy. I am not sure what Mummy would say either, so, right now, it is best to say nothing. Besides, all we really did was talk.

I am sure you will want to talk to someone about it as well, so please let it only be me! At the risk of becoming a bother, I will say it once more. You are sworn to secrecy! Write to me.

Your Faithful Sister Row

Cailin put Rowena's letter back in the envelope and put it in her pants pocket.

When Gus finished reading his letter, he gave a sigh of relief and wore the expression of someone who had eaten his first good meal in a long while.

"What did he say?" asked Cailin.

"He said a lot." Gus looked at the letter again then announced, "Daddy's a real hero!"

"I agree," said Cailin. "What has he been doing?"

"He said his aeronautical missions have made it difficult to find time to write."

"Yes, I'm sure he said exactly that word." She gave a sarcastic smirk. "I'm sure he's been extremely busy with the war and all, so go on. What does the letter say?"

"He said he's a full-fledged commissioned RAF pilot, and he's flying a Lancaster bomber!" Gus beamed. "From now on, we have to refer to him as Officer Campbell!" He saluted. "He just got finished with a two-day bombing campaign, which was a success. He destroyed two German fuel plants! And he said the war will be over in no time!" Gus jumped up and danced around, waving the letter and yelling, "My daddy's coming back soon! Officer Campbell will be back soon!"

Cailin leaned back, laughing. She was glad to see Gus in such a jubilant mood.

When he completed his victory dance, he added, "Oh yeah, he also said when he was at a pub in London, he saw the American pilot who introduced him to flying at Vernamfield. The sight of the pilot made him feel like he was back home in Jamaica." Gus let out a hope-filled sigh.

"Come on." Cailin got up from the bench. "Let's go riding on the beach."

Cailin slipped the remaining letters under Prime Minister's saddle. They mounted their horses and followed the footpath to the beach.

The sea lapped gently over the sand as though it were sifting for prize shells. With the crystal blue waters and a wide berth of sand between sea and soil, Oristano Beach was one of the most beautiful beaches on the western side of the island.

On reaching the firm, wet sand, Cailin signaled Prime Minister into a canter. Gus followed but spurred his horse into a gallop, passing Cailin.

"Hey! That's not fair!" yelled Cailin, and she tried to catch up.

Just before reaching the west side of the beach, where two families were enjoying the sun and water, Gus slowed to a walk, allowing Cailin to catch up.

"You should have given me some warning," she complained.

"No," replied Gus. "A good jockey doesn't need a warning. I won fair and honest."

He took off galloping again.

She shook her head and said to Prime Minister, "That boy thinks everything is a competition." She patted him on the neck.

As she was passing the second family, she overheard the mother say, "His mother has left, and his father's off to war."

Looking to see who had made the comment, Cailin was just in time to see a teenage girl wearing a two-piece bathing suit interjecting, "And he has to live up at that dreadful house!"

Their eyes linked.

Not knowing how else to respond, Cailin spurred Prime Minister into a gallop. She wasn't sure if she was more hurt at the intentional comment or aghast at the two-piece bathing suit. Her father would kill over the first. Her mother would die over the second.

As she neared the end of the beach, she saw Gus on his horse, speaking with someone. When she got a little closer, she realized it was Archie, but Gus was already steering his horse toward the road, leaving Archie behind. Her face went flush at the thought of speaking with him again.

Archie picked up a rock and flung it with a sharp, spasmodic movement far out to sea. Cailin thought back a couple weeks to when her father had kicked his bird shooting boot in a similar manner. *That damn boy*, he had said, then had left for Savanna-la-Mar.

By the time she reached Archie, Prime Minister was walking. Cailin was prepared to stop and say a few words to him, but all he did was nod and crack an emotionally absent smile. Again, she was reminded of her father two weeks prior when he had returned from Savanna-la-Mar in a foul mood. *What happened that day in Sav?* she asked herself.

Later that evening, she wrote a reply letter to Rowena.

10 February 1945

Dear Row,

I received your letter today. It was a nice surprise, but not as surprising as what you wrote in it. I wish you were here so I could ask you a thousand questions. Since you are not, I'll ask a few of them in this letter and hope you'll write back with answers.

My first question, what is his name? I remember from church on Christmas Day that he has light brown hair and a handsome profile. He strikes me as a Charles or a William. Include his last name also when you write. What were the most interesting things you talked about? Please don't tell me the conversation was sappy and mawkish. That would be disappointing. What does he like to do? Does he play sports? Which leads me to ask, why wasn't he playing football that day? Does he bird shoot or ride horses? I just realized I am asking questions that reveal the type of boy I would like.

Yes, I know that must sound strange to your ears. Cailin, who doesn't like dresses. Cailin, who wants to be outside on adventures with her brothers. Cailin, who gets embarrassed at a movie when a man kisses a woman. Well, I guess everyone must grow up, eventually. Not that I'm exactly there yet.

I have a secret of my own that I want to share. I hesitate to write it, but since you have confided in me, I know I can with you. There is a boy I like. It's strange to write it. I've thought it in my head but seeing it in ink is another thing. His name is Archie Price. He's the son of the innkeeper for Oristano Inn. I've seen him six times and talked with him three. He's handsome and funny. He says peculiar things like he's reciting lines from a play or something. Gus and I were on the beach today, and we saw him. Anyway, please don't tell a soul! Over the Christmas holiday, Ian met him and told me and Gus to stay away from him. He never said why. I've only talked with him once since then, and it's only because he's so charming. I couldn't help myself.

Anyway, now you're sworn to secrecy! We both have good reasons to never tell each other's secret.

I miss you and can't wait to see you over the Easter holiday.

Your "Secret" Sister,
Cailin

P.S. Mummy and I are making my new sky-blue dress. I'll wear it to church on Easter Sunday. We'll be the best-dressed sisters! I hope Archie comes that day.

SHARPE

MONDAY, FEBRUARY 12, 1945

Sharpe moved into his partially completed dwelling with only the land cleared and the walls and roof erected. The Cawdor gardener, who Malcolm had told to share his room with Sharpe until the dwelling was complete, was none too happy to be living with what he called "a rass murderer." He made it perfectly clear every night Sharpe came into the room. The gardener complained bitterly to Malcolm, to no avail.

Leaning on his new doorframe, Sharpe took in his early morning vista. It was much nicer than his old view in Hakin. Here he looked down into a thicket of trees with the far-flung ocean horizon cresting the top of the canopies. This new view filled him with the hope that one day he would scale past those trees and navigate toward a new life. One better than Hakin, Accompong, or even Cawdor had to offer.

There was, however, an ever-present gnawing blackness seated at the meeting of his chest and abdomen. He placed his right hand there, as if to mollify it. But he knew it would only continue to grow. Since the moment he had laughed at Mr. Lyn's macabre joke the day after the murder, the infection of the needle prick had spread little by little every moment of every day. He bent over slightly, as if to vomit it out, but there was no such relief.

His mind flashed back to the dream he'd had at the ceremony in Accompong. His tears turning to blood. His father choking on the blood. His father's face turning into Magus's face. Magus crying blood. He shuddered and sat down on his front step, closing his eyes.

As if in a vision, he could see himself as a boy. He and his schoolmates were sitting in the small Methodist church building with Mr. Aldridge reading from the Bible. He could hear Mr. Aldridge's voice, as though he were standing right in front of him: "What hast thou done? The voice of thy brother's blood crieth unto me from the ground."

Sharpe's body curled up like a salted slug. He lay on the ground moaning, wishing he could cry. But he couldn't.

He thought of Busha and the stories he had heard about Busha shooting a property worker for talking back to him. Before the man's blood had dried in the soil, Miss Abum had sent him to Savanna-la-Mar to take a ship to Cuba. *Did Busha feel the same blackness inside him? How him deal with it? Me would love to ask him about it, but him would never outright admit it.*

The only time Sharpe felt anything akin to relief was when he was in Essie's presence. This puzzled him, as lately she looked at him disapprovingly and scolded him at every opportunity. Even so, he needed a respite. After he managed to pull himself together, he set off down the hill to the Cawdor kitchen.

"Good morning, Miss Essie," said Sharpe, stopping at the kitchen window.

"Good morning," she replied, busily peeling a potato.

"You need help with anything?"

She stopped peeling the potato, cocked her head to the right, and, squinting, asked, "What is it you really want?"

He was taken by surprise, although he knew he shouldn't be. He answered, "Me…me just want to help. That's all. Me no ready to start work yet."

"Well, me will take you word for that." She went back to potato peeling and continued, "In any case, me feel say you want to talk, so me have a question for you."

"Go ahead," he consented.

"What you did really go to Accompong for?" She picked up another potato.

"Me did tell you already," he said, irritated. "But me will say it again. Me go to see me father and sister them."

"Yes, you told me that," she said calmly, then asked another question. "Why you come back so soon? If me never see me family for such a long time, me would stay to the last possible day. Why you come back so soon, eh?" She looked at him, frowning.

Feeling like she was putting him on the witness stand to testify against himself, he stepped back a pace and responded, "Then, Miss Essie, you look like say you accusing me of something."

"Me nah accuse you of nothing. But, like me tell you before, the Good Book say, 'The wicked flee when no man pursueth.'"

"And what that really mean, eh?"

"Alright then, mek me put it another way. When herring mauger, him bones show."[1]

"Then you accusing me!"

"Me nah judge you. Me only asking question. But you carrying on like say you guilty."

Sharpe's face grew hot. He snarled, "Miss Essie!" He caught himself and took a deep breath. With deliberation, he attempted to conclude these new proceedings. "Me would ask you to keep you question them to youself and stay out of me business."

"You business?" she chuckled, shaking her head. "Trouble deh a bush, Anansi bring it a yard."[2] Then she looked him square in the eyes and said, "Don't you realize this is now the whole property's business?"

Just then, an old voice was heard crackling like a wireless radio, "E-s-s-i-e! C-o-m-e h-e-r-e!"

"Miss Abum calling me, but we don't done with this conversation."

Sharpe harrumphed.

After Essie went into the house, Sharpe stood by the kitchen window, considering their conversation. This was the first time she had all but directly accused him of the murder. He knew there was no way to avoid her—neither did he really want to—so he would have to walk cautiously around her, being careful to steer any conversation away from Magus.

That name set his teeth on edge. He brooded, *Even in the grave, the old Obeah man after me!*

To avoid the green coffee beans the gardener was spreading to dry on the barbecue, Sharpe walked along the front side of the house. Abum's coarse voice transmitted through the hall, out the open door, and made its way to Sharpe's ears. "I'm not sure why Mass Malcolm didn't fire him after the murder."

Sharpe's feet halted.

"Probably for the same reason you never turn Mass Malcolm into the authorities but send him to Cuba instead," Essie sniped.

Abum responded, "How dare you speak to me that way! I have a good mind to let you go!" She paused. "Get back to the kitchen at once, and never make mention of that again!"

∼

After eating dinner that evening, Sharpe carried the pot from behind the kitchen, where Essie and Ruby cooked the servants' food. He placed it in the kitchen sink to be washed.

"Miss Essie, can I ask you a question?" Sharpe said with gentleness in his voice.

"Yes." She looked up at him. "What is it?"

"Why you stand up for me this morning in front of Miss Abum?"

She looked down and brushed the lap of her apron with both hands. "Me never stand up for you in particular. Me is always on the side of the truth."

"But you almost lose you job," he pressed. "Over me."

She looked up, speechless and seemingly knocked off-balance. Then she sucked her teeth and said, "She know she can't replace me. And beside, even though me nuh believe in murdering, that Magus was a man Jezebel!" She was on a roll. "And now the Kerry Mongoose them learn a lesson! Just like when Sampson crash down the house on the Philistine them." Then she added, "Me told you the Kerry Mongoose them was under condemnation."

"Miss Essie, you ever hear about one poem call 'Harlem Shadow'"?

"No, sah. Is what you know about poem?"

He sighed. "Never mind. One day me will read it for you."

"Me don't know about no Harlem Shadow, but me can tell you about one shadow that follow a man in the Bible till Jesus catch him and wash him clean of the murdering."

"Please, Miss Essie!" Sharpe raised his hands in frustration.

"No! Listen to me!" She stepped forward, grabbing both his hands and cupping them in hers. "If God can take a murderer like Saul and turn him into the Apostle Paul, then him can do the same thing with you!"

Sharpe froze. There was no use. She was convinced he had done it. He knew he had done it. She was throwing out what she believed to be a life preserver to a drowning man. He wasn't convinced it could help, but the blackness within him was growing and threatened to drown him from the inside.

The only thing he could think to say to change the subject was, "Me go to Missa Aldridge church back in December."

She let go of his hands. "That no nothing. Me already told you, that Methodist minister is a politics man, not a God man."

"I heard him talkin about Jesus and the Spirit of God. Then maybe him is a God man *and* a politics man. After all, him use the Bible to get the people them to vote." His face brightened at what he perceived to be a good comeback.

Her rebuttal was quick. "All his Bible politics bamboozling never get his man in. Instead, it get Busha man in." She laughed, then wagged her index finger at him. "Now, if you want to go to a real church, you can come with me to my Moravian church up in Beeston Spring."

He rolled his eyes and mocked, "Me know! Me know! You Moravian people was here before Columbus reach!"

She stood, arms folded and lips pursed.

Sharpe continued, "And anyway, how me going get leave to go to Beeston Spring with you?"

She sucked her teeth and exclaimed, "The Lawd done mightier things than that!" She nodded, raising her eyebrows. "Leave it to Essie and the Lawd."

CAILIN

FRIDAY-SATURDAY, MARCH 9-10, 1945

Ruby handed Cailin a piece of mail.

Row! At last, a response, she thought, immediately heading upstairs to read the letter. It had been a month since she'd written Rowena and had been anxious for a reply. She tore open the envelope and lay on her bed to read. By the end of the letter, her mood had dampened. She returned it to its envelope and tucked it under some old clothes in the bottom drawer of her dresser.

~

"Every time I see a sailboat, for a split second I think it's a U-boat," Gus said, sighing as he leaned on the back veranda railing and gazing into the clear, blue, afternoon horizon.

To cheer him up, Miss Recas responded, "You will be able to read about it in a history book before too long." She smiled at him, even though his back was to her.

This was one of the rare occurrences that Miss Recas joined the family on the back veranda, rather than going straight to her room after the school lessons were completed. Cailin would have preferred she did the latter.

Auntie Bitsy cleared her throat as she always did before she spoke. "Well, Young Angus…" Gus turned to Auntie Bitsy as she seldom spoke, and when she did, it was with good reason. "…tell us the latest news of the war."

Gus lit up, then he narrowed his eyes and said, "But, Auntie Bitsy, you read every paper I read and hear every BBC war report I hear. Why do you want me to repeat it?"

"That's a very good question," she replied with a chuckle. "I am an old lady. There have been enough wars in my years. This war, the Great War, although this one seems to have topped it, and the Boer Wars, just to mention a few. But now, I want to hear it from an unsullied mind."

"Well, Auntie, I think this war has sullied my mind." Smiling ear to ear, he immediately looked around for accolades, which he received from Miss Recas's beaming face. Cailin pursed her lips and shook her head.

"Touché!" Auntie Bitsy exclaimed. "You've got me there! But go ahead with your young, sullied mind and give us your perspective."

Gus put his hand on his chin, looking up at the raftered ceiling in thought. The March wind blew a tuft of dark-brown hair onto his forehead. He swept it back then said, "There are two things about this war that have sullied me." He waited a moment. "The first is that Daddy has gone off to war." Tears pooled in his eyes.

"That's okay, dear," consoled Auntie Bitsy. "You don't have to talk about it if you don't want to."

"I want to," he asserted. "That's the thing. I would talk about it all day, every day, if I could." A slight sob escaped, accompanied by a tear. "But I don't want to burden anyone. It's mine to bear."

Auntie Abum, who had been silent thus far, commented, "It is all our burden to bear, son. War touches everyone."

He wiped his eyes with his shirt sleeve, took a deep breath, then continued. "The other thing that has sullied me is the news of what Russians found when they entered the biggest German concentration camp." Gus tried to repeat the name as he had heard on the BBC. "Au-sch-witz, I believe it's pronounced. It's in Poland. They said it's the worst of the Nazi death camps. The conditions the prisoners were living in were dreadful. They believe up to six thousand people a day could be gassed to death there." He sighed. "Since I heard that, sometimes I lay in bed at night thinking about it and can't get to sleep."

Everyone was silent.

Gus continued. "Many of the people killed there were Jews. I've never met a Jew before. At least, not that I know of. I thought they were only in those Bible stories you read us, Auntie Bitsy."

"Oh no, dear. They have managed to make it through the pages of the Bible and onto the difficult pages of history. As a matter of fact, there are Jews who live right here in Jamaica."

"Well, why do the Germans want to kill so many of them?" puzzled Gus.

"Somehow, they see them as a threat to what they are trying to achieve. Much the way they see the British and the French and the Russians. A hindrance to German dominance over Europe. To bring back the old Kingdom of Prussia. That's what the Great War was about. They lost, and so here they are at it again." She paused, then in a sort of whispered prayer said, "God forbid it."

"It looks like that's just what he's doing," assured Helen, who had taken a break from her sewing machine to sit with them on the veranda. "I've been overhearing your conversation, which has become woefully gloomy. Let's bring the sunshine back by asking Ruby to bring some lemonade."

Cailin volunteered to deliver the request. On her way to the kitchen, it dawned on her for the first time that studying history had its uses. While the conversation had been enlightening, she had felt unable to contribute. Even so, at least she now had a historical background as to why the Germans were causing so much trouble for everyone.

Before the lemonade was served, the veranda party could hear Essie's voice calling out to someone from the front of the house.

Auntie Abum declared, "What the devil is going on outside?"

"I'll go check," said Cailin.

Gus followed her out of the house where they found Essie standing beside Archie, who was bent over, hands on knees, trying to catch his breath. Sweat dripping down his neck, staining his mostly untucked shirt. Cailin's first thought was Ian's warning to stay away from Archie. She looked at Gus, who looked back at her and was obviously thinking the same thing she was: *Why is he up at the house and in such a condition?*

Essie broke into their silent conversation. "Me believe you should take him in to see you mother." She urged the three of them in with a wave.

Cailin and Gus silently led the way to the veranda.

Before Helen could say a word, Abum asked sternly, "And who might you be, young man?"

"I'm the innkeeper's son," he said, not quite breathing normally. "The name is Archie."

Helen looked away through the railing balusters.

Abum looked him straight in his eyes and asked, "What brings you here, son, and why are you so disheveled?"

"It's Mr. Campbell," he blurted out. "I ran up here from the inn." He gushed the rest like water from a hose. "When he came to pick me up in Sav, he was drunk. Mr. Witcombe convinced him to let me drive. He insisted on going back to the inn where he'd been drinking for the last few days. After more drinks, Mother refused to give him anything else and told him to go home. He got angry. I offered to drive him, but he refused. Before he left, I ran up here to let you know. I didn't know what he'd do." He took a big breath.

"Oh, don't worry." Gus put his hand on Archie's back. "It's not the first time he'll be coming home drunk. When he gets here, he'll stumble to his room, close the door, and sleep it off until tomorrow."

Auntie Bitsy added, "He's a pleasant drunk. Thank God."

Archie looked disappointed and said, "I'm sorry then. I've never seen him leave the inn this drunk, and I thought…"

Gus patted his back. "Never mind. You've shown great gallantry."

"Yes," said Cailin, nodding in agreement. Their eyes met momentarily, then they both looked away.

Helen finally looked at him and said, "Thank you, Archie. Your thoughtfulness is appreciated."

"If you know what's good for you, you'll leave now before he finds you here," directed Abum. "Gus will show you another way to go home." Then she looked over and said, "Gus?"

"Yes, Auntie." Gus led Archie out toward the kitchen and to the west side of the house.

Shortly after, Malcolm's car overshot his parking spot and ended up on the barbecue, with the crunch of drying coffee under his tires. True to Gus's words, Malcolm stumbled into the house, made his way to his bedroom, shut the door, and wasn't seen until the next afternoon.

Cailin excused herself and went up to her room, where she lay down on her bed. She was unsettled. Questions flooded her mind. *What made Archie run all the way up from the inn? That's a long and difficult run! Does he care that much about us?* Then she had to be honest about what she was really feeling. *Or is it that he cares that much for me?*

Malcolm sat at the dinner table the next evening subdued from his lingering hangover. The only sounds at the table were the grind and grate of tines and serrations.

"Who the devil's coming up at this time?" Malcolm said with effort, as though every syllable was disconnected.

"I don't hear anything," responded Abum.

Cailin wasn't surprised at Abum's lack of hearing. Neither was she at her father's acute hearing. His ability to hear reminded her of Prime Minister, who would raise his head suddenly and rotate his ears one hundred and eighty degrees. She often wondered what he was hearing when on occasion he would refuse to go where she was leading him. She could only assume he was avoiding danger.

With his left ear directed toward the Cawdor road, Malcolm insisted, "Well, someone's driving up the road, and I would bet it's Kester." He straightened his posture.

Sure enough, within a few minutes, Kester walked into the dining room.

"I apologize for dropping in during suppertime," said Kester, "but I was in the area visiting a patient and found it opportune to pay a quick visit before I head home."

"Would you like to join us for something to eat?" asked Helen.

"No, thank you. Jane will be waiting for me," he said, sitting at an empty seat at the table. "I would love a glass of water, if it's not too much trouble."

"Not at all," said Helen, and she rang the server's bell to get Ruby's attention.

"How is everyone?" Kester asked, looking around. "You seem a bit glum this evening."

Malcolm answered, "We're fine." Then, obviously steering the discussion away from danger, returned a question. "How are things going with your practice?"

"All is well. As long as people continue to get sick, my practice continues to flourish," Kester said with a smile.

Gus chuckled and said, "That's a good one, Uncle Kester!"

"Yes," chimed in Malcolm, "your Uncle Kester was always a good one for corny jokes. Go ahead, Kester. Tell the one about the three-legged dog."

"If you insist." Kester smiled and turned to where Gus and Cailin were sitting. "A boy said to his father, 'Look! There's a three-legged dog. I feel bad for it.' The father replied, 'I don't see why. He's got one leg more than me!'" Kester's resulting laughter, not his joke, brought levity to the table. Malcolm laughed the hardest, which caught Cailin's attention.

After dinner, Kester said it was time for him to head back to Savanna-la-Mar. As Malcolm walked him to the front porch, Cailin overheard Malcolm say, "I'm doing much better now. I haven't had one in a while." Confused, Cailin excused herself from the table and quietly trailed behind them. She waited inside the house, eavesdropping.

"Are you sure? You know you can ruin your liver if you don't stop drinking?"

"Yes. You've made that clear," Malcolm replied. "I only have one drink every Friday night."

"How is the boy?" Kester said with some hesitancy in his voice.

"What boy?"

"Archie. You know who I'm talking about."

"I've got it all in hand, Kester," Malcolm said in a low growl.

"Malcolm. He's a good boy. He just needs some direction. If you need help—"

"Kester!" Malcolm took a deep breath, then continued calmly, "I've got it. Thank you for your concern."

"Very well," Kester said, "I'll be off then."

Cailin retreated up to her room, where she took Rowena's letter from the bottom drawer of her dresser. She found the part she had read at least ten times earlier that day. *You need to be very careful of that boy. If you become friendly with him and Daddy finds out, something serious could happen.* "That boy." Even though she knew Row's intention was to avoid mentioning Archie's name in case someone else read it, those two words stung her. As if said with scorn. She had not read it that way earlier in the day. But now, after hearing it through the filter of her father's conversation with her uncle, the tone had changed. "That boy!"

She mulled over the exchange. *I've got it all in hand...He's a good boy. He just needs some direction...I've got it. Thank you for your concern.* She wondered what exactly the relationship between Archie and her father was. Beyond the fact that he was the son of the innkeeper, who her father employed, she only knew that her father took him to school on Mondays and picked him up on Fridays. But her uncle seemed to imply her father had more of a role in Archie's life and that he may not be taking that role seriously. What was that role? And what direction did Archie need? Why should her father be the one to give it? She thought about asking her mother, but wiped the thought from her mind. Her mother wouldn't tell her father, but after both Rowena and Ian's warnings, she decided to keep it to herself. She slipped the letter back into the drawer, climbed through her window, and sat on the pitched, shingled roof, embracing her knees and staring out to sea.

31

CAILIN

SUNDAY, APRIL 1, 1945

There was nothing particularly special about Easter Sunday in the Campbell household. Cailin's mother and aunts had breakfast as they usually did at seven thirty. Malcolm slept in until nine. Heather, back from school the day before with Ian and Rowena for the Easter holidays, ate breakfast with the women of the house. Gus was in the cattle shed with Ian, who was overseeing the milking of the cows. Cailin had asked Gus if he was coming to church, but he merely echoed a statement Ian had made the night before: "There's a reason this Easter Sunday's on the first of April." So Cailin left him to his big-cousin worship, and she and Rowena mounted horses for the ride down to the church.

Earlier that week, with her mother's help, Cailin had proudly finished sewing her new sky-blue dress. Her grandmother had not yet embroidered the collar, but she loved the dress just the same. Remembering Esther from the film she had seen during the Christmas holidays, she felt like a lady in it, except for the fact they were not riding sidesaddle. They would have to dismount the horses several yards away from the church property.

The way down was not her usual ritual observance of nature with Prime Minister sauntering out bars and measures on the gravel road. Rather, from the barbecue, Rowena spurred her horse on, which prompted Prime Minister to take off in kind, jolting Cailin backward. She quickly regained her balance and caught up to Rowena and her horse in time to catch Rowena in the middle of a sentence, of which the last word was Munro.

Rowena began talking about the boy she had written to Cailin about. His name was George, who Rowena thought a royal name, reminding Cailin unnecessarily that the king's name was George. She went on about his being tall and that a lock of his dark-brown hair was always falling onto his forehead, which he was continually combing back with his fingers. She told Cailin she had seen him one other time since the letter she had written her. That time, the boys had come over to Hampton to a dance. Oh! What a wonderful dancer he was! She went on and on, ending her monologue singing the Munro fight song: "In Arce Sitam Quis! When we shoot, we never miss. When we cheer, we cheer like this, M-U-N-R-O!"

Just about the time Cailin was catching on to the song, they exited the Cawdor road. Rowena's demeanor changed instantly. She hushed Cailin, saying they couldn't be seen carrying on that way. A little puzzled, Cailin did as her sister instructed, thinking it fit the unusual way Rowena had been acting on the way down. Her sister, who had always been the epitome of relaxed and in control, was now excitable and unpredictable.

～

Before entering the church doorway, Rowena stopped for a moment, pulled her skirt taut to lessen the wrinkles from riding, and lightly patted her hair with her right hand. Then she strode up the aisle, stopped halfway, and slid into a pew on the left side, leaving room for her sister. Cailin followed her, realizing she had never sat that far up the aisle, nor had she been to church that early since her second visit. Even though she felt more confident in her new Easter dress, she still felt as if all eyes were on her.

Rowena shifted her head to the right and slightly back. Cailin instinctively did the same and saw a handsome boy on the other side of the aisle, one row back. Seated in a row with a man, a woman, and several children, he glanced at Rowena with a barely perceptible nod and then looked forward. A well-dressed family. She recognized two of the children as having teased her about her clothes the first few times she came to church.

Just then, the priest mounted the podium, stood behind the lectern, worded a prayer honoring the day of Christ's resurrection, and enjoined the congregation to sing the opening hymn as the organ breathed the first notes of "Christ the Lord is Risen Today." As everyone rose to sing, Cailin forgot about her nemeses and her sister's erraticism and good-looking boyfriend. She lost herself in the organ and vocal notes waltzing around her and right through the open stained-glass windows.

At the end of the service, the priest gave his benediction, then the congregation began to file into the aisles and toward the door. Rowena looked over to where George had been sitting. His family was standing in their row greeting another family who sat behind them, but George wasn't there. She urged Cailin to let her pass and pushed her way through the exiting congregants.

Cailin did her best to follow Rowena, but when she got to the back pew, her eyes fastened on Archie, whose facial expression gave away that he'd been waiting for her.

She was stunned and blurted out, "What are you doing here?"

"Can't a man go to church without being given the third degree?"

"Well…of course." She collected herself. "As the priest says, all are welcome in the house of God."

He stood up. "Thank you, Miss Campbell." Then he added, "My, aren't you looking quite the lady today? I believe this is the first time I've seen you in a dress."

She blushed. "Thank you. I made it myself."

"If I may be allowed to say so, it's impeccably made, and the color reminds me of the sky over Oristano Bay."

He offered her his arm, so she held on to it, followed him out the door, wavering between astonishment and embarrassment.

Outside the church doors, Cailin found Rowena staring blankly at George as he walked through the gate to the road.

Not being able to ask what transpired, as Archie was there, Cailin let go of his arm and said, "Rowena. This is Archie. He's Ms. Price's son. You know, the lady who runs Daddy's inn."

Rowena inhaled slowly and turned to Archie, saying, "Yes. I know who he is." She reached out to shake his hand. "Pleased to meet you. I'm Rowena." Then she looked back at the gate and said, "It's time to go, Cailin. Have a good Easter, Mr. Price."

As soon as they mounted their horses, Rowena spoke. "I thought I told you to stay away from him! If Daddy knows you are in any kind of friendly relations with him, he'll have your neck!"

"But why?" she demanded. "What's wrong if I talk with him?" She hesitated. "He's just a friend. And I don't have anyone else to talk with but Gus."

Rowena used her reins to signal her horse to move. "Just trust me. If Daddy finds out, you both will regret the day you ever met." Then she added, "Friend or no friend."

"You're a hypocrite! You just got snubbed by George, and now you want me to snub Archie?"

Rowena inhaled sharply, her eyes welling up.

Cailin spurred Prime Minister harder than she ever had, and he jerked into a full gallop. Cailin yelled, "I won't stop talking to him!"

There was no Easter lunch. No Easter egg hunt. It was just another Sunday. The only Easter ritual Cailin took part in was the egg-white-in-water rite. Before sunrise, an egg was cracked with the white skillfully separated from its yoke and poured into half a glass of water. The glass was then placed where the sun would shine on it at sunrise. By midday the egg white would have formed into a shape, and the partaker would then study the artifact and interpret their future. If a ship was seen, a journey would be probable. Money meant riches. A wedding ring meant marriage. A casket meant death. There was always that Russian-roulette aspect to it. No one knew anyone who had died shortly after seeing a casket, but older Jamaicans refused to participate—it was for the young. The only other person who took part in the ritual anymore was Gus. The others felt it was silly.

On arriving home from church, Cailin remembered her glass and went to read her egg white. She only played for the fun of it, having no use for a journey, money, a husband, and definitely not a coffin. Before looking, she paused and thought she might have use for a wedding ring. She laughed and looked in the glass. At first, all she saw was a mess of egg white. Then she thought she saw the ocean. She looked closer. It reminded her of the rough waves breaking over the Oristano Bay reef. She wondered what that could mean.

After dinner that evening, Gus, knowing the BBC schedule, asked to be excused from the table and turned on the wireless. News of the war seemed to be more encouraging of late. With a resolute tone, the announcer reported that during the previous day the Third Algerian Infantry Division had crossed the Rhine, leading the charge for the First Army. This was a promising development.

The family cheered while Gus danced about the room boasting, "Take that, Hitler!"

Everyone laughed and Auntie Bitsy chimed in with another supporting "Take that, Hitler!"

Pushing back his chair, Malcolm remarked, "Well, with all this victory in the air, I'll be heading down to the inn to do a little celebrating of my own." As he walked to the hallway, he signaled for Ian to come along.

Seeing this, Cailin asked, "Daddy, can I come too?"

Rowena, who was seated beside Cailin, elbowed her, then gave her a warning look.

"No," he responded from the hallway. "I'll be home late."

32

KIMBERLY, SOUTH AFRICA

20 AUGUST 1916

Dear Abum,

I am writing to give you the sad news that Cuddy has died in honorable service to His Majesty King George V. He was serving as a medical doctor with the South African First Infantry Brigade, and I am told, on 17 July during the Battle of Delville Wood in France, German artillery caused an explosion in the South African camp infirmary where Cuddy was on duty. I know this must come as a shock to you as it has been twelve years since we last corresponded, and you had no word he had joined the war effort. You can only imagine the effect it has had on me, left here in Kimberly with two children and no other family for support.

Yes, I mentioned two children. You know about Alexandra, but I had no opportunity to let you know of Lionel, who was born two years after his sister. The enclosed picture is of the four of us. It was taken shortly before Cuddy left for France. I hope it will help you and the children to remember him.

I regret that I had to stop writing to you. As you will remember, Cuddy forbid me from doing so. It hurt me to be cut off from you and my children. If you can find it in your heart, please write and let me know how they all are and what they are doing.

After the war is over, the children and I plan on moving to Scotland, where Cuddy's old professor has offered to put us up until we can get our feet on the ground. Oh, when will this horrible war be over?

Please give the children my address, so they can write to me if they are so inclined. I would love to hear from them.

Warmest Regards,
Winnie

$$33$$

ARCHIE

TUESDAY-WEDNESDAY, APRIL 10-11, 1945

icking himself up off the gravel pathway, Archie detained his embarrassment and frustration behind bars.

Yet things had gotten out of hand. Not only had he been tripped in front of the prettiest girl in the school and her friends, but it was by some no-name boy who had apparently been egged on by a group of other no-name boys. It would have been one thing if it had been his nemeses, Clive and Devon, or even someone from their wolf pack, none of whom were anywhere in sight at that moment. But now it seemed the entire school was in on this grand new game, and he was the leather ball.

Embarrassment and frustration bulging through his self-restraining prison bars, he could stand it no longer. Turning to the boy who had tripped him, he demanded, "What was that for? Who are you trying to impress? None of these girls even know who you are!"

The boy shot back, "Maybe so, but who'd want to know you —a murderer's bastard son!"

Archie didn't understand what the boy meant by *murderer*;

although he recalled Clive and Devon saying a similar thing a few months back. The part he understood, however, touched his rawest nerve. Embarrassment and frustration transmuted into desperation and rage, breaking through the bars and sending Archie hurtling toward the boy, spitting out a "son of a bitch," with his right fist swinging and connecting squarely with the boy's left cheekbone. The boy reeled backward to the ground. Archie was instantly on top of him, fists pumping like pistons against the boy's face.

The girls screamed.

The group of boys stared with mouths open.

For Archie, everything was in slow motion, including the blood that spurted from the boy's nose.

His next perception was of himself being pulled off the boy and his flailing arms being straitjacketed by larger arms harnessing him from behind.

Archie sat on a wooden chair outside the headmaster's office with his face resting in his cupped hands. He had preferred to stand because of the raw-bottomed caning he had received, but the headmaster had demanded he remain seated. Malcolm had been immediately sent for and now, late in the afternoon, he sat in the headmaster's office. The only sound coming from the closed door was the headmaster's muffled voice.

In less than ten minutes, Malcolm walked out of the office, and without a word, grabbed Archie by the arm, escorting him straight to the car. When the car pulled onto Beckford Street, all Archie could think of was eating and going to bed. This day had been more than he had bargained for. Malcolm, however, took a left turn on to Barracks Road, the road that led out of the town and toward Oristano.

An objection rose in Archie's throat but stuck there. He knew better. Malcolm's face was set like a sculpted ancient Roman bust, with the ends of the mouth slanted down in an eternal scowl. This was not just the usual silent car trip with Malcolm. This felt more like a silent-treatment journey, which was the longest kind.

Archie played a sort of game, to not have to think about what Malcolm would say when his scowl finally broke. He counted the landmarks along the way, anticipating each one. First, Ferris Cross. Next, the little one-car bridge. The big breadfruit tree. The enshrouding tunnel-like run through the impermeable vegetation. The ocean wall—he expected the waves to be crashing, but they were uncharacteristically calm. Like Malcolm. Before the storm. Oristano Beach. Left turn. The Inn.

The car pulled up the winding drive, which seemed extra-long today. About halfway up, his mother came out on the balcony above the porte-cochère, drink in hand and waving demonstratively.

When the car stopped, Malcolm spoke his first words. "Get out of the car."

Archie did as he was told.

Gracie stepped back in surprise and called, "Archie?" Then she addressed Malcolm, who was still in the idling car. "Why did you bring him back?"

Malcolm simply replied, "Your son won't be going back to Manning's." Then, without another word, he turned the car around and drove off.

Archie stood dumbfounded. This was the last thing he'd expected. Both he and Gracie stared speechlessly at the car as it drove back down the driveway.

For the rest of that day, it was Archie's turn to administer the silent treatment. No matter how his mother peppered him with questions—"Why are you back in the middle of the week? What did Mr. Campbell mean by you're not going back to Manning's? Did you do something bad?"—he wouldn't say a word except for those inferred by his demeanor. Not even

Abbie could get him to talk, much less eat. After refusing dinner, he left the house.

Turning onto the road, his legs took possession of him, flinging him into a full-on run. He didn't know exactly why, but he sensed that if he ran fast enough, he could leave behind the crushing feeling in his chest that had started as a twinge when Malcolm turned the car left toward the inn instead of going straight toward the Witcombes' house. The crushing feeling grew incrementally until it had amplified into an unbearable inner explosion that kept his feet moving in a mad dash to nowhere.

Still in his school clothes from the previous day, Archie got out of bed sometime after ten that morning. On his way to the kitchen, his mother, who was seated on the balcony, caught sight of him.

"Where did you go so late last night?" she asked, cigarette smoke accompanying every word. She puckered her lips and expelled the rest in one breath.

"Last night?" He paused in mock thought. "I can't recall. That was so long ago," He turned walking toward the kitchen.

Halfway there, he turned around and, looking at his mother intently, asked, "Is Malcolm my father?"

Gracie's torso spun toward him; her brow furrowed. "Why would you say that?"

Archie was quick to respond. "I don't know, Gracie. Maybe because he's been taking me back and forth to Manning's. Maybe because he brought us over here from Mobay to run the inn. Maybe because the boys at Manning's call me a bastard of a murdering womanizer. Hell, even Mick said Malcolm had a bastard son!" He held out his arms, palms up. "So, I must be it."

Gracie stubbed out her cigarette and rose from her chair.

She walked over to Archie and, putting her hands on the sides of his shoulders, said, "I am going to tell you who your father is not." Then she said with resolution in her voice, "Your father is *not* Malcolm Campbell."

"I would like to believe that, Mother. I would really like to believe that." He shook his head. "I've been trying to deny it myself, but everything adds up to Malcolm."

"Listen to me!" she squeezed his shoulders. "I was the one who gave birth to you, so I am the one who should know." Then she stated with slow, deliberate words, "Malcolm is not your father."

"Are you sure, Mother?" He looked into her eyes, trying to decipher performance from reality. "Are you sure Malcolm is not my father?"

She took hold of his face. "Archie. I am your mother. I know I have not always been the best of mothers. I have had to do things I am not proud of. Things that were done for our survival. But you must believe me when I tell you—Mr. Campbell is not your father."

As far back as he could remember, he had never heard her admit to doing anything wrong, although he knew she had. Thrown off the scent, he took a deep breath and said, "Okay." Then he resumed his walk to the kitchen.

"Mass Archie! Where you was last night? Me did stay up watching for you till you come in. It was so late."

He sat down at the table and after a while said, "Sorry, Abbie." Then he went silent again.

After serving him breakfast, Abbie bent down and stole a shoulder hug, saying, "What no dead, no call it duppy.[1]"

He appreciated her encouragement but could only return a feeble smile.

～

The early afternoon rolled around to the sound of a car making its way up the drive. Archie flinched at the thought of seeing Malcolm again, figuring he must be ready to talk. He covered his face with his bed pillow.

To his surprise, he heard a male voice that didn't belong to Malcolm. The voice called up the stairs from the porte-cochère, "Ms. Price? May I come up?"

The voice sounded familiar. Almost like Malcolm's, but with less gruffness to it.

The voice spoke again, "Pardon my unexpected visit, but I'm here to see both you and Archie."

Archie sat up in his bed, having matched the voice to a face. "Kester Campbell!" He jumped out of bed, pulled on his shoes, and made his way to living room.

Holding his hat with both hands, Kester said, "Archie. Glad to see you again. Sorry it has to be under these circumstances."

"What circumstances?" Gracie immediately questioned.

Kester hesitated, then said, "It's about Archie being expelled from Manning's."

"Yes, Malcolm left us without an explanation about that," she responded.

Looking at Archie, he said, "Sorry to hear it."

Archie shrugged and then pushed back the unkempt mop of hair that was resting on his forehead.

Putting his hat on the arm of the couch, Kester asked, "Do you mind if we sit down so I can explain what happens from this point?"

What happens from this point? The words caught Archie's attention. Over the last day, there were no thoughts of *from this point*. He thought the point a full stop. A period at the end of a sentence. He had imagined living and working at the inn until he was an old man. Like his mother, carrying on in grand old theatrical style. His life a farce. The thought came to him, *Just like Gatsby's*. Up to this point, he had been intrigued by Gatsby's life, but he had thought little about Gatsby's death, precipitated by the hypocritical house of cards Gatsby had meticulously built.

"A drink, Mr. Campbell?" Gracie offered.

"No, thank you, Ms. Price. As a doctor, I've seen what the stuff can do."

He sat down and began by asking, "Ms. Price, has Archie told you about what happened at Manning's yesterday?"

"I wish he had. Not that I haven't asked."

Kester looked at Archie, then said to her, "Archie got into a fight yesterday. He beat a boy badly. The boy was unconscious for a while, and there was some loss of blood." He paused. "The thing is, this is the second fight he's been in this year."

Gracie looked at Archie as though expecting an answer. He kept his eyes on Kester.

"What's more, apparently, Archie's grades were very good at the beginning of the school year, mostly A's. But as the year has progressed, his grades have declined." Kester breathed deeply, then started to ask Archie a question but stopped before a word came out.

"So, what's to become of him now?" asked Gracie, almost as if it were Kester's fault. "What's he to do about his schooling? I can't afford for him to stay here forever. He needs to make a living of his own."

"Ms. Price," Kester said firmly. "Please. The boy is right here."

"I'm sorry," she said with her head lowered. "It's just that…" she paused, not finishing her thought.

Kester looked at Archie and continued. "There is a plan from here on forward. The headmaster is allowing you to complete your classes from home. I've picked up your belongings and your schoolbooks from the Witcombes, and I've brought your schoolwork from your teachers for the rest of the week. Every Sunday afternoon, I'll come by with new assignments and pick up the work you've done from the previous week. At the end of the term, on the first day of summer holidays, I'll bring you to Manning's to take your exams. Your grades from the beginning of the year prove you can complete the year successfully." He looked directly at Archie and asked, "Are you willing to do this?"

"Of course he is," piped in Gracie. Then, in dramatic form, she got up to shake Kester's hand. "Thank you so very—"

Kester cut her off. "I need to hear it from Archie, Ms. Price." He kept his eyes on Archie, who sat silently balancing his thoughts as on a fulcrum.

When he achieved equilibrium, he said, "Yes," as if to himself.

34

CAILIN

TUESDAY, MAY 8, 1945

"Hitler dead! Hitler dead!" Cailin heard the shout as she brushed Prime Minister's hind leg in the early morning light.

She looked up to see Samfie running past the cotton tree and flapping his arms about. She laughed and said, "Why is he saying that? Doesn't he know Hitler already died a week ago?"

Sharpe, who was cinching Prime Minister's saddle, sucked his teeth and replied, "Samfie been missing for almost that long. Maybe him no know."

"I didn't realize he was gone," Cailin commented.

"That's because him never doing much of anything around here anyway."

When Samfie reached the barbecue declaring the last of his victory chant and looking pleased with himself, Sharpe questioned him, "Then you never know say Hitler dead from time?"

"Well, no…" He scratched his head then replied, "Me really just find out." Then, as if he remembered another juicy morsel, he leaned forward and announced, "The war is over!"

Cailin dropped the horse brush. "What? The war is over?"

"Yes," replied Samfie with a broad smile, as though he was expecting a tip.

Cailin spun on her heel and ran toward the house, where her mother and Ruby were standing by the front door and Essie was sticking her head out the kitchen window.

"The war is over! He says the war's over!" she announced, with a fraction of disbelief in her voice. "Turn on the wireless!"

Gus, who never seemed far from the wireless since Hitler's death, made it there first. When Cailin got there, he was coaxing the thing to warm up, which usually took about ten seconds but now seemed ten minutes.

The first sounds they heard were a mass of voices singing. But it was hard to tell the tune as the announcer kept speaking over them. He reported that the streets of London and areas around all the national monuments were packed with crowds singing, cheering, hugging, dancing, and, in some places, burning effigies of Hitler. He announced Parliament had declared the day Victory in Europe Day and that it and the following day would be national holidays.

There was a general sigh of relief in the Campbell household. They'd heard what they had been hoping to hear.

Cailin let out a cheer, but Gus hushed her.

The announcer enumerated the sacrifices of the six-year war—food and clothes rationed, cities bombed, the death of so many loved ones—but that now there was, all over Britain, the sense of great relief.

The programming continued this way for some time with a sort of unintended choral response back and forth between crowd and announcer. Then the announcer reported that the Prime Minister would make the formal declaration of Germany's unconditional surrender from 10 Downing Street at three o'clock that afternoon.

"Oh, that's such a long time from now," Cailin complained.

Helen and Auntie Bitsy chuckled, and Gus promptly

responded, "London is six hours ahead of us. That means the announcement will be given at nine o'clock this morning, Jamaican time. Just under an hour and a half from now."

"That's right, Angus!" Miss Recas said, beaming.

Cailin shook her head and blurted out, "Show off!"

"That's enough, Cailin," chided Helen. "Breakfast should be ready soon."

With that, Essie and Ruby left the doorway they had stationed themselves at and headed for the kitchen.

The high-pitched tone of the wireless marched victoriously throughout the house while breakfast was being prepared and then served.

Malcolm, who had been out on the property when Samfie brought the news, was heading to his office when he heard the radio playing. Walking into the house, he found the family seated for breakfast. "What's going on here? Why is the wireless blasting?"

"Haven't you heard?" asked Abum.

"Heard what?"

"The war in Europe is over," she replied. "They have pronounced it a national holiday in Britain."

Malcolm stood silent, then declared, "Well, well, the Reich has fallen. You have to give them credit for giving it their best shot." He pulled out his chair and called, "Ruby! Get me a plate!"

"But, Daddy, you already ate breakfast earlier," said Cailin, surprised.

Then, with eyebrows raised and arms stretched out, he said to everyone around the table, "This is cause for a second-breakfast celebration! If it's a national holiday in Britain, then as a colony of Britain, it must be a national holiday in His Majesty's favorite jewel!"

Ruby placed a plate and a knife and fork in front of Malcolm. "Here you go, sah."

"Ruby."

"Yes, sah."

"Go tell Sharpe to tell the workers I have declared today a holiday at Cawdor!"

"My, you're in rare form," scoffed Abum. "Why don't you hold a banquet and invite everyone from the highways and byways?"

"Well, I might just do that!" replied Malcolm with a jaunty laugh.

"Does that mean we have a holiday from school?" asked Cailin.

Miss Recas scowled.

"Yes, indeed!" replied Malcolm. "As a matter of fact, in celebration of the end of the war, Cailin, why don't you do one of your jigs for us?"

Cailin hesitated.

"Go on!" encouraged Malcolm.

"I don't know, Daddy. I'm still eating."

"That's never stopped you before. Go on," he insisted.

She paused, then said, "It's just that I'm getting too old for that sort of thing."

"Well, hallelujah!" interjected Abum. "The girl has finally realized it. Not that I haven't been saying it for some time now."

"Fiddlesticks!" responded Malcolm.

"She's right, Malcolm," Helen said. "She's past that stage."

He sat back and turned his attention elsewhere. "Okay then, Gus, how are you going to celebrate? I expect they'll be sending your father home on the next banana boat."

Gus sat forward. "Do you think so, Uncle Malcolm?"

"I don't see why not."

This time, Auntie Bitsy spoke up, "Now, Malcolm, don't get the boy's hopes up so soon. There will be more for the military to do before they're sent home. That is how it was with the Great War."

Seeing Gus sink back down into his chair, Cailin diverted the conversation. "It looks as though we have about half an hour until Mr. Churchill's announcement." Then she elbowed Gus. "See, you're not the only one who can read a clock, Mr. Know It All."

Gathered around the wireless, with Essie, Ruby, and Sharpe standing at the living room door, the family waited for Churchill to speak.

When he finally stepped to the microphone, there was silence, but for the scratchy crackling of the wireless, ever present in the background.

Yesterday...in the early morning hours...[1]

There he was, his voice paced and resolute.

General Jodl of the German High Command...and Admiral Doenitz, the head of the German State...

The Campbell household collectively leaned forward.

...signed the instrument of surrender.

Gus raised both hands in victory, making the V-for-victory symbol, while the rest of the household cheered along with him, sounding like the crowds in London.

Then Gus quieted everyone, while Churchill summarized the war—from Germany's attack on Poland in 1939, to Britain declaring war on Germany, to the occupation of France, to Russia's involvement, to the United States joining the effort, to almost the entire world fighting together against the evildoers.

At that, Gus jumped to his feet and exclaimed with unmeasurable pride, "Daddy fought against the evildoers! Daddy beat the evildoers!"

Everyone affirmed him with a collective, "Yes, he did!" while the Prime Minister's voice crackled in the background, expressing heartfelt gratitude and compliments to Britain's allies.

Churchill went on to encourage Great Britain to have its moment of celebration but then to remember the great challenge that yet lay before them—the challenge to subdue Japan for the evils she had wrought on Britain, America, and much of the world. Then, with Henry the Fifth band-of-brothers fervor, Churchill rallied the nation forward with the universal British cry, *God save the King!*

With that, everyone in the house, including Essie, Ruby, and Sharpe, proclaimed, "God save the King!"

Later that morning, Essie approached Helen in her sewing room. "Excuse me, Miss Helen. Can I have a word with you?"

Looking up from the foot-pedaled sewing machine, Helen replied, "Yes, Essie. What is it?"

"Me was thinking for some time now to visit with me people them in Beeston Spring. And, with celebration in the air, me did think this is a good time to ask."

"Today?" Helen asked, with eyebrows raised.

"No, ma'am. Me wouldn't do that to you," she replied a little defensively. "Me was thinking this Saturday and Sunday. And Ruby say she can manage the cooking."

Helen thought about it briefly, then said, "You're right. This is a good time with the victory celebration and all. Mass Malcolm will be more inclined to understand. I will tell him."

"Thank you, Miss Helen," Essie said, beaming.

When she got back to the kitchen, Sharpe was still hanging around as he had been doing most of the day "celebrating," as he put it, with her and Ruby. He'd been more like a circling fly she couldn't swat away, no matter how hard she tried. He knew her efforts weren't serious as every so often he'd catch the coy corners of her mouth upturned.

"Why you so happy, Miss Essie?" He imitated the skip in her step he'd seen as she crossed from the house to the kitchen.

"You think you is the only one can celebrate?" She brushed past him. "Well, Miss Helen just agree to let me go to Beeston Spring come the weekend."

"Oh?" he responded, a little at a loss.

"Yes, indeed. Me going see me family and go to church on Sunday. It's a long time me no get to go to church."

Steadying himself, he said. "Well, me tell you what. You going to need somebody to carry you suitcase and give you little company on the way." His confidence increased to the edge of cockiness. "And me know somebody who is just the right person to do it."

Essie spun around, hands on hips. "It's not everyone me like to play the fool with."

Sharpe felt the force of what she said but couldn't help feeling this was camouflage for what was beneath, so he tried the humble approach, saying, "Yes, Miss Essie, me know say you no like to play game, so what me telling you is that if you want somebody to accompany you to Beeston Spring, me will be glad to do it."

Essie looked out the kitchen window without giving a reply.

At that point, Ruby, who had been sitting on a kitchen stool chuckling, wisely excused herself and left the kitchen.

Sharpe stood there in the silence, determined to wait for an answer.

"Well." She looked back at him. "Truth is, me could use somebody to help me carry me things and the few things me want to bring me family."

Not believing what he had just heard, he leaned forward and asked, "Yes?"

"And sometime me feel a little afraid when it's me one passing by a big man."

"Me was goin say that, too."

"And me guess you could stay at me brother house up the hill." She looked up at him and stipulated, "But you have to go to church Sunday morning."

He nodded. "Me will do that."

She turned to look out the window again and said as if to herself, "Me have to pray about it first."

"Take you time, Miss Essie."

"But," she looked at him again, "even if God tell me yes, you have to get Busha permission."

"Of course. I will do it right now!"

Sharpe was out the door before Essie could give a proper objection to his impetuous response.

After Malcolm confirmed Essie's leave with Helen, he shook his head and slapped Sharpe on the back, saying, "You son of a gun!" He laughed and repeated, "You son of a gun, you!" Then added, "Just make sure things are covered for the weekend." And that was it.

Amazed, Sharpe walked away, looking upward, and said, "Thank you."

Later that afternoon, Cailin and Gus rode down to Oristano to see if there were any victory celebrations happening in the village. Nothing that was happening was particularly interesting to the children, except that there were more people at the rum bar than usual. She even recognized a couple of the property workers, who must have felt emboldened by their victory day off to forsake the Hakin rum bar and risk being ridiculed at Mr. Lyn's rum bar.

When Mr. Lyn saw Cailin and Gus, he called them into the shop, saying, "Come, children. Me have a special treat for you today." He handed them a box of Chinese sweeties and a pack of Paradise Plums.

Gus exclaimed, "Thank you, Mr. Lyn. This is the best treat you've ever given us!"

"Well," explained Mr. Lyn, "The war is over, and business should pick up again, so why not share some of the goods with me favorite customers?" He laughed, then added, "Oh, there is some mail for the big house." He went into the back room to fetch it and brought out three letters.

"Thank you, Mr. Lyn." Cailin said as she sorted through them. "One for Daddy, one for me, and..." Gus grabbed the third letter before she could say, "...another for Daddy."

When he saw it wasn't for him, he shoved it back in her hand, turned away, and walked out of the shop. They mounted their horses and headed down to the empty beach, where they ambled along in silence.

Eventually, Gus asked, "Do you think he's coming back?"

Cailin felt a bubble rise in her throat. She pushed it back down, then replied, "Yes. He's coming back for you, Gus."

"But Churchill said the war against the Japanese is still on. And besides, suppose he was killed at the end of the German war? Suppose he gets killed before midnight tonight?"

Gus was looking at her for an answer, which she found odd, as he was always the one giving answers, even when she hadn't asked for any. Besides, how could she be sure of her answer? But she knew she had to assure him. "Gus...your father is coming back. Believe me."

He looked toward the sea and asked, "How can you be so sure?"

"Because love is like a magnet. Remember what we learned about magnets in school? Well, Uncle Tam's north pole and your south pole are always pulling toward each other. That's why you can't stop thinking about him and sometimes even want to cry when you think of him." Cailin paused. "He feels the same."

He looked back at Cailin, wide eyed. "You really think so?"

"Yes." She put her hand on his shoulder.

Gus nodded slowly as if trying to believe.

After a while, he asked, "Who's your letter from?"

"Row," she replied.

"What does it say? Open it!" he demanded.

"Sorry, it's girl stuff," she said, patting her pocket to make sure the letter was still in there.

"Girl stuff?" he said mockingly. "What's coming over you these days? You used to tell me everything. If this is what happens to girls, then I don't think I'll ever get married." He threw his hands to the sky and repeated, "Girl stuff!"

Cailin's mind raced with thoughts of what could be in Rowena's letter, which led her to think about Archie. She hadn't seen him since Easter Sunday, even though Gus had told her he was no longer attending Manning's and was living at home. While she'd wanted to see him, she was reluctant to go to the inn, hoping instead that he would turn up at church on a Sunday. He never did. She now considered stopping at the inn, telling herself she only wanted to see how the war victory was being celebrated there. But Rowena and Ian's warnings about Archie kept rolling around her head.

As she and Gus approached the driveway to the inn, she straddled the fence on whether to take the left turn in. Just then, she spotted her father's car coming around the corner and heading toward them. She panicked, wondering if he was going to the inn. When he took the turn into the inn, her heart fell, not because she knew her father would be drinking and wouldn't come home that night, but because now she couldn't go to the inn—she couldn't see Archie.

On arriving home, Cailin rushed upstairs to her room and pulled out Rowena's letter. She learned Rowena had seen the boy again at the last Hampton and Munro dance for the year. He had explained to her he'd been feeling sick on Easter Sunday at the church. He told her sweet things about how beautiful she was and how she made him feel special. Then he kissed her, which made her head light with love. Oh! She was in love and looked forward to the next time she would see him, which would be over the summer in Oristano. The letter instructed Cailin to burn it as soon as she had read it so that no one else could read it, especially their father. Then she was again sworn to secrecy.

Immediately after reading the letter, Cailin went to the kitchen and threw it in the wood-burning stove.

3 5

CAILIN

MAY 12 - JULY 21, 1945

The old, fastidiously kept great house sat on a small hill that sloped gently to the road outlining the front of the property. The Lennox property itself was not as large as Cawdor, but it was large enough that Cailin and Gus always found plenty to do on their visits. This one was to be for a week.

Lennox was where Cailin's mother had been born and raised. She found it hard to think of her mother as a child playing on this land, yet there was something about the kindliness of it that reminded her of her mother—the cool inland mountain air, the soothing roll of the surrounding hills, the feeling that this place would always be just as it was at that very moment.

That day, however, Cailin had a headache, which she figured was from the long, bumpy car ride her grandfather had given them from Cawdor to Lennox. Upon her arrival, her grandmother scolded her for wearing shorts. She was in no mood for exploring the property with Gus anyway, so she complied, changing into her sky-blue dress. Her grandmother complimented her on it and agreed to embroider the collar. As the afternoon wore on, she became nauseous and asked to be excused to lie down.

That evening, queasy as she was, she came to the dinner table, but after two mouthfuls, she again excused herself and threw up in the enamel-covered metal wash basin in her bedroom. Helen assisted her with changing and put her to bed. By two o'clock that morning, she had a temperature of a hundred and two and was suffering from ague. Helen had put two and two together by this time and knew exactly what it was—malaria. Cailin would be experiencing recurring chills, sweating, fluctuations in temperature, and delirium with only brief moments of lucidity for weeks to come.

She woke up the next morning to everyone hovering over her bed and Helen complaining, "Every May I tell the children to stay away from the cotton tree as the rainwater pools in its roots." She felt a cool washrag on her forehead. Her mother added, "That accursed cotton tree!"

Cailin slipped back and forth through the thin veil that separates wake and sleep, hearing bits and pieces of Cissy and Mass Whim debating the exact wording for the telegram to the doctor. The last thing she remembered was her grandfather kissing her on her head, telling her he was going to Darliston to get her some quinine water and to send the telegram. With a chuckle, he whispered in her ear, "I'm jolly well going to write it my way." That was the last thing she remembered for quite a while.

The time in Lennox was a blur for Cailin. It was as though she was under a sheer funeral pall. From time to time she could dimly see and hear bits and pieces of what was going on around her, but she was mostly in a dark dream world consisting of chills and groans with the occasional interlude of black and white dream sequences, as though she was at the Doric Cinema in Savanna-la-Mar watching scenes from Cawdor and Oristano—her father, Gus, Prime Minister, Essie,

Rowena. Archie appeared in more than one scene. Once she was sitting beside him by the river behind the inn. But mostly, there was darkness.

Regularly, in the recesses of her mind, she would hear a familiar soothing voice, deep and jovial. There was a cadence about it. Not like Prime Minister's hooves keeping time. But there was regularity, nonetheless. Once, in a moment of clarity, she recognized her grandfather's voice. She opened her eyes and raised her head enough to see him sitting in the bedroom chair, reading a book out loud. Her head fell back, and she drifted off.

"What day is it today?" asked Cailin with the feel of cotton in her mouth.

The maid, who had been sitting in the chair nodding off, looked up and saw Cailin staring at her and yelled, "Miss Helen! Miss Helen! She wake!" She got up and ran out of the room. "Miss Cailin wake!"

A moment later, her mother and grandfather were in the room fussing over her, with her grandmother trailing behind in arthritic pain.

"My girl! My girl!" Helen kissed her forehead. "How are you feeling?"

"I don't know," replied Cailin in a soft and slow voice. "Like I've been lying underground," she took a breath, "and I've just popped my head out of the dirt."

Mass Whim responded with a laugh and commented, "Well, it's a good thing we didn't plant any of Cissy's Gerbera daisies on you. They would have been ruined with your resurrection."

Cissy corrected him. "She's not quite resurrected yet. She's got a good couple months more to go." Then to make sure he understood, she stipulated, "She is to stay in bed except to use the chimmy[1] and to take a bath."

"You're right, dear," he acquiesced. Then, with a twinkle in his eye, he asked, "Can I still read *Great Expectations* to her?" He gave her a playful hug.

"You obstreperous man," she said, pretending to swat him. "Of course you can. It will only do her good to hear you read Dickens and take her mind off her own troubles."

Looking around, Cailin asked, "Mummy? Where is Gus?"

"Grandpa took him back to Cawdor three weeks ago," answered Helen. She sat down beside her and stroked her hair. "You've been sick for a month. You've got malaria."

"Yes…I faintly remember you saying that…and something about the cotton tree being cursed."

"Yes, I did say that, didn't I," replied Helen thoughtfully. Then, returning to the task at hand, she asked, "Do you want anything, dear?"

"Well…since Gus is not here…perhaps you could send word…for him to write me."

"You know your sisters and Ian are back from school. Would you like to hear from them?"

"Yes…Anybody who'll write."

As her mother was getting off the bed, a thought came to Cailin. "Oh…and can you ask that all letters be sealed…for privacy?"

Her grandmother, taken aback, asked, "Whatever for? No one will read any of the letters."

Mass Whim piped in, "But, Cissy, she's a young lady now and deserves her privacy. You know she turned fifteen two weeks ago." He looked at Cailin, and said, "Happy belated birthday, my pigeon!"

~

The next day, Mass Whim peeped his head into the room, and seeing Cailin's eyes open, came in waving a book in the air saying, "Time for Dickens!"

While he sat on the chair and opened to the bookmarked page, Cailin said softly, "Sometimes…I heard you reading to me. It made me feel…safe."

He looked up and was speechless for a moment. Returning his eyes to the book, he said, "Well, maybe I should tell you what has happened up to this point?"

"Yes, please."

"It won't be a lengthy retelling as I could never tell it like Dickens. At any rate, I've been looking forward to the next chapter ever since I read to you yesterday. You see, there was a poor boy by the name of Pip and a rich girl named Estella…"

Mass Whim delineated all the salient points of the novel up to chapter twenty-nine, then continued reading one chapter a day to her. He brought the novel to life with his rhythmic cadence and vocal inflections. Cailin never knew books could be so captivating. This was so much better than reading the books Miss Recas gave her.

One morning when he was reading, Cailin weakly motioned with her hand and said, "Stop. Stop. Read that bit again."

"Which bit?"

"The part where he says, 'I loved her against reason.'"

Mass Whim found the line and read dramatically, "'I loved her against reason, against promise, against peace, against hope, against happiness, against all discouragement that could be. Once for all, I loved her nonetheless because I knew it, and it had no more influence in restraining me than if I had devoutly believed her to be human perfection.' There you are, my girl. How was that?"

"Good, Grandpa." Then she looked away from him, staring out the window. She thought about Archie. For some time, she had begun to think of him in similar terms—*perfection*. He had no flaws. She wondered if he felt the same way about her. "That was…beautiful. Would you mark the page for me so I can read it later?"

Shaking his head, he dog-eared the page and said, "I guess I was right. What I told your grandmother. You are a young lady, after all. I knew the day would come." Then he began reading again.

~

Within a week of her request for letters, Cailin received her first two.

Gus started his perfect cursive letter with the good news that he had received a letter from his father, saying he was stationed at Andrews Field in Essex and didn't think he would be sent to fight in the Japanese conflict. He hoped to be discharged from the RAF in the next few months. Of course, Gus expressed his eagerness to see his father. He went on to fill Cailin in on the happenings on the Cawdor property. Uncle Malcolm had allowed him to go along with Ian and the property workers to herd the cattle back from Negril Springs, as breeding season was over, and they would birth their calves at Cawdor. Cailin regretted missing the fun.

He ended his letter with a P.S. "Good news! Miss Recas has gone home for the summer!" There was a P.P.S. "This is Ian. Cheer up! When you get back, we can scare some of the Relax folks at the graveyard." There was a P.P.P.S. in Gus's handwriting. "Archie sends his greetings and wishes you a speedy recovery."

She read the last postscript again, then said softly, "He remembers me." Then she read it again.

When Cailin opened Rowena's letter, a photograph fell on the bed. It was of Rowena at the beach, posing against a coconut tree, wearing shorts and a shirt tied at the waist. Cailin's first thought was to make sure her grandmother didn't see it. In her letter, Rowena said she was bored as Heather was away interviewing for a position as a secretary at the sugar estate in Clarendon, so all there was to do was read and sew. She had sewn the blouse she was wearing in the picture and wanted to know if Cailin liked it. When she returned from school, she found Essie to be in unusually good spirits, always singing hymns or humming a tune. It all made sense to Rowena when she saw Sharpe hanging around the kitchen at every free opportunity. She was happy for Essie but concerned because of the rumors of Sharpe killing someone. Rowena's letter also had a P.S. "I haven't seen George since I've been back. I know I should be mad at him, but I still want to see him!"

Cailin's strength was growing, and she asked to sit in the bedroom chair so she could look out the window, but her grandmother insisted she stay in bed. Her mother agreed. Realizing she had to suffice herself with Mass Whim's daily Dickens readings, she sent for him. He opened to the day's chapter and began reading the part where Pip finds out Estella had accepted an offer of marriage from a gentleman scoundrel. Pip tells her that even though he feels sharp distress about her forthcoming marriage, she will always be a part of him. Cailin motioned for her grandfather to stop.

"Yes, I thought you would want me to dog-ear that part." Laughing, he flipped the pages of the book with his thumb then remarked, "There are more dog ears than corners on these pages." He marked the page and kept on reading.

After Mass Whim put the book on the bedside table and left, Cailin opened it back to the last dog-eared page and reread the words. Wondering about the way Estella had treated Pip throughout the novel, she recalled Pip's friend warning him about Estella. That lead to her thinking about Archie and the warnings she had received about him. *Why? What had he done? He's only a boy, not that much older than me.* She remembered him swimming in the river with Gus and how self-assured he was. But why shouldn't he be? He was handsome and seemed to be smart. She liked that he was willing to play with Gus, even though he was younger. Then a familiar question came back to her. *Why did he leave Manning's and return home for the rest of the school year?* He was a mystery. A handsome mystery, but a mystery, nonetheless. She continued trying to solve the mystery for some time until her eyelids shut slowly.

In Rowena's next letter there was no photograph, only a lament. She had been to church every Sunday since she had returned home but had not seen hide nor hair of George, even though she'd seen his family there. She missed Cailin and asked their father if he would take her to Lennox, but he said he was too busy with the cattle.

Gus's second letter was more lighthearted. He wrote about Ian not going on adventures with him but spending most of his time working on the property. It was increasingly obvious Ian was trying to impress Uncle Malcolm. He had also come home late one evening with Uncle Malcolm and didn't wake until after nine the next morning. This was a first for Ian, as far as Gus could remember. As a result, Gus and Archie had been on adventures together. On reading this, Cailin propped herself a little higher on the bed pillows. They had been soldier crabbing on the foothills, climbing trees, swimming in the river behind the inn, and Gus had even taught Archie how to ride a horse.

They seem to be bosom friends! Cailin thought. As if Gus was stealing Archie from her. As if he was hers to be jealous of.

Gus ended his letter informing her that the Japanese resistance in both Okinawa and the Philippines had ended. He declared this to be a sure sign that the Japanese would be quickly defeated, and his father would return home soon!

To Cailin's surprise, she received a letter from Heather, although she thought Heather would have been too busy to write as she prepared for her new life. Indeed, the letter said she had been offered a secretarial job at the Monymusk Sugar Factory and would leave in the next week. She had hoped to come to Lennox before leaving, but she only had a week to sew work clothes and leave for Clarendon. Although Cailin was three years younger than Heather and so was not as close to her as to Rowena, she would miss her beauty and strength of character.

Toward mid-July, fed up with being confined to the bed and feeling strong, when no one was in her room, Cailin pulled off her sheet, slid her legs slowly off the bed, and struggled to prop her torso up. She took a few deep breaths, then attempted to stand. *Thump!* She hit the floor.

She heard her grandmother's voice coming from the veranda. "What was that? Whim, go check Cailin's room."

He walked into the room as she had managed to pull herself halfway onto the bed.

"Oh, dear," he whispered. "We can't let your grandmother see this." He helped her back into bed and covered her with the sheets.

"Is everything alright?" called Helen.

"Yes, yes," he said, smiling at Cailin. "The book fell off her bed. That's all."

She looked at him sheepishly. "Thank you, Grandpa."

"It's nothing at all. It never happened." He gave her his

winsome smile. "Well, my pigeon, we've already had our daily dose of Dickens, but it seems like you need another." He turned to the end of the book. "The problem is, it's the last chapter. Maybe we should wait until tomorrow."

"No. Let's finish it today."

"Well, here we go then."

As the story closed, Pip and Estella were standing by the ruined garden wall. Estella's beauty had faded with the hard years of abuse from her husband, who was now dead, but for Pip, the splendor of her beauty was still apparent. They talked about the ruins of her mother's house where they were standing, then the conversation turned to their relationship, where they each found out they were still in love with one another. They walked away from the ruins hand in hand while Pip said, "I saw no shadow of another parting from her."

Mass Whim looked up at Cailin, who was staring at the book in his hand. "Well, pigeon, we made it! What did you think of the end?"

"It was lovely. I hoped, but I didn't expect them to end up together."

"Well, what if I told you there is more to the story?" asked Mass Whim.

"What do you mean? I know it's the end of the story. I already peeked at it a week ago."

"You mean you knew the ending all along?"

"I couldn't help myself! I had to know if they ended up together or not."

"You won't like what I have to tell you then." He thought for a moment. "Maybe I shouldn't spoil it for you."

"What? They don't end up together?" she said in desperation. "You have to tell me, Grandpa!"

"Alright, alright, but brace yourself." He sighed. "The ending in the book is not the way Charles Dickens originally wrote it. A friend of Dickens said people would hate his first ending, so

Dickens rewrote it. Here's how the story originally ended. Are you ready for it?"

"Yes. Go on, Grandpa."

He sighed. "Pip knew Estella's first husband had died, and she had married a poor doctor who had defended her during her terrible marriage to her first husband. Pip meets her on a street in London and sees in her eyes the great suffering she has been through and that she has learned what it is to have a heart."

"That's it?" Cailin balked.

"That's it, indeed."

She folded her arms and said, "No wonder he had to write another ending."

Her grandfather closed the book with finality and stated, "It only goes to show you," he got up from the chair, "you never know how things are going to end. Life isn't like a novel. Just because people want happy endings, doesn't mean they can rewrite their lives to get it." He put the novel back on her table and left her in the room to ponder his words.

Cailin received one last letter during her stay at Lennox. Rowena wrote to her and to her mother that Auntie Bitsy had died in her sleep. Cailin could hardly breathe at this news. The night before she died, Auntie Bitsy had asked if anyone wanted the last plantain, and Gus said he wanted it, but Auntie Abum had squashed the game, and a good thing because Gus would have felt guilty for it. Cailin laughed, then cried uncontrollably. She loved Auntie Bitsy. She was sweet and smart and funny. She also cried, along with her mother, because they couldn't attend the funeral. When she stopped crying, the thought came to her that she could no longer go to the graveyard at night with Gus and Ian to scare the people—she couldn't disturb Auntie Bitsy in her rest.

One Saturday morning, Helen woke Cailin and told her Mass Whim would take them back to Cawdor that day. Her face lit up, and she tried to get out of bed, but, again, her legs were not strong enough.

Her mother washed her and dressed her in the sky-blue dress with the new embroidered collar, which she loved.

The gardener carried her to the veranda, and with her grandfather's direction, put her in his big chair. There was an air of ceremony. Both her grandparents stood in front of her with their hands behind their backs.

Her grandmother stepped forward with the crack of a smile Cailin knew must have come from deep inside. She showed Cailin a silver V with a pin on the back. "This is a victory pin that we bought right after Victory Day. It commemorates Britain's victory over Hitler. But now, for you it has a second meaning—your victory over malaria." She bent down slowly and pinned it on the collar of Cailin's dress.

Cailin felt the pin on the embroidered collar and thanked her grandmother.

"I have something for you, too." Her grandfather stepped forward and, from behind his back, produced the *Great Expectations* novel.

She said, "I wondered where that had gone! Thank you, Grandpa!"

He pointed to the book, saying, "Look inside at the inscription."

Cailin opened it and read, "My Little Pigeon, you came here a girl, and are leaving a young lady. You have been bent and broken, but into a better shape."

Cailin looked up at him and said, "These are Estella's words."

"Yes," Mass Whim replied. "Keep on reading."

"As you go back to your own home, remember the lesson of this book. Love with all your heart and take what comes with it. Love, Grandpa."

Tears welled up in Cailin's eyes.

Once back at Cawdor, Cailin remained in bed for six more days while being taught to walk again.

When her father came in to see her, her first words were, "You didn't come to see me. Or even write."

3 6

ARCHIE

TUESDAY, AUGUST 21, 1945

"Archie!" Malcolm's numb lips slurred the name. "Make the old man another drink."

A female giggle followed Malcolm's demand.

Archie, sitting in the kitchen with Abbie, exhaled deeply and yelled back, "Don't you think you've had enough?" He was wearied by Malcolm at this point and didn't care to temper his response, so he added, "Besides, you've just about drunk out the entire stock of rum. There's none left for the guests!"

Something slammed on wood, and a yell boomeranged back, "Damn it, boy! This rum belongs to me! This inn belongs to me! So, pour me another drink!"

Abbie said in a low voice, "You better go do what him say. Him usually don't get mad when him drunk, but you no want test him."

Archie had lost count of how many drinks he had served Malcolm since his mother had left for Montego Bay three days earlier. She had gone to visit family and order some furniture for one of the guest rooms that needed refurnishing. She left Archie in charge of the house, saying he was a man now and could shoulder the responsibility until she returned on Friday.

When Archie handed him the drink, Malcolm said, "Be a good host and offer the lady another drink."

The young local woman declined, saying her head was still spinning from the rum the night before.

"You have one, Archie!" Malcolm commanded with a huge grin and his arms spread toward the woman, who was sitting on the curved-back leather chair beside him.

Archie was unsure if Malcolm was commanding him to have a drink or to have the woman. Not that he was opposed to either option, but at that moment he was boiling inside like the new pressure cooker his mother had brought back from her last visit to Montego Bay. Some steam had already been let loose when he had questioned Malcolm's need for another drink. But the pressure continued building at the thought of Malcolm picking up a woman off the street, bringing her to the inn, and taking her into his mother's room for the night—for the last two nights! The thought sickened him! On top of that, Malcolm was ordering him around like he was his personal lackey.

"No, thank you," he said with a sharp edge. *Pssst*—more steam released. He turned and walked into the kitchen before any more could escape.

"One more thing," Malcolm summoned. "Take my car up to Cawdor and get my children. We're going on a boat ride!" He laughed, and the woman echoed him with a giggle.

"Chicken merry, hawk deh near[1]," said Abbie.

"Yes," agreed Archie, then he reversed his steps back through the kitchen door toward the front stairs, saying under his breath, "And it seems it's a great advantage not to drink among hard drinking people—you get to be their chauffeur."

On the way up to the Cawdor house, Archie drove carefully. One of his mother's friends in Montego Bay had taught him to drive up and down the guest house's hilly driveway. Consciously reciting the near simultaneous motion of easing up on the gas pedal and pressing the clutch, he changed gears. He was in no rush to get to Cawdor House because he sensed the hawk Abbie referenced hovering. He didn't want trouble for Cailin and the others, but if he didn't bring them back, there would be trouble for him. Concerned they might not come if he told them their father was drunk, he decided not to say anything. Once they got to the inn, they could make their own decision about the boat ride.

Archie stopped the car just short of the barbecue where Gus was sitting and tying a springe together.

Gus looked up. "Why are you driving Uncle Malcolm's car?" Seeing there was no one in the passenger seat, he added, "And where is he?"

"He sent me up to bring his children down to the inn. He wants to take them for a boat ride."

He jumped up and said, "Ian's not here, but hold on, I'll get the others."

Before long, Rowena came outside, followed by Cailin and Gus.

Rowena looked at Archie with narrowed eyes and asked, "What exactly did my father send you to say?"

"I don't remember word-for-word, but he basically told me to drive up here and get you so he can take you for a boat ride."

"What kind of boat ride?"

"He didn't say."

Cailin put her hand on Rowena's shoulder and said, "What does it matter? It's a boat ride, and it's better than sitting up here sweating."

"I'm going too!" Gus exclaimed.

"Are you coming, Row?" Cailin asked.

"Well, something doesn't seem right," responded Rowena as if thinking out loud. She panned her head from Cailin to Gus and said, "I'm not letting the two of you go by yourselves."

Archie opened the car door and said, "Ladies and gentleman?"

He pulled the car under the porte-cochère of the inn and ran up to get Malcolm. Seeing that he wasn't there, he returned to the children.

"Your father isn't here. He must have walked down to the cove."

They drove to the cove, which was situated across the street from Mr. Lyn's store. Archie parked the car close to a seawall, where small waves slapped against the seawall, announcing the rising tide.

Standing with his one arm around the woman he had brought to the inn and the other holding a rum bottle, Malcolm was quarrelling with a man beside a fishing boat. Finally, with an exchange of money, the fisherman gave in and handed him two oars.

It was not a large boat by any estimation, and Archie wondered how Malcolm, the woman, and the three children would fit, but he held his tongue.

"Get in, children,"

"Daddy," Rowena objected. "The boat is too small for all of us. And, besides, why are we going on a boat ride?"

"Because you're my children. I want to do something fun with you!" he slurred. "Don't I have that right?"

Rowena turned to Archie with a questioning look, then said, "Why didn't you tell us he was drunk and with a woman?"

"If I had, would you have come?"

"No!"

"Exactly, and I would have had to put up with more of his abuse. I've had enough. He's your father. It's time for you to deal with him!" He knew his anger was misplaced, but he didn't know where else to direct it.

"Stop talking, and get in the boat," Malcolm commanded, silencing any further complaints.

Gus was the first to get into the boat, followed by the rest of the children and the woman.

"Don't just stand there, boy." Malcolm motioned to Archie. "We'll need your rowing power. But push us off first."

Not wanting to stir Malcolm's anger, Archie took the oars from him and placed them in the boat. Once Malcolm was seated, Archie pushed the bow off the sand and got in.

With the woman snuggled close to him in the bow, Malcolm held up his bottle of rum as though it were a scepter and gave an order. "Archie! Give Gus one of the oars and head out to sea!" Then he took a swig of rum and let out a whoop, ending in laughter.

Looking behind him, Archie saw Cailin's widened eyes and Rowena's furrowed brow. He was between a hammer and an anvil. He turned forward and started rowing.

Because of the difference between Archie and Gus's strength, the boat spiraled in Gus's direction, so whenever the boat was positioned parallel to the incoming tide, water would smack the side of the boat and soak those seated on that side. Then the boat would continue its spiral until the people on the other side got a good soaking. Each time it happened, Malcolm had a good laugh.

With every spiral, the boat progressed in an arc, projected to collide back into where the other fishing boats were anchored. The fishermen bellowed with laughter as the overloaded fishing boat corkscrewed toward them.

Rowena's clothes were soaking wet, and her salt-water hair was pasted to her head, framing her scowling face. Everyone except Malcolm could see her fury. Finally, she let out an I've-had-it-up-to-here screech, getting Malcolm's attention. "Get us back to shore, now!" she demanded.

"We're just having fun, Rowena," Malcolm shouted. Then he held his stomach, leaned over the side of the boat, and vomited right as a wave hit the bow, dispatching his lunch all over himself. The woman shrieked in disgust after Malcolm's vomit hit her square in the face.

Archie promptly took the other oar from Gus and rowed the boat to shore.

The children disembarked and, with heads lowered, walked through the crowd of laughing fishermen.

37

KIMBERLY, SOUTH AFRICA

25 SEPTEMBER 1916

Dear Abum,

I am disturbed to hear the news about Malcolm. How could you have let that happen? Getting a colored girl pregnant and shooting her father, a Cawdor property worker. My own son, a murderer! You have lost control of him. The one thing you did right was immediately sending him to Cuba. I hope he learns a lesson from this and does not do the same thing over there.

How can you blame Cuddy and me for this when you are the one who raised him? Cuddy was right, after all. Your favoritism has spoiled the boy. At least the other children have moved on from Cawdor and seem to be settling down. I am glad to hear Kester has followed his father's footsteps and gone to medical school in London. My, my, Saint George's. Cuddy would have been very proud.

If you are in contact with any of the children, please give them my address and encourage them to write to me.

Winnie

38

CAILIN

WEDNESDAY, AUGUST 22, 1945

The next morning at the breakfast table, it was as if the children were practicing being seen and not heard of their own volition. Helen asked if anything was the matter. They said no. Abum said silence was a welcome change.

Cailin excused herself from the table and went for a walk. She wandered through fields and wooded areas of the property as her thoughts meandered, trying to understand her father's actions. Why would he take them on a boat ride when he was drunk? Who was the woman he'd brought along and was snuggled up with in the bow? And why did he make Archie come get them?

Since she'd been back from her bout of malaria, she hadn't left the property until the previous day, so the boat incident had been the first time she'd seen Archie. She hadn't talked with him since Easter, but she'd thought a lot about him since then. Cailin wondered if he had thought about her.

Her wanderings led her through a bushy path and out to the gentle river running behind the Oristano Inn. Sitting on the large rock protruding from the bank's shoulder, she was reminded of the first time she met Archie. She replayed each of their meetings in her mind—how he looked, what they said to one another, the nuances of his gestures.

She was just at the part where he invited her to take his arm at church on Easter when she heard, "Well, what have we here?"

She looked up to see Archie pushing back the mahoe tree that served as a curtain between where she sat and the inn. "Oh," she reacted, feeling her cheeks flush.

"Sorry, did I disturb you?"

"Well, yes, but it's okay. I just have a lot on my mind."

"I understand…after your father's performance yesterday."

She sighed and looked down at a yellowed leaf floating past her.

"Mind if I share the rock with you?"

"No. There's plenty of room."

They sat in silence for a time, Cailin enjoying the secrecy of the canopied sanctuary and the comfort of Archie's company. Beyond his charming personality, in the silence he seemed different. Humble. She liked that.

Finally, Archie broke the silence. "Cailin, are you okay? After what happened yesterday?"

"No." She shook her head, "Not really." Archie sat looking at her. With another sigh, she opened up. "I guess it's that I'm disappointed."

"Why?"

"With my father." She threw a twig she'd been twirling between her fingers into the river. "But it's not so much about yesterday. I guess I'm beginning to see him in a different light, and I can't quite figure him out."

"If it makes it any better, at least you have a father to try and figure out. I have no idea who mine is. My mother won't tell me."

"Well, aren't we a pair?" she said, gazing into his eyes.

He met her gaze and gently put his hand on hers.

Cailin's heart raced as their bodies slowly leaned toward each other. She closed her eyes and felt the warmth of his breath on her lips.

Then he pulled away.

Opening her eyes, she watched as he got up from the rock.

"I'm sorry, Cailin. I don't know if we...I don't think we should...I'm sorry."

He turned and walked toward the inn. Cailin's heart sank.

39

───────

CAILIN

THURSDAY, AUGUST 23, 1945

"I'm going to the beach today," announced Rowena. "Who's coming?"

Cailin and Gus immediately agreed, but Ian replied, "Not me. I have work to do."

"What do you mean you have work to do?" responded Rowena. "All you've done this summer is work seven days a week. You know what they say about all work and no play, don't you?"

Helen chimed in, "She's right, Ian. You need a rest. Go with your sisters and Gus down to the beach. I'd like you to accompany them." Then she added, "Besides, before you know it, summer will be over, and you'll be heading back to Munro."

Ian mumbled under his breath, "I'm not going back."

"Don't let your father hear you say that," advised Auntie Abum.

"She's right," said Helen. "And, if you're concerned your father will think badly of you for not working today, I'll tell him I asked you to go for Cailin's safety."

The four children headed down the Cawdor road on horseback. Rowena motioned to Cailin to slow down, and when the boys were far enough ahead of them, she said, "Guess who's going to be at the beach?"

Cailin's instant response was, "Archie?"

"No! I thought you stopped thinking about him."

Cailin remained silent.

"George is going to be at the beach today!" Rowena said, almost too loud, then covered her mouth with her hand and looked at Cailin, giggling.

"How do you know?" Cailin asked matter-of-factly.

"On Sunday, I overheard his mother at church inviting another family to the beach on Thursday. She said George was arriving home on Wednesday from visiting family in New England, and she was planning a day at the beach."

"Why didn't you tell me when you got home from church?"

"I don't know exactly, except I've been hatching plans and thinking through all sorts of scenarios…what I'm going to do and say when I see him…what his parents will think of me… what I should wear. What do you think of this outfit?"

"I suppose it'll do."

"It'll do? This is my best short pants outfit." She looked at Cailin's expressionless face, then said. "Oh. I see. Are you upset because I'm talking about George, but you can't talk about Archie?"

"Well, as a matter of fact, yes!" Cailin snapped back. She wished she could tell Row about the time she spent with Archie the previous day, but she knew she'd just get another warning lecture.

They rode their horses in silence for a while but were soon talking and laughing again.

Cailin thought the beach was crowded for a Thursday, but then remembered people from the hot inner parts of West-moreland sought the sea breeze to escape the late summer heat. She thought about Lennox and how the weather there got hotter as the summer progressed and wondered how her grandparents were able to weather the August humidity.

Recognizing some girls from church who were there with their families, Cailin immediately thought about her clothing. The bathing suit she was wearing under her khaki shorts and blouse didn't compare with their fashionable swimsuits. She had never thought much about what she wore to the beach before. Her mind had always been on the sea and sand, not on clothes.

The four of them got off their horses and walked them along the shore with the waves lapping at their feet. Two younger children started toward them, obviously wanting to pet and perhaps get a ride on a horse, when their mother called out to them, "Children! Come back! Don't go near those horses." The children reluctantly returned to their mother.

A little farther down, she saw another mother in a tug-of-war with her child. The mother said, "I'll take you to the Watsons' to ride their horse, dear." As she rode farther, to where the parent must have thought they were out of earshot, she heard the mother say, "They're not the type of people I want my Tommy fraternizing with."

Cailin's brow furrowed. She turned to Rowena and asked, "Row, did you hear that lady?"

"What did she say?"

"It seems like she was talking about us. She didn't want her son to come up to us."

"Oh, never mind her. Some people don't know what they're talking about," Rowena responded, looking straight ahead with her chin held high.

Cailin had the same feeling she used to have in church before she started going late and leaving early.

"There he is," whispered Rowena and pointed with a nod of her head.

Cailin looked in the direction of her nod, and there was George floating on the water, face up to the sky.

"Hold my reins," she said, handing Cailin her horse's reins and slipping off her shirt and shorts, revealing her bathing suit. Cailin stood and watched as she waded elegantly toward George. When she reached him, she must have startled him because he sprung up from his horizontal position. There was a brief interaction between them. Then he dove into the water and Rowena stood blankly watching him swim the short distance to shore. She immersed herself in the water and didn't come back up for a long minute. Then, just as elegantly, she waded back to shore, gathered her clothes, and mounted her horse. Cailin knew the water trickling down her face was more than sea water.

They rode in silence, taking their time catching up to the boys, who had tied their horses to a tree that shaded one of the few empty patches of sand left on the beach. They joined them, and Cailin had a pebble-throwing contest with the boys while Rowena sat quietly on the sand. Eventually, Gus persuaded Cailin to go into the ocean with him. When they rejoined the others, Rowena's mood seemed to have changed for the better as she was laughing at Ian's stories about Munro.

Cailin spotted Archie walking along the seashore.

"Look there's Archie,"

She got up to speak with him, but Ian pulled her back down.

"What?" Cailin said, looking at Ian.

"You can't talk to him."

She pulled her arm from his grasp. "Why not?"

"Because if Daddy found out, you, Archie, and me would get a whipping. That's why."

"But," Cailin fired back, "that's just like those people on the beach who don't want their children playing with us. It's no different. It's all hypocrisy! They can't talk to us. We can't talk to Archie." As Cailin muttered those last words, Archie passed by. He looked over at them. Gus waved at him. Cailin gave an indecisive wave. Ian and Rowena nodded. Archie kept walking.

"Why? Why do we have to treat him like that?" Cailin challenged Ian. "And why do they," sweeping her arm toward the crowd on the beach, "treat us like that? I want answers, Ian, and I want them now!"

Ian looked at her, then looked out to the horizon where the light blue sky merged with the dark blue sea. He sighed. "Okay, I suppose it's time, but what I'm about to tell you, I wish I could spare you. You too, Gus. I think Row knows much of it."

Rowena nodded.

"You know Ms. Price? Archie's mother?" He looked at Cailin then Gus. They didn't answer, but they were all ears. "Well, Daddy brought her over from Montego Bay to run the inn, with the benefit of him conveniently visiting her any time he likes."

Cailin squinted her eyes. "So, are you saying she's his…his mistress?"

"Yes," Ian replied softly.

"So…what about Mummy?" she asked.

"She is his wife," was Ian's simple reply.

"I don't understand," said Gus.

"You will. Just keep listening," assured Ian.

Rowena took over at this point. "The fact is, Daddy has children all over the countryside, with women of every color. Mummy is his respectable white wife, and we are his respectable white children. Although that's not how the people on this beach see us—nor the people at church. Our father's reputation precedes him—and us."

"Yeah," Ian continued. "There was a time when Daddy was younger, probably a little older than me, when they say he shot and killed one of the property workers because he was angry, and Auntie Abum had to ship him off to Cuba before the authorities could do anything about it."

Cailin put her hands over her ears. Gus sat there motionless with a dropped jaw.

"Cailin," Rowena said, "you need to listen."

Ian continued. "While he was in Cuba for five years, he had another family. But when he heard it was safe for him to return to Jamaica, he left them there."

Cailin began to cry. "How could he? How could he do this to Mummy, to us?"

Gus, shocked by the revelation, asked, "Is that why Heather was so eager to leave after she graduated from Hampton?"

"Yes," answered Rowena.

Cailin, holding in her sobs, turned to Rowena. "You know, I've been wondering about Daddy lately. Now it makes more sense." She looked around the beach.

"I think it's time to go home," said Ian.

No one resisted the suggestion.

The ride home was filled with the chaotic rhythms of the four horses' hoofbeats. Cailin thought about what she had just learned and everything that had happened over the last two days—the crazy drunken boat ride, almost kissing Archie, learning her father had killed a man and had many illegitimate children. It eventually dawned on her that Archie could be one of her father's illegitimate children. Was that why Ian and Row had been warning her about him? She immediately shooed the idea from her mind, thinking it couldn't be. Just because Ms. Price worked for her father didn't mean they had anything beyond a working relationship. Then she remembered all the nights her father spent down at the inn, but she consoled herself with the thought that of the many times she had visited the inn, she had never seen any sign of Ms. Price and her father being romantically involved. She assured herself Ms. Price was far too respectable for that sort of thing. Her thoughts reverted to her father. *How could he?*

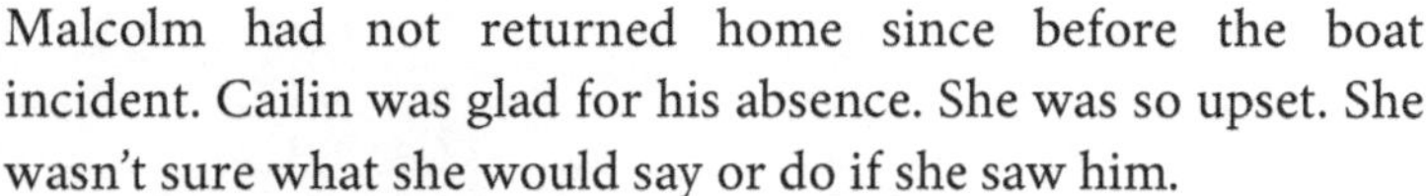

Malcolm had not returned home since before the boat incident. Cailin was glad for his absence. She was so upset. She wasn't sure what she would say or do if she saw him.

After dinner, Gus turned on the wireless and found classical music playing. He sat patiently, waiting for a news report. After about twenty minutes, an announcer apologized for interrupting the programming, and with an air of somber urgency, reported that the United States had dropped what was being called an atomic bomb on Hiroshima, a key Japanese military supply port, and that the entire city was covered with a colossal cloud of smoke. He reported that President Truman said if the Japanese did not accept the Allies' terms of unconditional surrender, they would be bombarded from air, sea, and land, in number and power they have not yet seen.

After the breaking news, Gus turned the wireless off and shouted, "Daddy is sure to come home soon!"

But Cailin couldn't help thinking about how many people must have died in such an unheard-of bombing. *The whole city is covered with the cloud from one bomb!*

That evening, with Rowena's muffled sobs escaping through her pillow and torn-up letters scattered over the floor, Cailin lay in bed, her mind exploding with thoughts of her father's destruction. She lay there covered in a cloud of despair. *How could one man do so much damage? How many others has Malcolm dropped a bomb on?* She tossed and turned for the rest of the night.

40

SHARPE

FRIDAY, AUGUST 24, 1945

Knocking on the dark mahogany front door of the inn and hearing the sound echo up the empty staircase, Sharpe reminded himself he was taking a chance checking on Busha. He had never dared do this before, nor had he ever thought of it. But it had been almost a week since Busha had been up at the big house, and Sharpe was concerned. He had heard about the boat fiasco from Mr. Lyn at his rum bar three nights earlier. The rum bar crowd was also talking about the local-colored woman Busha had taken back to the inn. And none of the children had said anything about it that day when he saw them walking home wet, looking as though they had gone swimming in their regular clothes. So Sharpe plucked up his courage and went looking for him.

"Come in!" he heard a female voice call.

He eased the door open. "It's me, Sharpe. Come from up the big house," he said loudly enough for his voice to carry up the stairs. "Me come to see Busha."

"Well," replied the voice now descending the stairs accompanied by the clicking of heels. "Your timing is impeccable."

Gracie opened the door with a look of disgust Sharpe

thought was intended for him, but her agitation erupted into loud protestations he realized were aimed upstairs for Malcolm to hear.

"He's all yours!" She flung the door wide open, waving her other hand up the stairs. "All his drinking! All his infidelities! All his foolhardy excursions! You can take him and them with you!"

Sharpe stood static. He was unsure what to do next. He had only ever entered the inn from the kitchen entrance, and it wasn't his place to go up into the inn to get Busha. On the way down from the big house, he had thought to tell Busha Miss Helen had sent for him but realized that would just get her in trouble. He hadn't been able to come up with a reasonable excuse.

"Go on," urged Gracie. "He won't listen to me. Maybe he'll listen to his foreman!"

He reluctantly entered the inn and began climbing the stairs. Halfway up, it came to him. He was indeed the foreman, but right now on the property, the cattle were being prepared for the journey to Montpelier in Saint James to be sold and shipped by train to Kingston. If there was any time Busha should be there, it was now. He was surprised he hadn't thought of it before.

At the top of the stairs, he found Malcolm sprawled over the couch, looking as though he were asleep but holding a half-filled glass of liquor upright on his chest.

"Busha," Sharpe said softly, then again, a little louder.

Malcolm turned his head and opened his eyes to a squint. Sharpe wondered if Busha even knew who he was.

"What are you doing here?" Busha managed to say, then put a hand on his forehead and groaned.

"Come, Busha," Sharpe moved toward him. "Mek me help you up. It's time to go back to Cawdor. The cattle them need you."

Malcolm lay motionless.

Sharpe looked back at Gracie, who was standing at the top of the stairs. She had let off her steam—and loud enough for Malcolm to hear—but now she was deflated, shoulders sagging, face worn. Sharpe knew there was nothing she could really do. It was not as though she could kick him out of the inn. She needed him as much as Sharpe did. Like it or not, he was their livelihood.

Malcolm shifted the glass from his chest to the coffee table, slipped a leg off the couch, tried to prop himself up, then fell back.

"It's alright, Busha. Me will help you."

Sharpe pulled him up and supported him to the stairs.

"Archie!" Gracie called. "You need to drive Mr. Campbell home."

"I thought he was home," Archie's voice carried from the kitchen.

"Enough of your cheek! Just come and do what I ask!"

Archie pulled Malcolm's car under the porte-cochère, and Sharpe assisted Malcolm into the car, then got in the back seat. On reaching Cawdor, Archie pulled up to the barbecue and saw Cailin on the porch watching Gus tie a springe together. Sharpe jumped out of the car to help Malcolm, but before he walked him to the house, Malcolm turned and leaned on the driver door, looking in at Archie, and slurred loudly, "Thank you...for taking care of the inn...while your mother was gone. You're growing up to be just like me...son."

Archie jerked his head back, then looked over at Cailin, whose face dropped.

Sharpe caught both reactions and thought back to something he'd overheard at Mr. Lyn's rum bar. Two local men were speculating that Archie was Busha's son. At the time, Sharpe had dismissed it as mere bar gossip, which he never paid mind to. But now he was hearing it from the horse's mouth.

The bulk of Malcolm's weight rested on Sharpe. With every step toward the house, Sharpe saw Cailin's face flaming with anger. He helped Malcolm up the porch steps. Cailin stepped forward, and before Sharpe realized what was happening, she slugged her father in the jaw, causing his head to flip back and Sharpe to lose his hold. Malcolm fell to the wooden floor with a thud.

"Now, get to bed, you drunken womanizer!" Cailin ordered. "Go to bed and sleep off your foolishness!"

Sharpe looked wide-eyed at Cailin while Malcolm groaned on the ground. Then, lifting him to his feet, he assisted him to his bedroom.

When Sharpe came out to the barbecue, he saw Cailin climbing further up the hill toward the sugar shack and Archie walking down the gravel road past the cotton tree.

Sharpe stood there. Mulling things over. Considering Malcolm's misspoken words. "You're growing up to be like me, son." The word "son" was a revelation indeed, but it was the four preceding words that caused his deliberation. "To be like me."

He distinctly recalled Busha's words to him which he had repeated as an incantation for much of the last year—*I chose you because I saw in you a seed of myself. A man who would do anything to get something.* He looked down and shook his head. *That's exactly what me did. And look where it lead me? Me separate meself from the people who take me in when me was young, and me murder a man out of revenge.*

Essie, who had been watching him from the kitchen window, called out, "Sharpe. You alright?"

He looked up and saw worry in her face. "Yes, Miss Essie," he replied. "Me just going for a little walk."

He headed to the path behind the kitchen that led along the mountain slope and didn't come back until sundown.

41

CAILIN

SATURDAY, AUGUST 25, 1945

Saturday morning arrived, and the dampened atmosphere from the day before lingered at the breakfast table. Cailin heard Malcolm's door open. She froze.

He sat at the table without a word and helped himself to breakfast. Everyone kept their faces toward their plates but watched him out of the corner of their eyes. He ate. He rubbed his jaw once. He said nothing. He got up from the table and headed outside.

There was a collective exhale.

After breakfast, Cailin spoke privately with Rowena. "Will you come down with me to the inn?"

"For what?"

"To confront Archie." Cailin's voice trembled. "How could he make me think he liked me when he knew he was Malcolm's son?"

"Well, it wouldn't be a bad idea to get everything out in the open, but you don't know that he did that on purpose." She paused, then said, "I think you should be careful not to go in there with your gun loaded."

"What do you mean, gun loaded?"

"What I mean is, don't go there accusing him of things you don't know for sure."

"I know he's Daddy's son! Why else would Daddy have called him son? And I know he was trying to make me like him." Then, just in case someone was listening, she whispered, "He tried to kiss me."

Rowena's eyes widened. "Did you let him?"

"No. But he was the one who actually stopped before we kissed."

Rowena looked at Cailin for a moment, chuckled, then responded, "Well, well, my little sister is not so little after all."

"No. Especially after the last few days."

"Well, almost-kissed and all." Rowena put her hand on Cailin's shoulder. "What I'm trying to say is…actually, better yet, this is the way it says it in the Bible, 'Be swift to hear, slow to speak, slow to wrath.' Do you think you can manage that when you see Archie?"

"I'll try, Row, but I can't promise anything."

Gracie came out on the balcony to see who was coming up the driveway. When she saw it was two of Malcolm's children, she went into character, waving and welcoming them gaily.

"What brings you here this morning, children?"

Dismounting, Cailin said flatly, "We've come to see Archie."

"Oh!" responded Gracie, surprised. "Yes…yes, come right up. I'll get him for you."

When the girls got to the top of the stairs, they heard a muffled conversation coming from the bedroom hall and caught the end of it as Gracie exited a room. "…and get yourself together before you come out."

Gracie came into the livingroom and smiled. "Archie will be out in a couple minutes. Can I get you some lemonade?"

"No, thank you," replied Rowena.

As Archie made his appearance, Cailin thought he looked like he'd fallen off a galloping horse. Hair disheveled. Shirt untucked and wrinkled. Dark circles under his eyes. For a moment, she felt sorry for him. Then her own pain worked its way through the pity like lava through the core of the earth.

Seeing Cailin's face, Gracie said, "Excuse me, ladies, I have something to attend to," and hastened to the kitchen.

Cailin's eruption broke through the crust. "Why didn't you tell me?" She didn't give him time to answer. "You're his son! You're my father's son!"

Archie stood there, overwhelmed by her accusation.

Cailin continued her rage, "How could you lead me on? How could you make me think you liked me? What kind of crooked person are you? To think you're my half-brother." She clenched her fists. "Oh! The thought makes me so angry!"

Rowena put her arm around Cailin and said, "You've said your piece. Now let him respond."

Cailin allowed Rowena to hold her while Archie shifted his feet and nervously ran his hand through his hair, not making himself any more presentable than before. "You're right," he finally said. "I did flirt with you. And I'm sorry for that." He sighed deeply. "But I didn't know I was your father's son. When I heard Malcolm say it yesterday, all the insults I heard while I was at Manning's finally made sense. I was just as surprised as you. As it is, my mother still won't admit it." He paused. "I wish I had done what you did to him yesterday."

Cailin wasn't ready to let him off the hook, and she didn't accept the roundabout compliment either. Pulling away from Rowena and leaning toward Archie, she interrogated him. "Why were you flirting with me in the first place? And why did you almost kiss me?" Her face burned red. Her voice shaking.

"To be honest…"

"Yes! Be honest!"

He hesitated. "My mother told me to get close to him—and now I understand exactly why. But then I took it a step further and thought if I got you to like me, I could be part of your family."

Cailin's heart sank. "Then you were using me."

"Well…yes…at first. But then I…I…I can't say it." He shook his head. "Now you're my sister, and it's all different."

There was a moment of silence, then Rowena asked, "Why would you want to be part of our family?"

He hung his head, shifting his feet again. "I was hoping I could have what you have…a home…a family…a father." A tear escaped his eye and fell to the wood floor.

Cailin's anger subsided, and she spoke frankly. "We do have a good life up at Cawdor. Or at least I always thought we did. But lately I've come to understand that Malcolm Campbell is no father at all and, as his family, we bear his shame—as outcasts."

Rowena, Cailin, and Archie stood there like three deflated hot air balloons until Archie called out, "Mother. Please come out here. I know you're listening anyway."

There was silence in the kitchen until Abbie could be heard saying, "Go on, Miss Gracie. You son need you."

Gracie came out of the kitchen smiling. "Yes, dear," she said casually. "What would you like?"

"I need you to…all three of us need you to answer my question."

"What is it, dear?"

"The same question I've been asking you since yesterday when I came back from the big house." Then he said emphatically, "Is Malcolm Campbell my father?"

Her casual demeanor cracked enough to show her agitation. In response she said, "It would be better if we talked about who your father is in private. After the ladies have left."

"No!" he demanded, "You'll tell us now! Right here! This has as much to do with Cailin and Rowena as me. You'll answer the question now!"

Speaking softly, Gracie asked once more, "Archie, please, can we speak privately?"

"No, Mother," he snapped. "Here and now!"

She inhaled deeply, her shoulders dropping on the exhale. "Yes."

"Yes, what, Mother? I need to hear you say it."

"He's your father."

"Who's my father?"

"Malcolm."

Silence.

"Thank you. You're seventeen years late, but thank you."

He sat down in the curved-back leather chair, looking as untucked and wrinkled as his clothes.

His mother stood where she was, unraveled, exposed.

After the foursome remained in silence for a time, Archie stood and walked over to his mother. With index finger pointed in her face, his words came out in rapid fire. "Why didn't you tell me before?" Then more tears escaped as he pleaded, "Why was it always such a secret? What harm would it have done for me to know?"

Gracie looked past him out the balcony doors toward the ocean and said with a whimper in her voice, "He told me never to tell anyone. Even you. He said if I played my cards right, he would make sure you and I were always provided for." Tears rolled down her cheek. She began to sob. Archie put his arms around her.

She chided herself between sobs. "Why did I accept his offer to move here? I should have stayed in Mobay where we were settled." She looked up at Archie. "Now you know...and apparently everyone else does too...and he'll cut us off...he'll cut us off!" she said, still crying.

Archie again wrapped his arm around her to console her.

"Now, Mother, you know he's doing no such thing. He needs this place, and he needs you to run it. Where else would he have his four-day flings? Drinking himself into a stupor. Having sex with any woman he can put his hands on!"

Cailin gasped, partly from the image Archie painted of her father and partly from his free use of such an unspeakable word.

Rowena held Cailin's hand.

Something took hold of Archie. He let go of his mother and started for the stairs.

"Where are you going?" Gracie asked in desperation.

"To confront him!" Archie barked.

"He doesn't like being confronted," Gracie called after him. "He'll cut you off, Archie!"

He turned around and replied, "Why should I care? There's nothing to cut off. He's never been a father to me. After all the years I've known him, other than ordering me to do something, I could count the times he's said anything to me on one hand." Then he added, "Besides, his brother offered to pay for me to go to Munro." He started down the stairs. "To hell with Malcolm!"

Rowena and Cailin followed Archie down the stairs.

"Archie!" Rowena called.

He didn't answer.

"Archie!" she called again. "Take my horse. I'll ride with Cailin."

The three horseback riders were silent for most of the ride up the hill, which gave Cailin time to think. Although she would have liked to have nursed her anger toward Archie, she found she couldn't. Not after what she'd just witnessed. She could have no idea what it was like to be Archie Price, with a mother like Gracie and a father like...well...her father. She thought about the change in her relationship with Archie—

from romantic attraction to brother—and wondered if she could ever really see him as a brother.

While she mulled it over, Rowena broke the silence. "Archie, I have a suggestion."

"What is it?" he asked, with less fire in his voice.

"Since it doesn't seem you have much of a relationship with…" she fumbled with her choice of words, then came out with "…Malcolm, what if I speak to him first, then we'll see where it goes from there?"

Archie breathe in deeply, then exhaled. "To be honest, I've been trying to think of what to say to him, but I can't seem to come up with anything he might listen to. After all those hours we spent driving back and forth from Sav, you'd think we'd be old pals."

Malcolm's office door was open. Cailin could see his head buried in an accounting ledger, pencil perched on his ear. Rowena stepped into his office with Cailin and Archie in tow.

"Excuse me, Daddy," said Rowena.

"What is it?" he replied without looking up from his ledger.

Rowena stood tall and blurted out nervously, "Daddy, why didn't you tell us Archie was your son?"

Malcolm looked up to see Rowena, Cailin, and Archie standing before him. He took the pencil from his ear, erased a figure from the ledger, and wrote in another without saying a word.

"Daddy!" Rowena resumed her already-failing inquest. "Why did you bring Miss Gracie and Archie to Cawdor's doorstep without telling us Archie is your son?"

He looked up at her and asked, "Is that it? Well, now that you know, you can shut the door on your way out." He bowed his head back to the ledger.

Archie demanded, "Why didn't you allow my mother to tell me…Malcolm?"

Cailin walked forward, firmly planting her hands on her father's desk, causing him to glance up at her. She lowered her head, looked him squarely in the eyes, and with flared nostrils, yelled, "How could you? How could you not care about how any of us feel? Neither us nor Archie. Not to mention your own wife!"

Malcolm locked on to her stare. "Every parent will disappoint their children at one time or another. Mine did, and you'll do the same to yours. Now, I'm busy." He rose from his chair, walked to his office door, held it open, and pointed. "The three of you, get out."

Dumbfounded, they did as they were told. The door shut firmly behind them.

"Miss Row," Essie called from the kitchen window.

Seeing Essie signal them over with a hand motion, they went over to her.

"What is it, Essie?" asked Rowena.

"Miss Helen say to tell you to come talk with her in the house." Then she added, "All three of you."

Surprised, Archie asked, "Me too?"

"Yes, Mass Archie. You too."

Cailin had never heard Essie use the title Mass with a young person before, except for her brothers and Gus. She marveled that Essie was now paying respect to Archie as Busha's son.

Helen was leaning over the dining table, cutting a piece of blue floral fabric to the specifications of a dress pattern spread across the table. Pointing to the dining table chairs with her scissors, she said, "Sit down. I need to speak with you." She finished the line she was cutting and sat down.

Cailin noticed Auntie Abum, who was sitting close to the door on the back veranda facing the ocean, turn her head so her right ear had full range of the conversation.

Helen continued. "I know what has transpired these last two days. This is not how I had hoped it would happen. Nevertheless, some things need to be explained."

Abum coughed loudly with the obvious intent of discouraging Helen from the path she was about to tread.

Helen looked down at her clasped hands resting on the table and said, "I had suspected all along that Archie was Malcolm's son." She looked at Archie. "I'm sorry to say you aren't his only child out of wedlock, and you probably aren't his last." She reached out, putting her hand on Archie's, and said, "I wish you could have found out some other way, but that's not how your father operates."

"How could you stay with him, Mummy?" Cailin asked with disdain in her voice. "Why did you stay?"

Helen looked at her with an amalgamation of pain and prudence and replied, "What would you have had me do?"

"Leave him!" protested Cailin.

"I did."

Cailin felt as though everything she knew about her mother had just turned on its head. She hadn't seen her mother as someone who could stand up for herself. She was the gentle, compliant type.

"After I found out about his many indiscretions, both before and after I had married him, I realized I was nothing more than his decent wife, who he could go out in public with. Yet, even in public—in front of me—he would make attempts at other women. At that point I did leave him, and I went back to my mother and father in Lennox."

"Then why'd you come back?" Rowena asked.

"Why? Aren't you glad I did?" Helen responded.

That broke some tension, and they all smiled, even Archie.

"I came back," Helen resumed, "because Heather was a year old, and he wouldn't let me take her. After two days without her, I had to come back." She looked at Rowena and asked, "How could I leave my baby?"

They were silenced by her rhetorical question, but Helen, anticipating questions they may have, said, "I suppose you could ask why I had more children with him. Besides the fact that he insisted on it, I selfishly wanted to receive love that he could never give—the love that all my children have given me."

Both girls got up and embraced their mother.

"Mrs. Campbell," Archie interrupted, "Thank you for telling me more about Malcolm… my father, but I need to go… I need to go see my mother." He got up from his seat.

"Archie, one more minute, please. There is more."

He sat down again.

Abum sat up in her veranda chair and turned around enough to make wide-eyed, head-shaking contact with Helen.

Helen went on. "When I came back from Lennox, Auntie Abum, who is your great-aunt, Archie, told me why your father was the way he was."

Abum coughed again.

Helen panned the children's faces. "His parents left him and his five brothers and sisters before his first birthday. They went off to South Africa, where his father took a position as a doctor in the diamond mines. They never returned to Jamaica, nor did they send for any of their children. Auntie Abum was left in charge of the property and the children. Over time, all the other children left and found jobs and lives for themselves, but your father didn't leave as Auntie Abum had long ago told him she would give him control of the property when he was old enough."

Abum's veranda chair scrapped against the wooden flooring as she pushed herself out of her seat. Helen stopped and looked over at her. Abum made her way into the dining room, then said, "Helen, you've gone too far! If problems arise from this, you will take full responsibility."

Cailin watched Abum walk toward her bedroom as Helen leaned forward and said, "Your father has always been Auntie Abum's favorite. She spoiled him rotten. In an odd way, I feel sorry for him. But he's hurt many more people than he'll ever admit to himself."

ARCHIE

SATURDAY, AUGUST 25, 1945

*A*rchie walked around the side of the inn to the back kitchen door where he found Abbie paring the fibrous skin off a large yellow yam. She looked up and saw him standing on the threshold, eyes fixed on her.

"Come in, Mass Archie," she said while wiping her starch-covered hands in her apron.

Her warm voice and soft eyes drew Archie into the kitchen, the only room in the inn that felt like home to him. He took his usual seat, the one facing Abbie, but his eyes were cast to the floor.

"I came back because I didn't want you to worry."

She poured him a glass of sweet ginger tea and sat in the chair beside him. Taking hold of one of his hands with both of hers, she said, "Nuh worry youself. Time longer than rope."

"I hope so," he responded, "because I'm at the end of mine."

Then he looked up at her, clasped her hands with his free hand, and said, "You know…you've been the only real mother to me." Then, with misty eyes and a bubble forming in his throat, he managed to add, "What would I ever do without you, Abbie?"

43

EDINBURGH, SCOTLAND

5 OCTOBER 1921

Dear Abum,

I received your letter today, forwarded from South Africa. As you can see from the stamp and return address on my envelope, I now reside in Scotland. Cuddy's old professor, Lord Joseph Lister of the University of Edinburgh, and his kind wife invited us to stay with them after they heard of Cuddy's death in the war. We only imposed on them until the children were able to find employment and we could afford a place of our own. Lionel has been apprenticed by an architect. He fell in love with the buildings in Edinburgh, and Lord Lister arranged for the apprenticeship. Alexandra is working in a dress shop and is being courted by a young professor. They hope to be married within the year. I couldn't be more pleased.

You write that things have blown over regarding Malcolm's misconduct, and he has returned to Jamaica, leaving a Cuban wife and children behind! This cannot be good. My advice is to make a match for him as soon as humanly possible. Find a decent girl from a respectable family of British descent. He needs someone to settle him down.

Oh, I should never have allowed Cuddy to talk me into leaving my children. They are an ocean and a lifetime away from me. At least

Susan and Kester have been in contact. Susan has been writing from before we left South Africa, and she encouraged Kester to visit me while he is still studying in London. He plans on visiting us for the Christmas holidays.

It is my dream to return to Jamaica one day and visit with all my children. Perhaps you and I will meet again at that time.

As ever,
Winnie

44

SHARPE

MONDAY-TUESDAY, AUGUST 27-28, 1945

*A*mid the stench of cattle, Sharpe had been walking in the August heat for what seemed an eternity. Two days earlier, Malcolm, Ian, Gus, and Sharpe, along with some other property workers, had set out to herd twenty-five head of cattle to Montpelier to be shipped for sale and slaughter in Kingston. Sharpe and the workers walked, steering the cattle, while Malcolm, Ian, and Gus drove slowly behind in the car—although Ian and Gus walked a good part of the way, getting back in the car only to rest.

Sharpe was surprised when Cailin chose not to go on the journey. She had been talking about it since the cattle were brought back from Negril Springs. The more he thought about it, though, the more it made sense. She had been keeping to herself lately. He could only figure it had to do with the whole Busha-Archie revelation.

When the cattle reached Ferris Cross, they rested for the remainder of that day and night at a property owned by a friend of Malcolm's. The workers also slept on the property, keeping watch over the cattle, while Malcolm, Ian, and Gus drove back to Cawdor, only to return early the next morning for the long journey's ascent up to Montpelier.

With the cattle safely delivered and herded onto train cars, Busha told Sharpe to ride back with him and the boys, since Sharpe was needed back on the property. The rest of the workers would have to make it back on foot. Glad for the respite from the heat and the smell of cows, Sharpe sat in the back seat with Gus, enjoying the rush of fresh air coming through the open windows.

For most of the drive, there was very little talk except for Gus asking Ian questions, which he answered briefly. The relative silence gave Sharpe the opportunity to reflect on things since last year's cattle drive to Montpelier. He thought about Marsha. He had heard she was now living with Ram Foot. And why not? He was the only other man Sharpe could see her with. He wished them well. Besides, things were going well for him in that area, too. He had met Essie's family in Beeston Spring, and they had taken to him. He'd overheard a conversation with her mother, who was encouraging the relationship. When Essie expressed concern that Sharpe was not a man of God, her mother told her she saw him singing in church and paying attention to the preacher's sermon, which was more than she could say for most of the men she knew. "Besides," her mother added, "Me going pray for him to change. God can do mighty things. Believe it, child!"

Essie answered, "That is me praying for.

Miss Essie right, thought Sharpe. *Me not good enough for her. What kind of man can kill another man and go on like nothing never happen?* He leaned closer to the window, letting the air blow hard on his face, wishing it would blow the memory of Magus's death right out of his head.

It was futile. The thought wouldn't leave. His only reprieve was the fact that Essie said she was praying for him. She was his light set on a hill that he heard the preacher talk about that

Sunday in Beeston Spring. He lingered on that thought for a time. Then he chuckled, causing Gus to look at him. The thought of Essie with her socks rolled down just above her shoes cheered him up. She was a strong, attractive, and unique woman.

His thoughts drifted to his family in Accompong. Was his father still alive? He hadn't received a letter since his visit. What of his sisters, and the people of Accompong? The people of the Kindah tree. He was drawn to the heritage and strength of his people, but he knew he couldn't go back there to live. Just like he could never even so much as step foot in Hakin again. It seemed to him he was always walking over bridges he could never cross again.

Bridges. Yes, the one Busha had invited him to cross. Now that he was well on his way over it, he was no longer sure it would lead him where he wanted to go. Was it too late to turn back?

Fatigue from the journey to Montpelier set in. His head bobbed until he fell into a tenuous slumber, soon to be awakened by the laughter of his fellow travelers who, as he soon realized, were laughing at him because of his snoring.

They were now halfway up the Cawdor road. Ian continued a conversation that he had apparently begun while Sharpe was sleeping. Sharpe sensed a tense urgency in Ian as he spoke about rearing the cattle, the upkeep of the property, what he had done on the property that summer, and what he planned to do for the rest of the year on the property.

Malcolm remained silent through Ian's well-rehearsed recitation. This seemed to only increase Ian's tension.

At the cotton tree turn, Malcolm tersely stated, "You're not staying. You're going back to Munro. You need an education."

Ian objected. "You never finished your education!"

"Listen, Ian," Malcolm said, his voice raised, "we went

through this last year, and we're not going through it again. You're going!"

"All the education I need is right here—at Cawdor. I don't want to become a lawyer or doctor like most of the boys at Munro. I have no plans to go to Kingston or to university in England. This is where I plan to stay."

Malcolm parked the car in front of the barbecue, got out, and headed for the house.

Ian got out of the car and firmly declared, "I'm staying here at Cawdor!"

Spinning around, Malcolm raised his voice. "You've overstepped your bounds, boy! You're going back to Munro! That's the end of it!"

Ian clenched his jaw, growling.

Malcolm turned and kept walking.

Sharpe put his hand on Ian's shoulder to calm him down, but Ian jerked away, marching toward the cotton tree and turning back down the gravel road.

Making his way to the kitchen, Sharpe heard Malcolm yell, "What in hell is she doing here?"

Malcolm marched out the front door, with Helen following, saying, "Kester dropped her off today. She's come from Scotland to see you. Please give her a chance."

Ignoring her, Malcolm got in his car, slammed the door, backed up, then sped off with gravel pellets shooting from his back tires. He didn't come back until five days later when word was sent to the inn that his mother had left.

45

ARCHIE

SUNDAY, SEPTEMBER 2, 1945

While Malcolm's mother visited the Cawdor great house, the days at Oristano Inn were somber. There was little talk. Malcolm didn't drink any alcohol but spent most of his time going over the inn's affairs. Archie spent most of his time in his room, avoiding Malcolm.

On Sunday morning, Archie woke up early to spend time with Abbie before having to leave for Munro. Later that morning, he would drive with Malcolm up to Cawdor to pick up Ian and Rowena, and from there they would be taken to their respective schools in Saint Elizabeth.

He had an emotional goodbye conversation with Abbie. She encouraged him to make the best of his time at Munro and promised him his favorite meals during the Christmas holidays. The last thing she said before hugging him was "Remember this—quatie buy trouble, pound can't pay for it.[1]"

"Oh, Abbie. You and your proverbs. But you're right. Manning's taught me that lesson. This time, I'll keep my nose clean. Besides, now I have Ian to defend me." He laughed.

With a tearful hug, she let him go.

Malcolm and Archie drove up to Cawdor in silence, which

Archie was thankful for. He knew Malcolm could never be a father to him. He wasn't one of his "respectable white children." When the car stopped at the barbecue, Malcolm honked the horn for Ian and Rowena.

Gus came out of the house with an envelope in his hand and ran over to the car. "Uncle Malcolm, my father's coming home!"

Malcolm nodded. "Good for you, boy. Now, where are Ian and Rowena?"

"I'm not sure," Gus replied, running over to Archie's side of the car to show him the letter.

Malcolm honked the horn again.

Rowena came out to the front veranda, with her mother and Cailin following. She kissed them both and headed to the car. While Archie was helping her put her suitcase in the boot of the car, Malcolm blew the horn again and yelled for Ian. Helen went into the house, then came back out and walked over to the car. She told Malcolm Ian was not in the house and that he might be out on the property.

Malcolm blew the horn again. "That damn boy!"

Sharpe, who had been sitting on the side of the barbecue sharpening a machete, got up and said, "Me will go find him."

It took ten minutes for Sharpe to come from the side of the house with Ian in tow.

"Where's your damn suitcase, boy?" Malcolm asked.

Ian inhaled, then said, "I'm not going back."

"You're not going what?" Malcolm swung the car door open and got out, marching toward Ian. "Get your suitcase and get in the car now!"

Ian straightened his shoulders and continued. "This is where I belong. I plan—"

Before he could finish speaking, Malcolm dealt him a blow to the solar plexus, causing Ian to keel over and drop to the ground. "That will teach you to disobey me. Now get up and get your suitcase."

Ian looked up and managed to say, "No."

Gritting his teeth, Malcolm said, "No son of mine will speak to me that way." Then he kicked Ian in the side, causing him to grab his side as his body closed in the fetal position.

In a quick stride, Malcolm moved toward the pimento room as Helen and the rest of the household ran over to Ian, urging him to get up. Malcolm grabbed the large chain used to secure the room at night and strode back. The circle around Ian widened, except for Helen, who pleaded with Malcolm to put the chain down.

Ignoring her, he erupted, "Boy! I'll teach you to disobey me!" and raised the hand holding the chain.

Before Malcolm could complete the swing, Helen threw herself on top of Ian.

Enraged, Malcolm swung the chain down on his wife's back, yelling, "And you need to stop protecting the children!"

Helen grunted under the lash of the heavy chain.

"Daddy! Stop!" cried both Cailin and Rowena.

Before he could lift the chain again, Sharpe grabbed Helen and pulled her back.

Ian, who must have realized what had just happened to his mother, tried sitting up but was met with a heavy blow of the chain to his chest and Malcolm hissing the words, "You will not...." Malcolm took a breath and raised the chain again for another blow, this time connecting with Ian's hands that were guarding his face. "...make the same mistakes I made."

From behind, Sharpe jumped on Malcolm's back, bringing him crashing down to the ground. Malcolm was momentarily stunned, giving Sharpe enough time to pull Malcolm's hands behind his back and wrap the chain around them. Sharpe pinned him to the ground with his body weight and kept repeating, "You can't do that to you family, sah. You can't do that to you family, sah. No, sah. You can't do that to you family."

Seeing Sharpe had Malcolm restrained, Archie called out to Cailin, "Do you know how to get to Kester's house in Sav-la-Mar?"

"Yes," she replied, obviously in shock.

"Come! Let's go get him." Then, heading to the car, he looked back and ordered, "Quick!"

With his minimal driving experience, Archie managed to back the car up and turn it toward the cotton tree, with the back tires flinging gravel.

They drove in silence, all his usual landmarks racing past in a blur. The only constant was the image of Malcolm bringing the chain down on his wife and son—like a gladiator in the Roman Colosseum, fighting for his life at the expense of others.

When they reached Kester's home, he had just arrived from church with Jane. After Cailin gushed some of the salient details, Kester took the wheel from Archie and told Jane to get his medical bag and follow in his car.

On arriving at Cawdor, Archie expected to see the scene as they'd left it, but the Colosseum was empty. Instead, they found everyone, except Malcolm, sitting sullen on the back veranda.

Kester immediately tended to Helen, who was sitting with a pillow behind her back. He diagnosed her with a bruised spine and gave her a weeks dose of aspirin, saying she also needed to ice it regularly. Since Cawdor didn't have facilities for ice, Archie left for the inn to get some. Kester then treated Ian, whose face, hands, and side were bruised and lacerated.

"You know you need to go back to Munro, don't you?" Kester said to Ian.

After a short silence, he replied, "I don't want to, but he'll never let me stay."

"No. He won't." Then turning to Helen, Kester asked, "Where is Malcolm?"

"In his room," Helen replied.

Cailin followed Kester to their father's room. He opened the door without knocking.

Malcolm was lying on his bed with one arm resting on his forehead, staring blankly at the wooden rafters. His eyes shifted over to Kester, then back at the ceiling. "What is it? Big brother come to save me again?"

"No," replied Kester.

"Well, what is it then?"

"I've come to take all my nieces and nephews to boarding school."

"I'm not paying for Cailin and Gus to go," Malcolm responded, still staring at the rafters.

"I offered to pay for them before, and I'm still planning on doing it."

"Do as you please."

Cailin turned to her uncle and asked, "What about Mummy? I can't leave her here. Not after what he just did to her."

Kester put his hand on her shoulder and looked in her eyes. "I know you're concerned for your mother, as you should be. But I'll make you a promise. I'll see to her well-being. Your Auntie Jane and I will visit her regularly, and we will invite her to stay with us from time to time." He turned to Malcolm and said, "You have no objections to that, I presume."

Malcolm grunted.

Gus, who had come up behind, said, "Uncle, but Daddy's coming home for me. How can I go to Munro?"

"Don't worry, son. When he gets here, he'll decide what's best for you. In the meantime, this is for the best."

Kester closed the door on Malcolm.

46

CAILIN

*E*veryone heard Kester's car as it came up the gravel driveway. He had picked up Archie from the inn and arrived at Cawdor just as breakfast was ending.

Cailin's eyes met her mother's. Her heart sank. In her whole life, she could not recall being away from her for a day, much less a school term. She realized she'd taken her mother for granted. Instead, she'd sought after her father's affections when her mother had always been there. She got up from the table, went to where her mother was seated, and embraced her from behind.

Helen reached up, tightening the embrace. She whispered in Cailin's ear, "You're going to be alright...I'm going to be alright...I love you."

"I know you do, Mummy. And I love you."

Cailin walked to the back veranda for a last look. She noticed how the sun shone against the green hills that were like a carpet rolled down to touch the multi-hued blue bay and spread out as far as Savanna-la-Mar to the right and Whitehouse to the left. How she would miss this. Her beloved Cawdor.

"Cailin!" she heard her uncle call.

She went to collect her suitcase and looked around her room one more time, memories flooding her emotions. One of those memories advised her to look in the bottom drawer of her dresser. There she found Rowena's letters safely tucked away. She retrieved them, picked up her suitcase, and went to the kitchen, where she threw the letters into the wood-burning stove. She watched them go up in flames, and thought, *Secrets my father will never know.*

"Cailin!" she heard her uncle call out again. "Everyone's in the car."

Sharpe, Essie, and Ruby were standing outside the kitchen, waiting to say their goodbyes.

Ruby gave her a quick hug, then made her way back into the kitchen, tears rolling down the length of her face.

Essie held both of Cailin's shoulders. "Now, don't forget where you come from. You is a Cawdor girl." They hugged.

Cailin reached out her hand to shake Sharpe's, and he took it in both of his large, rough hands. He spoke softly, so only the three of them could hear, "Me sorry to see you leave, Miss C. But me know is for the best." He held her hand firmly and added, "Nuh worry youself. Me will look out for Miss Helen. Nothing nah go happen to her."

"Thank you, Sharpe. Knowing that eases my mind," then she added. "And look out for Daddy, too. He needs you."

Sharpe seemed surprised by Cailin's words, so she added, "He does."

"Me will do that, Miss C." He let go of her hand. "Take care of youself."

Turning to leave, she saw her father and aunt standing in the doorway of the house. She wanted to run to him, but so much had transpired. She steered her feet toward the car, and as she passed him, she managed to say, "Goodbye, Daddy."

He breathed deeply and replied, "Goodbye, little girl."

She felt the guilt of betrayal. A bubble rose in her throat. But her feet kept walking.

Kester put her suitcase in the boot of the car while she hugged her mother. The words caught in Helen's throat, "My baby." Then she pulled apart from Cailin, nudging her toward the car, where Ian, Rowena, Gus, and Archie sat waiting for her.

As the car pulled off, her mother called out, "Don't forget to write!"

Sticking her head out the back-passenger window and looking back, Cailin shouted, "I won't!"

She watched the scene grow smaller—Ruby waving out the kitchen window, her father and aunt in the doorway, Sharpe and Essie, her sweet mother, her beloved Cawdor—until the car made the curve past the old silk cotton tree.

EPILOGUE

1973

"Miss Essie, your breakfast is even better than I remember," said Cailin, placing her silverware together on her plate. "Seeing you and Sharpe brought back such fond memories."

"And what about seeing me?" Archie feigned a complaint. "Bad memories?"

"No. Just memories of how incorrigible you can be—you and your Gatsby." She smiled.

Archie seemed to stop in his tracks, as though she'd hit a nerve. He quickly recovered and retorted, "Well, at least I'm not like your hopelessly lovesick Pip."

"That's enough, the two of you," Essie chided. "You sound like you did when you was teenagers."

"We do, don't we?" Cailin chuckled, then stood up. "Well, I guess I should be on my way. Harry and the children are expecting me."

Essie hugged Cailin, then held her at arm's length and said, "Tell me you going to come back and see we again."

"I will, and I'll bring Harry and the children next time."

"Now you two men take Miss Cailin bag and go see her off."

Archie walked with Cailin to her room to fetch her bag, then left for the car. Cailin lingered by the bureau where the bundle of letters sat. She reached out and took hold of them, clutching them to her chest. As important as Sharpe and Archie's stories were for filling in some gaps in her understanding of her father, getting to read the letters had meant the most to her. While she didn't have all her questions answered, and perhaps never would, at least now she had an idea of what had driven him—why, until the day he died, he had continued to hurt the ones who'd loved him the most. At that moment, her heart hurt. Not for her, but for a man who had never had the capacity to love or be loved. Tears welled in her eyes. The tension was gone, but the pain and the longing she had felt up until the last couple of days had only receded but a little. *Perhaps*, she thought, *as the years go by, it will diminish to where all that comes to mind when I think about him are the times he smiled and called me his little girl.* She sighed. *That will be the day.*

Outside, standing with Archie and Cailin at her car, Sharpe said, "It's funny what going back to your youth can do to you."

"Yes. I'm glad I came back. Getting the chance to talk about the past with both of you has been helpful."

"Well," said Archie, "as I said the day of the funeral, I still prefer forward ever and backward never. But I am going to miss the two of you."

As Cailin drove down the driveway toward the inn's gate, she looked in the rearview mirror and saw Sharpe and Archie waving goodbye. Waving back, the thought came to her, *No matter where the three of us go in this world, one man will always bind us together—Malcolm Campbell—for better or for worse.*

LEAVE A REVIEW

If you enjoyed reading *When Trees Fall,* consider leaving a review on the **online bookstore you purchased it from** or on **Goodreads.com.**

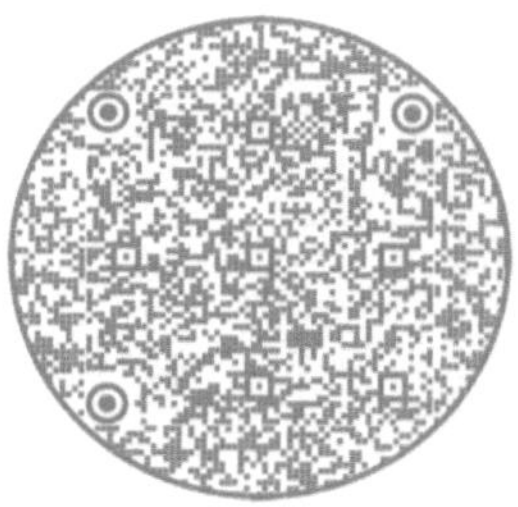

GoodReads QR code

To get updates on *Up From Mountains*, Book Two of the Wood and Water Saga, and to learn about Dale's other writings, sign up for his newsletter at DaleMahfood.com.

ENDNOTES

CHARACTERS AND SETTING

1. **Tainos** are the indigenous peoples of Jamaica. They migrated from South American into the Greater Antilles centuries before the European colonization of the Caribbean.

PROLOGUE

1. **Duppy** is the Jamaican word for ghost. The origin of the word is not clear. Some say it is of African origin and some maintain it is of Taino origin.
2. **Busha** is an informal title given to the owner of a Jamaican property. It is thought the word originated among the slave population as "obissha," which is an alternate pronunciation of the word "overseer." While Malcolm is the owner of the property and not simply an overseer, in the early days of Jamaica's plantations, English plantation owners, who disdained the idea of living in Jamaica, often hired Scotsmen or Irishmen as overseers to run their properties. Over time, some of these overseers became landowners.
3. **Sah** is the customary way for Jamaicans of all standings to pronounce the word "sir" when not addressing a male member of a higher class. It is often used as a word added for emphasis with no class or gender attached to it, as in the sentence this footnote refers to.
4. **Haul in you mouth mek me pass** is said to someone who is sulking and, as a result, pouting their mouth. Essie is using this humorously to bring levity to the situation.

3. SHARPE

1. **Quashie** originates from the Akan name Kwasi or Kwesi, given to boys who were born on Sunday. It became a pejorative term for lower-class Black Jamaicans, who were considered gullible by the white population.
2. **Patwa** is the name of the native Jamaican language, a creole language with mainly British, West African, and Taino influence. Variants of the spelling are "Patwah" or "Patois."
3. **Fass**, in Jamaican Patwa, means to be meddlesome and nosey.
4. **Pocomania** is a Jamaican religion that is over two hundred years old and incorporates aspects of African forms of religion with Christianity. The

practice of Pocomania during slavery in Jamaica is thought to have been a form of rebellion against slave owners and their European form of Christianity. Pocomania is one of the two main branches of what is called Revivalism. The other main branch is Revival Zion, which focuses more on Christianity but still incorporates African elements. Both branches of Revivalism stem from Myalism (explained in Chapter 24 endnotes). Some adherents in both Revivalism streams wear turbans and have been nicknamed **wrap-heads**. The etymology of the word Pocomania is uncertain, but some think it has Ghanaian roots while others think it was influenced by Spanish and may mean "a little madness." This may refer to practices of spiritual possession, dancing, speaking in tongues, and rituals of healing. Others say the word has nothing to do with Spanish as its phonetic pronunciation is closer to "Pukkumina."

5. **Obeah**, somewhat similar to Haitian Voodoo, was brought to Jamaica and other Caribbean countries by enslaved Africans, particularly those of the Igbo tribe. While it was said to manifest itself as both white and black magic, the word Obeah came to be associated primarily with evil occult practices. In 1898, the Obeah Act was passed, outlawing Obeah in Jamaica, yet it was easy to find an Obeah man or woman, particularly in the country parts, who would be willing to heal an ailment with an herbal formula, cast a spell, send a curse, or dispense a poison that would prematurely put an end to one's antagonist. Magus, Hakin's Obeah man, neglected many of the spiritual aspects of Obeah, focusing instead on the parts that served him well—mind-altering and poisonous herbs.

6. **Rass** is a crass way of saying "ass," but more commonly, it is used as a violent or abusive insult, though it can also be used as an expression of surprise or frustration.

7. **Chuh** is a Jamaican interjection used during times of frustration, annoyance, or disagreement. It can be used interchangeably with the sucking of teeth.

4. ARCHIE

1. *The Daily Gleaner*, established in 1834, was the main newspaper published in Jamaica. It still holds that status but is now called *The Gleaner*.

2. **Savanna-la-Mar** is the official name of the largest town in Westmorland. Jamaicans often shorten it to **Sav-la-mar** and some, with more familiarity, call it **Sav**.

6. CAILIN | SHARPE

1. **Baccra** is a term Black Jamaicans have used to refer to white Jamaicans. It carries a negative connotation and has a couple possible origins: Enslaved

West Africans from the Igbo tribe, who were taken to the Caribbean, are said to have used the word to refer to their white masters, and over time, the word referred to white people in general. In some parts of the Caribbean, and possibly in Jamaica, the word may have also been used to refer to Welsh, Irish, and Scottish indentured servants who, when in church, were only allowed to sit in the back row. Hence the pronunciation "back-ra."

2. **Ganga spliff** is a large cannabis cigarette, more akin to the size of a cigar.

7. ARCHIE

1. **Pickney** means "child" or "children" and is used to refer to children of any racial background.
2. **Rhaatid** is a Jamaican expression of surprise or annoyance. It's a polite expletive.

11. SHARPE

1. **Missa** is a Jamaican way of saying "Mister," which is not to be confused with "Massa" (see note below on "Massa").
2. **Horse-staring** is a term usually applied to a younger person who has matured physically in height and possibly even in strength. However, being that Sharpe is in his thirties, Mr. Aldridge uses the term to imply that Sharpe is old enough to call him by his first name.
3. **Put the handle to the cup** is a Jamaican saying expressing the need for a younger person to address someone older than themself using their title (Mr., Mrs. Sir, Miss, etc.). This also applies to a person from one social class addressing someone from a higher social class.
4. **Take me for mock** is a Jamaican expression meaning to make a mockery of a person.
5. **Claude McKay** was a Black Jamaican poet and author who had moved to Harlem, New York, in the earlier part of the century. McKay was one of the early influences in the New Negro Movement (later known as the Harlem Renaissance). He was also a contemporary of Marcus Garvey, but being a communist at the time, he was displeased with Garvey's ideas about racial separation. Instead, he focused his protestations on the plight of Black Americans compared to their white counterparts, in hopes of social change right where they already lived.
6. **Massa** literally means "master" but is used by Jamaicans of all classes to address everyone and no one in particular. It's more of an interjection than anything. In this case, Sharpe uses this word, rather than the more familiar interjection "boy" as an unconscious recognition of Mr. Aldridge's older

age and higher social status. "Massa" is not to be confused with "Missa" (see note above on "Missa").

7. **"If We Must Die"** was written by Claude Mckay in response to what has been called the infamous "Red Summer" of 1919 when white mobs in cities and rural areas across the United States killed hundreds of Black Americans. Sharpe is applying the poem to himself as many persecuted people have since it was first written.

8. **Putus** is a Jamaican term of endearment, similar to sweetheart.

9. **Quaco**: "In sections of Jamaica, the word 'Quaco' is the ultimate in disrespect. It calls up an Africanness, which is the subject of self-rejection. In parts of Saint Thomas, Quaco [not the fictional Quaco of this novel] is said to be the name of the man who betrayed Three Finger Jack, so a Quaco is also a traitor." (Amina Blackwood-Meeks)

12. CAILIN | ARCHIE

1. **Rolling Calf** is a dangerous duppy (ghost) that can change its appearance. It usually manifests as a bull or a goat with flaming eyes and a chain wrapped around its body that drags on the ground making noise.

2. **Neaga** is Jamaican slang for the word Negro. During the time period of this novel, depending on who was saying it and what the context was, it had several connotations, from friendly (one Black person speaking to another) to neutral (anyone—Black or white—using the word as a physical descriptor of a Black person) to derisive (as in a white person speaking down to a Black person.) In this case, Mass Whim is using it as a physical descriptor.

13. SHARPE

1. **Pull cat out of pregnant dog** is similar to the well-known saying "make something out of nothing."

2. **Ackee** is a fruit that comes out of a pod. When the pod ripens, it opens up and lets off a poisonous gas. If the ackee is eaten before it is ripe, it is poisonous.

3. **John Crow** is the common name for vultures in Jamaica. **Draw breaks** refers to the John Crow landing and leaving talons marks on the ground.

17. SHARPE

1. **Add house and land** is a Jamaican expression meaning a person is adding way more to what they are saying than is warranted.

2. **Facety** (pronounced fias-ty) is a Jamaican word that is akin to the word "feisty" but has more of an edge to it. Sometimes it is used to scold rude children, but it can also be used for an adult who speaks their mind, unconcerned with what others think (as Essie does with Sharpe).

19. SHARPE

1. **Chain** is a surveyor's measurement that is equal to sixty-six feet or about twenty meters.

23. SHARPE

1. **Myal** is most probably Jamaica's first homegrown religion, originating as an amalgamation of various religions the enslaved Africans brought with them from their ancestral lands. However, it is possible that Myal may have actually originated in Africa. It was instrumental as a uniting force for the enslaved Africans in Jamaica and proved to be an effective tool for resistance against colonialism and enslavement. After Jamaica's Great Revival in the 1860s, Myal evolved into what is called Revivalism, the two main branches being Revival Zion and Pocomania, both incorporating some aspects of Christianity. In this story, what Papa Rufus practices is a mixture of Myal, Revivalism, and without realizing it, some Obeah from his past.

24. SHARPE

1. **Bammy** is a small thick round flat bread made from cassava. It was a regular part of the Taino diet.
2. **Gizzada** is a small Jamaican tart-like circular pastry with an outer crust that is pinched around the edges and filled with sweet spices and coconut.

29. SHARPE

1. **When herring mauger, him bones show** is a Jamaican proverb meaning secrets will be revealed in the course of time. The word "mauger" (pronounced ma-ga) is a Jamaican word that comes from the word "meager," but when Jamaicans call someone mauger, they mean the person or thing is too skinny.
2. **Trouble deh a bush, Anansi bring it a yard** is a Jamaican proverb that means your personal troubles affect those around you, whether you want them to or not.

33. ARCHIE

1. **What no dead, no call it duppy** is a Jamaican proverb encouraging someone not to give up because they are still alive.

34. CAILIN

1. **Winston Churchill's character's words are in italics** rather than quotes, as they are not the actual words he spoke during his Victory in Europe Day speech on May 8, 1945. While paraphrasing liberties have been taken, I have made every effort to keep Churchill's intent. I plead poetic license before my avid history readers.

35. CAILIN

1. **Chimmy** is a chamber pot, a vessel used in a bedroom at night in a house without a toilet.

36. ARCHIE

1. **Chicken merry, hawk deh near** is a Jamaican proverb warning that too much fun can cause someone to be careless, making them vulnerable to negative consequences.

45. ARCHIE

1. **Quatie buy trouble, pound can't pay for it** is a Jamaican proverb meaning it's easy to get in trouble, but hard to get out of it. A "quatie" was what Jamaicans called the British three-halfpence coin.

CHARACTER LIST

CAMPBELL FAMILY

Malcolm (Busha) – *father; owner of Cawdor
    property*

Helen – *Malcolm's wife and mother of (in order):*

* Heather – *oldest daughter*

* Rowena (Row) – *middle daughter*

* Ian – *only son*

* Cailin – *youngest daughter*

Gus (Angus) – *Cailin's cousin; Tam Campbell's son*

Winnie – *Malcolm's mother*

Cuddy (Cuthbert) – *Malcolm's father*

Abum and Bitsy – *Malcolm's aunts*

Kester, Cameron, and Tam – *Malcolm's brothers*

Susan and Bonnie – *Malcolm's sisters*

Irma – *Malcolm's third wife and widow in 1973*

Jane – *Kester's wife*

Mass Whim and Cissy - *Cailin's maternal grand-
    parents*

PRICE FAMILY

Gracie – *Archie's mother; inn keeper of Oristano Inn*

Archie – *Grace's son*

SHARPE FAMILY

Sharpe – *Cawdor property foreman; from Accom-
    pong; living in Hakin*

Manu – *Sharpe's father living in Accompong*

Bena and Ama – *Shape's sisters living in Accompong*

OTHER CHARACTERS

(*alphabetical order mostly by first name*)

Abbie – *the cook at the Oristano Inn*

Alexander Bustamante – *Jamaica Labour Party
    leader*

Clive Taylor – *main bully at Manning's School*

Devon Blake – *other bully at Manning's School*

Essie – *the cook for the Cawdor great house; Sharpe's
    wife in 1973*

George – *Rowena's crush who attends Munro College*

Harry – *boy Cailin meets in the hardware store;
    Cailin's husband in 1973*

Leroy – *Sharpe's uncle in Hakin*

Linton Aldridge – *minister and schoolteacher for the
    Oristano Methodist church*

Lucy – *influential woman in Hakin; works on the
    Cawdor property*

Magus – *the Hakin village Obeah man*

Marsha – *Sharpe's girlfriend in Hakin*

Mick McFagan – *liquor salesman; Gracie's suitor*

Miss Recas – *Cailin and Gus's governess*

Mr. Lyn – *owner of Oristano grocery store &
    rum bar*

Mrs. Aldridge – *Linton Aldridge's wife*

Norman Manley – *People's National Party leader*

Papa Rufus – *Accompong Myal man (spiritual leader)*

Phibbi – *Sharpe's aunt in Hakin*

Pressy – *the Witcombe's cook*

Ram Foot – *Sharpe's friend in Hakin*

Robby Thompson (Robert) – *Archie's friend in
    Savanna-la-Mar*

Ruby – *maid for the Cawdor great house*

Samfie – *a Cawdor property worker*

The Witcombes – *board Archie in Savanna-la-Mar*

ACKNOWLEDGMENTS

Sitting around the dinner table listening to my mother tell stories about her youth for the umpteenth time, I announced I was going to write a novel that included, among other things, fictionalized versions of some of her stories. The whole family, young and old, encouraged me to do so. Little did I realize all the resources and people it would take to accomplish the task.

In the early stages of the manuscript, several people were beta readers: Michele Fievre, Joe Gallagher, Abbie Kopelowitz, Kevin Prescott, and Tristan Bradshaw. There were also members of the South Florida Word Weavers International Chapter who critiqued my first chapter: Patricia Hartman, Patrick Hartman, Dave Haun, and Jim Geiger. Each of you gave me honest feedback that has vastly improved the story and the quality of my writing. Thank you, all.

At the Miami Book Fair a couple years ago, I had the privilege of meeting Sara Collins, the author of *The Confessions of Frannie Langton*. Based on something she said in a later interview, I realized I needed to revamp my completed manuscript —much to my chagrin. In the end, Sara, you inadvertently challenged me to make *When Trees Fall* so much better. Thank you.

Over the last two years, through two Clubhouse app rooms, Jamaica Book Club and Good New Jamaica, I've become acquainted with many wonderful Jamaican authors and bibliophiles who have encouraged me on my publishing journey. Here are just a few: Nicky Lafayette, Cleveland Grey, Rosheen Salmon, Trudy Knockless, Natalie Corthésy, Andre Simpson,

Andrene Bonner, Charles and Judith Hyatt, Jeffrey Anderson-Gunter, and Lynda Edwards who has become like a sister to me. Jamaica contingent, I thank you, all. *Big up youself!*

I am also grateful for all my family and friends who have encouraged me along the way and for my many students who, over the years, have continually asked when the novel would be released. Well, here it is! Thank you for caring.

Often, while writing or editing the novel, I needed some quick information about everyday life in the southwest part of Jamaica during the 1940s. Besides my mother, who was my first go-to, I would text George Graham, whose mother had given birth to him two days before my mother was born—both in the Black River Hospital. Mom and George, thank you for adding the subtle flavors of old-Jamaica county life.

Four people were kind enough to share their knowledge of Jamaican culture and history with me: Rachel Manley gave me feedback on a couple of my chapters that included two important Jamaican historical figures she was well acquainted with— her grandfather, Norman Manley, and her relative, Alexander Bustamante. Amina Blackwood Meeks, the foremost living Jamaican storyteller, enlightened me on some of the nuances of Jamaican culture and language that I did not know. Anabella Seaga-Mian and Christine Reynolds provided invaluable information on Revivalism in Jamaica, giving me insight into what it would have been like for Sharpe to experience a "bands" meeting in Accompong. Thank you, ladies, for lending me your time and expertise.

Then there are my diamond polishers who made *When Trees Fall* presentable to the world. Janet, my wife, is my chief polisher. From the beginning, she has given priceless feedback from the big picture to the tiniest detail. Her name deserves to be on the cover beside mine. Junie, we really make a great team! I don't want to mention the next person as I'm afraid she'll become so popular and won't have time to edit my future novels, but, alas, I will—Grace Wynter. Thank you for being the most amazing professional editor who also gave me sensitivity feedback that makes the novel accessible to a wider audience. You're the best! The final polish was done by Dusan Arsenic, my cover designer, who lives in Serbia. Thank you for making the cover come to life.

Most importantly, I'm thankful for my family. I'll start with Theodore, the family dog, aka my son, who was always close by as I wrote the novel—a writer's best friend. Mary and CeCe, my daughters, you've encouraged me the whole way—from that first day I announced my intention to write the novel until now. You've given thoughtful comments on character names, the title, the book cover, and the story in general. Thanks also for teaching me how to use social media to get the word out. I could never have asked for more wonderful daughters. Janet, I bring you up here again because you are more than just my teammate—you are my soulmate. As we say in Jamaica, you and I are *batty and bench*. Mama, my dear mother, as I said on the dedication page, your influence on me is profound. There could never have been a *When Trees Fall* without you. Thank you for encouraging me my whole life, but especially with this labor of love. Papa, you've been gone these thirteen years, but I'd like to think your way with words lives on in me—until we meet face to face. *Family, I love you dearly!*

A big thank you to every reader. God willing, there's more to come in the Wood and Water Saga.

Most of all, I'm thankful for you Jesus—you open eyes so we can see clearly.

CULTURAL AND HISTORICAL SOURCES

What follows are the primary sources referenced while researching and writing *When Trees Fall*.

"A Moment in History - Jamaica Is Granted Universal Adult Suffrage -." diG Jamaica, August 16, 2018. http://digjamaica.com/m/blog/a-moment-in-history-jamaica-is-granted-universal-adult-suffrage/.which

"BBC on This Day | Front Page." BBC News. BBC, February 20, 2013. http://news.bbc.co.uk/onthis day/.

"Bustamante and Manley, the Fathers of Jamaica's Independence." Los Angeles Sentinel, August 23, 2012. https://lasentinel.net/bustamante-and-manley-the-fathers-of-jamaica-s-indepen dence.html.

Curtin, Marguerite R. The Story of Westmoreland a Jamaican Parish. *Jamaica National Building Society Foundation, 2010.*

Dickens, Charles. Great Expectations. *London, England. Chapman & Hall, 1861.*

Eaton, George E. Alexander Bustamante and Modern Jamaica. *Kingston: LMH Publishing, 2000.*

Fitzgerald, F Scott. The Great Gatsby. *New York, New York: Charles Scribner's Sons, 1925.*

Folk Music of Jamaica. *MP3. Jamaica: Smithsonian*

Folkways Records, 1956. Recorded and produced by Edward Seaga

Hill, Frank. Bustamante and His Letters. *Kingston: Kingston Publ., 1976.*

John, Hamilton B L St. Bustamante: Anthology of a Hero. *Kingston, Jamaica: Produced for B. St. J. Hamilton by Publication & Productions, 1978.*

Manley, Rachel. Drumblair: Memories of a Jamaican Childhood. *Toronto: Key Porter Books, 2008.*

McKay, Claude. Harlem Shadows. *New York: Harcourt, Brace, 1922.*

Palmer, Colin A. Freedom's Children: The 1938 Labor Rebellion and the Birth of Modern Jamaica. *Chapel Hill: The University of North Carolina Press, 2014.*

Salkey, Andrew. A Quality of Violence. *London: New Beacon Books, 1978.*

Seaga, Edward, and Francis Saighoe. "Revival Cults in Jamaica, Notes towards a Sociology of Religion." Yearbook for Traditional Music *15 (1983): 180. https://doi.org/10.2307/768661.*

Seaga, Edward. Edward Seaga: My Life and Leadership (Clash of Ideologies). *Vol. 1. Vol. Vol. 1. 2 vols. Macmillan Education, 2010.*

Seaga, Edward. "Folk Music of Jamaica (Liner Notes: Ethinic Folkways Library Album No. FE 4453)." New York, New York: Folkways Records and Service Corp., 1956.

"The Rt.. Hon. Sir Alexander Bustamante (1884 – 1977)." National Library of Jamaica, n.d. https:// nlj.gov.jm/project/rt-hon-sir-alexander-busta mante-1884-1977/.

Tortello, Rebecca. Pieces of the Past: A Stroll down

Jamaica's Memory Lane. *Kingston, Jamaica: Randle, 2007.*

Weil, Martin. "Sir Alexander Bustamante, 94, Jamaican Leader, Dies." The Washington Post. WP Company, August 7, 1977. https://www.washingtonpost.com/archive/local/1977/08/07/sir-alexander-bustamante-94-jamaican-leader-dies/2f8af0b7-ec0b-4b3b-a957-264fb580f280/?noredirect=on&utm_term=.740c843c3337.

"William Alexander Bustamante." Biography. Your Dictionary, n.d. https://biography.yourdictionary.com/william-alexander-bustamante.

www.ingramcontent.com/pod-product-compliance
Lightning Source LLC
Chambersburg PA
CBHW020348220726
48290CB00014B/1364